The Author has drawn upon his childhood memories as a "spotter", his encounters with the preservation movement and long-standing involvement with model railways in order to present "The Club".

This story concerns a group of similarly dedicated individuals, brought together from many walks of life. The reader follows their everyday trials and tribulations which are inevitably entwined with the world of steam, modelling, exhibitions, day-trips and a yearning for the past.

The result is their membership of the Surbiton Railway Club.

Books by the same author - writing as Anthony Mann

- From Where I Sit

- As I Was Saying

- The Further Thoughts of Chair Mann

- Last Mann Standing

These titles are non-fiction (humour).

There are also two talking book CDs

- A Mann at Last

- A Mann for All Reasons

Published by Trouser Press and currently in print.

For further details please see back pages.

MEL REES

THE CLUB

- An Everyday Story of Trainspotters -

Best wishes

Arthur Adams.

TROUSER PRESS

A Trouser Press Paperback
First Published 1995

Reprinted 2011

© Copyright Mel Rees 1995

Cover Design - Jill Wadsworth
Typesetting - Tim Harvey

British Library CIP Data
A catalogue record for the Book is available from the British Library.

ISBN 978-0-9516501-2-7

Printed in Great Britain by
MPG Biddles Ltd., King's Lynn, Norfolk

ACKNOWLEDGMENTS

Thanks are due to all the enthusiasts I have met over the years for providing the inspiration to write this book.

Thanks also to those who gave assistance with medical advice and police procedures.

To David Shepherd, a special thanks for supporting the project so wholeheartedly and also to my wife, who lived through every word.

REVIEWS

THE CLUB –
An Everyday Story of Trainspotters
By Mel Rees

"I have to own up that I approached this book with the wrong attitude! Although personally not embarrassed at being a trainspotter, I expected this, involving a presumably ficticious Surbiton Railway Club, to be a rather a second-rate effort; I was at fault in mentally pigeon-holing the author as an 'anorak' - I could not have been further from the truth. From the opening page, Mel Rees proves he is a fluent, erudite, inventive writer, with an eye for detail and an ear for dialogue, which I know to be difficult to carry successfully. Some of the characters I recognised from my forty years as a spotter, but the situation in which he places them are human, humorous and imaginative, while staying within the bounds of reality. I warmed to descriptions such as: 'They all looked the same - pasty, unfortunate faces, hidden under a camouflage of encrusted acne.' The author does not take himself too seriously and neither does he allow his characters to; there is an honesty about them that is refreshing and the interaction between club members both amusing and realistic. The people herein are ficticious but a guest appearance by David Shepherd and reference to other 'realities', such as popular records, give a credence to the story, which in sum is highly entertaining. I struggled to put the book down - well done, Mr Rees! - *Railway Magzine*

"There is humour found a-plenty in Mel Rees's novel, The Club - *Sunday Express*

"The author has discovered a rich vein of comic drama, a highly readable story unfolds ...David Shepherd's appearance adds a further touch of authenticity to a believable story" - *British Railway Modelling*

"Light-hearted, barbed but not vicious and entertaining – don't blame me if you find yourself in the pages" - *Railway World*

CHAPTER ONE

"Mrs. Seagrave - Room 22", boomed the receptionist as she craned her neck through the hatch like a captive bird in a crate. Her eyes darted back and forth until the scraping of a chair indicated that Mrs. Seagrave was indeed aware of the directive.

A small girl swung her feet, occasionally scuffing the floor; a young boy seated beside her alternated his movements between poking her in the ribs and picking his nose.

Albert Buchanan sat opposite, attempting to glean more about the latest soccer sleaze sensation, as reported exclusively in "The Sun", when he suddenly became aware of a female arm emerging from nowhere, stinging the boy's arm. "Mum", shouted the aggrieved child, as he clutched his multi-coloured jacket, festooned with so-called designer labels.

"How many times have I told you about that?", chided the mother, eyes conveying indignation.

"Didn't 'urt 'her".

"I mean, picking your nose!"

All eyes focused on the family. The daughter ignored her slightly older brother as he continued to rub his arm, his face one of continuous frown. An internal door squeaked open. Vi Buchanan walked towards her husband. She smiled. Albert stood and folded his paper.

"'Ow d'you get on then, gal?"

Vi shrugged her shoulders. "Doctor's still not sure, but they're making an appointment for me to see someone at the hospital - a specialist he said - so we'll just have to wait and see".

Out in the street Vi squinted, the bright sunshine being in direct contrast to the rather sombre surgery. It had been a warm, dry start to May and today was no exception.

Arm in arm they made their way through Kingston market. Vi

stopped to buy apples and oranges, then queried a fruit she had not come across before. On being given a potted history and an abridged description of its taste, combined with cooking instructions, Vi thanked the stallholder prior to Albert leading her towards the bus stop. "Bit fancy for us", she said.

"Bit like the price", muttered Albert.

"You down the Club or the Hippodrome tonight, Alb?"

"Hippodrome, Friday night's Karaoke night. All the Elvis's and the Tom Jones's 'll be there. All doing their level best to destroy their idols". He chuckled, wagging his finger. "The thing is, Vi, that they all think they're the bees knees, that's what's so funny, they all think they're it!"

Vi seemed sympathetic. "Well, they think they've got something, Alb".

"By the look of some of 'em, I reckon they have. Just pray you never catch it yourself!"

Vi looked up at her husband and tutted. "I'll make us a nice cup of tea when we get home".

The bus was, to their surprise, almost on time. Albert showed their passes to a driver, whose interest appeared to extend only as far as getting under way with the least effort and consideration for those travelling. The Buchanans took to their seats. Albert was mockingly scolded for casting too long an eye in the direction of a young girl sitting close by. "You'd have looked good in one of those skirts when you were her age", whispered Albert affectionately.

"Don't know why she bothered to put it on. Leaves nothing to the imagination!"

"Well, I was imagining you in it", responded Albert.

Vi smiled, squeezing her husband's arm.

The bus was hot, the journey littered with traffic lights and traffic jams. The Buchanans prepared to alight as, having left the leafy avenues along its route, the bus once again mingled with the teeming populace going about its business - Surbiton was alive and well!

Albert glanced subconsciously as the bus passed an unassuming side road, on the corner of which stood a sign; erected in all its grey utilitarian glory, it offered guidance to those wishing to visit the Surbiton Railway Club.

*   *   *   *   *

The Railway Club was, as usual deserted at this time of day, save, that is, for one solitary member. Greg Wagstaffe sat on a bar stool surveying his surroundings.

"Clubs would give a lot for premises like these", he thought. His mind wandered, his distraction only being broken by tapping on a window, followed by a voice akin to that of John Major.

"Meter reading", the voice shouted.

As the words were uttered Greg noticed that an officious looking little man was accentuating his oral movements to back up his announcement, in case he wasn't being heard. Greg had heard him. He half-smiled as he raised his body from the stool and walked towards the door. He felt that he now knew what it was like to be a foreigner when confronted by a Brit - if you don't understand English, he'll shout at you!

The door was unbolted and the semi-uniformed, bespectacled official made his way inside. He was ushered into the kitchen where in the corner lay the gas man's quarry. He knelt awkwardly, his torch came alight and the immortal numbers "3- 1- 8- 6" were announced.

"You work here, do you?" enquired the gas man.

"No, I'm on holiday".

"Funny place to come for a holiday".

"No, I'm not on holiday here. I'm ..... oh, it doesn't matter!" replied Greg.

The gas man continued. "Of course, half my problem relates to gaining access, you know". He stood upright. "Estimated bills", he announced.

"Pardon?" replied Greg, curtly.

"Estimated bills", the gas man repeated. "When we fail to procure entry estimated bills have to be sent, and do you know, that despite computer calculations they are sometimes out by up to one thousand units".

"Fascinating", Greg remarked, with a distinct lack of enthusiasm.

All the way through this detailed analysis of a gas man's lot, Greg continued to slowly retrace his steps, followed by the limpet-like official.

"Well, I mustn't keep you", said the meter reader.

"That would be too much to expect", mumbled Greg.

The gas man was still talking as he got back into his van. Greg feared that this could be the cue for an intense comparison between his newly acquired company steed and previous models. He quickly signed off his side of the conversation by shouting, "Yes, that's right", assuming that it was the expected answer. Judging from the thick end of ten minutes' one-sided conversation, the part of the brain that took stock of answers appeared to be missing in the gas man. "Too much sniffing leaking valves", Greg mused!

Back in the bar the head of Greg's pint had all but disappeared. He resumed his position on the stool and supped his still imperial-measured Fuller's ESB. As the last crisp was devoured, he crushed the packet and walked over to the notice-board. Among the array of dog-eared timetables and for-sale ads were the list of trips being run by the Surbiton Railway Club.

The outer door was pushed open. "Ah, hello, there". It was Colin.

"Oh, it's you. I was hoping it would be someone more interesting, but there we go!"

"Don't tell me", Colin smiled boyishly. "You're looking to see who's going on the trips before you commit yourself".

"Commit suicide, you mean! Honestly, looking at some of the names on the sheet - it reads more like an outing from MENCAP".

"Oh, that's a bit cruel", countered Colin, as he walked briskly towards the notice board. He perused the list of names under the various tour headings and gave vent to a few sighs and several umms. "Well, there are a few people listed with whom one would rather not be travelling. Mind you, in the thirty-nine years the Club has been going we've probably had our fair share of characters".

Greg's look towards Colin was intense. "Yes, the SRC does have a lot to answer for".

Colin murmured - a sure sign that he was thinking. "It doesn't spell anything, does it?"

"What doesn't?"

"SRC - I've got a friend .... ".

"Which is something in itself", interrupted Greg. Colin ignored his fellow Committee member.

"I've got a friend who has recently joined the newly formed Andover Railway Circle, although when he initially applied they were going to be known as the Andover Railway Society". Colin laughed fatuously.

"That amuses you, doesn't it?" Greg shook his head slowly. Colin continued to chuckle. "The trouble with railway clubs is that whilst they are a good social leveller, they do still endear themselves to some odd sorts". Greg voiced this thought as they walked back to the bar. To be accurate, Greg walked, whereas with Colin it was more of a bounce. He always seemed to walk on his toes, with his head bowed, as if checking whether the next two feet or so were clear. It had been mentioned by members of the Club that two feet in front of him were, in fact, as far as Colin could see on most issues, but he had the Club at heart and fairly preened when able to announce his name, adding, "Clubroom Manager **and** Secretary" to anyone who asked his status.

For two years he had been known across the length and breadth of the one hundred and twenty or so members as Colin Clubroom, but the added responsibilities had necessitated, in his eyes, the carrying of a clipboard whenever he walked within the confines of the Club's buildings. "Colin Clubroom" was by many henceforth rechristened plain "Clipboard".

"So why are you here during the day?" enquired Colin.

"Holiday".

"What, time off in lieu for services rendered?"

"Colin, I'm a sales manager, not a prostitute!"

"Ah", said Colin at length, unsure of whether Greg was genuinely irritated or merely feigning annoyance. Colin began to bounce more noticeably. "First visitor of the day, then?" he said.

"No", came the reply, "The gas man beat you to it".

Greg described the said official, suggesting that the only other job he would have been qualified for was that of traffic warden.

"The frightening thing is, that he actually resembled several of our members - petty, boring and humourless - a bit like you, in fact! No, that's not quite right, you do have a sense of humour, it's just that it's never progressed beyond the level of seaside postcards!"

"Aaah", repeated Colin.

Greg frowned. "That gas man typified all the enthusiasts at Paddington Station in the fifties and sixties - long raincoat, holdall for the sandwiches which his ageing mother would have packed for him; notebook, spotter's books, Ian Allan ABC's and well-honed pencil. And that's not forgetting his tape-recorder and camera slung around his neck. They all looked the same - pasty, unfortunate faces, hidden under a camouflage of encrusted acne. Straight, greasy side-parted hair that teemed with dandruff ....."

"And glasses", chipped in Colin.

"Yes, and glasses. And they were so ungainly - arms and legs never

11

seemed to be co-ordinated".

Colin was thoughtful. He put his left index finger to his lower lip. "I wonder what happened to all those types".

"Judging from their looks, most will be serving time for paedaphilia".

"Still, there's not so many of them around nowadays", suggested Colin hastily.

Greg slowly finished his pint and laid the glass down on the bar top. "You wouldn't think so, would you?" he said with more than a degree of resignation, "But come an SRC tour and they all burrow their way out of the woodwork".

"What about you?"

"What about me - I don't look like that!" Greg's reply was sharp.

"No, I mean which trips will you be subscribing to?"

Greg pondered. "I'll tell you what - you put your name down against the one's you are going on and I'll go on the others!"

Colin cast his mind back to the lists of the notice board uttered one of his more positive comments, "Hmmmmm".

Greg picked up his empty glass and crisp packet and walked into the serving area. Having rinsed the glass he threw the packet into the waste bin beside the sink. Colin bounced behind him, scrutinising the list of forthcoming events which were to be held at the Club.

"Colin, you're almost sitting on my shoulder".

"Ah, sorry. Just noticed we're a bit thin on the ground for bookings. There's a Rotary Club meeting tonight, but nothing tomorrow. In fact, the next one's the 14th of May. Mmmmm, it appears that the Wesleyan Chapel Players are rehearsing Macbeth".

"Don't they use the church hall any more?"

"No, not since it burned down".

"Aha", said Greg knowingly. "So, one of the big supermarket chains is looking for a new site!"

"You are cynical".

"Just a realist, Colin, just a realist".

Colin continued with his scrutiny. "Aaah, on the 21st we have one of those dreadful singles nights, and on the following Friday, the hall is being hired out to the Phyllis Enwright Fund for research into elephantitis ...."

"They want to fund research into a shorter title, first!" replied Greg, as he stood with his back to the sink.

Colin continued undeterred. "On the following Monday is our Committee Meeting, then there's nothing until the middle of June - Rotary again".

"It's always stimulating hearing the list of events being read with such enthusiasm and interest".

"Do you think so", Colin replied eagerly.

"No, not really", Greg continued. "I was just practising the line for another conversation - bound to come in useful some time".

"Aaah", said Colin, rubbing his chin with his left hand, bouncing nervously. He looked at his watch and then at the clock behind the bar, before his eyes reverted to his watch once more. "Ten to two, better be getting back or I'll start to use up all my accrued flexi-time".

"So soon? It seems only five hours ago that you arrived!" The sarcasm completely washed over Colin, who bowed his head as he backed out of the door.

"See you Wednesday".

Greg half lifted his right hand in acknowledgement and began walking back towards the library where he was to recommence his filing activities.

"Greg, Greg!"

He turned. "What now, Colin?"

"You didn't notice, did you?"

"Notice what, Colin?"

Colin plucked his lapel with his left hand, whilst pointing enthusiastically with his right.
"Oh, go on, I give up".

"My new badge. I got it in the post this morning. It's a reproduction Spotter's Club badge". His zeal was not shared by Greg.

"That's nice", he said, in a disinterested fashion.

"1963 they last came out, you know".

"You've been waiting all these years to get one, have you?"

"Well, I lost my original one on a trip over the Settle and Carlisle in 1967, so it's sort of deja vu, so to speak".

"Not only a replacement badge but a chance to speak a foreign language as well! - Colin, hadn't you better be going? Your accrued flexi-time - remember".

"Aaah, right. 'Bye".

Greg thought back to the time long ago when an ex-schoolfriend of his joined a company called Triumph Investment Trust (TIT). Still, knowing his friend, they probably deserved each other. There were, he felt, looking down the list of names pencilled in against the various tours on offer, a number of tits in the Club. Two of the biggest belonged to the tour organiser, the only woman on the Committee. It was Doreen who, along with husband, Derek, spent a lot of time suggesting destinations, obtaining quotes from various coach companies and then playing mine hostess and host, organising games, sing-songs, videos and snacks on the journeys and often to keep an unappreciative travelling public happy.

There were Club members who supported every trip, those who were discerning in their choice and those who never set foot on a coach. Greg placed his left hand on the wall by the side of the notice board and leant heavily as his mind drifted back to one of the photographs he had unearthed. It was a 7" x 5" blow up of a scene taken at a long-closed branch line station. An ageing steam engine had been brought out of its stored condition and life breathed into her, enough life to haul four coaches, the inhabitants of which had climbed or jumped down onto the tracks, so that this group photograph could be taken. Everybody had crowded around the Club's most prized asset, the locomotive headboard. Those in real authority had both hands clasped around the carved, wooden plaque which read, "Surbiton Railway Club, Last Day Tour, 3rd October, 1956".

"I was only three", Greg said to himself. Without exception everyone appeared to have said "Cheese" on cue. This had resulted in an extremely staged effect being enacted. To Greg, however, it mattered not. What he would have given to have been able to reboard that coach, and travel off behind a veteran of the steam era, when the sun always shone and there was every chance that you would not be subjected to an assault on the local train home at the end of it all.

Greg glanced once more at the names on the notice board and muttered, "Of all the places in all the world, and they have to live in Surbiton!"

* * * * *

Almost two hours had elapsed before the peace was shattered. "Bastard" was the expletive which accompanied the door being pushed open.

"How did you know I was in here?" asked Greg dryly, his eyes still fixed upon the dusty Meccano magazines languishing on the floor.

Now standing just inside the Club library were Mick Clayton, the

Treasurer, and Robin Harmsworth, the Chairman, who sniggered at Greg's comment. "You just caught the tail end of one of Mick's rantings", commented Robin.

"Oh, that makes me feel a lot better. You think you're in for a nice quiet day, and it's been busier than Clapham Junction. Are you two an item, or did you just happen to arrive together?"

"Oh, I just popped in to pick up the post and bumped into Mick by the main gates".

"No work?"

"Well, there are no lectures this afternoon, if that's what you mean".

Mick stood as usual with his legs apart, hands by his side; the left hand held a cigarette. It had often been noted that his aggressive stance mirrored that adopted by cowboys when facing each other for the final showdown. "You have more free periods than your students, no wonder the country's over-populated by uneducated oiks and over-paid educationalists!" He turned towards Greg. "So this is how you spend your holiday".

Greg looked up. "Members seem to dump their unwanted journals quicker than we can sell them".

"That's why we needed someone with your willingness, zest and dedication", added Mick.

Greg pointed a finger. "If I remember rightly, all I said was, 'it's a pity the magazines aren't in order', when hey presto, there's a vacancy created and filled before I get a chance to say 'no thanks'".

"We never said it was a democratic committee", added Mick, who turned suddenly towards Robin as he headed off down the corridor towards the main office. "Can you see if there's anything in my tray while you're there".

Robin returned and handed Mick the contents of his tray. "Circulars, circulars - it would be nice to discover some invited correspondence for a change. Aha, here we are". Discarding the previous mail, Robin opened a buff envelope and digested the contents. "Greg, listen to this. We've just got a reply from the railway club in York re the September show. They're quite prepared to meet the expenses you listed for taking "Southworth", three-star accommodation for five operators, lunch and beverage vouchers - non-alcohol, naturally ....."

"Naturally", offered Greg and Mick in unison.

The Club had two 'OO' gauge layouts, "Southworth" and "Pennytown". The former name was acknowledged by many as being uninspiring, to say the least, but the core of the layout's operators lived either in Surbiton - South Biton as was - or Tolworth. It seemed, however, to keep everyone content, if not ecstatic.

Robin continued. "They go on to say how pleased they are that we are running a coach for our members and other enthusiasts".

"And how is our Outings Secretary doing on that score", enquired Mick, with more than a hint of sarcasm.

"Well, she's reserved a 56-seater, and apparently over 40 people have pencilled in their names so far. Not bad, is it".

Mick lit up another cigarette. "No doubt you'll impart that information to the vibrant throng that manages to prise itself from in front of their televisions come Wednesday night".

"Of course I will be mentioning it", said Robin. "It's very good news having one of our layouts accepted for display at such a prestigious event".

Mick sighed. "Yeh, it's just the thought of Doreen standing beside you like a bitch on heat, waiting to elaborate on everything you've said".

Robin looked towards Greg, who was pulling in his back in an effort to relieve the discomfort of kneeling for a considerable period. "Shouldn't be doing that at your age", suggested Mick.

"You can always help, you know - volunteer, a bit like I did".

"No thanks, I prefer to cook the books, not read them".

"Seriously, though", offered Robin, "There are always members whinging that the Committee doesn't do enough for them. Surely this will be a weekend few will want to miss. You are sure you'll get enough to man it, aren't you, Greg?"

It was Mick who replied. "Free travel, board and grub - 'course they'll go. Mind you, if some of them had to contribute towards it themselves ....."

"Oh, that's unfair, Mick", interrupted Greg. "We pay in regularly to keep "Southworth" up to exhibition standard".

"What, including Harold?"

"Yes, even Harold".

"Well, if you say so", acknowledged Mick, grudgingly.

"You're just judging everyone else on the standards set by the N gauge lot", said Greg.

"Tight bastards. Psychiatrists would doubtless say that's why they play with small toys. They feel they're getting better value for money".

Robin sighed. Mick mumbled a drawn out "Well", before

continuing. "You have to have your suspicions about any group who call their layout "Much Furtling"."

Robin, always a conciliatory type, said, "I'm sorry, Mick, but I believe the Club should be all things to all men and that it should embrace all interests with equal enthusiasm".

"Pompous sod", exclaimed Mick. "Liberal voter, are you?"

Both Greg and Robin raised their hands to their mouths indicating mock boredom. Mick stubbed out the cigarette. "Right, I'm off. I'll see you and the rest of the unappreciative bilge on Wednesday".

Robin busied himself in the storeroom which housed the various Club layouts. This area was part of an extension added just under four years ago. Most of the materials, from bricks to timber, from plaster to flooring, had come from a source which had never been aware of the contribution it had made to the Club's rateable value. Peter, the materials provider, or to give him his working name, Pete, always knew somebody. He was a car salesman by trade, if not profession and appeared to live by his wits. It mattered not what the industry was, for he generally had a man in the trade who "owed him a favour". In the case of the Club room extension it had been a several thousand pounds favour!

Like many of the Club members Pete was in his early forties, but unlike those members, who had accepted the ageing process, Pete intended to stay in his twenties, both in dress and mentality. He was of average height with dark, wavy hair parted in the style of the day. Years of conducting his business in public houses and hotels had given him more than a slight paunch, although Pete's vision of himself was far from that of an ageing Lothario. He subconsciously pulled in his stomach every time he was introduced to a member of the opposite sex, but the curled waistband around his trousers and the straining belt that encircled them still failed to see the light of day under the excess of fat.

If not in a formal suit Pete would arrive in a track suit of the gaudiest kind, mobile phone in hand regardless. His wife, Rita, who had just turned thirty-five, was known to all as "Reet". If anyone should address her as Rita she would quickly tell them, "Everyone calls me Reet". Psychologically she felt that by rhyming the names Reet and Pete they would be considered more of a unit - an item. Despite fifteen years of marriage she had every right to feel insecure. Whilst she was outward going, attractive and enjoyed male company, she was fiercely loyal - and expected that loyalty in return. Pete, however, was not endowed with the same sense of devotion. His reasoning was that if it wore a skirt and was aged between sixteen and sixty, then it was fair game, neither extremity of age limit required to be strictly adhered to! Pete was not, however, unaware of the need to keep his extra curricular activities, as he called them, hidden from Rita. She knew deep down that he had eyes (and hands) for other women but preferred to ignore all the signs and stay smiling, avoiding any confrontation that might bring matters to a head.

Although Pete did have a genuine interest in railways, the Club provided him with an alibi when philandering. Not uncommon were the occasions when Rita would ring and a Club member would have to cover for her husband. Imaginations were being drained of excuses as to why Pete couldn't get to the phone to answer her call. When all was said and done, how many times could the beer be blamed for someone's continued occupancy of the lavatory!

Greg sat in the office chair and thumbed through the telephone directory for Pete's works number.

Pete Balfour stood beside a recently resprayed "F" registered Austin Maestro.

"Oh, yes, it's an absolute gem of a motor. You won't find better this side of, well, the High Street!" He laughed raucously. The potential customer smiled. "And, of course, the mileage is 100% guaranteed".

The customer was not convinced. "It is unusual to find a four year old vehicle with such low mileage".

Pete put his arm around the man, who visibly shrunk under the pressurised insincerity.

"The previous owner was a titled gentleman".

"Really?" He was now impressed.

"Yes, really - so, you're happy with the colour, you're happy with the drive and you're happy with the mileage. So what will it be? Cash, or would you rather take advantage of our amazingly easy terms?"

The interested party drew back from any form of commitment. "I would rather like my wife to see it before I take the plunge".

Pete raised both hands. "No probs. Give me your address and I'll run it round tonight".

"I'm not sure of my wife's movements".

"Well, what time does the little lady get your dinner?"

"We always eat at 6.30".

Pete clapped his hands as if solving the final clue in a Times crossword. "Then I'll be round at 7.15. Give you time to digest your prunes". He cackled.

"Oh, right".

Pete, smiling smoothly, led the man through to his office. "'Ere we go, write down your address". The phone rang. Pete lifted the receiver. "Balfour's Beauties, purveyors of quality horseless carriages, how can I help you".

Greg listened in amusement. "Do people actually fall for that line? Hello, Pete, it's Greg".

"Well, you must have, you bought one of me motors - so what's new, pussycat?"

"The York weekend, it's on. Good news, huh?"

Pete put his hand over the receiver. "And your phone number".

He continued his conversation with Greg. "Boys' weekend away, that'll do for me, Tommy".

"You coming Wednesday evening?" enquired Greg.

"Yeh, bringing Reet, give her a night out".

"Oh, that'll be a bundle of fun for her. Look, I'll give you all the info then. Okay?"

"Yeh, fine. See yer".

"Bye".

Pete's attention refocused on the possible sale of his Maestro. "Right then, sir, see you at 7.15". The customer stood his ground.
"Just one thing before I go. May I have a look at the log book, please?"

Pete hesitated. "Er, certainly". He pulled open a cabinet drawer and extracted a folder. "'Ere it is".

The log book was scrutinised for what Pete considered an unacceptably long time.

"I thought you said the car had a titled owner?"

Pete beamed. "That's right - Mister!" His laugh was ear-piercing. The man looked uncertain.

With arms around shoulders once more, Pete steered the seemingly hesitant individual out onto the pavement and followed his progress as he headed off along the high street. "Prat", he mumbled.

*   *   *   *   *

The Rotary Club had been and gone. Lessons had been learned by the Committee as to which bookings were accepted and which were tactfully rejected. Eighteenth birthday parties were barred, twenty-firsts

19

were welcomed, providing the hirer lived in what was considered to be a decent area. If, however, the enquirer gave his address as being that which formed part of the local council estate, then the date was immediately, and as if by magic, found to be previously booked - as were, of course, any other suggested alternative dates. It was unfortunate that the Club had to bar all activities generated by what Mick called the CH factor. CH stood for council house and there were no grey areas as far as the Treasurer was concerned. Nine roads made up the council estate and nine roads contained morons of low mentality and high violence levels. Mick's all-embracing phrase for the residents was to describe them as "pond life".

The trouble was that whilst this was a somewhat over- simplification of the truth, it had to be said that whenever the Club weakened with the lure of money being dangled over the phone, the resultant morning's clean-up cost more than the profit made the previous evening. The regular cleaner, known to all as Mrs. M., worked miracles, getting the hall, corridor and toilets back into some semblance of order by the following mid-day, when her departure time was officially due. Mrs. M. was a lady of few words, in her mid-fifties and blessed with a lounge whale of a husband, whose only known activities, other than using the toilet when pressed to exercise his bodily functions, was to accept huge platefuls of food in between quaffing mild and bitter, and lighting up cigarettes. The resultant ash would forever fall on the settee or floor around his body, whilst the butt would be flicked into the fireplace; simply stubbing out a cigarette in an ashtray had never been considered as an alternative worthy of pursuance. It had, however, been many years since the chimney breast had been bricked up, rendered, and a gas fire fitted.

The consequence of this action was that the stub invariably hit either the bars protecting the elements or the "realistic log effect" covering that played such a part in making this heat generator the centre of conversation to all-comers - new or old - even if it were to be continually surrounded by the fallen butts.

Mrs. M. had chosen it because she liked the idea of a posh, mahogany finish. She hadn't thought of it as posh, until the salesman in the gas showroom mentioned the word as he stood to one side of the said appliance, bending over it lovingly with both hands gripping the corners. That four letter word had sold it to her - something posh on the estate.

It had always been a source of amusement that someone like Mrs.

M., who's two teenage children were anything but socially acceptable, would agree with every word said about her fellow neighbours of the nine roads. In fact, she actively discouraged bookings in case the Club was damaged, or its bar staff injured. Mick always maintained that she considered herself to have been elevated out of the social level that governed the estate, by dint of her working, which was in itself a major change in policy from that adopted by the majority of its residents.

The Clubrooms remained unopened on Saturday, other than to receive Mrs. M.'s attentions. Sunday saw a few members pottering around tidying up some electrical work on the "Pennytown" layout. This group's members were very gregarious and generous in nature. Ridiculed throughout the Club it was known as "Anytown" since it was not based on anywhere and it did not comply with any of the rules of thumb that governed layouts. It was not set in a particular period, trains ran at scale speeds of 150 miles per hour - from start to stop - and buses, lorries and cars from Victorian times to modern day, could be seen grouped together over the hastily completed and garishly coloured scenery. It was, however, the layout on which everyone was welcome. Would-be members, tempted to test an ageing Hornby Dublo or Triang Locomotive, or a newly purchased ready-to-run model, were encouraged to "let her rip", a phrase used by all four group members with gusto - and generally in unison.

It was not, perhaps, surprising that the railway layout was so nebulous in its parentage, for all custodians hailed from north of Watford, the line across which no southerner traverses without making comment. A Brummie, a Jock and one from each of the red and white rose counties made up their number. They were the true "take us as you find us" types.

The Club would open its doors at 7 p.m. on Wednesday and by 7.30 p.m. without fail all four would be ensconced by the bar, and there they would stay until closing time. This routine was only broken when it was their turn to set up "Pennytown" for its running night.

Over the four Wednesdays in any given month each layout was given an allotted date when it would be up and running. If there was a fifth Wednesday in the month then an extra activity, such as a film show or a talk, would be organised. The Committee had tried an auction on a couple of occasions, whereby the vendor retained the profit, less ten per cent fee for each item sold, which was supposed to swell the Club's coffers. Railway modellers are not generally thought to be a wealthy breed, and if they are, then not the most generous.

Mick had probably tried more than most to generate some enthusiasm and salesmanship when he offered to act as auctioneer. Once again, it was left to the northern element to stick up their hands, not because they necessarily wanted to own everything they bid for, but because it was fun, an aspect lost on many of the check-jacketed brigade who frequented the Club.

These members were mainly in the older age bracket. Some were satisfied only when in the company of real steam. Some were modellers, referred to as rivet counters due to their obsession with accuracy, and some were ex-modellers, this state being forced upon them by failing eyesight or some other medically inhibiting factor.

They all had their likes and dislikes but the subject which united them all was a loathing, in some cases bordering on hatred, of the "Pennytown" layout. The one thing you didn't do was "let her rip", or compete in races around the track. One trick considered by check-jackets to be childish was Jock's love of "tail chasing". This consisted of a locomotive hauling so many coaches that the train filled almost the complete circle of track. This resulted in a gap of only a couple of inches between the front of the engine and the last coach. Jock's comment that, "It's sniffing its own airse!" did nothing to lighten their view of the situation.

Come an Open Day, however, and "Pennytown" came into its own. There was never a dull moment. Parents and children alike would stand for some considerable time watching the antics of Thomas, Percy and James the Red Engine doing battle with each other - and all at 150 mph.

The check-jacket members who did still model were part of another four-man team that made up the fourth indoor layout. This was their pride and joy - a rivet counter's dream. Everything was "just so". Every detail of the station and environs was as near as one could get to perfection. Every tree took on an identity of its own. The oaks looked like oaks, the willows like willows. It was the epitome of the archetypal, rural country terminus. Based on a fictitious village in the Cotswolds the layout's name, "Chipping Waltham", conveyed the atmosphere and period feel for this Great Western branch line set in the 1930's.

The down side of this situation was that the members refused to run anything other than a realistic timetable, even at the one New Malden show they had attended. They claimed that a branch line like theirs would have been served by six trains each way, Monday to Friday, with four trains running on a Saturday, and no Sunday service at all. The result of this obsession with reality meant that on the Saturday of the show they ran only eight trains all day. One visitor to the exhibition likened the lack of activity on the layout to the famous ASLEF strike nearly forty years previous.

Complaints were made to the organisers, the chairman of which had his job cut out trying to stop them using Sunday as an excuse not to run anything at all. The four members just did not like the idea of running two Saturday timetables on successive days. It just did not seem right to them. The chairman's offer of free cream teas melted their mouths, if not their hearts. One member, overcome with the thought that they were getting something for nothing, proffered the suggestion that they might include an unscheduled train sometime during the day. No-one said a word, looks were enough to cancel the proposed addition to the timetable.

*   *   *   *   *

At 6.30 p.m. on another fine May evening, Albert, walked slowly up the drive which led to the Club. He was, besides Mrs. M., the only other paid "employee" at the Club, both being engaged as casual staff.

The ex-army sergeant had just celebrated his 70th birthday, years of "testing the barrel" were beginning to take their toll. Everybody liked Albert. There was nothing he would not do for anyone, he was considered everyone's friend. As he approached the double gates Albert subconsciously viewed the live steam line that bordered the longest, straight section of fencing surrounding the Club's grounds. The track was just long enough to justify it being used to shuttle children up and down on the Open Days that were infrequently held and usually when the question of increasing membership came into play.

The track was used mainly by its builders for testing their latest example of precision engineering. The half dozen or so members who made up the "crew", as they liked to be called, were a fairly dour lot. It would actually be a mistake to call them a group, because that was the one thing they definitely were not. As individuals, they built their locomotives, and as individuals, they operated the line. Information and advice were freely given and received, but each looked after his own. Few were friends in the true sense of the word - it was more a case of sharing a love of large scale modelling. Their general dislike of anything

23

small and electrically operated was, however, a bonding factor, and one which reared its head whenever a fault developed on one of the popular gauge layouts being operated in the hall.

To their credit, they were, along with their wives, on every tour that visited a steam railway. At least twelve names could be relied upon to be on the list. It goes without saying that they block-booked seats on the coach, as the last thing they wanted was an interloper sitting amongst them from what they considered to be the lower orders. That attitude set the scene for the rest of the day out. They would tour the works together, inspect pistons and coupling rods together, and naturally sit together, exchanging technical data on the preserved railway's train ride. The wives went along with their husbands in uncomplaining style as if it had never occurred to them that there were other people to talk to.

Albert unlocked the back door, turned off the alarm and walked through to the bar. Once inside he released the protective grille that ran between the ceiling and bar. He turned on the lights. Although the Club house had been built using pre-fabricated materials during the 1970's, it lay on the site of a Victorian dwelling. The opportunity had been taken during construction to utilise the remaining cellar for the storage of beer and lager.

Having checked the barrels, turned on the gas and placed ash trays and mats on the bar, Albert pulled himself a half pint of real ale. The brewery who supplied the Club with its beers was associated with a number of smaller, independent concerns and very often a non-local brew would appear, its origins being hand-written on the card attached to the pump. This latest delivery included a barrel from the Welsh brewers, Felinfoel. Albert had tapped the barrel Monday morning before his trek to the Hippodrome Arms, named after a variety theatre long since demolished and only remembered in the artwork that contributed to the pub's sign.

He raised his glass to the light, inspected the clarity of the beer and sipped slowly. Albert never drank quickly, just continuously. He considered it sacrilege to pull through the first pint of a new barrel, and then be forced to decant the generally frothy liquid into the sink. It was only when the yeast began to take on a life of its own, appearing in larger than acceptable globules, that he accepted the sink to be the only possible option.

Albert glanced up at the clock behind him. It was just turned 7 p.m. He walked from the serving area to the main doors, unbolted them and left them unlocked so as to facilitate entrance by Club members.

Keyholders were strictly appointed by the Committee. Apart from representatives of the various groups Albert and Mrs. M. were the only other entitled holders. The responsibility of such high office was not lost on Mrs. M., who prized them in the same manner as most women would a diamond ring. It had been said that if she came to choose between her husband and the keys, then the metal objects would have remained with her - a preference, to be fair, which would have been taken up by anyone who knew her other half!

Albert walked to the layout which stood in the middle of the hall. Tonight it was "Pennytown"'s turn to grace the floor. Its operators had erected it the previous evening so as to gain maximum running time on Club night. They would, in fact, be leaving the layout up at the end of the evening, meeting again on Thursday night in order for it to be dismantled.

Although not an enthusiast, Albert treasured the rare moments when he had been able to bring his grandchild down to the Club. The last occasion was over two years ago, shortly before his only child, Graham, emigrated to Australia with his wife and Jamie, who would now be seven. The occasional letter, containing the odd photograph, was the extent of contact from down under. Albert and his wife, Vi, telephoned and wrote regularly, but it always appeared to be inconvenient for conversation with their grandchild. Albert and Graham had never had a close relationship. They were not the sort to embrace each other. A hand shake at arm's distance was the closest they got to personal contact. A rift prior to emigration had stifled what little there was between the two men, but Albert stepped back from breaking all ties for fear of never seeing Jamie again.

Albert turned, sighed and walked back to the bar shaking his head. His mind was far away in Australia. From his jacket, which hung behind the bar door, he removed a wallet. His fingers worked rapidly as he extracted the latest photo of Jamie, sent just over six months ago. He rubbed his thumb over the glossy smile and then suddenly, as if being tapped on the shoulder by an unknown hand, quickly returned the photo back into its sheath. As he straightened the jacket his hand moved to the regimental badge, which adorned his left lapel. Of the three loves in his life, only Vi was absent.

Albert took hold of his keys and turned towards the storeroom. It was usual to unlock the double doors early on, as there was always someone wishing to stack, unstack or generally fiddle around in the room.

Two cars pulled up simultaneously. There was a frenzied banging of doors before the "gang of four" strode through the entrance. Something had amused them for there was much mirth and back-slapping. Albert returned to the bar. One of their group ordered four pints of "Feeling-Foul", as he pronounced it, much to the amusement of his colleagues. As the straight-sided glasses were filled, one of "Pennytown"'s creators leant forward from the stool until his eyes were level with the bar top. Looking directly into a full glass he observed, "There must be something wrong with this beer, it's clear, no bloody bits. Normally need glasses to see through your beer!" He looked around with a wide, self-satisfied grin in order to soak up appreciation of his witticism.

The barman raised his body and looked above their heads towards "Pennytown".

"I always need glasses, tinted ones 'an all, to look at your layout. Bloody colours you've got it in!"

Jock looked sombre, his eyes narrowed. "Colours, I'll tell ye of colours. Have ye nae visited the wild expanses of Rannoch Moor in autumn? Heathers of every hue, their colours revealed by the clearing mists playing host to the ghosts of battles past".

There was an eerie silence as Jock's hands wavered menacingly in mid air.

"No, can't say I have", replied Albert, bringing the others back to life. "You?"

"Aye, just the once. Rained solid for three days, could'nae stand the place!"

The back slapping and laughter recommenced. Albert poured out the last pint. Isn't it time you lot started playing with your train set before the Fat Controller gets the hump!"

"Oooooh", they mouthed in unison.

"Someone got off the wrong side of the barrel rack", retorted Yorkie.

Albert sneered, took the price of a half from the change and muttered, "Thanks very much, don't mind if I do".

It was all taken in good part. After a few minutes dedicated to exchanging stories and gossip, one of their number made his way over to the wall socket, fitted the plug and switched on the power. The others took their cue and beer in hand made their way under the circular layout until they were surrounded by track work. Within seconds, locomotives of differing parentage and generation were zooming around at speeds which would have caused a Health & Safety Officer apoplexy, hauling stock that differed in every conceivable way. Time-honoured roars of "let her rip" echoed throughout the hall, as trains weaved their way around tracks to the pure delight of its operators, and to a purist's worst nightmare.

As the evening progressed, members trickled in and lively banter, debate and exchange of memories held sway around the Club rooms. On average, around half the Club's membership were present on any evening. Many of those absent were country members, who stayed in regular contact through infrequent visits or via the Surbiton Railway Club News. This was a quarterly news sheet compiled by the Clubroom Manager and Secretary. Some of the membership were life presidents, rarely seen. Some were just never seen, others were dead!

As was tradition in the Club, come 8.30 p.m. and Colin would set about selling raffle tickets to members present. For 50 pence one would receive six tickets. For one pound, thirteen would be extracted from the book. It had recently been a source of bewilderment to the Committee that something as innocuous as a raffle should bring about such strong feeling. At the last AGM the subject of general accounts had taken up little space and time on the agenda, compared to that afforded to the raffle. Whereas there had not been the expected long debate on the financial situation, which was not nearly as healthy as it had been some twelve months previously, a motion had been proposed by a vociferous section, who maintained that if one purchased one pound's worth of tickets, an extra raffle ticket should be issued. The proposer said this would be an encouragement to buying yet more, thus contributing further to the Club's coffers. It had not gone unnoticed by many that the proposer, seconder and their supporters, all regularly bought twelve tickets, and obviously felt aggrieved that their generosity was not being fully acknowledged.

It was "Pennytown"'s finest hour. They may not have had a layout to be taken seriously, but they had forced the Committee to discuss a change in the rules, which would have been unthinkable only a few years before. Colin had stood up at the AGM, saying that in his view, and his capacity as Clubroom Manager **and** Secretary, it was a perk to receive one extra ticket when spending 50 pence, because if purchased separately, each ticket cost ten pence. He went on to remind the attendees that it had only been five years since the extra ticket had been granted by the Committee, due to pressure being brought to bear at a previous AGM. Colin asked where it would all end.

Mick had leaned towards Greg and whispered, "With a hot poker up his arse, if he doesn't stop boring everyone!"

Colin never fully heard the comment but knew instinctively that he was the butt of Mick's aside. He then proceeded to hold his hands aloft and fall silent.

Swearing wasn't particularly prevalent at the Club, which made Mick's comments all the more colourful. At the end of most discussions held with him, Mick would sigh dismissively and with pained expression the word "bastard" would be vented. It was rare to find Mick laughing with anyone, but not uncommon to find him laughing at someone. His sense of humour could readily be brought alive by witnessing some unlucky soul dashing fifty yards for a bus, leaping for the platform and missing by a hair's breadth. He was, in fact, the sort whose longevity of mirth was exceeded only by the embarrassment and humiliation of the victim, left spreadeagled in the gutter.

Mick had sat at the Committee table throughout the AGM, stretched out in his usual manner, hands behind his head. He had stood up only to deliver his report. From the attended throng a spotty-faced newcomer, in awe of Mick's presence and style, asked for his opinion. Mick duly obliged by commenting that it wasn't surprising that raffle tickets should hold such staying power as an item, when one took into account that its protagonists were "northern bastards", used to pettiness, unions and going underground - where, if they had any consideration for others, they would have stayed! Nods and grunts ensued and after much discussion the motion, likened by Colin to Maastricht, was carried on a show of hands.

Despite changes to the system some members stuck rigidly to their 50 pence per week purchase. One long-established member, Harold, had since time immemorial, handed over 10 pence every week. He would dig deep into his check-jacket pocket, a jacket worn regardless of condition or temperature, and extract a tan purse. It was one of those which doubled over. He would prise it apart as if stiff from lack of use and slowly empty its contents into the lower half, now forming a tray.

Colin had learned to grasp the coins quickly before Harold found, tucked in a crevice, another penny to join the lone example he had previously located but unable to find a soul mate, had rejected in favour of a ten penny piece. Harold always felt he was spending more if a coin of a higher denomination were to be surrendered.

Tonight was no exception. "I don't know why you don't buy 50p worth, Harold. You do get an extra ticket free".

"Look, Colin, you only need one ticket to win first prize".

"But have you ever won a prize?"

"Not yet, no".

"But that's my point, the more you buy, the more ....."

"Colin".

"What?"

"Bugger off and irritate someone else!"

Colin accepted the three 2-penny and four penny pieces. "Aah, right".

The total sum contributed would be split into three or four varying amounts, decreasing in value and offered to the members as prizes. There was nothing so unsavoury as cash, however. A receipt for the amount won was issued from the bar till and could be used against the purchase of a Club tie, T-shirt, sweatshirt or books. Doreen administered the funds and recorded who won what, and when.

Just after 9 p.m. Colin stepped back into the hall and on tiptoes surveyed the gathering. Satisfying himself that everyone had been nobbled he returned to the office. The evening's takings were emptied from the beer mug onto the desk. The sum totalled £31 in one pound coins and silver, plus of course, six pennies and two two-pences. Doreen entered.

"How are you getting on?"

"Nearly done", replied Colin, checking over the piles once more with his fingers.

Doreen agreed the tally and divided the total into three prize amounts. It was at this point that Robin enquired as to whether anyone wished to make an announcement. As Clubroom Manager **and** Secretary it was Colin's job to co-ordinate members - Committee or otherwise - who wished to make a statement at Chairman's Announcement Time.

At approximately 9.30 p.m. Colin walked behind the bar and rang the bell. This was the signal for trains to slow to a halt, or in "Pennytown"'s case, screech to a halt. All conversation ceased, all eyes focused on Robin, who entered the hall clutching his list of notes. All eyes, that is, except for Fred, who unfailingly continued to sit in the corner under a section of board that he painstakingly wired and rewired on a weekly basis.

It wasn't always the same board but the level of activity remained constant. Fred usually arrived around 8 p.m., set himself up and from then until approximately 10.30 p.m. the sighting of his person was limited to his shoes and lower trouser legs. His upper torso was always shadowed by the board held above him by virtue of the portable legs, which entered the building with him every week and were taken away again at going-home time. Several weeks ago Fred had emerged from under the board, prematurely by his standards, and a Club member had asked Colin if he was new to the SRC. "Oh, no", Colin had replied, "Fred's been coming here for many years now - before me, in fact. Let's think, his membership number is 1169 and I'm 1340".

Somewhat perplexed the enquirer said he felt sure that he'd never seen this Fred chap before and that he had been coming down for nearly six months himself. As Fred packed away his snippers, volt meter and other assorted electrical paraphernalia, Colin pointed to Fred's shoes. "Haven't you seen them before?" he asked.

"No, why?"

"Thought you might have recognised them", said Colin, becoming excited. "And the turn-ups, thought they would have given the game away". Colin was positively bouncing now. His fellow member, however, wished he had never started the conversation. It had only been a passing remark, after all. Colin sensed a distinct lack of interest beginning to shroud the proceedings.

"You generally only see Fred's feet and turn-ups under that board over there". Colin rubbed his chin with his left hand, looked at his watch and then turned to the clock behind the bar. "Mmmmm", he added, "It is unlike him to go home this early". His eyebrows furrowed.

"Doesn't look like the sort to be on a promise".

"Aaaah", said Colin, not knowing how to answer the sexual intrusion which had just entered the conversation. He was, however, spared further deliberation as a pat on the back and a "See you later" ended the verbal exchange.

Colin had never been able to handle references or overtones of a sexual nature. He was 33 years of age and lived with his mother. Colin's father had left the family home when he was very young. Mrs. Mabey and her son lived in a semi-detached, in a very pleasant tree-lined cul-de-sac full of 1930's built dwellings. The surname "Mabey" suited Colin well. His generally accepted lack of decision led to his office nick-name of "Maybe Mabey". He was the sort who would spend his life tagged to a nick-name, if not his mother. Mrs. Mabey had tried introducing her only child to friends' daughters some fifteen years ago, but to no avail. Colin had never found the confidence to look straight into a girl's face when talking to her, let alone considering asking her out.

When he was twenty-two Colin was involved in an incident which led to him being the hero of the hour. Whilst walking up the stairs which led to Platforms 9 and 10 at Clapham Junction Station, a young lady ran past him in a hurry to catch a train. She slipped, trapping one of her high-heeled shoes on the edge of a step. Her ankle twisted and she was knocked off balance. Falling sideways and stumbling down the steps, two people behind her moved swiftly away from the tumbling body. It wasn't that they didn't wish to help, it was just the natural reaction not to become entangled. Whilst would-be passengers looked on, Colin hastened towards the screaming female and, almost wrestling with her, pulled her to the side, where his left hand grasped the hand-rail to prevent her falling any further. Other members of the public now crowded round. Colin held her whilst she composed herself. Offers and suggestions were voiced, but Colin remained in control.

"Can someone please get a cup of tea for the lady", he ordered, "and would someone else please find a member of staff".

The tea was the easier request to comply with, even if the tea-room assistant had demanded 20 pence before handing over the elixir of life. By the time tea arrived Colin had calmed down the young lady, who was now sitting on the step, knees together, her hands clutching a tissue, with which she wiped her eyes. It transpired that she was travelling to Victoria in order to attend an interview. She would still go, despite the torn tights and grubby coat. Colin offered to phone the company and explain why she might be late. The small crowd now began to disperse. Colin held her arm; she was still shaking as he led her slowly up the stairs. There appeared to be no broken bones, although she complained of feeling sore down her left side. After another cup of tea in the refreshment room they exchanged good-byes. Still flushed from the impromptu success of his handling of the situation, Colin turned quickly. "Wait, can I phone to see how your interview went?"

The young lady smiled coyly and hurriedly extracted a piece of paper from her handbag, writing her telephone number upon it. This she handed to Colin, who beamed and said, "Good luck".

Her train screeched to a halt. Doors opened, people busied themselves, the doors slammed closed. Within seconds she was gone. Colin stood there as the 11.13 faded from view. He couldn't believe he had done it. The initial reaction on the steps was instinctive, but to ask for her phone number was something different. That move was calculated.

He had mentioned the incident to his mother over a Sainsbury's haggis at tea time but omitted the proposed phone call. Colin left it a few days and finally rang her one evening when his mother was out visiting a family friend. The phone rang twice. He heard her voice and replaced the receiver. At home the atmosphere was different. His hands were sweating. He rang again. She answered again. Colin announced himself. Her voice came alive. She asked if it were Colin who had rung a few moments previously. He said that it was, but that he had dropped the phone, adding that he had just finished washing up and his hands were still wet. Colin considered this to be a reasonable excuse for his shyness.

"Wonderful", he exclaimed, as she told him the good news.

"In a way I think it helped".

"What did?" asked Colin.

"Looking helpless", she laughingly replied. "I think they felt so sorry for me that they had to offer me the job".

"Nonsense", said Colin. "You're doing yourself an injustice. They offered you that job on merit".

A long silence ensued and despite several attempts by Colin to utter the words, "Can I see you again" - words he had practiced for days - he ended up wishing her luck, saying "Goodbye".

He had detected her trying to continue the conversation but ignored the signs that would have been so easily responded to by a less sensitive person. Colin lowered the receiver onto its base and walked slowly back into the kitchen, where he inspected the state of his newly painted Maunsell coach. He knew that he had failed to achieve what he had set out to, but consoled himself with the thought that the preparation of his works' social club minutes would take up most of tomorrow evening anyway, the evening he had set aside for asking her out. He would ring again, he told himself, but he never did.

*   *   *   *   *

Doreen stood next to the Chairman who, having shuffled his list of notes and cleared his throat, commenced his announcements.

"Firstly, for all those who felt guilty about not attending last year's Working Sunday, please don't forget that this year's effort is only four days away. I hope to see as many people as possible turning up. Starting time is 10 a.m. ....."

Mick, adopting his usual stance, butted in. "I'd like to point out that the more of you who get up off your arses, the more money the Club saves. Everyone here can paint and use a hammer, so even the most worthless example of DIY failures amongst you should come, even if it's only to help with the tea". Doreen frowned. The Chairman regained the initiative. "Thank you, Mick, for that untimely intervention, you almost took the words out of my mouth. Anyway, you never know, you might just enjoy it! Now, to the important part of the day, that of food. Doreen has kindly offered to prepare snacks and lunches. Albert will be here after work to refresh the parts, etc. and the Club will be providing supper at about 7.30 p.m." Doreen looked up at the Chairman. "Once again, thanks are due to Doreen for organising our meals". Doreen preened.

"Now", said Robin, "We need a couple of volunteers to man the pumps on the nights Albert isn't available. Any offers?"

Two hands shot up from the "Pennytown" layout.

"Thank you", said Robin. One hand belonged to Jock, the other to Lanky. "Colin will give you the details later. Robin paced himself, took a deep breath and said, "And this is where the really exciting news begins. The Club's premier layout, "Southworth" ....

He did not get any further due to the cat-calling and mock abuse which emanated from members of the other layouts.

"What's so bloody premier aboot something based on the Southern?" shouted Jock.

"At least it's based on somewhere, even if it's not a **proper** railway", retorted a dyed-in-the-wool Great Western fanatic. The well- meaning barracking subsided amid laughter, as each corner attempted to outdo the other with badly reasoned argument and Fascist style salute.

"Quiet, you rabble!" shouted Robin. "As I was saying, "Southworth" has been chosen to represent our Club at the prestigious York show in September. As many of you know, we are running a coach to the exhibition. There are some seats left but book now to avoid disappointment". He motioned to Doreen. "Our Outings Secretary will be on hand to answer questions about the options available but first, the raffle".

Doreen interjected. "May I just have a word while we have everyone's attention, Robin".

"Certainly", said the Chairman, taking one step back. This was Doreen's cue to announce further information previously unavailable to her.

Assured of everyone's attention she explained, "I don't know exactly who it will be yet, but the coach drivers will be SRC regulars. I have asked if John is available. You'll remember him from last year's trip to the Isle of Wight, when he led the singing all the way back from Petersfield, and who could forget Yorkie's rendition of 'My Way'. Our coach will naturally, once again, be of the luxury type, with on-board catering and toilet facilities".

"She could have said all this afterwards", one member was heard to remark.

Mick, standing close by retorted, "Yeh, but with a much smaller audience and not such a captive one!"

It meant a lot to Doreen that regular drivers were used, as it increased her stature and her ability to control a situation. It was not unknown for her to map out a diversion to somewhere, or something, she felt would be of interest to the travelling throng. This add-on enhancement, as she called it, a term which had impressed her when heard at work, was her idea, and one that could be kept to herself until the driver signalled that time was available. Only Derek would be party to this scheme. If an unexpected delay occurred, then the add-on enhancement would be hastily discarded.

"Lastly", said Doreen, "I'm going to announce the provisional date for our annual mystery tour". She looked around the room before adding, "And it's no good asking me where we're going, because I'm not telling you!" She laughed at her little joke and adjusted her bra strap.

Colin had bounced his way from the office, having folded all the raffle tickets and deposited them into an ice bucket. He stood alongside Doreen. "Ready?", he said, holding the bucket aloft. Doreen raised her arm and dipped her hand into the vessel, pulling out a pink ticket, much to the verbal dismay of green ticket holders.

"Third prize, for £8.10, pink ticket number 38", she announced in measured tone, extracting the maximum suspense without attracting accusations of over-acting. An arm was raised in the corner.

"House", shouted the winner, who came forward to collect his prize till receipt. For reasons unknown to anyone, Harold's odd pence contribution was always tagged on to the third prize. Colin surmised that a figure free of penny excess held higher station. Clasping his till receipt in one hand, the "bronze medallist", as Colin referred to him, dipped his free hand into the bucket and withdrew another pink ticket, which he duly handed to Doreen. She looked around for complete silence and attention, then only when satisfied, announced, "Second prize, for £10, pink ticket number 69".

Pete, who was sitting at the bar alongside his wife, shouted, "That's Reet's favourite number". Rita smiled knowingly and smacked him on the arm. Supporters of a base sense of humour laughed encouragingly. That element of the check-jacket brigade who did understand the significance of the comment, stayed silent, as if they hadn't heard. To them it was bad enough   having a car trader in the Club, let alone one who was openly smutty.

The "Pennytown" group gave a roar as Jock exclaimed, "Aye", before diving under the layout to receive his winnings. Shouts of "fix" echoed around the hall as it was the third time in four weeks that Jock had won a prize. He followed the previous examples but extracted a green ticket. "Green, 183", he called. Doreen butted in. "You haven't told anyone how much it's for". Jock looked to her for the amount, but Doreen was having none of it. His arm moved involuntarily as Doreen made a grab for the ticket. "Thank you", she said, as he finally relented. She glared at the Scottish member, composed herself and then smiled insincerely. "For £13, green ticket number 183".

A further roar from the centre indicated that yet another group member had won a prize. Lanky held up his ticket and made his way under the boards to collect his winnings. More mock groans followed. Jock announced to anyone who cared to listen that justice had been seen to be done as they had both volunteered to stand in for Albert. The two men were showered with redundant raffle tickets.

Robin thanked everybody for their time and attention. Doreen waited to be accosted by members seeking information about the York trip. She hoped that some would-be travellers would ask about the destination of the mystery tour. There was no finer moment than being able to reply, "You'll have to wait until we get there". This situation epitomised Doreen's love of authority. The fact that no-one else had wanted to organise the excursions had never occurred to her.

As soon as Jock and Lanky had resumed their positions once more within the confines of "Pennytown", the controllers came to life and the united strains of "Let her rip" resounded around the hall.

Robin, Mick and Greg made their way to the office. Colin remained in the hall, giving details of bar duties to Jock and Lanky.

"You coming Sunday?" Robin asked Greg.

"I'll be there".

Robin turned to Mick who was leaning against the filing cabinet. "And you could hardly not attend after what you said!"

Mick sniffed, moved towards the desk and stubbed out his cigarette. He sat down, stretched, then rocked the chair on its back legs. "Well, there are so many prats. They all want nice club rooms, they all want nice, manicured lawns but when it comes to doing anything about it ....." He stopped, sighed and muttered, "bastards".

Greg looked at Robin. "I knew it was coming, it was just a question of when, really". Both men chuckled as Mick raised his arms and placed them behind his head. He added nothing to his comment but shook his head slowly from side to side, exuding an expression of complete indifference.

There was a knock on the door which stood slightly ajar. They waited for someone to enter. No-one did. "Come in", said Robin at length. A wizened hand grabbed the inside of the door, pushing it open. A small, slightly hunched figure in its early sixties entered, and looked at each of the men in turn.

"I wonder if I might indulge your attention for a minute?" he asked. His speech was measured, every word uttered precisely. "This Sunday, isn't it, the Working Party?"

"Yes", said Robin, deliberately avoiding looking in Mick's direction.

"Only, I wanted to know what time, approximately, you, well, we, are to make a start".

"About ten".

"Ah", said the man, lifting a single finger into the air, as if to signify a dilemma. "Well, there we, well I, have a problem. You see church service doesn't commence until 9.30 a.m. and this week I'm taking the collection".

"Where, home?" chimed in Mick.

"I'm sorry, I didn't quite hear that", retorted the church-goer, as he edged towards the desk.

"Which church", said Robin, "he asked which church". He glowered at Mick.

"No, not Whitchurch, it's St. Paul the Apostle, Motspur Park".

"Christ, you could spend the rest of your life having this conversation", muttered Mick.

The church-goer was determined to sort out times. "I should be able to get here by 11.45, if that's all right - should I bring any tools?"

"Just some fishes and loaves, oh, and if you can summon up some **real** wine from the cardboard boxes labelled "Liebfraumilch", you know, the stuff that tastes like gnat's piss, then you'll be very welcome ....."

Greg interjected. "Anything that you think will be useful, brushes, screwdrivers, etc."

"Well, that's a weight off my mind, I don't mind telling you. I hate being late, people not knowing whether you're turning up or not. Well, I'll see you all at approximately 11.45 on Sunday". He waved to all three individually as he backed out of the office.

"Why did he knock", asked Greg.

"He probably does that when seeking an audience with God".

Greg pulled open the door so as to make his way to the bar, but stopped and looked back at the others. Above the general cacophony of noise, two voices could be heard, both female. One was Rita's, who, on a rare visit to the Club, was taking advantage of the attention being paid to her, the other was closer, and louder. Doreen was holding court with several members keen to add their names to the list of those wishing to join the mystery tour.

"No, no, I'm not going to tell you if it's the seaside or not! It could be, but I'm not saying". She was in her element. Derek was beside her, telling interested souls that tea and coffee would, of course, be served on the coach, as usual.

"We've done that", said Doreen, "they all know about refreshments".

"I don't", said the churchgoer from the back of the gathering. "I got here late".

"See", Derek uttered. Doreen ignored him.

"All I **will** say is that you should take warm clothing with you". She threw in this little teaser and remained open mouthed and smiling, revelling in the fact that she knew something they didn't.

Gwladys Bowen appeared with husband Reg in tow, and picked up on Doreen's last comment. "Told you", she gloated, "it's Paignton - always need warm clothes for Paignton".

"It's **not** Paignton", Doreen replied before she could stop herself.

"Well, at least we know where it isn't!" chided a cheerless Gwladys.

Doreen stood with hands on hips. "If you remember correctly, the last time you complained about Paignton, we were actually in Weymouth - although I'll give you half a mark as they're both seaside towns! You're always quick to complain, but you're still at the front of the queue for the next outing".

Glwadys's strong, undiluted Welsh accent rose above the general level of noise. "Well, someone's got to provide the snacks and my Welsh cakes go down a treat. Everyone says so, don't they, Reg?"

Reg was looking suitably embarrassed.

"Don't they, Reg?" Gwladys was more forceful.

"Yes. Yes, dear", he replied hesitantly. Gwladys nudged her husband.

"Righto, Reginald, let's be getting 'ome. I've recorded 'Coronation Street' and I don't want to be watching it at 2 o'clock in the morning".

"Only because you should be out on your broomstick by then!" muttered Doreen to her husband, as she watched Gwladys's imposing figure walk away into the night.

"Great, super", beamed Derek.

Reg mouthed "goodbye" and turned to follow. "I expect it'll be a good day out wherever we're going", he said, nodding to the Outings Secretary. Gwladys had heard her husband's comment.

"Well, wherever it is, it's going to be cold - they said so!"

It mattered not where it was, for nowhere could compare with Porthcawl. A fiercely proud south Walian, Gwladys condescended to accept that the English could live in England but judged that buying a holiday home in her native principality was akin to stealing food from a starving child. She liked to impose her dominant brand of Welshness wherever the opportunity arose. A regular chapel-goer and knitter of Reg's jumpers, she was an all-round prophet of doom.

Gwladys would often venture off into some story concerning a chapel visit to her beloved Welsh coastal resort some forty years previous, as if it were last week. During the Club's travels Reg usually slept, or pretended to. It had not gone unnoticed by many members that Gwladys always placed her name first on the outings list, and that of Reg's, second - and in smaller print.

The three Committee members had continued to eavesdrop by the main door.

"Make's you wonder what on earth Reg saw in her, doesn't it?" enquired Greg.

"I think she raped him and he didn't like to say no after that!" retorted Mick.

They looked at each other and after a moment uttered an elongated "Yuk", whilst grimacing as if to support their verdict. Colin entered, witnessing their animated faces but not aware of the reason for it.

"No, that wasn't a comment on our own - our very own - Clipboard", said Robin.

"Mind you ....." drawled Mick, once again ensconced in the chair. Robin glanced him the look that says, "You never give up, do you?"

Greg walked to the bar and ordered two pints of the Welsh brew and a half of lager for Robin. Colin had missed out. He turned to see Pete pinning a sheet of paper on the notice board. It was a list of cars for sale. He invariably had something that suited someone - even if it didn't once they had bought it! Pete's terms and conditions for purchasing a car from his home address were simple. There was no warranty - implied or given. His guarantee extended to his gate, or three feet - whichever was the sooner! He actually sold a lot of cars under these conditions. It wasn't legal, of course, but this straightforward approach meant everyone knew where they stood. If you wanted a warranty, you went to his garage. If you didn't, you could save yourself a lot of money - and sometimes it even worked out that way. From the showroom, of course, he was obliged to follow certain guidelines and legal requirements. These naturally were kept to a minimum.

"How's business, Pete?"

Pete threw his arms around Colin. "Can't complain, Clipboard, can't complain".

Colin stood on tiptoe in order to peruse the list in its entirety. "Mmmmm, I see one of the cars on your list has been crossed through. A recent sale?"

"Should have been but unfortunately the punter decided to ring the previous owner".

"What difference did that make?"

"Apparently there was a slight discrepancy in the mileage".

Colin's finger ran under the deleted description. "It says 15,000 here".

Pete became reticent and pulled a face. "Yeh, somehow the five and the one changed places".

Colin smiled broadly. "Oh, I see, caught with your trousers down - or rather with your Black & Decker in reverse gear!"

Pete shook his head in mock bewilderment. "Complete mystery to me!"

Still grinning, Colin continued on tiptoes towards the bar. Pete finished pushing home the drawing pins and turned his attention towards his wife. Rita was still in conversation, perched upon a bar stool, her skirt riding ever higher, much to the pleasure of the "Pennytown" group locked within their railed environment and all inexplicably facing the bar. The check-jacketed brigade were not so united on this issue. Some felt it was just "not on" to allow women into a club where manly subjects, such as the life and times of Woking Station or the rebuilding of the Mansfield to Nottingham line should be discussed with solemn reverence. Others found the sight of a well-formed female delightful, if not distractive. Colin hadn't really noticed.

It had just turned 10.40 p.m. Rita finished her Malibu and Coke and stepped off the stool, adjusted her pencil skirt and followed Pete who beckoned her to the door. They bid goodnight and made their way to the car park. Albert started to clear the glasses from around the hall and the various rooms. Mick and Colin added up the night's takings and walked back to the office, Colin carrying the till drawer. It was his job to make out the paying in slip and bank the takings through the night deposit box on his way home.

Robin and Greg were looking at the vehicles available on Pete's sales list. "You ought to charge Pete for advertising space", suggested Greg.

"It's a service to our members".

"Many would say a dis-service".

"Maybe ...."

Suddenly the car salesman burst back through the door. "Any chance of a push - flat battery".

Two or three members laughed as they made their way outside.

"Not the Maestro?" enquired a would-be helper.

Greg looked back at the list and shouted, "Is it the Maestro 1.3L, one lady owner, genuine 27,000 recorded miles?"

"Yes, that's it", said Pete, slightly peeved.

Greg was on a roll. "You mean the 27,000 recorded mileage example in metallic blue, mint condition, sun-roof, recently serviced and a snip at £1795?"

"Yes, yes, that's the one". Pete was now openly put out.

"I thought it must be" teased Greg, "'cos I couldn't see another Maestro listed that included a buggered battery amongst its attributes".

Pete muttered something and left. The hall erupted in laughter.

Within half an hour the last switches were turned off, leaving on only the security lights. Colin held his clipboard in one hand and the night deposit pouch in the other. Albert walked to the entrance, waited for Colin to leave in his Metro Vanden Plas and re-attached the clasp of the padlock through the bar that connected both gates. Having checked them he made his way along the footpath that conveniently linked the Club rooms with the road that led to his bungalow. Albert looked at his watch. "Just time to have a quick cup of coffee with Vi before bed", he thought.

*   *   *   *   *

CHAPTER TWO

Robin had timed it nicely. Peter Skellern was just finishing the last track on side one of the cassette his wife had bought as a Father's Day present from their youngest. He indicated left as he approached the lane leading to the Club rooms. A smile developed as he remembered his lad's face when unwrapping the flat gift. "Thanks", he had said, "thanks very much, Toby. You must have known that Skellern is one of my favourites".

"Skeleton?" replied Toby, bemused.

"No, Skellern, Peter Skellern", Robin had re-iterated, brushing his hand through Toby's hair.

By this time Robin was having to compete with an early Sunday morning showing of Tom and Jerry and he was becoming a very poor second.

"Never heard of him", said Toby, eyes glued to the box. "Mum got it".

"At least I'm not the first", the Chairman thought to himself, on seeing the Durdles unloading Derek's car. Robin wondered just how many members would rally to the cause. Perhaps Mick's interruption had put off some of the newer faces. Time would tell.

Derek grinned inanely as he handed an outer of plastic cutlery to his wife. "He's good, isn't he?"

"Sorry, who?" asked Robin, as he walked towards the main door.

"Peter Skellern, 'You're a Lady'. Heard it being played on the radio - or was it a tape? Terrific song, great, smashing".

Robin smiled amiably and recounted the cassette's history.

"Nice story that, great", enthused Derek.

"And they say women talk! Come on, Derek, there's food to shift. We don't want the workers complaining, do we?" Doreen smiled insincerely. She looked up over the trees and squinted slightly. "Still, the sun's coming through nicely. You can always rely on Suzanne Charlton to give you a nice day". Robin looked puzzled. Derek grinned.

"Mind you, it's surprising", added Doreen, as she struggled with a box of tomatoes.

"Why", enquired the Chairman.

"Well, she's a footballer's daughter, isn't she. And a Northerner!"

Robin looked perplexed but decided not to enquire further.

Within half an hour around twenty members had turned up. All the Committee were there, the five males to work manually and Doreen to provide sustenance and female company. At least that was the way she saw it, but not necessarily in that order.

Mick noticed Derek's car when arriving and walked over to Robin. "The dreadful duo are here", he stated.

"Yes, Doreen has come along. You want feeding, don't you?"

Mick put his hands in his pockets, looking vacant. "At least with her here no-one will be thinking about sex! When you think of it, they never needed to add bromide to solders' tea, did they. A cardboard cut-out of Doreen in every trench would have sufficed!"

Robin looked straight at Mick and in a low voice replied, "What have you got against Doreen?"

"Only Derek, with a bit of luck!" The conversation was halted by the arrival of willing volunteers seeking guidance.

Colin had spent several weeks making out lists. He made out lists as a matter of course, whether they were needed or not, and generally they were not. Today's lists were in two parts. Part one, itemised jobs required under the following headings - plumbing, painting, timber, fencing, gardening and car park. The second part contained specific requirements, sectionalising the ground into zonal areas. A computerised map, to scale, had been produced with asterisks marking the areas where attention was required. The asterisks were of various colours. Plumbing was blue, timber was brown, and so on. With Colin's usual optimism, he had produced fifty photocopies of each part, with correctly coloured asterisks, painstakingly stuck to each part two. He had considered asking volunteers to line up in front of temporary wooden signs, which would have indicated the aforementioned headings. The only reason the idea had not been carried through was due to time being against him. He had voiced his proposals to Greg on Wednesday night. Greg had asked, tongue in cheek, if the signs were to be painted in the same colours as the asterisks. Colin had replied, "Of course", with total sincerity, not understanding the comical implications of files of men armed with forks, spades, hammers, brushes, etc. - all in separate lines. Greg had asked Colin if he ever watched "Dad's Army". Colin had furrowed his eyebrows, stating that he didn't watch much television. As Colin had walked out of the office, still trying to understand the reference to the vintage sit-com, Greg had shaken his head. It wasn't so much another way of life, more a different life form.

Robin approached Colin. He wished to appear tactful. "Just a thought, Colin, but I wonder if it might be a good idea if you worked out how many men would be required for each task".

Colin appeared puzzled and referred to his clipboard. He prised from under the clip several A4 sized documents that would not have looked out of place during an army exercise.

"The basis of the day is all here", said Colin.

"Yes, I understand that, but the natives are getting restless, so to speak".

"Aaaah", said Colin, replacing the paperwork.

He then walked purposefully across to where many of the members stood talking and waiting. A few minutes' discussion, a brief resume of the map and a walk around the grounds brought about some semblance of order. Mick and Greg had not waited for the farce to end. From the top of their ladders placed at the far end of the building, they had already commenced repairing the ageing guttering. Both men watched Colin bounce his way, clipboard in hand, followed by a pack of eager-beavers. They walked around the Club rooms twice, the first time it took on the appearance of a tour, with Colin's arms jutting out optimistically. One wag in the group of followers shouted, "Didn't King Harold stop off here on his way to Hastings?"

Colin didn't join in the laughter, he'd heard words but hadn't really listened. A universal groan replaced the mirth as one of the more scholarly members wearing a check-jacket, reminded the rest that if Harold had been going to Hastings, he would have had to change trains, what with Surbiton being on the western section ..... His attempt at a joke trailed off as the groans increased.

Gradually things settled down, small groups and ones and two's got stuck in to their allotted tasks. At precisely 11.47 a.m. Greg's attention was drawn towards a vehicle slowing entering the car park. It was the man who, on Wednesday, had knocked on the office door and bored everyone stiff by his ramblings about his E.T.A.

44

"What is his name?" asked Greg.

Mick looked down to see the hunched figure locking each door of his L-plated, sweetcorn coloured Austin 1100.

"Prat, I think".

Mick resumed his position and continued work on the newly assembled guttering.

A voice known to all beamed out of the entrance. "Come on lads, break time".

It was Doreen, holding a tray of teas and coffees. From where Mick was perched the tray appeared to be supporting her breasts as well. Greg noticed Mick's downward gaze and the subject of his mutterings.

"I suppose that's the price middle-aged women pay for having such adornments when they're young".

"Adornments?" replied Mick, looking in Greg's direction with more than a hint of incredulity. "What sort of word is that? It's like that prat - and no, I don't know his name - who's just arrived. I couldn't believe it when he finally hauled himself into the office last Wednesday evening. What was it now? Oh, yes, "I wonder if I might indulge your attention?"? If I'd known he was going to keep on like that, I'd have said no".

Greg sighed. "Where do they find phrases like that?"

"Where do we find people like that?"

Both men descended their respective ladders and joined the resting workers.

"How are the bells?" Mick asked of the late arrival, as he sought out Committee members.

"Sorry, I didn't quite catch that".

"I said, you got here all right?"

"Oh, yes, thank you and virtually on time. Mind you, if I'd been trying to catch a train ....."

"Yes, you'd have missed it", interrupted Greg.

"Quite", came the reply.

Colin was heading towards the only volunteer who had not been allocated a task. "We're one short on car park lining", he shouted. "Would you be able ....." He was cut short.

"Ready, willing and able", said the hunched figure. "I appreciate that when you're late you have to take what jobs you're given".

Colin apologised for not knowing his name and waited with pen poised above his clipboard for an answer.

45

"Oh, right. It's Gittings, Cedric Gittings".

"Gittings, C. Number 1497", confirmed Colin, entering the name on his list under the black asterisk which signified car parks.

"Why are you being so formal?" asked Greg.

"Oh, it's easier for me to look up the membership by surname. I can then amend their work record".

"I thought we were supposed to enjoy this", suggested Mick.

Colin led Cedric over to the car park team. Mick put down his cup and looked at Cedric who was now in conversation with his newly-found colleagues. Mick listened. "I could swear he just used the word 'indulge' again, so at least the 'git' part's appropriate" He turned towards Greg. "I bet he's the only male this side of Stoke Poges who irons his shirt on a wok".

"Everyone got a cup?" asked Doreen, poking her head through the serving hatch in the kitchen. Most people were sitting around the tables that Colin had set out earlier, although some had taken chairs outside and were enjoying the sunshine. Cedric put up his hand to indicate a lack of liquid refreshment. Doreen didn't notice his signal. It was more important to her that she received attention. Cedric was encouraged to walk over to the kitchen and ask Doreen for his share of the spoils.

"Now", said Doreen with relish, "as you've all been working so hard I've got a little treat for you".

"She's going home?" asked Mick of Greg and Robin.

"If you'd all like to form a queue, I've got some lovely cakes for everybody". Just then Gwladys appeared in the main doorway, blocking out most of the sunshine.

"I've brought some cakes myself. Proper ones, mind, not plastic! Anyone can **buy** cakes, but then, making them takes practice and experience ....."

Gwladys always wallowed in the praise received from fellow members, much to Doreen's chagrin - and today was no exception.

There then began a heady round of cake offering as both women vied for position of "Top Dog", to see whose cake tin could be emptied first. This "race" was lost on most members, whose only concern was that of obtaining examples from both kitchens - Gwladys's and the supermarket - via Doreen!

Reg nearly fell foul of Gwladys when he dipped his hand into the tin held our by her rival. His initial verbal reaction, "Don't mind if I do" was followed by, "I'd better not make a pig of myself Thank you", his hand retracting slowly. Reg's plate contained only home-baked Welsh cakes and that was the way Gwladys liked it. Derek, never one to fully appreciate an under current took examples of both, saying, "Lovely, ta, thanks very much".

Gwladys returned her tin to the car, muttering damnations which would not have been out of place during a chapel service.

Robin finished off his tea, announcing that if it was okay with everyone else lunch break would commence at 1.30 and last for about forty-five minutes. Work would then recommence until about 6 p.m. Money had been set aside from Club funds to provide salads - ham and cheese for lunch, plus rolls and butter. The ace up Doreen's sleeve was the provision of variously filled sponges which emanated from the same supermarket that had provided her mid-morning offerings. She was certain that there was no more ammunition left in Gwladys's tins.

Tea cups were returned and thanks given to both ladies. Robin asked to see the list that Colin had compiled concerning the day's activities. Twenty-four members had attended. Colin pointed out that the five-man team allocated to the gardens had been formed by the group that operated "Pennytown". Despite contributing the loudest, most raucous and very often the most juvenile of conversations, the variation of accent was always pleasurable to those around. Although the occasional clod of earth had been thrown at a fellow group member and the more than occasional head strimmed off a flower, the lawns, shrubbery and beds were starting to take shape.

"Mmmmmm, yes", said Colin. "I did mention that they might like to transform the overgrown shrubbery into some kind of topiary. I suggested they might consider a Great Western locomotive as a basis for their effort, but they apparently can only do Donald Duck - which I didn't feel was appropriate".

Robin looked bemused. "You don't think they were sending you up, do you?"

Colin was taken aback. "No, why would they do that?"

He was aware of Robin mumbling, "Doesn't matter" as the Chairman walked away. Colin frowned, somewhat perplexed.

Three members of the live steam crew had appeared and asked to work on the fencing. The fencing that is, that ran alongside their railway line. Other sections required equal attention, but that, in their eyes, was not their problem. All four members who manned the "O" gauge layout were there, in check jackets, older examples of their clothing relegated for use when painting and decorating.

One of the areas requiring attention concerned the ridge tiles on the Club room roof. Although of pitch construction the angle was very gentle. A light man could easily negotiate the ascent by virtue of the decking which ran the entire length of the roof on both sides, allowing access to every tile. Reg was a small man, light and wiry. Despite his sixty plus years, he was still very nimble. His main failing was deafness. Many members considered this to be a blessing, one of God's kinder acts, as it protected him from the continual condemnations, put-downs and the general verbal diarrhoea that Gwladys heaped upon his every waking day. Reg had spent his working life in the building trade and proudly kept every tool from tape measure to hammer in pristine condition. Lovingly oiled, serviced and stored, their age defied belief. He only worked in Imperial measurements and ordered paint by the pint, even though it was sold in metric units.

"O.85 Imperial pints of your best Dulux" would be his request at the local store. "One litre of Dulux coming up" would be the reply, totally disregarding Reg's loyalty to a foregone era. But Reg would persist. Very little perturbed, let alone upset, Reg. Metrication, however, continued to be his Achilles heel. He could not let go of Imperial weight and currency or Fahrenheit, any more than he could his beloved tools.

It was shortly after 12.30 that the sound of high heels were heard coming around the back of the building. Mick and Greg had commenced replacing a down pipe and were now back on firm land. Greg looked around to see an anguished Rita standing behind him.

"Hello, you two, d'you know where Pete is?" she asked.

Greg glanced at Mick and then turned to Rita. "No idea, love".

"I thought he was going to be here all day".

"Well, half the day's gone. He's not been here so far".

"But he left at nine saying he wanted to be here early".

"Oh, he was coming in the Maestro, was he?" quipped Mick.

"No, I'm in that - or was. Bloody thing broke down just before the A3 at Tolworth".

"But that's just round the corner from home. Why didn't you walk back?" enquired Greg.

Mick turned his attention once more to the down pipe.

"I left the house keys indoors, that bloody thing stalled and would it start again, would it buggery".

"So, how did you get here? Why didn't you phone?"

"I did but the answering machine was on. All I could hear was Doreen mouthing out the times of opening and a list of tours". Rita half smiled adding, "For once I'd have welcomed listening to Doreen live".

"'Fraid it comes a very poor second to listening to Doreen dead", chimed in Mick, not taking his eyes off the newly connected Osma piping.

"So where the bloody hell is he?" Rita was clearly irritated. Greg had forgotten the original question.

"We haven't seen him. You must have misheard. He's probably selling a car somewhere". Greg offered this possibility more out of hope than a genuine reason in which he believed. "So how did you get here?"

"Oh, I got a lift. Just stood on the kerb looking pathetic and helpless".

"And still they whine on about equality", said Mick, as he knelt, attempting to fit a curved section to the down pipe.

"Well, I did allow my skirt to ride up a little", Rita added, sensing interest from Greg in her last comment.

"Ride up a little what?" enquired Mick.

"Don't take any notice of him", said Greg raising his eyebrows, "it's the wrong time of his month!"

"Is there a right one. Prats, lost husbands, broken down cars, is there no end to this misery?"

Greg ignored his male companion. "So how are you going to get in?"

"Well, my neighbour's got a key but they're out 'til this evening". Her expression changed to one of distinct annoyance. "But if I knew where Pete was I just **might** be able to get in a bit earlier - you don't think he's hurt or anything, do you?"

"No, as I said, he's probably got waylaid by the sniff of a profit. You know what he's like".

"Yes, I do", Rita replied with resignation. "Look, I'll just pop and see Robin, see if he knows anything". She looked at her watch. "I won't be able to get to my sister's now. S'pose Doreen could do with a hand preparing the lunches".

Greg looked at Mick who was grinning. "Don't say anything".

"See you later, then", shouted Rita as she walked towards the rear entrance. Greg continued to look in her direction as she turned the corner of the building. Reg appeared carrying his tool box. "Ah, the ladder's round here".

"No", replied Mick, following Reg's gaze. "It's the same shape as everywhere else".

It took a second, then Reg laughed heartily. "That was quick".

"Oh, don't encourage him", urged Greg.

With the appearance of a man who knew exactly what he was doing, Reg deftly moved one of the ladders, balancing it upright as he walked to the far end of the building. Having checked that the ladder was safely positioned he climbed to the walk-way where he surveyed the required work on the tiles.

As one o'clock approached, an almost peerless sky had developed. In spite of Colin's efforts to overburden everyone with paperwork, the contents of which only he, and eventually the inside of a wastebin, would be privy to, the various activities had been progressive. While the sounds of lawnmowers, strimmers and hammers overshadowed the efforts of those wielding brushes in terms of volume, the smell of freshly applied paint in the gents' lavatory went some way to counteract the continual problems caused by a less than satisfactory drainage system. One Club wag had observed that the odours generated by the continual blockages were well past their "smell by" date. His jocular offering had been met with groans of derision and the mock pulling of toilet chains.

"We'll have this done by 1.30", said Greg as he struggled with a section of piping. Mick, who was kneeling on the ground, looked at his watch.

"So, ten minutes until Doreen gets all the attention she craves. Perhaps for cabaret tonight she and Gwladys can entertain us with some nude mud wrestling". He looked up at Greg, and after a brief pause, both men shook their heads from side to side and exclaimed, "Naah".

"Mind you, we won't finish at all if you don't get your arse into gear and get that hacksaw out". Mick continued to look in the toolbox.

"What do you think I'm looking for? It's not here".

"Well, it was there earlier. Someone must have borrowed it. Reg'll have one".

"Not up there, he won't. They've apparently progressed from cutting tiles with hacksaws".

"I'll put your jibing down to you being over-tired. Anyway, I'm bloody starving. Sod the ham and cheese, what I really fancy is a rump steak".

"That's Freudian". Mick suggested. "What you **really** really fancy is a piece of rump - Rita's to be precise!"

"What?" said Greg taking one pace back.

Mick, still absorbed with his plastic tubing continued, "I've seen you, whenever you talk to her your tone changes". He mimicked. "Can I buy you a drink, Rita? Can I take you home, Rita? - can I take you to bed, Rita?" He resumed his normal speech pattern. "Don't worry, your secret's safe with me".

"What secret? Pete's a mate", Greg exclaimed, somewhat put out by this observation, which wasn't fully without a degree of truth.

"Pete's a mate until she says 'yes'". Rising from the now closed toolbox Mick looked Greg straight in the eyes. He became serious. He pursed his lips before speaking. "Greg, if you ever want to talk about it, you know, a friend who'll understand ....." He placed his left hand on Greg's shoulder. "You know I'll always be there as a friend - one who wants to help, one who'll listen to you, one who wants to know what colour her knickers are, one ......" He could not keep a straight-face and burst into laughter. Greg took hold of a 3 foot length of plastic piping. Mick took to his heels. He ran to the end of the Club rooms and around the corner, with Greg in hot pursuit, wielding the brown tube in a manner not dissimilar from that of a warring Zulu tribesman.

Doreen stood in the doorway alongside Robin, she was expanding on her ability to catch a cold regardless of the time of year. Suddenly Mick and Greg raced by. "Boys!", Doreen exclaimed, turning her head as she watched them disappear around the side of the building, before looking up at Robin. "What's got into those two?"

"I'd put it down to the mid-day sun if I were you", suggested the Club Chairman. A head bobbed between them.

"The mmmmmm, one-thirty sun, I think", added Colin, bouncing as if in anticipation of a big event. Robin wiped his hand around his face.

"It was a figure of speech, Colin, not the Greenwich Time Signal".

"Aaaah", mumbled Colin.

All three looked on as the piece of plastic tubing flew through the air before landing in the car park.

"There ought to be a health warning about acting like that at your age", said Robin, as Mick and Greg entered the Club rooms. They were breathing heavily. Both looked quite drained.

"Lucky that tubing didn't land on the newly painted lines", observed Colin. "One of you would have had to go and tidy them up again".

"Oh, I don't know", gasped Greg. "I could have used the pipe to wipe that self-righteous grin off your face!"

Colin tried manfully to stifle his mirth as the other two continued to bend, hands on knees, while they recovered from what Doreen described as "being silly".

Individually the workers re-entered the building, many taking advantage of the gents', with its now "less than obnoxious" odour, before commencing lunch. The four members from "Pennytown" entered the loo together. Three of them were still adjusting their flies as they walked back down the corridor towards the hall. As usual, there was much pushing and shoving.

Colin, still standing in the doorway, ticking off the workforce on his clipboard, turned to Robin. "I suppose it must be something in the northern make-up which makes them so loud. They're always touching each other as well, I've noticed". He hesitated. "Not exactly touching in the way psychiatrists would have you think of it ....."

Robin helped him out. "I know, it's a strange phenomenon. It's like a tribal blooding with that lot. Still, they enjoy themselves".

"But is that what it's about?" enquired Colin, looking up at Robin, who frowned.

"Oh, I think so, don't you? I mean, you have enough aggravation at work. This is where you are supposed to relax. 'Chill out' as my kids say, enjoy yourself".

Colin wasn't convinced.

"Is Clipboard being a pain?" asked Clive Davies, the Brummie, looking across towards the door.

"No more than usual", said the Club Chairman, wondering why on earth Colin wanted to check off members as they came in for lunch. Brummie continued.

"Oi was just saying, that's a noice job they've made of the loo. Beige is a good neutral colour, unloik the smell".

This was all Robin wanted to hear, as everyone sat down to their salads prepared by Doreen, with the assistance of Rita and Gwladys. It wasn't that Gwladys wished to help Doreen, it was more a case of not wanting to be accused of being unhelpful - it didn't go with the chapel image.

The "Pennytown" group had by now taken to seats close to the kitchen.

"Never sat this far from bar before", said Lanky.

"Aye", replied Jock. "You can still breathe the scent of Eau de Dulux".

Someone else chimed in. "Don't you mean **Odour** Dulux?"

A voice nearby offered. "Better to be odorous than odour arse!"

Groans engulfed the hall. Lanky carried on. "I'm surprised bog weren't painted pee green". He emphasised the "pee" in case anyone missed his pun - few did.

"Aye, state of the art is this", offered Yorkie, not to be outdone.

"As opposed to state of the fart - God, even I'm doing it now", Greg quickly added.

"No wonder variety died", commented Mick, standing with hands on hips, legs slightly splayed. "Look at them, come tonight most of this lot will pretend to be drinkers. Half the tossers struggle with a Kaliber Top".

Doreen was nothing if not fair. Everyone had exactly the same amount of cheese or ham, accompanied by lettuce, cucumber, half a tomato, cut in two, and a pickled onion. One member offered to give back his onion, advising Doreen that they repeated on him, but Doreen just said, "Give it to someone else on your table". After the said member had left the serving area she turned to Rita. "Honestly, men, they want you to do everything for them". Rita's thoughts returned to her husband.

"Where are you, Pete Balfour?" she said to herself as she stared blankly. A hand waved in front of her. She blinked.

"Cooee, you're more on Fuller's Earth than this one", said Doreen. "Harold's been standing in front of you for ages". She looked at Harold, smiled, then added, "You'll starve, won't you?"

Harold appeared embarrassed. "It's all right, I've only just arrived at the hatch. It's not as though I've been waiting long".

"Sorry", offered Rita.

"Well, we don't want to keep the queue queuing, do we", advised Doreen.

"Oh, that's all right. Cheese for me, please". Harold looked at Rita. "It's a pity your name's not Louise, I could say, 'cheese, please, Louise', couldn't I?"

Rita smiled, Doreen cut in. "But you can't can you. Next!"

As the stragglers continued to eat their salads Colin walked up to the servery. "By my calculations there should be only two more lunches required. I've ticked off everyone except Reg and myself".

"Does Reg know it's lunch time?" asked Rita.

"Yes, I've shouted up to him".

"But did he hear you?"

"Well, I shouted from the top of the ladder. He was just going to finish mending a tile - or whatever you do with them".

"Yes, but did he hear you. He is slightly deaf".

"What?"

"I said, did he hear you, he is ....." Rita fell in, Colin chuckled.

"Right, then, Colin. Ham or cheese?"

"Aah. Decisions, decisions", he replied, scratching his chin.

"Oh, give him the cheese", said Doreen impatiently. She looked him straight in the eyes. "You're thinking, aren't you, I've seen that look before".

"Yes, aah, right. I was just curious as to why you suggested the cheese in preference to the ham".

"Because you remind me of a rodent", Doreen replied sharply.

"Marginally better than reminding you of a pig, then", countered Colin, who then grunted swine-like. Doreen tutted.

"Right, then, cheese will do nicely, thank you". Colin continued to say thank you as he walked over to where Cedric Gittings was seated.

"Makes you wonder how he ever gets dressed", said Doreen. "Never got married did he. Not even a girlfriend, according to Derek. I wouldn't be surprised if he's one of those trans-whatevers. You know, dresses up in women's clothing when he's by himself".

Rita laughed. "I think he's just shy, that's all".

"Well, you never ....."

Doreen was interrupted. "That's not for Reg, is it?" asked Gwladys, prodding the lone ham salad with her index finger.

Doreen looked at the now indented ham. "Well it was".

Gwladys dismissed her. "Don't bother about him, I've brought some tuna. I knew the cheese would be pre-packed and the 'am's more water than pig". She looked at Rita and then at the ham. "It's not so much sweating, as flooding".

With that Gwladys brushed past the other two females and began to make up tuna salads for Reg and herself. Doreen shrugged her shoulders as she and Rita continued to eat their respective lunches. As the spent tuna tin was thrown into the waste bin Gwladys explained how, in her youth, Pontypridd was a mecca for hams. "'Ung up in rows, they were. Evans Family Butchers was one, mind, Price's were another, du,du, there was quality then. Mam always made 'am sandwiches when we went to Porthcawl ....."

Doreen and Rita walked quietly out of the kitchen, leaving Gwladys staring out of the window, picturing only the beaches of her youth.

"Give me a hand with the table, will you", asked Doreen. Rita looked quizzical.

The table was directed into a clearing to one side of the hall. Doreen settled it in a precise manner and walked to the cleaner's cupboard, from where she withdrew a large box. This was taken to the kitchen where one by one she extracted several sponge cakes. These were unwrapped, some cut into portions, all were set onto plates. She proudly laid them out on the table and fussed around them until there wasn't a member left in the hall who was unaware of the cakes and their provider. Looking around, Doreen announced loudly, "They're not home-made, but then you do know they're fresh and baked under hygienic conditions". Gwladys appeared in the hall.

"Are you insinuating?"

Doreen put up a hand, as if to rebuff any comment. "Not at all, I'm merely pointing out ....."

Robin leapt to his feet, wiping his mouth with a serviette. "I think it's a very nice gesture. Both Doreen and Gwladys have contributed greatly to today's work-in". He clapped his hands. Others followed. The two women glared at each other.

"Oi loiks sponge cakes", said Brummie, still chewing the remains of his buttered roll.

Colin looked at his watch. "Reg not here yet?", he said to anyone who cared to listen.

At that moment there was a terrific thud above the hall. A shriek went up as a foot shot through a polystyrene tile. A length of aluminium support gave way at one end, falling towards the floor, its progress being halted as it landed on the table piercing an uncut sponge. All eyes focused skywards. Gwladys made her way across the hall.

"Is that you, Reg?" she shouted without a hint of compassion.

Reg was bicycling in mid air. Robin, Greg and Colin rushed around to the ladder at the end of the building. All three made their way along the decking to where they found the newly removed broken tiles and a large hole in the felt.

"Help, help", shouted Reg. His body was dangling between two joists, around which his arms were locked. He vainly attempted to push himself back onto the roof.

"I can't reach his arms", said Colin, stretching tentatively from the decking.

"You might do if you put down that bloody clipboard", shouted the

Chairman.

"Ah, right", said Colin, as he quickly but gently placed it against the railing.

Anxious hands grabbed Reg's arms as his rescuers struggled to prise him from the loft. He panicked slightly and knocked the edge of a polystyrene tile, which completely dislodged itself and struck the table below before collapsing onto the floor. Reg's final kick just prior to being lifted clear caught the end of the aluminium support. This caused the free end, still embedded in the cake, to jerk itself from the table and despatch the sponge several yards away in a spray of jam-clad crumbs at the feet of Doreen, who stood there speechless. Putting her hands to her mouth she looked towards the ceiling, her gaze slowly returning to the table. Dust, highlighted by the sunshine pouring through the hall windows, quickly followed consigning the sponges to an inedible finale.

Rita stood open mouthed, Mick stood open legged, cigarette in hand. "As it happens, I'm not overly keen on sponge anyway", he said and walked towards the bar.

Doreen turned to Gwladys. "You did this on purpose, they're ruined". She started to cry. Rita led her along the corridor and into the ladies' toilet. Reg was helped down by Robin and Greg. Colin clasped the clipboard close to his chest. Reg looked embarrassed when confronted by his wife. He raised both hands from his side but said nothing. Gwladys tutted, shook her head and said, "Lucky it was salad, otherwise it would be cold by now".

Everyone, with the exception of the "Pennytown" group went quietly about sorting out the hall. Plates and cutlery were washed, tables and chairs stacked along the walls, the floor cleared of debris. A ladder was brought through and the aluminium angle iron lifted back into position. Colin bounced towards the office, delved into the filing cabinet and extracted a file marked "Maintenance". He pulled from it an inventory of spares. His index finger ran down the listings - "Paint Exterior", "Paint Interior", "Tools. "Aaah, ceiling mats", he muttered. "Section 3, subsection 1". He hastily opened another file, thumbing through for the appropriate page. There, under Subsection 1, appeared the latest update on ceiling materials. "Polystyrene tiles, 3 of", it read. Colin took a pencil and turning it upside down rubbed out the "three" and replaced it with a "two". He blew the resultant spent rubber and then smoothed his hand across the page. Colin replaced both book and file. Satisfied that the correct rules had been adhered to, he walked to the cupboard and raising himself on tiptoe, discovered only two sections of tile. He counted again. His mouth fell open. "Cripes, I must tell Robin", he said aloud. He hurried back along the corridor shouting, "Robin, Robin". On entering the hall he found the gap in the ceiling had been filled. Although of a slightly different hue, due to discolouration, it was as if nothing had happened.

"Oh, I thought someone had either stolen a tile or even worse, a wrong entry had been made". Colin was puzzled.

"No", said Mick, who grinned and patted Colin on the head. "While you were following correct administrative procedure, someone else was following tradition, you know, doing something about it while you were writing about it".

Colin looked despondent."Oh, I see".

"You probably don't, but never mind".

Reg was sitting down sipping a cup of tea. Members still fussed around him. "I took my eyes off what I was doing for just a second - just a second". Reg was visibly annoyed with himself. I just stepped back, see, and lost my bearings".

"Still", said Mick predictably, "at least you didn't lose your balls!" He put down his cup, stubbed out his cigarette and walked out into the sunlight.

Besides the minor setback of fitting replacement felt and insulation progress was continuous. Reg bore no ill effects other than being slightly shaken, suffering less from hurt pride than Doreen.

Afternoon tea was served at 4 p.m., along with Digestive biscuits. Rita sat in the empty hall with Doreen, who was by now coming round to being her usual ebullient self. "I know it wasn't Reg's fault, no-one would purposely fall through a roof just to ruin some cakes. It was just that bitch". She looked around. "I saw her gloating. She wasn't the least bit concerned about Reg".

Rita put her arm around Doreen. "Thanks, Reet", Doreen continued. "You've been a brick today. I'll tell you now, I wasn't looking forward to having Fanny Ann for company in the kitchen. I'd rather have done it all myself".

"That's all right", replied Rita, dunking her Digestive into a very milky cup of tea. "I wasn't going anywhere. Mind you, still like to know where my Pete's got to".

"Does he often go out without telling you where he's going - or rather, not going to where he's told you he's going - if you follow?"

Rita smirked. "Yeh, that's more like it".

Doreen pressed. "Oh, it's not unlike him, then?"

"Well, he's always got a bit of business going on somewhere but after all these years it would be nice if he told me occasionally".

"You've been together a long time, then?"

"Yeh, childhood sweethearts. Been married just over fifteen years".

"Never had any children?" Doreen asked tentatively.

"No". Rita looked ahead as she played with the teaspoon.

Doreen hesitated. "Didn't you want any?"

"Oh, yes, but not at first. I had this awful feeling that I'd never get my figure back, 'cos I married at twenty. After a few years, when I really wanted something else in my life, what with Pete being out all hours, he never seemed interested in a family". She looked directly at Doreen. "Pete used to say kids was all right if you had time for them, but he only had time to make money". Her eyes lit up. "Mind, you can't have everything. He's never been tight. We've been to America, Australia, Cyprus and we go every year to Lanzarote". She stopped suddenly, looking blankly at the wall. "Wish I hadn't been so bloody vain about my shape, though".

At that moment Colin entered and lowered his eyes between the table and the two women.

"I wondered when you two ladies would like a hand arranging something for supper. Doreen got up quickly, smoothed her dress and then rubbed her hands together. She was now totally composed.

"About 6.30, please". Rita continued staring at the wall.

"Right", he said, "I'll commandeer a couple of chaps to report to you then - then!"

He smiled, coughed nervously and bounced his way back into the car park.

Mick and Greg had completed all the repairs to the guttering and down pipes - with the aid of a borrowed hacksaw. It niggled Greg that a comment should have been made about his feelings towards Rita, even if in jest. He had contemplated offering her a lift home, nothing more. Now, in a way, he wished to distance himself from her. After all, he thought, if Mick had noticed, had anyone else? He scratched his head and reflected on the number of times Rita had actually been down the Club. Greg satisfied himself that he was getting everything out of proportion, but he still cursed Mick for what he had said.

As the heat of the sun subsided a light breeze sprang up. The sky was still blue and the lawns looked uniform and well-groomed. The gardening team had sown bedding plants of the hardy variety. The ex-Southern railway seat had been repainted and now looked resplendent, although Colin was not convinced that the shade matched that worn when in the former company's ownership. The white lines in the car park stood out, the fencing no longer invited attention from would-be vandals or other intruders, whose interests would be more severe.

One by one over a period of half an hour the members wearily trod back into the hall, the tables had been arranged with white paper cloths, bordered in red, neatly placed upon them. The atmosphere in the kitchen had been somewhat cooler than the heat. Chicken or sausage, with chips and peas, mushy if preferred, were on the menu, with mince or apple tart and custard to follow.

"Whatever you say about her, she's worked hard", whispered Robin to Mick, as they took their turn in the queue.

"But at what cost? We'll be thanking her for months". Both men chose sausages.

Mick followed Robin from the servery. He noticed the direction that the Chairman was taking. "Steer clear, the Hunchback of Motspur Park's sitting over there".

"Cedric wanted a word earlier, now seems as good a time as any".

"You're becoming more like a sodding vicar with his flock than a Chairman".

"Bless you, my son", replied Robin with mock solemnity, adding, "Although in your case there's no hope of a reversal in after-life fortunes. For you it's a case of Paradise Lost". He grinned. Mick smirked. Both men sat down at the table laid for eight. Colin, Derek and Harold joined them half-way through a conversation.

"Reaming and riveting", exclaimed Cedric, "and very interesting it is, too. I've made a study of reaming over the years, you know".

"There can't be many who haven't", considered Mick. "That doesn't include Clipboard, of course".

"Mmmm", mumbled Colin, not being too clear about the Treasurer's remark.

Cedric persisted. "I've always found reaming very therapeutic in times of stress".

Mick opened his mouth to speak.

"No", said Robin, pointing his knife at the Treasurer. "Don't even think about it". Mick grinned and shook his head.

"You get in a lot of reading, then?" asked Derek keenly.

"I do now, yes", replied Cedric.

"You're not still working?"

"No, I'm retired".

Mick turned to Robin. "He meant retarded, surely".

"The first book was written in 1922", explained Cedric, "followed by three reprints, the second being amended to include more modern techniques and methods ....." His flow was interrupted by an eruption of laughter at a near-by table occupied by the "Pennytown" group. Lanky had pushed Yorkie, his red rose companion, who in turn, had pushed Brummie. The laughter subsided until the point was reached when Yorkie was about to take a mouthful of sausage. Brummie then pushed back and the sausage leapt across the table.

"That's stupid", said Colin, frowning. Greg walked over and joined Colin's table. Derek hastily swallowed a forkful of mushy peas and looked up at Greg.

"Oh, while I think of it, there's a book I saw recently on landscape modelling. D'you think the Club could order it for me?"

"Can't see why not".

"Ah, great, thanks, ta".

"Well, what's it called then. Who's it by?"

"Well, its actually called 'Landscape Modelling' and it's written by Barry Norman".

This part of the conversation was overheard by the "Pennytown" group who decided to tap out the theme tune to "Film '94", whilst humming an accompaniment.

"It's not that Barry Norman", said Derek, who appeared impressed with the loud, albeit unmelodic, interruption. "Great, terrific, nice one".

It made little difference to the northern element. Their enthusiasm was not about to wane. Mick stood up and stretched.

"Took your sausage somewhere else, did you?" he enquired of Greg.

Greg sensed pressure being placed upon him as Mick grinned and lit up yet another cigarette. "Actually, I was sitting with Reg and Gwladys".

"She's married as well, so it's not just Rita who takes your fancy. Two in one day, huh", chuckled Mick.

"You've enjoyed today, haven't you?"

"Well, it's been different. I've seen Doreen go red, and I've seen Colin go red, and you've gone a darker shade of crimson on more than one occasion".

Greg ran his fingers through his hair. "Rita's just rung home again, actually. Pete's still not in, but next door should be back soon and they've got a key, so I'm going to give her a lift home, **and that's all!**"

Mick continued to grin. Greg heard the shutters of the bar being raised. "D'you fancy a pint?"

Mick looked at his watch and nodded. Albert was serving Cedric with a mineral water.

"Could I have a slice of lemon in it, please?"

Albert raised his eyebrows as he speared a slice with a cocktail stick. He handed Cedric the glass, lemon astride the rim. "Might I have some ice?" Cedric continued.

The old man walked to the other end of the bar and brought back the ice bucket which bore the name "Lamb's Navy Rum". "Help yourself".

"A cherry always goes down well with that", said Greg.

"Does it? Well, I don't mind trying these things", said Cedric. "It never hurt anyone to explore new horizons, I say".

Albert opened the jar, making several attempts before finally skewering one of the many bright red fruits and delivering it into Cedric's glass.

"Thank you", he said, turning to Greg and Mick who were by now perched on two of the bar stools. "I was just saying to Colin, I read recently that no matter what breed of dog or its size, they all scratch at five to the second".

"Five what?" enquired Greg.

"Five scratches".

"Oh". Mick appeared numb.

"God moves in mysterious ways", observed Cedric, as he walked back towards his table.

"And God's got a lot to answer for, lumbering us with arseholes like him!" said Mick.

Albert sought to catch their attention. "Two pints with everything, is it? You can also have a parasol each, if you like".

"No, just the two pints, please. One plain and one Worcester sauce, as well". Greg looked at the hand pump, devoid of label. "What's on, anyway?"

"Oh, Clipboard hasn't made out a new card yet but tonight we have 'Charles Wells Bombadier'. Nice pint, that".

Albert then poured two pints which the men supped quickly.

"Needed that", said Greg.

Reg acknowledged the pair as he ordered half of bitter and a port and lemon. "Feeling okay now?" enquired Albert.

"Yes, fine thanks. You just feel such a fool".

"One pound, seventy five, please".

Reg looked at Greg. "Thirty-five shillings. Thirty-five shillings for two drinks". He shook his head as he walked off across the hall to rejoin his wife.

"Rita still talking to Doreen I see", said Mick. "Her knight in somewhat tarnished brass still an unseen villain".

"Well, he's obviously been out with a somewhat tarnished brass himself, hasn't he", Greg pondered. "Honestly, Mick, would you bother having a bit, or bits in his case, on the side when you had someone as loyal as that at home? Good legs, good figure, nice face, long hair ....."

"It's a bit mousy", interjected Mick.

"Well, okay, so she's not a blonde, but you wouldn't kick it out of bed, would you?"

Mick glanced in Rita's direction. "No", he answered after a brief pause.

Greg continued. "It might not be Joan Bakewell between the ears but she's good-hearted. I just don't think she deserves to be treated the way she is by Pete".

Mick crunched a crisp. "How long have you known them?"

Greg thought. "Well, Pete's been a Club member for about four years - at least. He's been in the "Southworth" group for over three. Whatever you say about him, he's an extremely good modeller. I was surprised by the standard of his locos, builds everything himself".

"What about that Black Five?"

"Yup, that an'all. There's a few bobsworth there".

"Shows the profit he makes selling cars", remarked Mick. "Which reminds me, how's your Balfour Beauty going?"

"What, the Cavalier?" Greg placed the two glasses ready for a refill. "It's been fine, touch wood. Sally must have done over ten thousand miles since we bought it. Of course, Pete's got a garage, well, showroom really, just outside Hampton Court. Can you believe it, the sign over the entrance actually says 'Balfour's Beauties' - that's not to be confused with 'Balfour Beatty'".

Mick joined in with the refrain. "I said **not** to be confused with 'Balfour Beatty'".

At that moment Colin appeared in the bar. "'Balfour Beatty, huh.

Our Department's had dealings with them. They ....."

His flow was interrupted by the Treasurer. "Colin, there's always a down side to a conversation, and you're it!"

"Aaah", said Colin before turning to Albert. "So, what lagers are on tap, so to speak?"

"Harp and Fosters", came the reply.

"Mmmmm, and what bottled beers have we got?" Colin stretched over the bar in order to get a better view of the lower shelves. Albert indicated with his fingers as he read from left to right. "Grolsch, Becks, Budweiser, Worthington White Shield, Light Ale, Brown Ale, Guinness, Mackeson ....."

He looked at Colin, who rubbed his chin, tapped a dispenser and at length said, "I'll have a half of dry cider, please".

Albert shook his head in despair. Rita appeared between Greg and Mick. "I've just rung home, Greg, and there's still no answer. D'you think I could take you up on that lift you offered me?"

"Yes, of course. D'you want a drink before we go?"

"Thanks, but I'd prefer to get home tonight, you know, just in case".

Greg noted her concern. "Yeh, I know what you mean".

Mick looked on whilst he remained sitting on the stool, finishing his second pint. "You coming back, Greg - going home, or what?"

"I'm going **straight** home". Greg ignored Mick's intonation.

"Oh, right", said Mick, looking into his beer glass. Rita furrowed her eyebrows.

"Good night, Mick", she said. Mick acknowledged them both before turning to Albert, who stood wiping a lager glass.

"So how's things with you?"

"Not so bad", replied the barman, straightening up.

"Everything all right at home?"

"Well, Vi's not been responding to that course of antibiotics, but she's no worse. She's going for tests next week, so we'll know more then, hopefully".

"Well, send her our love, won't you. Heard anything from Graham?"

Albert tutted. "Last time he wrote was months ago. Sent us a photo of Jamie, though. Here, I'll show you".

Mick had seen the photograph more than once but was not about to say anything. Albert walked over to his jacket and took out the most recent photograph of his grandson. "Good looking lad, isn't he?"

"Yes, he is. Bloody sight better than his grandfather!"

Albert didn't respond.

"Any chance of Graham coming back in the near future?"

"Wouldn't think so. There's no reason for him to be here. We've nothing to say to each other".

"That's a pity", sympathised Mick.

"You having another?"

"No, I'm off home. Kate will be restless. Pines, you know!"

"I'd have thought Kate'd be bloody pleased not to have you under her feet".

Mick grinned. "Good night, Albert. Give our love to Vi".

"Night, son".

*   *   *   *   *

Greg's Ford Mondeo swept around the corner that led to Rita's home. It was situated along a wide avenue brimming with up-market neo-Tudor style houses. As they slowed and turned into "Ballocks", security lights lit up the paved drive, an area wide enough to accommodate eight cars.

"Shouldn't these things come on only when it's dark", suggested Greg.

"They're supposed to but the bloody timer's up the cock. Pete bought them from a mate who ....." Greg joined in "....... owed him a favour". They both laughed. "Pete's reputation goes before him", said his wife.

"And after him", added Greg spontaneously.

"Right, I'll just pop next door and get the keys".

Greg walked around the car taking in the tranquillity of the summer's evening. Rita's high-heeled shoes click-clacked as she walked back up the drive, keys dangling from her right hand. She opened the door and disarmed the alarm system.

"Coming in for coffee?"

Greg hesitated before answering. "No, I won't, thanks Reet. Been a long day. Sally'll be wondering where I've got to. Besides, it's school tomorrow. I'd like to see the kids for a few minutes before they go off to bed. 'Quality time', I think they call it these days".

"Okay, goodnight, Greg, and thanks for the lift".

Greg smiled, turned and walked back towards his car. He spun around abruptly. "Reet", he shouted, as she was shutting the door. "If Pete doesn't come home soon or you get worried, you know, give me a ring".

"Will do. Goodnight".

* * * * *

As members began to make their way home Colin walked around the Club rooms with Robin, inspecting and checking the day's work.

"Wasn't a bad effort". The Chairman was encouraged.

"No", replied Colin, grudgingly.

"You don't agree?"

"Well, it's the general lack of tidiness. I've just put away two hammers, a screwdriver and a pair of mole grips, plus - **plus** that lot who were painting the gents' didn't wash out their brushes properly. I shall make a point of mentioning it in the next issue of the SRN". Colin was put out.

"I wouldn't make too much of a fuss about it, Colin. Not everyone's a perfectionist".

Colin quickened his pace, head bowed. "No, but they could be trying a little harder".

Robin stopped, watching Colin as he walked purposefully across the hall. "No-one could be more trying than you", he thought.

Those still present were thanked for their achievements and bidding goodnight to everyone Robin drove home. Colin took the cash tray out of the till and started to count the night's takings. Albert went about collecting glasses from the hall.

* * * * *

As Rita paced the lounge, headlights darted across the drive. A car door slammed. She walked swiftly to the latticed windows and pulled back the maroon curtains that glided silently along the gold-coloured runners. Pete was hurriedly walking towards the porch. His wife stood in the hall, arms crossed, as the front door slammed shut.

"'Allo, love".

"Where the bloody hell have you been?"

Pete was taken aback. He grinned inanely. "Down the Club. Where d'you think I've been?" He looked back towards the door. "'Ang on, where's that Maestro? You haven't pranged it, have you, 'cos I've got a Billy Bunter giving it the once-over tomorrow".

Rita locked her arms against her thighs. "You have **not** been down the Club, Pete Balfour, so don't lie to me again".

Pete started to laugh nervously. "Again? What d'you mean again?"

"Well, if you've been down the Club you must have had a pretty good disguise. What did you go as - a lawnmower, a ladder, or were you that bad smell in the gents' loo!"

"What?"

"Well, that's where you're supposed to be when I ring you on a Wednesday". Tears welled up in her eyes. "I don't ring you for nothing, do I, I'm not checking up or anything. I only ever call because someone's rung about a car". Rita start to cry. She turned and leaned on the G-Plan table placed in the middle of the dining room. Several seconds elapsed as she stood looking through glazed eyes into the highly polished surface. Pete walked over to her, attempting to put his hands on her shoulders. She rebuffed his advances. He stepped away. Wiping away the tears, her sobbing gradually subsided. She became aware of an uneasy silence. Pete half-raised his arms as a token gesture.

"I thought you were going to Homerton", he asked, trying to take the heat out of the situation.

"You can blame that bloody Maestro for that", replied Rita, looking up at her husband.

"You have pranged it", he shouted.

She clenched her fists in anger and stood upright.

Pete retreated slightly. "Okay, where's the car?"

"It stalled, just before the A3 at Tolworth. It's quite safe. Two men helped me push it into a layby. Tried it time and time again. It just clicked".

"Did you check the battery leads?"

"Sod the battery leads, I'm not a bloody mechanic! If you remember, it broke down Wednesday night at the Club, Thursday night as Asda - you're supposed to be a motor dealer. You keep telling me how you look after your customers, but when it comes to me, all I get's the crap".

"That's unfair". Pete pointed a finger.

"Unfair? I never get a car that's complete. I can't rely on you or your cars ....."

"That Sierra was all right", interrupted Pete.

"It was all right until I tried to get out. Central locking, you said. It's supposed to central lock from the outside, not with me in it". She paused, eyes venomous. "Or is that it? You use that for your 'bits on the side'. A safety precaution in case some silly bitch says 'no'".

"That's out of order, Reet".

"Is it? Is it? I've turned a blind eye for years, I just don't like my nose being rubbed in it. Thinking about it, perhaps it was a good job the Maestro broke down after all".

"Yeh, how d'you make that out?"

"Well, I'd have come home from my sister's none the wiser. Pete, it broke down at 10.30 this morning. I got a lift to the Club. No-one **had** seen you, no-one **has** seen you. I stayed all day helping Doreen. I can think of better things to do ....."

Rita stopped suddenly. They were still standing several feet away from each other. Calmly Rita asked, "Pete, I want an explanation". She crossed her arms as she waited for an answer she felt she didn't want to hear.

Pete smiled coyly. "Did you try rocking it? The starter motor might have jammed".

"Did I what?" bellowed Rita, as she turned, picking up a single rose vase from the centre of the table. She hurled it with force across the room. Pete jumped to one side shielding his face with his hands as the vase crashed against the door.

"Christ, Reet", he exclaimed, "that was a present".

"What, one a previous bit didn't want anymore?" She thought quickly. "Most prostitutes only take money".

Pete looked angry. "Leave it out, Reet, you don't know what you're talking about".

"Then bloody well tell me what it's about", Rita screamed.

She watched as her husband walked slowly over to the table, pulled out a carver chair and sat down. He massaged his forehead.

"Reet, I didn't want you to know".

Rita looked anxious. "Is this where you let me down gently?"

"Who's telling the story, you or me?" Pete placed both hands on the table, palms spread. "No, I didn't go to the Club". Rita was about to interrupt again but Pete's look told her to listen. "It has nothing to do with a woman. It's Dad".

"Go on". Rita took a seat next to her husband.

Pete took a deep breath and continued. "I went to see Dad. He's in trouble, Reet. He rang me at the office during the week and asked me to go over and see him. Said it was important, like. He wouldn't tell me what it was about. All he said was that it wasn't his 'ealth and I wasn't to tell you."

Rita looked hurt. Pete sensed her feelings and placed a hand on hers. She began to withdraw but he clenched it tightly. "He's got money troubles, Reet". Rita looked for an explanation.

"Mum's been gone two years now, hasn't she?"

Rita nodded. "So?"

"So Mum used to look after all the bills and since she's died 'e's hardly paid any. Anyway, when I gets over to Ilford Dad shows me all these final demands, gas, electric ....."

"Not all from two years ago, surely".

"No, not all from then. Mostly over the last year or so. I've sorted through everything, it's about two grands' worth".

Rita's mouth opened, her eyes widened. "Two thousand pounds?" she repeated.

"'E's not paid all 'is Poll Tax, let alone Council Tax".

"Surely the Council would have sent someone round?"

"Oh, they 'ave, several times but, 'e's pretended not to be in".

"Didn't they write to him?"

"Oh, yeh, but 'e's just torn up all the letters. 'Oped everything would go away I suppose".

Rita shook her head slowly. "It just doesn't seem like Dad, he was always so on top of everything".

"I think Mum going knocked it out of him. Anyway, the Council have served summonses and now 'e's panicking".

"But why didn't you tell me, Pete?"

"'Cos 'e didn't want you worried or thinking of him as an old fool. You know what Dad's like - he's got his pride".

Pete sunk back in the chair. "I'm going to ring the Council tomorrow. Once they know the facts, it'll all be straightened".

"Still wish you'd told me". Rita looked dejected.

"Reet, I would've done. Christ, until I got there I didn't know what the problem was".

Rita reflected as she blew her nose. "I had you run over, lying in a ditch injured - dead, I don't know what". She looked him in the eyes and squeezed his hand. "Come on, I'll make some coffee". After a second, she added disarmingly, "I ought to get that dustpan and brush out as well, hadn't I?" There was a slightly longer hesitation. "D'you fancy a little something before we call it a day?"

"You call it what you like, gal, but I still fancy it!" Pete guffawed loudly.

Rita drifted into the kitchen. Pete relaxed and breathed a sigh of relief. "That was a close shave", he thought, "better have a word with Dad tomorrow!"

*   *   *   *   *

Colin finished making out the paying-in slip. "Eighty eight pounds fifty, Albert. Not bad for a Sunday".

"Yeh, well you're half of cider and a bag of roasted nuts helped considerably".

"Mmm, well, every bit helps".

"And that was only a bit". Albert tutted as he locked the doors. Both men made their way into the car park.

Colin unclasped the Krooklok from the steering wheel, placing it neatly on the back seat. Albert made his way along the car park out of the glare of the security lights, timed to allow the key holder ten minutes to vacate the premises before being plunged into darkness. Colin's Metro Vanden Plas slowed as he passed Albert. He lowered the window and said goodnight. Albert waved before locking the car park gates. He had enjoyed the evening. "Charles Wells Bombadier" had gone down a treat - all several pints of it! As he turned to walk along the footpath his thoughts travelled to Australia and his grandson. Suddenly, two men approached. Albert sensed trouble and bowed his head as he tried to pass them. They blocked his path. Before he could say anything he was on the receiving end of a vicious attack. The barman gamely but unsuccessfully tried to protect his face as he was subjected to a rain of blows about the head. Crying out in pain he slumped to the ground. One of his assailants then kicked him in the ribs whilst uttering expletives. His watch was forced from his wrist, his pockets pulled open. He became disorientated, little resistance being made as the wallet was extracted from his jacket pocket.

Both men ran off laughing as Albert lay in a semi-conscious state. Several minutes passed before he heard footsteps. He covered his face in fear but the passer-by stepped over him, assuming the prone figure to be drunk. It was a neighbour who, whilst out walking his dog, came to Albert's rescue. An ambulance was summoned, the journey taking several minutes longer due to motorists parking on both sides of a narrow street, halting its passage.

* * * * *

Robin sipped his early morning coffee as he finalised notes made for a lecture later that day. The phone rang. "It's a Vi Buchanan for you Robin. Says you know her".

It took Robin a couple of seconds to realise who it was. "Oh, Vi", he said to the college secretary. "Put her on".

"Oh, no, I am sorry", commiserated the Chairman, as Vi described the previous night's assault. She gave him the hospital and ward names.

"How are you going to get there for visiting?" Robin enquired.

"I've got a neighbour who can take me in the mornings", replied Vi.

"Look, you'll be needing transport for evening visits. I'll ring a couple of the chaps and sort out a rota. Listen, Vi, we both know Albert well enough. He'll pull through all right". His voice was encouraging.

Vi had not been looking forward to ringing Robin. Both she and her husband had known Mick for many years, but she had not received any reply when attempting to contact him. She knew Robin only in passing but his concern had comforted her. The Chairman made arrangements with Mick and Greg to visit Albert that evening. "Bastards", was all Mick had said on being told of the assault.

Vi had been too optimistic. Albert was not well enough to receive four visitors. Robin took hold of Vi's arm as he led her into the ward. He placed two chairs by the bedside. Mrs. Buchanan sat holding her husband's hand which lay prostrate across the bedsheets. His head was heavily bandaged, his cheeks swollen. Albert's nose looked reddened and sore. His eyes were shut. The right eye, having been on the receiving end of a particularly vicious blow, was very blackened.

"It always looks worse on an older person, because the body can't take it as well". Robin put his arm around Albert's wife. She sighed.

"How could anyone do this?" she asked softly.

"There's no respect". Robin rubbed his hand gently up and down Vi Buchanan's arm. The ward sister walked by. On seeing the visitors she came across to them. "He's comfortable", she said.

"He's sleeping a lot, isn't he?" Vi countered.

Sister replied. "We woke him at tea time and he ate a little. He was asking after you and Jamie - oh, and he mentioned something about a photograph. I think he's still a little bit confused, but it's only to be expected".

70

"Oh, I know what that's about", nodded Vi. "Those thugs stole his wallet and it had a photo of our grandson in it. That's what that's about".

Sister smiled again, sensing Vi's concern. "It looks a lot worse than it is. There's no broken bones, although he's obviously very bruised. He'll be kept in for observation until Thursday or Friday. Then depending on what the doctors say, he'll probably be able to go home before the weekend".

"Oh, that's good". Vi smiled weakly, somewhat relieved.

Robin looked towards Albert. "We'll make sure someone take's him home from now on. I assume he'll want to come back to the Club".

"You won't keep him away, Robin, he loves it, you know that".

"Yes, I know".

Sister repeated that Mrs. Buchanan could come in at any time as the hospital had a policy of open visiting. She had been told this during her morning visit but like much of what had been said, she hadn't fully taken it in. Robin helped Vi to her feet. She kissed Albert gently on one of the few areas of facial skin devoid of bruising. She blew a kiss from the end of the bed as they walked silently towards the swing doors. Greg and Mick were sitting on a bench in the corridor. Both men stood as Vi and Robin appeared.

"That was hard for you, wasn't it, Mick?"

"What d'you mean, Vi?"

"Not being able to smoke", she replied with a grin.

Mrs. Buchanan was escorted by the three men back to Robin's car. "Sorry it was a wasted journey", she said to Mick and Greg. "I hope'd he'd be awake. I know he'd have wanted to see you".

"Plenty of time for that", said Greg as they drove back to the Buchanan's house. All three accepted an offer to "come in for tea, coffee or something stronger". Robin and Greg sat around the square table in the living room, Mick helped Vi with the beverages. It was the first visit Greg had made to the Buchanan's home. It reminded him of a 1950's set for a television play. Pride of place on the mantlepiece was given over to a photograph of Albert and Vi on their wedding day.

"I was just looking at your photo. Love at first sight, was it?" enquired Robin.

"No, not really. I always fancied Jack Buchanan, and Albert looked like being the nearest I was going to get to the real thing - well, in name anyway!" Vi giggled.

Mick and Robin were still chuckling when Greg added, "So you never got to Hollywood?"

"No, furthest I got was Cricklewood, and that's when I caught the wrong train - should have been Oxford Circus!"

"What about the photo next to your wedding, is that Jamie?" enquired the Chairman.

"No", said Vi as she brought through the tray. "That's our Graham".

"Only child?" asked Greg as Vi walked back into the kitchen to collect a tin of biscuits.

Mick leant towards Greg and whispered, "If they'd known how he was going to turn out they'd have had him aborted and tried again".

"Hob Nob, anyone?" she asked.

All three stayed until just after 10.30, when Robin suggested that Mrs. Buchanan should get a good night's rest. Her neighbour was due to collect her in the morning to visit Albert and the police were calling back to ask more questions. He had only been able to give a thumbnail account during the initial enquiry. It was agreed that Mick would give Mrs. Buchanan a lift on Tuesday evening, whilst Greg would assist on Wednesday. Having said goodnight, she waved out of her window for several seconds after the cars had departed.

*   *   *   *   *

As they walked up the stairs to the ward where Albert had spent his two days' confinement, Vi Buchanan's spirits had been lifted by a marked improvement in her husband's condition during that morning visit. The police had managed to obtain a statement from him and he had been able to give some details of his assailants. Mick and Vi waited in the corridor until the doctor had finished attending to Albert. After a few minutes they were allowed into the ward. Curtains were pulled back and a bespectacled doctor smiled warmly. Before he could say anything, Vi introduced Mick as a family friend. Both men shook hands. Vi and the doctor had a few words while Mick pulled up a couple of chairs. Albert opened his eyes.

"'Allo, Mick, thanks for coming".

"Only came to make sure you're not trying to bunk off".

Albert managed a snigger, but it hurt. "Thank Robin for helping out yesterday, won't you". He paused. "I hear you and Greg had a wasted journey last night. Sorry about that".

"I'm just sorry Vi couldn't get hold of either of us. Always the way, isn't it? Kate had an outside appointment and I was in that continuous traffic jam they call the M62. Still, Vi had the presence of mind to ring Robin, which reminds me, Greg'll be bringing Vi up tomorrow".

Vi joined them. "Doctor reckons you'll be out either Thursday or Friday". She was openly smiling.

"Told you you're a selfish sod, taking up someone else's bed", joked Mick.

"Don't, Mick, it hurts". Albert attempted to stifle another snigger. "Mind you, I'd rather die laughing than die at the hands of those two bastards".

"Mind your language, Albert Buchanan", scolded his wife, as she looked around.

"Have the police any idea?" asked Mick.

"No, they just say what I've heard them say on telly - 'it's one of the most vicious attacks the local force has had to deal with' - that's until the next attack, of course".

"Did they hold out much hope of catching them?" enquired Vi.

"Well, you know what it's like. I told them everything I could remember. White, young, local accent, or no accent, you know. I gave them their approximate height and build, but that's all I could tell them. 'Appened so quick!. Albert allowed his head to sink into the pillow as he closed his eyes. "What beer you got on for Wednesday, Mick?"

"Morrell's Varsity", Mick replied, grinning at Vi.

"Ah, that's a good pint", enthused the barman, licking his lips.

Mick placed his hand on Albert's. "Look, I'll wait outside while you two have a chat. Oh, and Albert, thanks for the grapes!"

Albert opened his eyes. "Bloody typical that, Robin brings them and you scoff them!" He smiled. "Thanks again, Mick".

Mick winked and walked towards the swing doors. Albert attempted a wave. Mrs. Buchanan moved up a seat to be closer to her husband.

"They're a good bunch down the Club, aren't they?" he said.

"Yeh, better than that lot down the Hippodrome. Not a ruddy soul, 'scuse my French, has been near nor by. I rang them, said you wouldn't be in, told them why 'an all".

"Well, it's not the pub it used to be", whispered Albert, now somewhat tired. "It's all these managers nowadays, that's the trouble, don't even know their staff. Not like it was when they had landlords, proper people as Mick would say. Bloody greedy breweries".

"He looks better than this morning", said Vi, as she and Mick walked towards the exit, "but do you know, what he wants back more than anything is that photograph of Jamie. The thirty pounds and his watch was bad enough". She clenched her fists. "Oh, it makes me so mad. Albert asked the police if they would be able to find his wallet, but they said it could be anywhere". They walked down the hospital steps and into the car park which had recently become subject to a Pay & Display scheme.

"I know Albert and Graham have had their differences but it's at times like these they should be together".

"You have rung Graham, haven't you?"

"Oh, yes, I've told him all right, and I can't say he didn't seem concerned, 'cos he said that if there was anything he could do I was only to let him know ....." Mrs. Buchanan did not complete her sentence.

"That's bloody big of him", thought Mick.

As he opened the door Vi turned. "He considers you more of a son than Graham, you know". Tears came to her eyes. For once Mick did not have a ready retort. He smiled slightly, feeling embarrassed and humbled by the comment. He also felt it to be a shame that someone should feel that way about their only child.

As they drove home Mick enquired, "These tablets they've been giving you for your indigestion, Albert says they've stopped the pain. You're not feeling any worse now, are you?"

Mrs. Buchanan sniffed, evading the question. "Yeh, look on the bright side, eh. No good me getting meself worked up when I've got him to look after, is there".

Mick lit a cigarette as they approached the Buchanan's house. He saw Vi inside, staying a short while for tea before setting off. He drove only a few hundred yards before parking close to the entrance to the path where the assault took place. Locking his car Mick walked down the footpath until he turned into the lane which led to the Club and open land. The police had searched the area but had drawn a blank. With the Club house behind him Mick retraced the steps Albert would have taken, stopping several feet short of the junction where the path met the side road. Walls hemmed in the footpath, acting as a boundary for a recent housing development that had left the centuries-old right of way almost continually shrouded in shadows. Mick, well built and a little over 5'10", placed his hands on the yellow brick parapet and hoisted himself up until he had a good view of some twenty back gardens. He completed the same exercise on the opposite wall before deciding it was impossible

74

to lever himself up some forty times and still not be in a position to oversee every garden. Shortly after arriving home he made several phone calls.

* * * * *

Mick picked Robin up from his home at 7.30 p.m. on Wednesday. They drove to the Club rooms. Derek and Colin arrived separately. They split into pairs and walked to the two closes, separated by the pathway, each starting at opposite ends. They rang bells and knocked on doors for nearly two hours, asking owners and occupiers if they would mind looking around their gardens to see whether the wallet had been thrown onto their land. With the exception of two houses which failed to reveal occupancy, they had covered the entire area. They met back at the Club rooms.

"I felt sure we'd get a result", said Mick, somewhat dispirited. "I mean, how long would you keep a wallet. I'd have thought they'd have emptied it pretty smartish and lobbed it over the wall".

"There's still the other two houses", noted Robin.

"Yeh, I'll go and see them tomorrow".

"It was a bit like J.R. Hartley and his fly fishing book", observed Colin. "You know, keep coming away from everybody nodding their heads apologetically".

"I think it's been quite an adventure", said Derek. "The mission itself might have failed but I managed to pick up quite a few good tips on begonias. Great, terrific".

* * * * *

Reg and Gwladys had looked in on Albert during Wednesday morning. Mrs. Buchanan had once again been taken to the hospital by her neighbour. Albert was clearly on the mend as he insisted on asking Reg to pass on a few messages concerning the order in which the barrels were to be used.

As Chairman's Announcement Time arrived word of their barman's condition had spread to virtually every member attending. Fred surprised everyone by clearing up his boards early as a remark of respect.

"He's in hospital, not a mortuary", exclaimed Mick on being told of

Fred's decision. "What possible difference is it going to make to Albert whether Fred wires up a board or buggers off early! Prat!"

Robin and Colin worked out a rota to cover forthcoming events. Several members offered their services behind the bar whilst Albert was incapacitated. Colin, never one to enjoy bar work, inadvertently found himself placed at the disposal of the singles club, who met on a monthly basis. Their next disco was scheduled for Friday night.

Colin approached the bar and commenced chinking money around in his pocket, a sure sign that a liquid purchase was imminent. Mick, in his capacity as acting barman reacted quickly, and poured out a half of cider. Colin looked surprised when he realised it was for him.

"I didn't ask for that", he said stonily.

"I know, I'm just dispensing with all the time you waste fart-arsing about looking at every bottle before deciding on cider".

"Aaaah", said Colin, and duly handed over eighty-five pence.

Greg walked into the Club room witnessing the tale end of the saga. He looked at Mick as Colin bounced away, sipping his half pint of Herefordshire produced tipple.

"I wouldn't mind if he chose anything else, but he always ends up with cider".

Greg smiled shaking his head.

"How is he, then?" asked Mick, his arms leaning on the bar top.

"Well, as Reg has no doubt told you, he's a lot chirpier".

Colin walked back to the bar. "You put me off my stroke. I'd like a bag of nuts as well, please". He turned to Greg. "Just come from the hospital?"

"Yeh, I was just saying to Mick, he's a lot better. The doctor told Vi that he'll be taken home by ambulance on Thursday or Friday, depending".

"Still got ambulances?" offered Mick sarcastically.

"Mmmmm", said Colin, "I would have liked to have gone and seen him myself".

"I wouldn't do that", replied Mick, "they're trying to make him better. A visit from you could set him back weeks!"

Both he and Greg laughed. "Don't take it so personally", said Greg as Colin opened his packet of beer nuts.

"No, it's not just Albert", suggested Mick, "a visit from you could set anyone back weeks".

Despite being a beautiful evening, Albert's situation had temporarily dampened the members enjoyment. Gwladys wanted to bake Albert a cake, with an engine iced in green. The "Pennytown group who were unusually subdued, thought of having a collection and buying him a present. Doreen suggested that Albert and Vi be treated to free tickets for one of the Club's tours, as a "little something".

Robin thanked everyone for their suggestions and advice - a commodity that was in abundance. Most of the latter involved a variety of punishments for the offenders. One member felt that it was society's fault and therefore those found guilty should be helped, not punished. On hearing these views expressed Mick said he assumed the person concerned was a Liberal voter, and therefore not entitled to be considered a proper person. Some felt that a long period of square bashing would be in order, but most felt that a bloody good hiding should be meted out. Mick, never one to shy away from the more radical viewpoint, offered nothing less than the "cutting off of the goolies" as a punishment, on the grounds that at least that way they wouldn't be able to produce other little bastards.

"Pete not coming tonight?" asked Robin.

"Dunno", replied Greg, "haven't spoken to him since last Wednesday, when the Maestro wouldn't start".

"I wonder where he was Sunday", mused Mick.

"Well, wherever he was, you can bet your life that some silly bitch was thinking she'd fallen in love, whereas we all know she'd just fallen out of her pram".

"He does like them young, doesn't he?" replied Mick.

"Oh, any age, I think. It's all such a challenge", remarked Robin ruefully.

"It's Rita I feel sorry for", commented Greg without thinking.

Mick smirked. "That's the second time in four days you've felt sorry for her".

Greg's reply was cut short as the front door swung open.

"Evening all", said Pete, grinning from ear to ear and rubbing his hands together.

"You look like a man who's lost fifty pence and found a thousand quid", remarked Greg.

"Ten shillings in real money that was", observed Reg as he waited to be served.

"Just sold the Maestro".

"What the 27,000, one lady ....."

"Yup, that's the one. I keep telling you, there's a punter out there for every car, it's just a question of matching them up".

Mick was thoughtful. "What, you mean like Colin in a Metro, Reg and Gwladys with their Lada, Cedric with an Austin 1100, and show-offs with mobile phones like you, swanning around in BMW's that never need to use indicators because it's beneath them".

"Gawd, I only come in here for a pint".

As Greg bought Pete a drink he unfolded the story about Albert. Cedric walked through the hall bidding goodnight to everyone as he went. Some five minutes elapsed before the jerky movements and noise of his car caught the attention of members nearby. Cedric's Austin was heaving its way towards the gates. They all listened for the excessive revving and crunching of gears as he made his way home. There was silence.

"Has he stalled?" asked Robin, looking out into the blackness.

The 1100's headlights were on. Cedric appeared to be scrabbling around by the bonnet. As Robin made his way out of the building Cedric walked towards him.

"Here", he said, "I've just found this wallet. Might it belong to anyone at the Club".

Robin took hold and knew immediately from the description Vi had given him that this was Albert's. He felt inside. There was no money but the photograph of Jamie lay untouched. Fellow members huddled around. There was much back-slapping, although Cedric was unaware of what he had found until it was explained to him.

"It was just lying by the gate, in this bush. My headlights, dipped, of course, picked it out. I thought to myself, 'that looks like a wallet, and what a strange place for it to be'".

"The main thing is that Albert gets his photo back", interjected Robin, thanking Cedric once more.

"Just one point", said Greg with mock severity, "both your fingerprints are on the wallet. None of us saw you pick it out of that bush. I'd say we've found the culprits. Albert did say there were two of them".

Cedric looked concerned. Those around kept straight faces. Robin sniggered. Slowly a half-smile developed on Cedric's face.

"It's a joke", said Mick, putting his arms around Cedric's shoulders. "Let me explain it to you ....."

* * * * *

CHAPTER THREE

"Manford & Bayliss, Doreen speaking, how can I help you? - oh, Trevor, ' morning". It was the coach company. Trevor, Doreen's contact, had rung to confirm the date of the mystery tour. It was to be the last Sunday in June. "I knew John would want to come. Who's the co-driver? - Dave? - oh, yes, we've had him once before. Quiet sort, bit of a mystery himself", she chuckled. "Still, a long journey with us should bring him out of his shell. What's that? Don't you be so saucy, Trevor Arnott, perhaps you ought to come on one of our tours. You'd enjoy it - okay, I'll hold you to that, well, I'll hold something anyway!" She laughed coarsely and replaced the receiver.

That same morning Mick had collected Albert from the hospital. There was a shortage of ambulances which caused a lengthy delay for home runs. Albert was weak but cheerful. Unbeknown to him, however, the results of Mrs. Buchanan's tests the previous day were not good. Cancer of the stomach had been diagnosed. It had spread to the point where time was not on her side. Mick had driven her to the consultant's and was the only person she had told. Graham had not yet been informed, her only thought was to nurse Albert back to health. She wanted him to be strong when the time came to break the news.

"You've stayed long enough Mick, you'd better be off back to work". Vi cleared away the teacups, Mick looked at his watch.

"In a minute". He still felt devastated by yesterday's news and wondered how long she could keep it from Albert, who sat in his favourite chair, relaxed, seemingly contented, his bony fingers clasping the edge of the arms.

"Anything on tonight, Mick?" he asked.

"Oh, a singles do. Colin's in charge of the bar".

"Oh, my Gawd. I 'ope they make their minds up quicker than him". Albert tutted. Mick smiled.

"I think he's sweet", said Mrs. Buchanan, who paused before adding, "a bit odd, but sweet".

"You thought that rat was sweet", remarked her husband, prodding the fire.

"Ah, yes, but that's because I thought it was a mouse". Vi laughed.

"Bloody big mouse", said Albert raising his eyebrows. He held out his hands to indicate the size of the rodent.

"Don't exaggerate, it was never that big".

"It was". Albert looked towards Mick and increased the distance between his palms. "It was probably this big".

"If you keep your hands like that, I'll wind up balls of wool on them - mind, his heart's in the right place, though".

"Whose, the rat's?" queried Mick.

"No, Colin's".

Mick rubbed his chin. "I suspect that if someone dissected him, they'd probably find that it was the only organ that was in the right place".

"His brain's up his arse for a start!" added Albert.

Vi tutted. "Don't be so unkind".

"That's it", said Mick getting to his feet. "Back to the grindstone".

He looked at Albert, whose face was taking on a patchwork of colour. The deep black and reds were giving way to yellow as the bruising began to subside. "Don't forget, anything you want, just ring. Kate or I will pop round with it. Take care now, Albert".

"I'll see you out", said Vi getting up. As they approached the front door, Mick whispered, "When are you going to tell him. Isn't this where care in the community should count".

Mrs. Buchanan shrugged her shoulders. "I don't want any busybody poking their noses in. They're all wet behind the ears and young enough to be my granddaughters. I've had my fill of them. I've seen that programme 'Casualty'".

Mick smiled, squeezed her arm and left. Having spent the rest of the afternoon in the office, Mick arrived home to find Kate in the back garden with her feet up, sipping a vermouth. "You've started early".

"Just starting the weekend the way I mean to go on - beer?"

"No, not for me, thanks".

"That's not like you, taken the pledge?"

Mick loosened his tie as he slumped into one of the garden chairs.

"You all right", enquired his wife as she took off her sunglasses.

Mick tapped the table, his face impassive, yet conveying the look of suppressed anguish. Eventually he spluttered out, "Vi's got cancer".

Kate put down her drink. "What? Has she just been told or ....."

Mick looked skywards, drumming his fingers slowly. "She told me yesterday, as soon as the consultant had finished with her".

"Why didn't you tell me when you came home?"

"I don't know, Kate. Wasn't deliberate, not to tell you. I suppose I needed it to sink in myself really. Not an announcement that's made every day, is it? The ironical thing is Albert doesn't know yet. It's only me - us".

"Can it be cured, is it curable?" ..... There was a pause. Kate gestured with her hands unable to expand on her question.

"No".

"Oh, Mick, that's awful. She's told Graham, surely?"

"No, only me". Mick looked directly at his wife. "I think she only told me because she had to tell someone".

Mick pondered. "Puts your own problems into perspective, doesn't it?"

*   *   *   *   *

As Colin arrived at the Club rooms, a transit van with roof extension blocked the entrance. Colin walked around to the off side. The window was lowered. "You the cleaner, mate?"

"No, I am not", said Colin disdainfully. "I'm the Clubroom Manager **and** Secretary and this evening I'm manning - or should I say 'personning' - the bar". He peered into the van. "And you're the musical accompaniment, I presume?"

The driver looked at his passenger, and then at Colin. "We're the disco, if that's what you mean - Darren's Disco, to be precise".

Colin stepped back and pointed to the body panels. "Well, there's nothing to denote that here. You're Darren, then, are you?"

"Yup, this is an evening job, bunce money. During the week we're plasterers". He smiled amiably.

"Mmmm", said Colin suspiciously. He unlocked the gates and ushered them through impatiently. Having gone through the motions of checking the bar stock, float and barrels he unlocked the grille. "I suppose you drink lager?" he said as the two men approached the bar, having set up their equipment.

81

"Two St. Clements, please", asked Darren. "Dave sometimes drinks Budweiser, but not when we're working".

"Oh", said Colin, somewhat miffed by his inability to put the pigeons in the right holes. "I assumed you'd both be lager drinkers".

"Never could stand the stuff, or any alcoholic drink come to that". He turned towards his assistant, who was grinning inanely. "Well, we're all set up, time for testing".

"It's not going to be loud is it?" Colin commenced distributing the ash trays.

"Well, they won't hear it in Kingston", said Dave.

"That's Kingston, Jamaica!" added Darren.

During the course of the evening single males and females, others in two's and three's continued to enter the building, all stopping at the desk placed by the organisers just inside the main doors. Club membership cards were shown, visitors signed in and raffle tickets sold. Colin was kept busy until 10 p.m. when there was a lull due to the raffle. It afforded him the opportunity to wash up and clear away glasses and bottles. Emptying the ash trays was not the most pleasant of tasks to be performed. He found it necessary to wipe the bar top after every drink was served. Colin hated drips or splash marks. Empty crisp packets always seemed to be surrounded by greasy crumbs. He tutted constantly. During the course of the evening several single men had sat by the bar drinking and smoking, but never dancing. Colin had understood the evening's festivities to be a disco. That to him meant dancing, even if it were of a most precocious nature. He noticed that after the break those previously sitting started to circulate, seeking out would-be mates, as he thought of them.

What he found odd was that for each seat vacated at the bar by a male, a young, or not-so-young female would take their place, nearly all smoking as well, he observed. Colin noticed that there were examples ranging from the apparently shy to the extremely gregarious, covering both sexes within the hall. He wondered if many of them held down what his mother called a "proper job".

One young lady he took to be in her mid-twenties, with blonde hair tied in a pony tail, took up temporary residence on the bar stool nearest the desk. She looked hot. "Half of lager, please", she said, fanning her face with a hand.

"In a lady's glass?"

The female laughed. "You what?"

"In a lady's glass", Colin repeated, showing her his chosen vessel.

"Yes, that's fine. I don't usually drink out of mugs, you know". She laughed.

"Ladies don't usually drink lager", Colin said to himself as he poured.

She took several long gulps then lit up a cigarette. A young man who had consumed several pints during the course of the evening swayed as he walked across the hall towards the girl. "Come on, I wanna 'nother dance".

"Well, ask someone else!"

"I said **you**". He pointed his finger at her.

"Go away", she replied, before turning her attention towards the bar.

"Come on, get your arse off that stool ....."

"Excuse me", said Colin, "but that's no way to talk to a young lady".

"You what?" said the young man, who spun round menacingly towards the stand-in barman.

"I **said** that's no way to ask a lady if she wants to dance, and it's obvious she doesn't". Colin was very emphatic.

"Are you looking for a smack ....."

His aggressive flow was halted by the arrival of friends, who broke off from dancing and hastened across to him.

"Leave it out, Terry, no-one wants any trouble".

"I think he should go home", said Colin. "He's annoying the lady".

They muttered apologies, each grabbed an arm and led their friend outside. A short while afterwards there was a screech of tyres and a black Escort XR3 roared out of the gates. The organisers confirmed that all three were now off the premises.

"Thank you for that", said the girl at the bar.

"Well, it's not on", replied Colin, adjusting his tie.

"You **can** smile, can you?"

"Yes, why?" remarked Colin tersely.

"Will you have a drink with me as a thank you?" Her smile was disarming. She reverted to Cinzano and lemonade.

"That won't be necessary".

"It might not be necessary but I'd still like to say thank you".

"Oh, mmmmm, okay, I'll have ..... mmmmmm ......"

Colin surveyed the pumps and dispensers, then turned and studied the bottled beers before announcing in the positive, "I'll have a half of cider, thank you".

"Couldn't make your mind up, huh?"

"Oh, yes, I always drink cider".

Tanya looked confused. "So what's your name?"

"Colin, Colin Mabey".

"I'm Tanya, pleased to meet you". She extended her hand.

"Ah, hmmmmm, yes, likewise".

Colin felt it was only right and proper to engage in small talk now that glasses were being recharged more slowly. The dances were becoming longer and more intimate as the lighting grew dimmer.

"Do you come here often?" he asked at length.

"That's an original chat-up line!"

"That wasn't a chat-up line", Colin replied coldly.

"I was only joking. You want to loosen up a little". She took a sip from her glass and looked into the hall. "You're not very busy now, how about a dance?"

"I don't think that would be right, I'm not here to enjoy myself".

Tanya was thoughtful. "D'you ever enjoy yourself?"

"Of course".

"Married?"

"No".

"Have you ever been to a disco or dance, you know?"

"No, it's not my scene. That is what they say, isn't it?"

"What is your scene?" she teased. "Leather, rubber? ....."

Colin reddened. "Certainly not".

"Two pints of Varsity, one orange juice and a rum and Coke, please", asked a young man.

Colin was glad of the distraction. He looked at his watch. "Nearly time to wind things up", he thought. He raised the hand bell, ringing it with vigour. "Time everybody, please, it's five to eleven".

Tanya still sat, legs crossed, her short skirt revealing well formed thighs encased in black mesh. She eyed Colin as he pulled the shutter down one notch, indicating his verbal intent.

"Have I got time for a quick one?" Tanya asked, doe-eyed.

Colin was wiping a beer mug. "Sorry, I didn't quite catch that?"

"Have I got time for a last drink?"

"Ah, yes, certainly. Same again, is it?"

"You've remembered". She fluttered her eyelids. Colin turned towards the optics.

"After seven of the same, you tend to remember", he thought to himself. "Ninety-five pence, please".

Tanya made a meal out of counting the coins into Colin's hand. "I think that's right - you'd better check it".

"I'm sure it's correct", Colin replied, ignoring eye contact.

The hall was in darkness save for the subdued yellow, red and green spotlights picking out couples dancing as one. He watched as Darren played "Lady in Red". The scene reminded him of an advertisement on television for deodorant, where a naked couple blended into the surrounding trees or rocks. It was of the few advertisements he had ever noticed. Colin could not remember the name of the product. He just couldn't understand the validity of nudity at tea-time.

The shutter was lowered and locked into the uprights.

Someone on the floor shouted, "One last number, Darren". Darren duly obliged and played the "Last Waltz". Englebert Humperdinck's voice reverberated throughout the hall. Colin looked at his watch once more. Quick as a flash Tanya was off her stool. "Come on, you can't get out of this one".

"What?" said Colin irritably. "Oh, no, there's too much to do".

He picked up a tea-towel as if to substantiate his comment. The bar door opened. Tanya grabbed Colin's arm. "Don't be so stuffy". He was dragged onto the dance floor.

"I'll have to lock the door", protested Colin, "someone could dip their hands into the till". He pulled himself away from her clutches and turned towards the bar door. A bunch of keys rattled. Colin took his time selecting the appropriate bronzed-coloured object. Tanya stood several yards away on the dance floor, hands on hips. This had never happened to her before. No-one had ever made excuses about a slow dance. He walked back, head bowed and held out his arms. She pressed her body to his as Colin's outstretched arms flailed around in mid air.

"Ah, right", he said, whilst treading on her red, high-heeled shoes.

"Have you got two left feet or are they webbed?"

"Mmmmm", said Colin looking down, wondering what to do with them.

As the record came to an end the lights gradually grew brighter. Colin pulled away. "That was short", she said. Colin smiled apologetically but said nothing. He attempted a bow, then made for the bar door. She walked lazily back to where her handbag sat at the foot of the stool. She made much of her gently swaying hips. Colin didn't notice.

"Ceremony of the keys time again?" she enquired.

Colin remained silent as he once again went through the motions of discounting examples until he came across the correct key.

"I, mm, don't drive", Tanya announced nonchalantly as Colin ran a cloth around a series of ash trays.

"Don't you?", he said, not looking away from the draining board.

"I'll have to get a taxi - unless, of course, I could get a lift".

"Mmmm, well, the phone's on the wall over there". Colin pointed loosely in the direction of the pay phone.

"Right, thanks", said Tanya.

Gradually the congregation departed. A cabbie emerged from the darkness. "Taxi for Miss Richards!"

Tanya collected her jacket, whispered, "Thanks for the dance", and left. Colin forced a laboured grin as he wrung out a bar towel on which he had inadvertently spilt a half of lager. As the taxi driver opened the door Tanya looked back towards the hall. She had never encountered such resistance. It annoyed her. It also interested her. She liked a challenge.

Darren and Dave completed moving all the equipment out into the car park, where it was once more loaded into the transit. Darren returned, handing Colin a red card printed in gold.

"If you need a disco for yourself, give us a ring. Always do you a special deal".

Colin glanced at it, said "thank you" and waited for them to disappear before condemning the card to the waste bin. He tutted.

Having counted the takings and deposited the float into the floor safe he walked into the car park. Colin had just unlocked the driver's door on his Metro Vanden Plas when he espied a vehicle tucked away behind one of the sheds that ran parallel to the perimeter fencing. He closed his car door slowly and walked over. He could just make out the front edge of a bonnet and bumper. Colin heard giggling. He approached the driver's side of what he now knew to be a G-plated brown Vauxhall Nova. Colin stopped suddenly. A female leg was protruding through the driver's window. A red shoe dangled loosely on the foot. He back- tracked and walked quietly to the near-side. "God, there's another one", he said to himself. Colin scratched his head. Both female limbs were rocking. Hands on hips Colin took stock of the situation. The Nova swayed gently. "Looks like one of mother's jellies", he thought. Colin was impressed by the suspension - no squeaking. He looked at his watch.

"They could be doing this all night".

Walking to the back of the car he extracted a ten-penny piece from his pocket and tapped loudly on the rear window. "Excuse me, but I'd like to lock up". A surprised male face stared at him from the other side of the glass.

"Bloody hell".

"Oh", exclaimed Colin. The feet retracted immediately. A shoe fell onto the asphalt. There was much fidgeting and muttering within the confines of the Nova. Colin walked, head down, around the car. The passenger door opened, a young man glared at Colin. Colin handed over the shoe.

"I presume this is the young lady's", he said, once more adjusting his tie. Without a further word he walked back towards his Metro. He was aware of the young man cursing.

The headlights went on, the Nova burst into life and sped out of the gate at high speed. Colin watched them disappear down the lane in disbelief. He shook his head. "I don't know how anyone could do it. Fancy buying a car in brown. It's always such a difficult colour to keep clean!"

*   *   *   *   *

Greg flung back the curtains, the early morning sun filtering through the leaded lights of the bedroom window. Sally lazily rested her head on the palm of her left hand as her elbow slumped into the pillow. Greg scratched his testicles.

"If you have to do that, can you do it with the curtains drawn?"

Greg turned towards his wife and in mock anguish said, "You've never wanted me to have any hobbies. You've always stopped me from seeing friends!"

"Only friends who do that", replied Sally laughing.

Greg walked the few paces to their bed very slowly. He lay next to Sally, rubbing her cheek. "Tea?"

"Oh, yes please".

"No, I meant, will you make some?"

"We'll have less of that, thank you". Sally hit him with a pillow. They lay on their backs.

"Another Sunday consigned to the railway club - will you be home for lunch?"

"No, I'll pack some sandwiches. Have dinner when I get back".

"Fine", said Sally, "7.30 to 8, will that be all right? So who's going today?"

"Oh, Derek, Colin, Pete and Harold - a full set, in fact".

"Pete's going? I thought he was always missing these days".

"Oh, he was only missing on the working day, well and some Wednesdays, but he always comes down when there's work to do on the layout. Anyway, I think he quite fancies the weekend in York".

"Oh, yes, York. I thought you'd finished building your train set".

"Train set? Train set?! "Southworth" is a scale model of a prototypical Southern Railway line set in the early sixties - at least, that's what it says in our publicity blurb". Greg shook his head. "That train set, as you call it, took three years to build. Just think of the work that's gone into it".

Sally turned away. "That's why I thought you'd have finished it by now. Not very quick, are you?"

Greg turned to face Sally pointing an admonishing finger at her. "A model railway is never completed, just look at the buildings. We've been replacing all those card models with new ones built from embossed plastic. It all takes time. Lift the roof off the signal box and you'll see all the levers and mechanism. It's complete with table, desk, chair - even the resident cat's sitting by the fire".

"What colour's the cat?"

"Black, why?"

"I prefer tabbies".

"Well, our signalman prefers black cats, so there!"

"That's got Christmas sorted out at least".

"What?"

Sally smirked. "Well, I can buy you a big doll's house, then you can lay the kitchen tiles and carpet the sitting room and then you can put in the tables and chairs - through the square window!"

"You're not taking my hobby seriously, are you?"

"Well, honestly Greg, you're like a big kid".

"Big kid, huh?" Greg jumped to his knees and straddled Sally's legs. "Big kid, big kid?" he repeated as he vigorously tickled his wife's midriff. She giggled as Greg's hands moved more quickly. "Stop it, let go".

"Am I a big kid?" he demanded to know. "Am I? Give in, give in!"

She banged her hands on the pillows to signify submission and the couple lay back, his fingers gently stroking her curves through the fine material covering Sally's body. "Mmmm", she murmured as she snuggled next to her husband. "What time is it?" she whispered.

"Time to teach you a lesson, time to show you that little boys can also play grown-up games. Time to show you what happens when you don't bring your old man tea and toast". Sally screamed. She threw the covers over their heads. The playful seduction was abruptly ended by a tapping on Greg's back.

"Dad, dad - you in there?"

Greg and Sally fell silent.

"Dad, dad". The name was accentuated. Greg peered out from under the duvet.

"Oh, good morning, Tom. Nice timing! Well, what's so urgent? Has Poland been invaded again? Has your sister broken your Game Boy or are you surprising us all with breakfast in bed?"

"What?", said Tom totally perplexed.

Sally surfaced, adjusting her attire. "Don't take any notice of daddy", she mocked, pinching Greg's cheek, "he's a silly daddy, isn't he?" Sally continued to chide. "He's always silly when he doesn't get his Weetabix!"

Greg pinched his wife's bottom and gritted his teeth. "Close. I'm only a silly daddy when I don't get my oats". He sighed and looked at Tom. "So what do you want?"

"It's grandad, his door's open but he won't say anything". Greg looked at Sally and jumped out of bed.

"Okay, Tom, just, ummmm, go back to your bedroom for a minute, will you". He pulled on his dressing gown and ran downstairs, quickly followed by Sally. Her father did not respond to their calls. Greg searched his bedroom, sitting room and bathroom. The three-roomed annexe had been built four years previously after Sally had finally persuaded her father to come and live with them. His outside door, however, was unbolted.

Sally subconsciously played with her neckchain as she followed in Greg's footsteps. She gripped his arm. "Where can he have gone?"

"He might just have gone to get a paper".

"Should I ring the police?"

"No, not yet, I'll get the car out and have a look round first".

Greg dressed quickly and took to the roads, scouring the avenues and local parks. He stopped and asked pedestrians. All replies were negative. Greg thought back to his father-in-law's previous excursions. He had once been found by a neighbour who was walking his dog in the local park. On another occasion a police car stopped him from entering a demolition site, which in former times had housed a row of terraced buildings. One of these two-up, two-down red-bricked dwellings, number twenty-four, was where Sally's father had been born and raised prior to the family moving to Banstead.

"I wonder", thought Greg, whilst reversing his car into a private drive. Proceeding at speed he turned left into Mill Lane, before slowing at the approach to the old football ground, due for redevelopment as a superstore. The seven elm trees bordering the roads stood proud, still appearing to protect the terraced area and rusting stand. These trees were currently the subject of a controversy between developers and residents who wished to see them protected whilst the speculators wished to tarmac the entire area as a car park.

The football club's achievements could be counted on the fingers of one hand. Local residents still remembered the time when the stand played host to their local MP, dignitaries and sundry officials. Just prior to the second world war an unprecedented run in the F.A. Cup qualifying matches found them drawn against Chelsea in the third round. One thousand, eight hundred and fifty people crowded into the Mill Lane ground to see their side lose 7-0 but the result hadn't mattered. Sally's father, Alan Hargreaves, had been there. He'd spent most of his life telling Sally and her mother about that match. For the past four years he'd taken to telling the story to his grandchildren.

Greg pulled up, opened the door and stepped onto the verge. The grass was damp under foot, the street was deserted, save for a cat which clattered atop a dustbin lid, then jumped up onto a flat roof close by.

The paling fencing was intact for short sections, others had been removed by vandals and thrown onto the erstwhile embankment. Concrete crumbled and weeds abounded. The centre-piece of the stand, which stood on the far side, was a large clock, still showing 5.42 p.m. It had been stopped as the whistle blew at the end of the final match. It was now three years since that last Saturday meeting. Alan Hargreaves had told his son-in-law that if Willis, their centre forward, hadn't feigned injury trying to attract a penalty, the game would have ended at precisely 5.40 p.m. They still lost 3-1, against very poor opposition. As is usual at last rites that ultimate game of the season which ended in relegation and eventual financial ruin, had been attended by the largest crowd for many years. Seemingly everyone but the directors knew it to be the final match.

Greg side-stepped the larger fragments of concrete waste. He looked towards the peeling stanchions that still supported the rusting, corrugated iron roof.

There, arms resting on the wooden balcony, above where players once entered the arena, stood Alan Hargreaves. He didn't notice Greg kicking his way through the debris that lay about the stand.

"Dad, what are you doing here?"

"Hallo, son, I ...." His face lined as he narrowed his eyes.

"How long have you been here?"

"I don't know". Alan looked around as if awakened from a deep sleep.

"Do you remember walking here?" asked Greg, taking hold of his father-in-law's arm.

"No, son, not really. Did you bring me?"

"If you want to go out, all you've got to do is ask".

"Yes, son. All right".

Greg guided Alan along the terracing towards his Ford Mondeo.

"New car, son?"

"No, you've seen ....." Greg checked himself before continuing, "Yes, it's quite new".

"Did I ever tell you about the time we played Corinthians?" Greg opened his mouth to reply but Alan proceeded, "That was before they merged with the Casuals, of course. Funny name Corinthian Casuals, isn't it?"

"Yes", replied Greg as he opened the passenger door. In less than ten minutes they were home.

"Grandad's back", shouted Jenny, pulling back the downstairs curtains. Sally rushed to the door. Now fully dressed she wore an apron which sat neatly upon her plaid skirt.

"Dad, where've you been?" She hugged him. Tom and Jenny crowded round. Greg shut the door.

"He's been to the football ground". Sally stepped back.

"The football ground? What time did you start out?"

Alan Hargreaves shrugged his shoulders. "I was thinking of the team last night in bed. Followed them man and boy, and d'you know what?"

"What?"

"Don't think I ever saw them play well". So saying he walked through to the kitchen, leaving his family standing in the hall. "Wouldn't say no to bacon and eggs!"

Greg arrived at the railway club shortly before 10 a.m. Colin and Derek were already assembling the layout. Harold arrived shortly afterwards. "Southworth" was oval in shape, affording continuous running. The public viewed the front boards and both sides. A partition prevented them from observing the fiddle yards situated on the rear boards. It required four of the group's five members to operate the layout. A fifth person, however, was essential at exhibitions to relieve one of the operators at any time. This system allowed for lunch breaks and walk-abouts to be taken without disruption to the timetable. This Sunday's activities concentrated on minor scenic projects and tidying up chipped plaster that "scarred" the landscape, as Colin put it, plus the renewal of certain trackwork and electrical switches.

Harold decided that before any electrical work could be carried out, a pot of tea should be brewed. Derek and Greg commenced attacking the polystyrene and plaster-based scenery that showed signs of wear. Like most portable layouts continuous assembly and subsequent dismantling meant that knocks were common place. Chimneys were often found to be missing, fencing broken and bushes stripped from hillsides.

At any two-day show they had attended the layout would suffer teething problems, which traditionally lasted from the time of opening until an hour before closure on the second day when, as if by magic, everything would run like clockwork. Greg had ignored Colin's bouncing around the layout for the first few minutes but as his shoes squeaked to the point of annoyance Greg commented, "I think I heard Harold calling you from the kitchen".

Colin stood there, tapping his lips with his index finger.

"Hello, hello, is anyone in?"

Colin looked around. "Aaaaah, mmmmmm".

Greg looked at him but said nothing.

"Mmmmmmmm, I was just considering the possibility of listing the various work required under a continuous maintenance programme schedule - we'd all have copies, naturally".

"Naturally", replied Greg.

"You know, scenery infrastructure - which would obviously be sub-sectioned "railway" and "non-railway" - that sort of thing".

Derek glanced at Greg. Both men looked exasperated as they continued to scrape away at a hillside, through which a small lane was to be extended, linking two newly-built cottages with an existing road.

"Tea up", said Harold, bringing through the tray.

"Lovely, ta, thanks", said Derek, taking a cup with all the enthusiasm of a small boy accepting a surprise gift.

The main doors burst open. "Morning all, sorry I'm late, 'ad a Billy Bunter on the Montego. Nice chap".

"Oh, he bought it, then?" said Greg smiling.

"Another satisfied customer?" Colin asked in measured tone.

"Well, I'm satisfied, mate". Pete rubbed his hands together.

"The Montego cost him two and a half grand and 'e only rang about a Fiesta at twelve ninety-five".

Derek looked up, scalpel in hand. "But a Fiesta is a hatchback".

"I know", replied Pete. "That's the beauty of selling someone something they didn't know they wanted. I think of it more of a social service, 'elping people to dig deeper into their inner selves, identifying what they really want ....."

"I think you mean digging deeper into their pockets", suggested Colin.

"Oh, yeah, that was it". Pete laughed heartily. He removed his tan leather jacket to reveal a stone-washed denim shirt. He and Greg spent some minutes discussing the required repairs to the tracks.

"So, anything exciting happened, any news?"

"Sally's dad went AWOL again", said Greg as he cut a large chunk of polystyrene from a sheet some two feet in length.

"What do you mean AWOL?" asked Colin, quickly adding, "Well, I know what AWOL means, but I'm trying to connect the phrase with your father-in-law".

"Oh, his mind's going. He's suffering from senile dementia. It's in its early stages but he's got the habit of buggering off, not telling anyone and leaving the doors open".

"Happened this morning, did it?" enquired Harold.

"Yes, found him in the stand at the old football ground in Mill Lane".

"No mother-in-law to look after him?" enquired Colin.

"Sally's mum's dead".

"I remember you saying", said Pete. "How long's he bin widowed?"

Greg looked upwards. "Ooh, about eight years now. He's no trouble generally, only these little lapses".

"You'll need to try to contain him during the winter", said Colin, as he bent down to measure the front boards.

"He's not a prisoner".

"No, I know that, I just felt that going out and leaving the doors open could play havoc with your heating bills".

"Frankly, I think that comes a poor second to his dad-in-law", commented Pete.

Colin mumbled as he made his way along the boards.

"Bowels and bladders!" exclaimed Harold.

"What?" asked Greg.

"Bowels and bladders, that's when you'll have your work cut out. When he's forgotten he's been - or when he's forgotten he needed to go".

"Thanks for the advice, I'll remember that". Greg looked at Pete. Both men raised their eyebrows.

"Yeh, good tip that", said Derek, grinning. He gave the thumbs up sign as an added mark of approval.

By 1 p.m. Pete had replaced three sections of the track damaged when a board had been accidentally dropped. The new lane had been formed by Greg with Derek's assistance and the plaster was now in the process of drying, ready to accept paint on resumption of work. Harold had repaired several dry joints and replaced two point motors. Colin offered the services of his mother who, he had advised, would willingly run up some curtains for the front boards. He'd brought along sample swabs of material, holding them up against the legs. "What about this colour?" he had asked on several occasions.

"Fine" had been the unanimous reply for every example exhibited.

"So I'll choose, then, shall I?" Colin had asked eventually.

"Up to you", said Pete.

Murmurs of agreement were echoed by the others.

"Aaah, right, then. In that case I think dark green - or maybe the cream, perhaps brown?"

Harold made another pot of tea and lunches were unwrapped. Colin pulled open the foil which encased his wholemeal rolls. He removed the top half with precision and announced, "Let's see what we have here. Mmmmmm, tuna".

"You like tuna, then?" asked Derek enthusiastically.

"No, not really, but mother does".

"But she's not eating it, you are", quizzed Pete.

"I know, but it's difficult for her to accept that it's not my favourite filling".

"You've never thought of making them yourself?" suggested Greg.

"Mmmmmmm, that's a thought". Colin paused, took a mouthful then replied, "but then it wouldn't be a surprise".

Everyone tucked into their lunch boxes.

"Went to the All Star last night", said Pete.

"Where's that?" asked Derek.

"What's that?" asked Colin.

"It's a nightclub-theatre. They have alternative comedians".

"Alternative to what?" queried Colin.

"Alternative to ......" Pete fumbled for an explanation. "Well, they're not mainstream ....." He tailed off.

"What, like Ray Allen and Lord Charles?" offered Harold.

"No, not a bit like them".

"I've never quite worked out which one's the dummy", said Greg.

Pete thought as he waved a pickled onion about on the end of a cocktail stick. "Well, they don't tell sexist or racist jokes and they don't take the mickey out of the disabled or minorities".

"What about traffic wardens?" asked Harold.

Pete thought. "I don't think they mentioned them, so they could be included - although as they didn't, maybe they're not!"

"It's difficult to find anything left to be funny about", suggested Greg.

"Yeh, I can't remember any of their jokes but they were really good".

"So, who was it, anyone well known?" asked Harold, carving a tomato with his penknife. "Like Little and Large, were they, or Cannon and Ball?"

Greg interrupted. "Well, they're hardly alternative".

"I've heard Cannon and Ball sing", said Derek, "and that sounded alternative. Great".

"Like I say, they were Channel 4 types. There was a bloke called Ray Piste and a woman comedian who's name - you'll like this - was Jenny Taylior, like Taylor but with an 'i' in it. Get it?"

Pete laughed loudly. "Great names for comedians, aren't they?"

"Well, if she was a woman she would have to be a comedienne", stated Colin.

"Yeh, right", said Pete, forcing a large lump of Red Leicester into his mouth.

Derek pointed eagerly towards Pete. "You should do a turn on the stage, those jokes you come out with here, they'd go down well in a club. You've got the gift of the gab".

"Got just the right stage name for you as well - Roger Ring", suggested Greg. "Appropriate, I'd say. After all, you've spent a lifetime stuffing your customers".

Pete howled with laughter, assuming the inference to be a compliment. Derek nearly choked on his egg mayonnaise roll. Harold felt slightly awkward about the comment, while Colin said he understood the reference to the car trade but didn't quite see where the name Roger was relevant, or Ring, come to that.

"The hall looks a lot cleaner since it was painted", observed Harold, changing the subject. Everyone agreed.

"I suppose you had a customer on one of your Balfour Beauties", said Colin, "which would account for your being conspicuous by your absence last Sunday". Pete grinned knowingly.

"Let's just say I was otherwise engaged!" He looked towards Greg and winked.

Greg frowned. "Actually, Rita was very concerned".

"Yeh, I know, but I've sorted 'er out. She's okay now. Anyway, ours is a marriage of convenience - neither of us was doing anything that Saturday!" He laughed loudly and insincerely. "So, my little Clipboard, 'ow did Friday night go? I 'eard you was doing the singles disco".

Colin looked up. "Well, it went". He related the story of the drunk and in passing commented that he had disturbed a couple "doing it" in a brown Nova.

"Yeh, but this bird with the drunk, this Tanya sort, sounds as if she fancies you - seeing 'er again?"

"Certainly not. She was a very pleasant young lady, but not my type".

"Being female wouldn't have helped, of course", joked Greg. Pete laughed raucously. Harold smiled.

"Good one that, great, yeah", said Derek. Colin sat po-faced.

The rest of the afternoon saw the desired progress achieved. Harold had tested all the point motors to his satisfaction. Pete's endeavours with the track work provided faultless running. Greg and Derek completed the lane. Fencing had been erected, scatter material now covered the painted plaster and shrubs bordered the modelled tarmac. Colin had worked tirelessly on completing his work schedule and estimating the amount of material required to screen the legs of the boards from the viewing public, the colour of which he had still not decided upon.

Having dismantled the boards and stored them, the five group members made their way to their respective cars. Harold started up his Austin Princess. The engine roared but the car merely trickled forward.

"Try first, not third", shouted Greg.

"I think the clutch is going", replied Harold. Pete was standing alongside a BMW 520i that he had continually made reference to throughout the day. The "steal of the century" was how he described this acquisition. Pete took off his sunglasses and sauntered towards the Princess.

"You wanna get that seen to before you have no clutch left".

"I know, it's just that, well, mechanics - who can you trust not to rip you off?"

"You need to speak to Baz", suggested Pete.

"Baz?"

"Yeah, he does all my mechanics, very cheap 'an all. Look, I'll give 'im your phone number and you can talk to 'im about it. I'll tell 'im you're a mate. He owes me a favour anyway".

"Thanks Pete", said Harold as his car slunk away, leaving behind a cloud of noxious grey smoke.

"Can you throw in a replacement engine as well?" shouted Greg, as he waved away the fumes.

Pete laughed and swaggered back to his BMW, sunglasses sticking out of his breast pocket. He acknowledged Greg as he roared out of the gates, front windows lowered, sun-roof open, "Dire Straits" blaring.

"Right", shouted Greg, "see you Wednesday".

"Great, yeah, good day's work", acknowledged Derek, rubbing his hands together before giving Greg the thumbs-up sign. Both men left Colin to lock up. He was still folding the plaid-patterned blankets that had carefully been placed over the seats to protect them from the sun.

*   *   *   *   *

As the shadows became longer and the bird song more frenetic, Albert Buchanan sat relaxing in his back garden. On the table beside his chair lay a copy of "Bee Keeping Weekly". He had found it strange that a well-meaning neighbour should offer this publication to him as something to read, when his only encounter with a bee in over seventy years was to have been stung by one at Margate in 1936. Still, he pondered, as Vi said, "it's the thought that counts". Albert's eyes remained closed as he reflected on the fact that it had been only a week since the attack. Most of the swelling had subsided, the pain now less severe. The exception to this improvement concerned his ribs, which still hurt considerably when he moved.

"Tea up, Alb", said Vi as she brought through the tray.

"Got something to dunk?"

"Not much wrong with your appetite". Vi smiled.

Albert opened up his eyes. "That's better, it's the first time I've seen you looking 'appy all day".

She sat beside him. Was this the right time?

"You're all right, aren't you?"

"Me, oh I'm fine, just a little tired". Vi said nothing more, allowing the chance to pass before she'd even realised it was there. She had been unable to tell him. One voice urged her to unburden the weight of knowing, another felt it selfish to inflict personal problems when her immediate priority was to see Albert well again.

They'd had corn-fed chicken, with potatoes, carrots and peas for Sunday dinner. Albert said the bird looked as though it had jaundice.

"According to the lady on the checkout, that's what a proper chicken should look like".

"Only when it's dead, surely", Albert had observed drily.

"You're looking forward to going to the Club on Wednesday, I bet", said Vi, taking a sip of tea from a willow-patterned cup.

"Yes, it'll be nice to see those reprobates again". Albert had a look of contentment as he dunked a digestive. His mind wandered off. "Gawd", he said, as half a biscuit fell into his cup.

"You're supposed to dunk it, not give it swimming lessons!" Vi was no longer waiting for an appropriate moment to chance itself. She would bide her time, it was now her turn to relax.

"What time's Mick coming round for you?"

"Eight o'clock - and I won't be out all night, I'll probably only feel like a half or so".

"If you come back only having had an 'arf, I'll reckon you'll have had a relapse". They both giggled.

Albert leaned over and pointed to the magazine still lying on the table. "Old Nobby doesn't keep bees, does he?"

Vi picked up a crew-necked jumper she had recently started knitting.

"No", she said thoughtfully.

"So where did he get it from?"

"How do I know. He probably had it given to him", Vi said in exasperation.

"Yeah, possibly".

"Does it matter?"

"No, not really, it's just bees, that's all".

"Well, if you're so concerned, ask Nobby when he calls round".

"Yeah, I'll do that". Albert seemed satisfied.

"We could always invite Miss Marple up for the day if Nobby doesn't know where it came from".

"All right, woman". Albert closed his eyes. "She must think I'm getting better or she wouldn't have been so sharp", he thought before drifting off to sleep.

An hour had elapsed before Vi prodded her husband's arm. "Come on, love, it's starting to get a bit chilly".

"Right-o", said Albert, rubbing his eyes. She helped him to his feet and he followed her towards the back door. Albert turned around. Only the tables and chairs devoid of tea-cups, biscuits and knitting remained. For an instant he could see Jamie sitting on the far side of the white garden table, his head just proud of the rim. The boy's face was smiling. He was holding a knife and fork upright in anticipation. The archetypal TV ad kid. The beaming face that had so much love to give was in direct contrast to Graham's. His was cold and bitter, the face of someone who blamed everybody but himself for his own inadequacies.

Even that last meal together two summers ago had been rushed. Albert and Vi thought their son and daughter-in-law were to stay the whole evening, but they left as soon as the meal was over, using Jamie's tiredness as an excuse to leave. Jamie had said he wasn't tired and appeared upset, but Graham did as he always did, he shouted at him. Their grandson cried. Albert could never remember seeing Camilla smile, she only ever scowled. They'd never known what their son had seen in her. She was pretty, but so distant. Cold eyes and hard lips. She generally stood with her arms crossed, forever on the fringe of a conversation, always giving the impression that she would rather be elsewhere. Neither parent ever seemed to talk to Jamie, only at him.

Albert and Vi had always wanted a daughter and naively assumed that Graham's marriage would fill that void. They had nothing in common with Camilla, and there was nothing common about Camilla.

She looked down on Graham's parents, only giving one word answers and being generally dismissive to any suggestion or ideas put forward by them. Even presents were accepted with scant regard for the thought that had preceded their purchase, let alone any financial consideration. Albert remembered how hurt Vi had been when, on one occasion a present given to Camilla, had been left on their dining room table. When, some two weeks later, Vi had telephoned reminding her of its whereabouts, Camilla had replied, "Oh, yes, I remember you giving me something. What was it you bought me, again?"

Vi had cried that night. She felt embarrassed and humiliated. That incident was, in fact, the straw that broke the camel's back. Albert rang Graham and told him what he thought of his wife's callousness but Graham, as besotted with her then as he was the first time they had met, still considered that she could do no wrong. It was shortly afterwards Graham casually announced that they were to emigrate to Australia.

*　　*　　*　　*　　*

Five forty-two, Colin's watch told him. He tutted as he walked from his car along the tarmac driveway to collect his trolley. He usually arrived by five-thirty at the latest, but this Tuesday's drive from the office to the supermarket had been fraught. "Women drivers", Colin muttered to himself, as he observed a female gamely trying to execute a manoeuvre which should, in his opinion, have been completed in two attempts. He had counted five instances where her reversing lights blinked their eyes in conjunction with the graunching of the gear box. Colin fumbled in his pockets in an effort to find the one-pound coin holder that was always about his person. It was eventually located in the inside right-hand pocket of his jacket, or off-side, as he referred to it.

Having extracted a trolley from the row of some thirty examples, he glanced back into the car park, only to see the same woman still trying to park her Nissan Micra between a Metro and a Renault Clio. Colin tutted again. "Glad that's not my Metro", he thought, "I would have to go back over there and check that she's not scraping my paintwork!" He wondered how she would have fared if both cars either side of her had been Volvo Estates. "Shouldn't be driving", he said to himself, as he prepared to enter the store between the revolving glass doors.

"Cripes", he said aloud on looking down and realising that he was in possession of a lame trolley. He knelt, attempting to free the near-side rear wheel, but to no avail. It was stiff to the point of solid. Colin looked around and noticed a security officer just to the left-hand side of the entrance. He raised his finger. "Ah, excuse me, I appear to have obtained one of those chaps with a gammy leg". Colin demonstrated by rocking it from side to side.

"Not a problem, sir", said the guard who promptly limped it to a side wall, against which another trolley already leaned, devoid of a front wheel. The chain was attached and Colin's one-pound coin released. They walked swiftly to the slightly reduced line awaiting the arrival of temporary custodians. Colin thought the guard looked rather smart in his uniform but felt intimidated by the peaked cap, which created a shadow over his eyes and nose. The one-pound coin was inserted for a second time. Colin tested it for stability and ease of movement, and when satisfied said, "If you have any WD40 handy you may find that it will assist the seizure. It could, however, be a dry bearing, of course. 'Timkins'!"

"Sorry".

"'Timkins'", repeated Colin, "'Timkins' roller bearings. Take a tip from British Rail, or Railways as I prefer to think of them. If they're good enough for **their** wheels they should be good enough for you. Remember, 'Timkins'. I know if I worked here, I'd make a note of it and put it in the suggestion box". He leaned forward, tapped his nose with his index finger and whispered, "Promotion prospects should be enhanced".

The guard smiled weakly, thanking Colin for his concern.

Colin pushed his newly acquired trolley once more between the revolving doors. "Been here before", he said as they stopped abruptly. A woman shopper making her way out had run into the door opposite, a loaf of bread shot into the aisle. "Typical", thought Colin, "they always drive too close!"

Once inside he withdrew a shopping list from his back pocket. Items required were noted alongside a number. These referred to the aisles, along which the necessary article could be located. The floor plan had been drawn up and reproduced in computerised form by Colin for his convenience, amendments only being necessary should the supermarket's management decide to move their stock around. Fruit and vegetables always seemed to remain just inside the entrance.

Colin rested his unerring trolley by the Cox's orange pippins, as he surveyed the various headings. He subconsciously dismissed anything

French, regardless of quality, and Golden Delicious were no exception.

"Ah, Granny Smith's", he said to himself, proceeding to turn them in his hands to check for signs of bruising. He chose four and placed them in one of the polythene bags provided, but not before he had struggled manfully to open the said bag. He rubbed the top with both hands, attempted to prise it apart with his finger tips. He tried blowing on it. Eventually, having checked that he had it the right way up, the bag finally submitted to the continual pressure and parted itself. It was as the fourth apple was being placed neatly into the bag to avoid damage that Colin felt a tap on the shoulder.

"Hello", said a female voice. Colin spun around. His foot kicked an unseen trolley. He furrowed his eyebrows. Two females were standing before him - one he recognised. It was Tanya. She smiled. Colin felt this to be an invasion of his privacy.

"This is Colin", said Tanya. "He's the one that saw off that pest at the disco the other night". Her face beamed.

"I wouldn't say that ....."

"Don't be so modest". Tanya turned to her companion. "Debbie, meet Colin. Colin - Debbie".

Colin bowed his head, his face reddened, he tried to avoid direct eye contact. "Aah, hello".

"So, the hero emerges from behind his trusty steed", Debbie said theatrically.

"Well, from behind his 'Timkin' bearingless shopping trolley, certainly".

Both females looked mystified. Colin's left hand played with the supermarket name-tag on the handle.

"Aren't you going to ask me if I come here often?" asked Tanya. Debbie giggled. Colin felt they were playing with him. "I'm only joking". Her eyes were wide and laughing.

"Oh, right".

"I'll go ahead then, shall I?" suggested Debbie.

"Okay, I'll catch you up".

"Don't let me stop you", said Colin, wondering why they needed to go shopping together anyway. Tanya ignored his offer.

"Look, d'you fancy going to the pictures?" She lowered her head and allowed her left foot to skim the floor from side to side.

"What?" said Colin, loudly enough to attract the attention of two women standing nearby. "You mean ....." Tanya looked up. Colin pointed to her and then to himself. "Us?"

She widened her eyes again. "Yes, us, the cinema. There's a film I'd like to see - 'Dracula' and it's, well, it's the sort of film I'd like to see with a friend".

"Why don't you go with Debbie?"

"A man friend, I meant".

"But ....."

"But what?"

"Well, we hardly know each other and ....." Colin's voice drifted into a suppressed muffle.

Tanya placed her slender hands on her hips. She tossed her hair, still tied in a pony tail. As Colin began to speak once more a woman pushed between them. "Have you seen the courgettes?"

"Over there", said Colin irritably, pointing to the far side of the aisle. The woman smiled and turned away. "Honestly, don't they know the difference between fruit and vegetables?" He continued to look in the woman's direction.

"And what?" reminded Tanya.

"Aaah, yes - and, well - well, there's a difference in age, in case you'd not noticed".

Tanya looked bemused.

"I mean you're ..... you must be in your early twenties, and I'm thirty-three".

"So?"

"Well, it does make a difference".

"Look, I'm asking you to take me to the pictures, not marry me!"

"Aaah, mmmmm, well, the only night I'm generally free is Friday - and when I say free ....."

"Friday's fine". Tanya flashed her eyes provocatively.

"Oh", exclaimed Colin, somewhat startled.

"The film starts at ten-past eight, it's on at the ABC". With that she hurriedly wrote her address on a scrap of paper. "Here, pick me up at, say, seven thirty".

"Well ....."

"That's the fourth time you've said that".

"Sorry, it's just that - well".

Tanya extended all five digits of her right hand. Colin half-smiled. "That's settled, then. Seven thirty, okay?"

"Yes, fine, mmm, right". Colin watched her shapely legs as she walked quickly to the far end of the aisle. She didn't look round. He stared at his shopping list for several seconds, as if in a state of shock. He then looked at the slip of paper containing her address. Colin blinked a couple of times, then headed off towards the seedless grapes.

Despite being in the store a further forty minutes he never encountered either female again.

*   *   *   *   *

Mick's just pulling up", said Vi, as she peeped out of her front window. Albert stood up slowly and pulled his tie straight. He ran his left hand across his silver-grey hair.

"Do I look all right?"

"You'll do", his wife said with concealed pride. She helped him on with his jacket. The bell rang and Vi walked to the door.

"Come in, Mick". The Club Treasurer gave her a peck on the cheek.

"How are you?" he asked.

"Oh, I'm all right, 'an all the better for knowing he's going out and enjoying himself". She smiled and brushed the collar of Albert's blue jacket.

"Right", Vi said, looking up at her husband. "You're all ship-shape and Bristol fashion. Off you go!"

It was the first time that Albert had set foot outside his house since the attack. The air in the street smelled different from that in his back garden. He rubbed the cuff of his jacket over his regimental badge before settling into the car. Mick drove smartly towards the Club house.

"They're no nearer finding anyone", said Albert gloomily.

"Trouble is, you're just one in a thousand, Albert. Sad to say, but you're just a statistic. Vi looks better, are those tablets working now?"

Mick fished for an indication as to whether anything had been said.

"She was a bit tense at the weekend but she's been better this week, so perhaps they are".

Mick pulled up, walked around to Albert's side and opened the door. Helping him out, Albert stretched before making his way towards the double doors. He was about to push them open when they were pulled aside by unseen hands. Albert walked inside and stopped suddenly. He looked around, his mouth dropped. A banner was draped across the hall - Welcome back, Albert", it read. He looked around. Bunting criss-crossed the ceiling, in the corners balloons hung like giant plums. "Is this all for me".

"No, it was left over from the weekend - 'course it's for you", said Greg.

The large crowd that had gathered clapped vigorously. Robin stepped forward and shook Albert's hand. "No speeches, but I would like to say on behalf of everybody here, as the banner says, 'welcome back'".

Albert stood slightly stooped, his eyes misty. "So what are you having?" asked Robin, leading Albert towards a seat near the bar.

"What have we got on?"

"Fullers E.S.B."

"Ooooh, that's a nice pint. I'll have half, please".

Over the ensuing couple of hours many offers of drinks were forthcoming, few were refused. Albert was correct when he predicted only drinking a half of beer, for it was whisky that passed his lips during that time - several singles and more than the occasional double. He was patted on the back, arms and shoulders but the alcohol anaesthetised the body.

During the evening, as Colin was groping around in a packet of beer nuts, Pete walked over to where he was standing. He was dressed in a purple and silver shell suit with purple and white trainers completing the ensemble.

"So, you're taking that Tanya sort out, I hear".

"What? But, I mmmmm ....."

"News travels fast, my little Clipboard. You can't keep a good story like that secret for long. And there was me believing it when you said she wasn't your type". He tutted mockingly and slapped Colin on the back.

"Do you mind, I could have choked".

"Gawd, you'd do anything to get out of Friday night, wouldn't you?" Pete laughed raucously.

"How do you know, anyway?"

"You know my mechanic, Baz".

"I know **of** him".

"Well, his girlfriend's Debbie, the bird who was with Tanya".

"Oh, I see".

"Well, she told Baz and Baz told me. Bloody dark horse, aren't you?"

He mimicked in a falsetto voice. "Oh, no, she's not my type. A nice

105

young lady, but not for me - lying toe-rag!"

"It wasn't like that. I just said I didn't generally do anything on Friday night and before I knew it she had suggested a time to pick her up".

"So, what are you going to see?"

"Dracula, apparently".

"Oh, you're in luck, then. That's a good cuddling film, she'll be 'olding on to you for grim life - or is it death?"

Pete raised his arms then bent them, opening his mouth in a manner so as to imitate the legendary character.

"Oh, very good", said Colin, obviously underwhelmed. "I assume you adopt that role when persuading your customers to part with their pennies".

"Don't forget, we'll all need to know 'ow you got on, blow by blow - you know, nudge, nudge, wink, wink!"

"God", exclaimed Colin as Pete walked back to the bar, smirking.

"'Ere, Greg, guess what ....."

Colin heard Pete commence telling his snippet of gossip to anyone who cared to listen - and most members did.

At ten o'clock Gwladys came through from the kitchen with a cake iced in white, with a green engine standing astride two chocolate coloured railway tracks. As everyone was offered a sliver of home-made cake Doreen appeared with an envelope.

"Albert, this is for you from the Club", she said.

He looked up, took the envelope and said, "Thank you". His hands were shaking as he opened it. Inside were two tickets for the mystery tour and thirty pounds to replace that which had been stolen. There was silence. Albert looked around the hall, then slowly his eyes returned to the tickets and the three ten pound notes.

"We had a whip-round", said Robin.

"You're not making out of this", commented Mick, "You're only getting back what was taken". Everyone laughed, except Albert, who was still taking it in, although his ability to fully comprehend the situation had been somewhat negated by the liberal doses of Scotch. He looked at the gathering, raised his glass and very softly said, "Thanks everyone, getting my photograph back was my only concern, but this is, well, the icing really. Thanks".

Albert beckoned Mick across. "Can you take me home now, son. I'm feeling a bit tired".

"I'm not surprised, after what you've consumed", said Mick.

Vi was standing by the window, like a mother awaiting the arrival home of a daughter from her first date. Mick saw Albert indoors and left him to go to bed. Albert slept well that night.

* * * * *

The journey into London was without incident. Rita kept her eyes on the dashboard dials in order to be one step ahead of a potential disaster. When the vehicle had been handed to her the previous evening Pete had, as usual, given the appearance of trying to sell his wife the car. All she'd asked for was his assurance that it wouldn't let her down.

"Baz's checked it, it's A1", Pete had said, but then Pete said that about every car, whether or not Baz, or any other mechanic, had checked it over.

From Tolworth, along the A3 and through south London it had been overcast but dry. By the time Rita had reached the City it was spitting with rain. Now, however, as she travelled ponderously with dipped headlights, pinned in the middle of a conveyor belt of traffic, rain leapt off the bonnet and puddles appeared to widen the border between pavement and road. "Bloody Baz", shouted Rita, punching the steering wheel as she crawled along the Romford Road towards the North Circular interchange. She pursed her lips and cursed. The windows were constantly steaming up. No matter how she tried to apply the controls neither heat nor air were forthcoming. The only way to contain the misting up was to lower one of the windows, which meant getting wet. Throughout the latter part of the journey her right hand had to continually depress the wiper arm, as only the intermittent stage appeared to work. Traffic gradually dispersed and Rita finally pulled into the side road, just off Green Lane, Ilford, where Pete's father lived.

She walked the few yards from where her car was parked, passed the iron railings that bordered the dull, red-bricked terraced house and up the steps to the front door. A puddle had formed on the bottom step where the ravages of time and wear had shaped a shallow bowl. Rita pulled the cast knocker, hitting the blue four-panelled door twice. Pete's father had never seen fit to install a doorbell. She heard movement. "'Who's that?" said a voice from within.

"It's me, Reet". The door opened slowly.

"'Allo, love", said Bert Balfour, his eyes lighting up.

"Hallo, dad". Rita held out her arms. She kissed him lightly on the cheek as he ushered her inside.

"You should've rung, gal, I'd 've got some dinner on the go".

"I wasn't sure how the traffic would be and I didn't want you getting all worried about me not being on time".

"Well, it's a pleasant surprise anyway. Come on through. It's a good couple of months since I've seen you. You're looking as good as ever. Things all right?"

Rita smiled. "Yes, fine, I'm doing a sort of round robin. I'm off to see Marcia later, but I thought I'd call in and see how you are".

Having gestured Rita towards an arm-chair, Bert Balfour asked, "Tea, gal?"

"Oh, yes please". Rita stretched her arms and yawned.

"You're old man keeping you up late, is he?" Bert laughed.

"No, it's just that - you know what it's like after driving a long way".

"Well, I might if I drove, gal". Bert laughed loudly.

"I know where Pete gets his sense of humour from", she thought.

Bert returned from the kitchen with two steaming mugs. "Go on, gal, get that down you". Bert's smile was infectious. He liked company and wasn't short of any, either. He was well known in the "Green Man" and the "Slug and Lettuce", formerly the "Royal Star", as well as the local British Legion club, where he also stood in occasionally as M.C. when Ernie Ricketts was indisposed.

"So, 'ow's your Marcie?"

"Oh, Still the same. Too few men and too many kids!"

"Not up the duff again, is she?"

"No, but the bigger they are, the more bloody hassle they are".

"Oh, no need to tell me that. Look at your old man". He laughed. "'Ow old are Marcia's lot now, Reet?"

"Well, Damien's fourteen, Cindy's twelve, Warren's six and Darren's four - bloody handful he is".

The rain had eased up. Rita could see patches of blue appearing as she looked through the lower half of the sitting room window. It was of the traditional pattern. Bert noticed Rita looking at the sash cord. "Next door 'ave 'ad them PVC double-glazed jobs fitted. Cost 'em a packet, it did".

"Sash suits these houses, though, dad".

"Yeah, but they aint 'arf bloody draughty, wind goes right through me some nights. You should 'ear 'em rattle". He gesticulated.

"Gor'blimey, gal, you'd think the bleeding place is falling apart. Nah, I thought about it, like, but I can't see me getting none".

Rita felt awkward. She didn't want Bert to know that Pete had mentioned his father's predicament. She thought carefully before replying. "No, you've got to mind the pennies, dad. I understand that".

Bert looked vague. "I'm not that brassic". He put down his mug. "You for another cup, gal?"

"No, I'm all right, thanks, dad". Bert sat back in the chair, his hands clasped behind his head.

"No, I've got a few bob stashed away for a rainy day, but not a windy one". Bert laughed again. Rita smiled politely.

"It's all right, dad, you've no need to pretend with me ....."
She hesitated, looking down at her hands. "Pete told me about your difficulties, I just wish you felt you could have trusted me. I mean, after all the years we've known each other". She let the sentence slip. Bert leaned forward, the springs in the arm-chair squeaked.

"Rita, can you tell me what you're talking about?"

She looked unclear. "Pete told me about the poll tax, the gas and the electricity".

"Told you what?"

"Well - that you were having problems finding the money. Dad, this is awkward, I don't mean to pry, I just felt hurt that you couldn't tell me things like you would have done, had mum been alive".

Bert stood up and paced the room. He scratched his head. "What poll tax, what electricity? I'm not behind with anyfink. It's not easy, I'm not saying it is, but I've managed". He continued looking at his daughter-in-law.

"But you phoned Pete about two weeks ago, asking him to come and see you. He told me".

"Rita, I haven't spoken to Pete for three weeks at least, I was going to give you a bell over the weekend, see 'ow you are, like".

Rita took a deep breath. "I'm sorry, dad, I must have got the wrong end of the stick, only I thought Pete said he was coming over to sort things out, the Sunday before last". Rita was fishing.

"Sunday before last, uh?" Bert rubbed his chin. "What date was that?"

Rita replied without hesitation.

"You must have got it wrong", he said, returning from the kitchen, from where he had sought verification of the date. "I was at me sister

Dolly's in East 'am. She put on a good spread, 'an all".

"Right", said Rita with resignation. She stayed for just over an hour. No mention of the previous conversation was uttered by either party. Rita kissed her father-in-law goodbye and drove back down the Romford Road, through Stratford, arriving at her sister Marcia's flat in Homerton shortly before 3.30 p.m. Having walked up four flights of stairs that smelt strongly of urine Rita felt relieved as she made her way along the balcony. Many of the glazed brown and cream bricks had been subjected to graffiti. Stickers informed tenants of forthcoming anti-racist demonstrations to be held in Bethnal Green.

Rita stopped outside number fourteen Pevensey House. Erected just before the last war the six blocks that constituted the "Sussex Estate" were all named after seaside locations within the southern county. Originally called "Pevensey Buildings" it was, along with its counterparts, renamed in an expensive P.R. exercise during the erstwhile G.L.C.'s tenure of office. Rita placed a shopping bag which contained small gifts for the children on the damp floor whilst she rang the bell. It didn't work. She knocked on the mesh glass window. A child was screaming. She knocked again.

"Coming, coming", shouted Marcia, somewhat distraught. The door opened. Marcia stood with a young baby in her arms. She beckoned Rita inside. Marcia's straight, bleached blonde hair hung lank across her eyes. The flat was a cacophony of noise. Warren and Darren ran from room to room, unaware of their aunty's presence. The baby belched. Marcia patted its back as the two women walked through to the kitchen, which looked out onto a vandalised space of mud and trees. Directly opposite them, on the other side of the square, stood "Beachy Head House".

"You've got your hands full, Marcie - who's this one?" Rita toyed with the baby's hands.

"This is Charlene. I'm looking after her for a couple of 'ours. 'Er mum's the one two doors up". She pointed in the direction.

"What, the kid with the tattoo in the funny place?" They both laughed.

"Yeah, that's the one - Ingrid".

Rita thought before replying, "But she can't be more than seventeen".

"Sixteen, actually".

"You never told me she was pregnant last time we spoke".

"No-one knew she was pregnant, not even 'er mum, 'til she started getting pains".

"Bloody hell", replied Rita in astonishment. The baby was placed in a playpen, retained after Darren's baby days. Marcia had commented at the time that it would be a pity to dispose of it as, "You never know when we'll need it again".

The front door opened and closed. Footsteps were heard in the hall. "'Allo, mum, 'allo Aunty Reet". It was Cindy. "Didn't know you were coming this afternoon".

Rita smiled. "How's my favourite niece".

"I'm only your favourite 'cos I'm the only one you've got".

"Oh, that's right", said Rita snapping her fingers. "I never thought of that!" They hugged each other.

"S'pose your starving, as usual?" Marcia looked at Cindy.

"Yeah, 'course. School meals are crap".

"Well, look after Warren and Darren and I'll get something in a while. Reet and I want to 'ave a chat".

She turned and opened a cupboard. "You can 'ave some crisps", Marcia said, throwing two packets towards the door, where Cindy now stood. Cindy made a good mother hen for the two youngest. Having called them through, she led them down to the communal swings. These had recently been painted in red and blue but were already becoming the subject of more vandalism and spray paint. Marcia lit up a cigarette and looked out of the window.

"Right, come on through to the lounge". She used the word mockingly. As Rita sat down on the settee, acquired via Social Services, Marcia carried through the baby and proceeded to lay her in a cream-coloured cot, positioned behind the armchair which Marcia used nightly as a refuge from the outside world. As she slumped down, placing an ash tray on the arm, she looked across at her sister. "You all right, Reet, you're a bit quiet?"

Rita sat twirling her necklace. She opened her mouth but remained silent.

"'E's not turned you out, has he?"

"What, Pete? No, 'course not. I went to see his dad before coming here and to tell you the truth, Marse, I don't know whether I'm coming or going". Rita recounted the events of that Sunday, how she felt she'd misunderstood the situation and now, having heard what Bert Balfour had to say, had realised that her initial gut reaction was correct. Marcia

111

listened intently as Rita poured out her heart.

"You know what I think?" said Marcia at length, placing both hands on her knees. "I think you ought to look at what you've got, then look at what I've got, and accept that if Pete's got a bit on the side, then tough! 'E still comes home to you, don't 'e. 'As done for fifteen years. It can't be all bad". She pointed a finger. "I tell you what, I'd settle for that". She stubbed out her cigarette with purpose. Rita looked shocked.

"You what", she said, looking up.

Marcia looked around her. "No-one would choose to live like this would they? Where's Damien and Cindy's dad now, where's Warren's dad, where's Darren's dad, huh?"

Rita opened her mouth to answer, but Marcia continued. "They've all buggered off, 'aven't they? Left me holding - and feeding - the babies. Men only want one thing at the end of the day, Reet, and you're lucky your Pete stayed with you. So, 'e's got a bit on the side, so bloody what! I'd be 'appy knowing there's a bloke coming home regular - think about it".

Rita was thinking about it. She had expected sympathy. She had received none.

"Do you think I want to look after her?" asked Marcia, pointing behind the chair.

"No". Rita's reply was almost imperceptible.

"No, 'course not, I do it for the money, Reet, not bloody pleasure".

Rita remained silent.

"You got out of this 'ole, you've done well. I'm pleased for you, really, but I feel it's like rubbing me nose in it, coming 'ere and telling me what a sod your old man is". She paused. "'Cos you got no intentions of leaving 'im, have you? You've got a lovely home, with central heating, a patio and a jacuzzi. Christ, you can't even have a bath 'ere some days unless you're prepared to shiver in cold water". Looking across at Rita, she took hold of her sister's hand. "It's always good to see you Reet, but we've got different - whatsits".

"Priorities", said Rita looking straight ahead.

"Yeah, them. He'll still be there for you tonight, won't he?"

"Yes". Rita felt somewhat divorced from the conversation. "Yes, he will". She was still thinking about what Marcia had just said. "Rubbing my nose in it". Rita had said that when arguing with Pete, and that's exactly what he had been doing. The question was, what should she do about it.

*   *   *   *   *

Bert Balfour picked up the telephone and dialled his son's number. It rang just once.

"Balfour's Beauties, purveyors of quality horseless carriages, how can I help you?"

"Cut the bollocks, son, it's me, dad".

"Oh, er, 'ello, dad, I was meaning to ring you". Pete was cut short.

"I bet you were. What's all this you've been telling Reet".

"Why, what?"

"She called in lunchtime, son. She's under the impression I've got trouble wiv me bills - what've you bin telling her. Gal's got a right to know".

"But ....."

"No buts, son, if you're seeing a bit of skirt after hours, don't use me as an alibi, I don't wanna know. It won't wash. We've been all through this before. I like Reet, lovely gal, too bloody good for you, yer git. Your mum and I always said so".

"Dad, I was going to ring you but you know 'ow it is".

"Oh, I know, son, you couldn't be bothered. When you going to grow up? Rita's probably the only woman you've been with who aint got one of your kids ....."

"That's not fair".

"What you're doing's not fair. Anyway, you'd better be on your best behaviour when she gets 'ome. Reet's not going to be very happy to say the least".

"All right, dad, I ....."

Bert Balfour slammed down the phone.

*   *   *   *   *

Rita arrived home shortly before 8 p.m. Pete wasn't expected until 9. He was to deliver a Honda Prelude to a customer in Claygate. Baz was taking a second car to run Pete home once the vehicle had been accepted. She couldn't remember driving back through London. Her mind had been whirring. The options, the blame, was it really all Pete's fault? As time progressed Rita came to believe more and more that any inadequacies lay with her. Perhaps she was losing her looks. Staring into

113

the full length bedroom mirror, Rita adjusted her bright green dress across the shoulders, her hands smoothed over the stomach. Was she putting on weight there? She half-turned and ran her hands across her buttocks. They still appeared firm, and felt firm. Was she deceiving herself?

Rita sat on the edge of the bed picking at one of her fingernails. She resolved not to say anything to Pete for the time being. After a few minutes she jumped up and said aloud, "Let's be positive". Looking at her watch Rita made her way briskly to the kitchen where she started preparing Pete's favourite meal.

In determined mood she drew the curtains in the dining area and switched on the subdued wall lights, the bulbs of which peered through Spanish porcelain bowls. Shafts of light brought long shadows to the tables and chairs. Rita lit the candelabra, placed with precision as a centre piece.

Place mats and cutlery were neatly arranged; serviettes, pushed through gold-plated holders, were laid at angles across the Port Meirion side plates. These dishes had been bought as part of a complete set when they visited the village of the same name. Pete had always wanted to see where "The Prisoner" had been filmed. Their visit had impressed him to the point where he had started to collect Italianate statues. They now dominated the patio in the rear garden. "If it ain't got arms, it's Kosher", Pete would say, as yet another example was being delivered.

Rita turned on the CD, inserting a Whitney Houston disc. She looked around. She was pleased with the atmosphere she had created, the mood was being set. She subconsciously clenched her fists. "I'll fight back", she said to herself, "and it starts tonight with peppered steak".

*   *   *   *   *

Colin drove slowly along the road where Tanya resided. "Thirty-two, thirty-four, thirty-six and thirty-eight", he mumbled as he indicated, pulling in towards the curb. Small box houses crowded the area which had once been home to grand Victorian dwellings, with tall oaks and elms spaciously situated behind high walls and fencing. Newly planted saplings struggled to make an impact between the yellow brickwork which covered the estate. Tanya lived in one of the maisonettes, number thirty-six.

Having secured the Krooklok Colin adjusted his tie, and looking in the rear view mirror brushed his blazer collar in case there remained any traces of dandruff. Locking the Metro Vanden Plas he bounced along the pavement, head bowed, and opened the wooden gate which led to Tanya's house. He tutted. "This wood won't last any time at all", he said to himself. "Unseasoned softwood!"

He looked at the door, then at his watch. It was precisely 7.30 p.m. Colin felt full up. He rang the doorbell. "Perhaps she's out. I could get on with weathering those coaches and ....."

The door swung open. Colin was taken by surprise. Tanya stood there, her blonde hair parted in the middle. It fell naturally onto her shoulders, forming curtains around her face. Her eyes sparkled. She wore a light blue, sleeveless, knee length summer dress, with matching high-heeled shoes. A fine chain encircled her neck. On her left wrist she wore a gold watch set off with Roman numerals, whilst on the other, a bulky bracelet sat somewhat conspicuously.

"Ah", said Colin, not making eye contact. "Five foot two, eyes of blue".

"Five foot four, actually".

"Yes - of course". Colin coughed nervously. "It's just that five foot four doesn't rhyme".

Tanya broadened her smile. "Shall we go?"

"You still want to visit the cinema, then?"

"Well, Dracula's not going to visit me, is he - not unless I get lucky, of course!" She winked enticingly.

"I suppose not", said Colin, now resigned to watching the film, the subject of which he considered unsuitable for females.

They arrived in plenty of time. Colin suggested he bought some popcorn and orange drinks to take in with them.

As the suspense grew, and the scenes became more menacing, Tanya edged closer to Colin who remained upright, knees together, holding the now half-empty popcorn carton on his lap. Tanya watched intently as a door creaked open, causing the audience to gasp out aloud. She grabbed Colin's hand and the popcorn flew everywhere. Colin turned to the patrons sitting behind. "Sorry", he said. He instantaneously leapt forward to those in front. "Awfully sorry", he whispered, as the man concerned brushed popcorn from his trousers. Colin placed the now-empty carton beneath his seat and turned towards Tanya. "Sorry".

She stifled a laugh. Seizing the initiative Tanya took hold of Colin's hand and held it firmly on her lap. He didn't try to pull away. He didn't encourage her. They remained that way until the film ended.

"Well, how did you enjoy it?" asked Tanya as they milled with the crowd down the steps leading to the foyer.

"It was, well, mmmm, different, I suppose".

"He's very sexy", added Tanya. This comment threw Colin.

"Oh", he replied, "unsound was the word that sprung more readily to mind. Still ......"

As they walked out side by side, Colin was conscious of the fact that he was lower than his companion, on account of her wearing high-heeled shoes. "It seems unfair", he said to himself, "without those shoes we'd be almost the same height".

She slipped her arm through his as they walked back to the car. Having unlocked the Metro and unfastened the Krooklok Colin drove steadily, arriving at Tanya's home some fifteen minutes later.

"Well, thank you for asking me to accompany you, it's been, well, a very pleasant evening".

Her eyes widened. "Aren't you coming in for coffee?"

"I think not, it's getting late".

"Colin, it's only 10.15".

"Mmmm, well, er, I must say, imbibing in liquid sustenance would round off the evening". Tanya laughed.

"Does that mean you'd like a coffee then?"

"Ah, yes, well, thank you".

Tanya opened the door and waited on the pavement as Colin re-attached the Krooklok. As they walked up the path towards her maisonette Colin said, "Tanya, d'you mind if I say something?"

She turned quickly, her face inches away from his, her hair flowing in the light breeze. "No, what?" she asked softly.

"Your gate. It's constructed of extremely inferior quality wood. If I were you, I'd think about arranging a rolling maintenance programme, covering both your gate and boundary partitioning". Colin bent down and pushed firmly on the white-slatted fencing which divided the houses. "Softwood today, no wood tomorrow", he added gloomily. Tanya looked bewildered.

"Right, I'll bear that in mind. Thanks".

She opened the door of number thirty-six. They walked into a small entrance lobby. Tanya took Colin's blazer, hanging it on one of the hooks. Colin pulled it straight and checked that the side pocket flaps were sitting correctly. He then followed her through to the sitting-cum-dining room, which was tastefully but not expensively furnished.

"Make yourself comfortable", she said, beckoning Colin towards the settee, part of a small three-piece suite covered in beige and brown patterned Draylon. He sank into the soft material and sat with his arms folded.

"Coffee, tea, something stronger? I've got lager, but no cider, I'm afraid. You can have a short if you like". She was waiting by the kitchen door for an answer. Colin's eyes lit up.

"Oh, that's nice of you, remembering I like cider. Mind, even if you had any I wouldn't be able to partake ....." His hands shot forward, indicating that they were clutching a ghost steering wheel. Colin smiled.

"So, coffee, tea?"

"Ah, sorry, coffee will do nicely, thank you".

"You sound like that man in the credit card ad, you know, the one where he hands it to the receptionist and she says, 'that'll do nicely'".

Colin didn't know of the advert. Tanya made small talk from the kitchen, whilst the kettle was filled, plugged in and the cups set out. "I'm just going to pop into the bedroom for a minute", Tanya announced.

"Oh, okay". Colin was puzzled. "Why would she want to go into the bedroom while the kettle was boiling", he thought.

"The minute" turned into four. Colin had counted them.

The bedroom door opened slowly. Tanya re-appeared. She was devoid of dress. Colin froze. She was wearing a black basque which enhanced her firm figure; black pants, suspender belt and stockings completed her attire, save for a pair of high heeled shoes. She threw her hair from side to side and exaggerated her hip movement as she walked slowly towards Colin. Her eyes, heavily made up, never left his. He could look nowhere else. He was transfixed.

"Well?" she asked, seeking reaction.

"V-v-v-very nice. Very fetching!" Colin sat, knees clenched together, hands by his side. He gulped. Tanya stood, legs astride his, bending down towards his face. Her eyes appeared to be half-closed and slightly glazed.

"Do you have problems with contact lenses?" enquired Colin.

She ignored his question. He could smell the peppermint on her breath. "Well, Colin Mabey", she said with due suspense, "let's see what we can make of you, then". Tanya was almost clinical in her delivery of words. Bringing both hands to his neck she loosened his tie and undid the top two buttons of his shirt. Colin blinked but did not resist. Grabbing his left hand she hauled him off the settee and pulled him towards the bedroom. Pushing the door open with her free hand, Colin followed meekly. A hurried appraisal revealed a double bed with black sheets, subdued lighting cast shadows over the black furniture. Pictures of naked men extracted from ancient Greek paintings abounded.

Tanya led him to the left-hand side of the bed; the black duvet was pulled back. He felt dominated by her size. She seemed taller than when they walked into the cinema. He looked down at her shoes. "Those heels must be four inches high at least, they'll do her feet no good at all!" he thought.

Everything was happening so fast - even though Tanya worked slowly, she worked purposefully. Colin's head was spinning. Before he knew it, his shoes, socks, trousers and shirt had been taken off and discarded on the floor. Colin stood in his white Marks & Spencer's underpants, his hands meeting across the "Y". Tanya never took her eyes from his as she once more took hold of his tie and repositioned it around his neck. She tied it slowly.

Colin look away at the wall behind her. He was aware of her smiling in a way he considered lewd.

She pulled the knot tight, but not uncomfortably so. The two ends were smoothed over Colin's naked chest. It was a red and green striped tie, with a single, circular motif. Within it the letters "MBSC" were picked out in cream.

"So, what do they stand for?" Her fingers stroked the lettering. "Is it 'Manly, Brawny, Sexy Colin'?" Her hands slid temptingly to his stomach. She commenced rubbing them over that part of his anatomy. Colin felt breathless and had difficulty in remembering just what they stood for.

"Mmm, Municipal Bus Spotters Club, actually", Colin spluttered out at length. Her hands ran round his shoulders and down his back. He looked around. "I see you quite like black". Again, Tanya ignored him, her fingers quickening their pace. He was aware of his arms standing proud of his body. "I feel like a penguin".

"You **look** like a dummy in a shop window that's about to be dressed - only you're not!"

Tanya flashed a wicked smile.

"Oh, right".

Suddenly, without warning, she pushed him onto the bed. He moved up slightly, his palms pressing into the sheets. Tanya leapt on him, straddling his stomach. She bent her head and kissed him, her hands pushing Colin's shoulders, forcing him to lie back.

"I'm not used ....."

"Coming up for air, are we?" She continued. Her kiss was long and passionate.

Colin's arms flailed like a swimmer in distress. After what seemed an eternity Tanya raised her face from his, but remained kneeling. Looking him straight in the eyes in a way so as to mesmerise and disarm, she spread her knees, gently lowering her bottom onto his stomach. Colin raised his head from the bed. Tanya noted his response.

"Aaah", said Colin, moving his hand deftly between her parted legs.

"Ooooooh", she sighed, letting her head fall back, her mouth open. "That touch", she breathed heavily.

"Yes, I'm terribly sorry about that", Colin said apologetically, but you're sitting on my tie".

Raising the index finger of his free hand he pointed towards his stomach and retrieved the thicker of the two ends from between her thighs. "There, you see, there's a crease running diagonally across my motif". She never heard him. Her hands moved to her bodiced top. She made much of undoing the laces, which bound the garment together. Her mouth formed a perfect "O" as she pulled apart the top lace, revealing slightly more of her cleavage. "Is there anything in particular you fancy?"

Colin thought the phrase slightly odd. Tanya raised an eyebrow and wiped her tongue across her top lip. It glistened. He pulled his left hand to his face and looked at his watch.

"Well, mother and I usually have cocoa about now", he said. She looked deeply into his eyes. Colin's mind was racing.

"But cocoa's not on the menu, is it?" Her voice was seductively silky. Colin was perspiring.

"Mmmm", she sighed, her eyes now closed, her nostrils flaring noticeably. "I like a man who smells of hard-earned sweat".

"Ah", croaked Colin, "well, a clerical assistant's job is fairly demanding.

"I'm demanding too, Colin, and I demand your body". Tanya's eyes were now wide, bright and piercing.

"Oh, I see". His voice became more positive. Colin's eyes darted from side to side. Using his feet for leverage he slid his body between Tanya's thighs and having extricated his head, hauled himself back into a standing position. Tanya looked down between her open legs. "What are you doing", she exclaimed, somewhat confused.

"Look, I'm sorry", Colin replied, as he hurriedly attempted to push his feet through the legs of his trousers, "but this isn't me".

"I thought ....."

"Obviously, and I thought that going to the cinema meant - well, you know, watching a film". Colin was indignant. Taking off his tie and quickly putting on his shirt, he added, "I'll assume it was the erotic nature of the leading man that caused you to act in such a manner".

Tanya's mouth fell open. She said nothing but stood up and grabbed a dressing gown. Following Colin through to the sitting area she witnessed him hobbling about the room, first on one leg and then the other, as he gradually brought each sock over his heels and around the ankles. He struggled to put on his brogues, but thought twice about asking for a shoe horn! Grabbing his blazer from one of the hooks in the lobby he bowed subconsciously by the inner door and mumbled, "Better be going, then".

"I don't believe it", said Tanya shaking her head.

"Ah", said Colin, as he backed out of the front door, once more raising his index finger. "Now, I know that one. It's Victor Meldrew - 'One Foot in the Grave', isn't it?"

"Aaaaaaaaagh", screeched Tanya, who promptly slammed the door in Colin's face. The letter box flap was lifted back.

"Well, good night, then", shouted Colin. Tanya ignored him. Returning to her bedroom she straightened the bed clothes, her face a mixture of resignation and bewilderment; never before had she suffered such humiliation. She walked into the kitchen and reboiled the kettle.

Discarding the second cup Tanya conceded, "Coffee for one, after all".

*   *   *   *   *

CHAPTER FOUR

"She's nice, isn't she, that Mrs. Maynard", said Vi Buchanan.

"Who?" replied Albert, as he skipped through the pages of the Daily Mirror once again.

"Mrs. Maynard", repeated Vi, her hands tightly clasping a dish, half of which lay submerged in soapy water. "Your cleaner", she added.

"Oh, Mrs. M. Yeah, nice of 'er to come round and see us, I didn't cotton on, Vi. She's never known as Mrs. Maynard down the Club".

"What's her first name?"

Vi continued washing up the dinner plates.

"Gawd knows, never asked". Albert's eyes rested on an article he had overlooked first time round.

Vi walked through from the kitchen, drying her hands on the Paisley patterned apron that covered her skirt. "Albert, I want to have a chat".

"Uh?" he replied from behind his paper.

"Albert", Vi said more forcefully, taking his paper away. "Listen to me".

"This sounds ominous", he said smiling. Vi played with the hem of her apron as she sat opposite her husband.

"Look, about Graham ....." Vi was cut short.

"I don't want to discuss him". Albert got up clenching his knuckles. His face hardened.

"Sit down". Vi pointed to the chair. "We've things to talk about".

Albert sighed, rubbed his forehead and slumped into the chair. "We've had a nice Saturday morning, why spoil it?"

"I don't want to, Alb, but we need to mend fences - be a family again".

"All he's got to do is get rid of those planks he carries around on his shoulders, start to care about our grandson, and about us. Not asking much, is it?" Albert's tone was bitter.

"Don't". Vi screwed up her apron. "It's bad enough 'im not phoning, but I don't want to argue with you".

Albert relaxed slightly. "I know, I'm sorry. It just seems so unfair. It's Mick we turn to all the time, isn't it?" He gestured with his hands. "And it's not just 'im. Robin, Greg, any bloody number of the blokes down the Club, and the Hippodrome come to that, would make better offspring than Graham, and have done. He doesn't think about us from one month to the next. He hasn't phoned to see 'ow either of us are. I mean, we know those tablets are working, 'cos the doctor's pleased with you, but he doesn't know that, does he?" Albert almost shouted out the last few words. Vi flinched at the reference, but still she couldn't bring herself to mention the unmentionable. They remained silent for several seconds.

"We're both getting on, Alb", Vi said softly. "I want, **need**, to be friends, even if it means paying lip service to Camilla. After all's said and done, he married her for better or for worse".

"Yeah, an' we all know which one we got!"

"That attitude's going to get us nowhere. We've got to face facts, one of us is going to go, we both are sooner or later. I don't want to pass on never having made up". She paused. "I know it's not easy, but he's our only son, our only child". She looked directly at Albert and shook a finger at him. "If you or I want to see Jamie again, we're going to have to make peace and at our age it's got to be sooner rather than later".

Albert looked intently at his wife. "Did I get beat up worse than I thought, then? Is there something I've missed?"

"No, you daft ha'peth, but you can't go around fooling yourself. We neither of us are getting any younger".

"I know", muttered Albert, seemingly distancing himself.

Vi leant forward. "So what are you going to do?"

Albert raised his hands, feigning submission. "Okay, I'll ring him later - it'll be nice if Jamie's in". Albert was warming to the idea. Vi smiled contentedly as she handed her husband back his Daily Mirror.

During the afternoon Nobby called round for a chat.

The evening dragged in anticipation of just what the outcome would be. Albert usually drank a few beers during one of his rare Saturday nights away from his bar duties, but tonight, he had been told to restrain himself. Vi did not wish for any slight niggle to be exaggerated by the effects of alcohol. At 10.45 p.m. Vi said, "Okay, Alb, ring now". He walked over to the phone and dialled Graham's number. As it rang he took hold of the lead, dragging it to a nearby chair. Vi sat looking on. She played with the beads which hung around her neck.

""'Allo, Graham, it's me, Dad". Listening intently whilst looking for signs on her husband's face Vi could tell that the conversation was strained. She heard her husband broach the subjects of forgiveness and family bonds but she also noted the raising of his free hand in exasperation. Vi understood from the way he shook his head that Jamie wasn't available. After some few minutes Albert uttered a begrudging, "Bye", and slowly replaced the receiver. Vi looked pleadingly towards her husband.

"Don't ever ask me to eat humble pie again". Albert walked through to his armchair. Vi joined him.

"What did he say". She had tears in her eyes.

Albert looked up at her. "Very little, really. Jamie's apparently stayed overnight at a friend's house - excuse number 32, I believe! But the funny thing is, when I asked after Camilla he said, 'Next question'. I took the hint, so I didn't press".

"Did he seem all right, though?" Vi was now sitting beside her husband.

Albert reflected. "No, I wouldn't say so. He seemed sort of furtive".

"You know what he's like".

"Look, it was as much as he could do, to ask how you were".

"Didn't he want to know how your injuries were clearing up?" Vi was indignant.

"No, I don't think we mentioned me at all, come to think of it".

Vi shook her head in despair. She had built up her hopes and they had not been fulfilled. They went to bed shortly afterwards.

"Damn", said Albert, as he turned out the light and walked over to his side of the bed.

"Stubbed your toe?" enquired Vi, half asleep.

"No, I still didn't ask Nobby why he brought round that copy of Bee Keeping Weekly".

*   *   *   *   *

Mick peered out of the French windows that led to the rear garden. "Another fine day in Gotham City", he said aloud. Kate passed by him and whispered in his ear, "Claygate, dear, I think you mean Claygate".

Mick turned. "There used to be a time when you could talk to yourself, enjoy the solitude, but now ....."

"Come on, look sharp!"

Kate was bustling around him. "It's eleven thirty, you'd better go and pick them up. **You**, more than anyone, knows how Albert likes his lunch time drink".

"Lunch time swim, more like". Mick looked at his watch. He checked himself as he walked out. "Oh, Kate, don't forget, as far as I'm aware, Vi still hasn't said anything. She certainly hadn't up to Wednesday, so for Christ's sake say nothing unless they do".

The Buchanans were all but waiting on the doorstep. Having deposited Vi, who insisted on helping Kate prepare dinner, Mick and Albert visited the local hostelry. "Wonder what they've got on today", asked Albert, rubbing his hands in anticipation.

"Six real ales". Mick pointed to the hand-chalked board standing just inside the entrance.

"Well, half a pint of each should keep us going for an hour or so!"

"If you remember, Kate did say that dinner would be served today".

Albert laughed as he nudged Mick's arm.

*   *   *   *   *

"You go and sit down", instructed Kate.

"But there's all the washing up", replied Vi, eager to help.

"We've got a dishwasher for that. Honestly, go and sit down".

Happy that no-one could accuse her of not pulling her weight Vi sat outside with Mick. Albert was already asleep and if previous performances were any indication, he would be until teatime.

"That was a lovely dinner, Mick. Thanks for the invite".

"Pleasure".

Kate brought through three coffees. They sat, saying little, basking in the summer sunshine.

"Another month's nearly gone, doesn't seem possible", said Vi, as she added a little more milk. She then took a corn plaster from her handbag and applied it to the small toe on her left foot. "Giving me gip something rotten, it is".

"Why don't you go to a chiropodist?", suggested Kate.

"Can't pronounce it, let alone spell it", replied Vi chirpily.

Kate was about to suggest a local practice when Vi added, "Anyway, I always use an old scalpel, carve it up occasionally - that usually does the trick".

Kate winced, Mick grimaced, Albert snored.

"Isn't it quiet, you can't hear a thing", said Kate, looking about her.

"Perhaps the world's died", replied Mick, before realising the possible implication of a throwaway remark.

Vi hadn't appeared to notice. She was still fiddling with her toe.

"Usually a few lawnmowers to disturb the peace", he added, more to satisfy himself than anything else.

Having achieved a satisfactory, if temporary, solution to her corn predicament, Vi asked if she could be taken on a tour of the garden. As Kate pointed out the various seasonal additions Vi blurted out, "I expect Mick's told you about my - well - problem?" Kate looked embarrassed. "It's all right, dear", Vi continued, "If he hadn't told you, I'd have thought something was wrong. Husbands and wives, and children, should talk".

"Albert doesn't know yet?"

"No, I've not found the right time to tell him". They paused at a corner given over to alpine flowers. Vi approved of them. They walked on slowly. Holding her handbag in front of her with an air of authority and intent Vi expanded. "I'd worked out that it would be best if Alb and Graham were to get back to being friends again. I thought that way, it'd be easier to tell 'im".

Kate looked at Vi. "So, what's happened?"

"Alb rang Graham last night". She gesticulated. "So, it was breakfast time out there and d'you know, Graham didn't even ask 'ow his dad was, 'ow he was feeling, or nothing. And when Albert asked how Camilla was, 'e just said, 'Next question'. Seems a funny answer to me".

Kate was relieved that Vi had broached the subject. No more pretence. "So, what did the doctors actually say at the hospital? I mean, Mick told me it was cancer, stomach cancer, but nothing else".

"I didn't tell Mick much else, Kate - mind, there isn't much else to tell". They stood at the furthest point from the house where a large willow draped itself over a rustic seat nestling in the shade. "This is nice", said Vi.

"Did they give you any idea about treatment?" Kate skirted around the phrase that Mick had used - "Time is not on her side".

"Oh, they were very nice. Gave me the options, such as they are, and then, what's the word, eliminated them". She looked hard into Kate's eyes. "At the end of the day, we all know what it means at my age. I told

Mick what they told me. Time is not on my side. They could operate, cut me about, and give that therapy-whatsit afterwards ....."

"Chemotherapy?"

"Yes, that's it". Vi raised a finger in acknowledgement. "At best I've got six months, at worst, two". Vi looked straight ahead and commenced walking ponderously. Kate was stunned. She thought they would have been able to operate, extend her life by a couple of years at least. She caught up with Vi.

"But you look so well". She could have kicked herself. "Oh, I'm sorry, Vi, that sounds so crass".

"It's me inside, love, not me outside", she replied in a detached manner.

"You can't keep this to yourself, Vi, you just can't. You've got to tell Graham, even if it means ringing him without Albert knowing".

"That's why I asked Alb to ring last night, but what's the point?"

Kate took Vi's arm as they admired the rose beds which lay to the left of the path.

"You won't say anything, will you, Kate? Promise me you won't tell Albert".

"Of course not", Kate reassured her.

"It's got to be me what tells him. The only wish I have is to see our grandson - just once more. You know, I want him to remember   us ....."

Kate sensed Vi becoming emotional. They walked past Mick, who by now had also fallen asleep. They made themselves a cup of tea.

*   *   *   *   *

As Mick and Kate lay in bed they discussed the way in which they felt the Buchanans should approach their dilemma. After much soul searching Mick came to the conclusion that Albert should go along with Vi to her next hospital appointment. Mick would take them. He also decided that it was about time he had a chat with Graham.

Mick remembered the times he had been invited as a child round to the Buchanans for tea. It had taken some time to realise that he went because of Albert and Vi and not because of their son. Graham never really had friends. Mick lay thinking. Even as a thirteen year old he had felt sorry for Graham's parents, due to the way their son treated them. Toys paid for with hard-earned money were broken needlessly. A kind word met with a sulky reply at best. But more usually, an aggressive, abusive response was forthcoming. "What rotten luck", he thought, "to have spawned such a selfish, arrogant little shit". Decision made, Mick turned over, bidding goodnight to Kate, who couldn't settle and remained restless before finally succumbing some time after 3.30 a.m.

*   *   *   *   *

Colin arrived some fifteen minutes before the other Committee members. This had enabled him to arrange the tables and chairs in the centre of the hall in readiness for the monthly meeting. He provided pens and paper, as usual, for notes to be taken.

"Ah, full turn out tonight", said Colin, as Mick ambled in.

Everybody obtained a drink from the bar and walked towards their respective places. Colin headed his minutes page in the fashion of a schoolboy not wishing fellow pupils visual access to his scribing. Head bowed close to the page, his left arm embraced the minute book. He looked around. "Those present", he muttered, "Robin Harmsworth, Mick Clayton, Greg Wagstaffe, Derek and Doreen Durdle, Reg Bowen - me".

Robin sat at the top with Colin and Mick opposite each other. Next to Mick sat Greg and Reg and across the table were Derek and Doreen.

"Eight p.m.", announced Colin. "Shall we commence, Mr. Chairman?"

Robin bid everybody an official "Good evening" and spent a few minutes welcoming Reg, who had recently been co-opted onto the Committee to oversee the maintenance of the buildings and grounds. Colin then read out the minutes of the last meeting before looking around for comment. Everyone nodded acceptance.

Mick slowly raised himself from a lounging position to one of purpose. His statement concerned the present financial position. It transpired that £2,158.28 was currently on deposit, whilst £1,206.59 pence was showing on the current account. Average bar takings on a Wednesday night continued at approximately £150 per session, and the various organisations hiring the hall over the past few weeks had provided another £680. The Singles Night had produced the best individual result, some £385 passing through the till, whilst the Phyllis Enwright Fund for Research into Elephantitis accrued only £2.26. Half of this sum had been raised by the sale of four Mars bars and a Twix to a rather large lady, who uttered the words, "Fine by me" to every suggestion - according to Derek who had manned the bar that evening!

"At least we took £25 for the hire of the hall that night", observed Greg.

Mick placed his arms behind his head and relaxed once more. "Mind, if Albert had been on duty it would have cost us money to provide the facilities". Impersonating his friend he held an imaginary glass to the light. "I'll just test another barrel".

Everyone chuckled knowingly.

"Do we know when he's coming back?" asked Colin, waving his pencil between thumb and index finger.

"Yes, next Wednesday. He's starting back at the Hippodrome tonight".

"Did anyone go round to see him, after all?" enquired Robin.

"Yes, they did", Mick drawled. "Took the Hippodrome's manager about a week to realise Albert wasn't there, apparently, but they sent round a barman with a card and a bunch of grapes".

"Big of them", commented the Chairman.

"Well, it's better than a kick in the futtocks!" added Greg.

"Futtocks?" repeated Colin, pencil poised.

"I wouldn't bother to minute that", suggested Robin dispassionately.

"Ah, right". Colin hoisted his pencil into the air in acknowledgement.

Robin addressed the subject of the York exhibition. Greg assured the Chairman that "Southworth" would be up to the required standard well in advance of the September weekend. Various other points regarding layouts were discussed before Greg gave his account of the library, book sales and the ongoing restoration of the Club's euphemia. A break was partaken whilst glasses were recharged and an assortment of crisps brought over by Derek. Doreen inspected the packets.

"Don't have any cheese and onion", she whispered to her husband.

"Is it private or can we all join in?" enquired Mick.

"Oh, Doreen was just telling me not to eat any cheese and onion, they make me ....."

Doreen nudged him with her elbow.

"..... they give me - a gippy tummy".

"What, they make you fart a lot, do they?" suggested Mick.

Robin smiled. Greg and Derek chuckled. Reg laughed heartily. Doreen frowned. Colin looked concerned.

"My turn", Colin said at length, as Mick once again sank back into his chair, a newly lit cigarette hanging between his fingers. "Membership", Colin announced. "We had 118 members at the start of the month. There have been 2 applications for membership". He produced the relevant forms. "The first is from a Stan Gunning, lives in Kingston, aged 53. He apparently heard about the Club when he read Doreen's advertisement for the York trip in the local press".

Doreen smiled, with more than an air of self satisfaction. Colin continued.

"He lists his interests as the Easingwold light railway and, quote, 'all things German'."

"Nazi, with Yorkshire tendencies, is he?" asked Mick.

"I suspect he was referring to the much-lamented German steam operations", replied Colin, straight-faced.

"Sieg Heil", shouted Mick and Greg, stretching their arms and stiffening their hands in mock salute.

"They want seeing to", said Doreen indignantly.

"Not by you!", Mick responded.

"Anyway, he seems a nice enough chap", added Robin. "I spoke to him two weeks ago when he first came down here".

"Are we all happy?" asked Colin, looking around for approval. "Right, next is a real odd-ball!" He emphasised the "real".

"Well, he can join then", interrupted Mick.

"Oh", enquired Robin, "why's that?"

"Because if he appears odd to Clipboard, he'll appear extremely normal to everyone else".

"Ah", said Colin in acknowledgement.

"Carry on, Colin", requested Robin, his patience being tested.

"Thank you, Mr. Chairman. Well, this chap came last Wednesday and he had - long hair". Colin indicated with his hands. "**And** he's interested in diesels". He sighed markedly. "He travels around the country with a group of chaps who go shed-bashing and when they traverse the countryside on these rail tours, they go behind, well, diesels".

"So?" asked Derek.

"Well, it is a bit odd, you know, diesels!"

Robin leaned forward, his elbows on the table. "Perhaps that's an area we should look at more closely", he suggested. "After all, steam was our yesterday, diesels are our today, and total electrification will be our tomorrow".

"Did you just think that up, or was it a pre-planned speech just waiting to happen?" asked Mick, rocking back on his chair.

Robin exuded a self-satisfied grin. "Mmmm, not bad for an impromptu observation, even if I do say so myself!"

"And you did say so yourself", retorted Mick and Greg in unison.

"Are those two a double act?" asked Colin somewhat irritably, before taking a sip from his second half of cider. Mick smirked, Colin tutted, Robin clapped his hands sharply.

"Can we get on, please".

Mick self-mockingly slapped his left wrist with his right hand. "Basil, Basil!" he shouted, to everyone's amusement. Colin continued.

"So do we want this Dave Warburton chap, or not?" He waved the application form around the table.

"I've had a chat with him, seemed a pretty decent sort. Fine, great, yeah, let's have him", suggested Derek.

"I can't bring him to mind. How old is he?" asked Greg.

"Twenty four", replied Colin.

"If he's prepared to pay his £25 like everyone else, why should we turn him away?"

"All agreed, then?" said Robin, as he looked round for any signs of dissent.

"So, we've hit the 120 mark", observed Greg. Colin looked sheepish.

"No, not quite. Still one hundred and eighteen, actually. I've received a letter of resignation from member number 1286, Simon Hanwell. He's moving to Telford, Shropshire. Work, I presume, he doesn't say".

"Well, you wouldn't go there out of choice, would you?" commented Mick.

"Shropshire's very nice", countered Robin.

"It would be if Telford could be shifted - preferably to France!" replied the Treasurer.

"So that's one hundred and nineteen", said Derek hurriedly. "Who's the other one?"

"Ah, yes". Colin twirled his pencil with increased zest. "The other member is number 182 - one Arthur Draper. He's dead!"

Everyone was at a loss to put face to name. All eyes turned to Colin, whose pencil sprung from his grasp and flew over Mick's head. "God moves in mysterious ways", noted the Chairman, with due reverence, clasping his hands together.

"If that was the hand of God, I want to know why it missed". Colin chuckled boyishly. "Anyway, it seems that Arthur Draper passed away three years ago but he paid by Standing Order and his wife thought the SRC was an insurance policy and kept it going. She wrote to us a fortnight ago wondering if she could cash it in!"

"Still, that's seventy-five quid we wouldn't have had otherwise", quipped Mick.

"I don't think that's in very good taste", moaned Colin.

"Did anyone ask you to think? You see, you just take it into your mind to do something and there's no stopping you ....."

"Mick, can we get on, please", implored Robin, his patience beginning to flag.

Maintenance proposals were outlined by Reg and Clubroom matters discussed at length.

"Next item - 'Outings'", the Chairman announced. He gestured to Doreen. Derek sat back resolutely.

"Now", said Doreen, beaming. "We have a full coach for the mystery tour, which is only four weeks away, and I've started a reserve list for that and the York trip - which is also full".

"Any other destinations in mind?" asked the Chairman.

Doreen looked at her husband knowingly. "Well, Derek, shall we tell them?"

"You don't have to if you don't want to". Mick sounded disinterested. He sprawled himself out and blew a smoke ring above the table.

Doreen ignored him. "We're thinking of running a December trip to France, to stock up for Christmas". She looked at each member in turn.

"A ferry", added Derek, still crunching his way through a packet of crisps.

"I didn't think we'd be swimming", said Greg.

"Derek was referring to the option of Euro-tunnel", replied Doreen stonily.

"You don't think it will have been flooded by then, do you?" queried Mick.

Robin banged at the table. "It sounds like a good idea".

"Well, don't pencil in my name", instructed Mick. "If anyone thinks I'm spending half a day trapped in a coach, surrounded by what most observers would take to be an escapee party from Broadmoor, they've got another think coming. The on-board entertainment will consist of guessing the correct number of cones we encounter - to within three-thousand, of course. Honestly, does anyone **really** enjoy driving through that building site called Kent. You then have to queue to find a space on that floating car park, having had your doors dented on both sides by ill-bred pond life, desperate to explore every orifice. You then struggle to find a seat that's not been covered in spew, donated by drunken louts on the previous sailing, which arrived four hours' late due to inclement weather. The only souvenirs worth taking home are the ship's embellishments found lying around the deck, having been dismantled by Millwall supporters ....."

Robin raised his hand in an effort to intervene, but Mick was having none of it.

"..... and when you get there, you pour out of the coach, everybody stopping to thank, and tip, the overfed licensed bandit for doing the job he's paid for. Everyone fights to get a trolley, so they can stack their Stella Artois and all the other cheap beers as high as possible without the thing collapsing!"

Colin raised his hand as if in a classroom, but was ignored.

"And we've all seen the size of them. They're three times bigger than those you get in Waitrose. The French trolley is designed for arseholes whose sole interest is taking home as much of the gassy, pee-coloured muck as they can load into the transit van they hired from some poor, unsuspecting sod ..... And the women are no better". Mick waved his arms. "They buy hundreds of sticks of French bread, French cheese and French wine. You try finding decent German wines in their hypermarkets - they just don't stock them. They could always buy their bread and cheese in Safeways or Tesco's, but, oh no, they would have been denied the pleasure of struggling half way across Europe with their booty. And why? You get a better selection of wines in any of our supermarkets". Mick tapped the table. "Bulgarian, Hungarian, South African, Australian - their reds knock the French into a cocked hat ....."

"But French wines are cheap", butted in Derek. Mick looked at his fellow member.

"Of course they're cheap! They're cheap because they're no bloody good!" He gestured. "You all come back exclaiming, 'Look at that wine we've bought, guess how much it was' - and no-one can guess that low, then after all the due suspense has evaporated, you astound your guests by announcing that you paid £5 for ten bottles. You then push home your savings - 50p a bottle, you gloat".

"Ten shillings in real money", offered Reg without expression. Mick glanced at him and continued.

"And it tastes like urine!"

Doreen grimaced. "Well, we like it!" she said indignantly.

Mick pointed a finger at his fellow Committee members. "And all the way through Kent you've been deluding yourselves. It isn't really cheap. While you've been wallowing in self-gratification, admiring your Chateau Gnat's Piss '94 at 50p a bottle ....."

"Ten shillings", repeated Reg.

" ..... you've not taken into account the fare across. What you've spent in the duty-free gift shop that's anything but, what you've squandered on the one-arm bandit because you never do that at home, what you ate in that pretty little back street cafe you discovered, and then proceeded to photograph, and that's not to mention the booze you consumed all the way there and back, to deaden the boredom of the cone counting". He raised his arm. "Oh, and then there's the presents for the kids, because they do like to have something brought back from abroad". Mick paused for breath. "All that way, you never know what time you're going to arrive, or whether there'll be a ferry back that day, due to a light gust of wind outside Ramsgate. And if you do remain sober the only thing to scan the horizon for is the shipwreck that half blocks your entrance to the French port. You take snaps for the folks back home". Mick mimicked intermittently. "'Oh, look', you say, diving into another pack of two-hour processed photos, 'do you remember that ship that went down last month? Yes, that's it, the one with six hundred people on board - most of them were foreigners, so they don't count. The few Brits that were among them were drunks from Luton, so no-one's going to include them in any tally'. There are photos from every conceivable angle, it's like a watery version of 'Match of the Day's Goal of the Month' and so it goes on - bastards!"

Mick slumped back and lit up another cigarette. The hall fell silent momentarily. "So, you're not going, then?" asked Greg.

"Better than a cabaret, that", enthused Derek, nodding in Mick's direction and giving the thumbs-up sign.

"Oh, don't encourage him", urged Colin, breaking the lead in his pencil.

A rumbling noise could be heard coming from Derek's direction. He looked embarrassed and instinctively covered his mouth with his left hand. Doreen sniffed and frowned at him.

"I think that was me", Derek said in a low voice.

"What did I tell you about cheese and onion!" Doreen picked up the empty packet that lay in front of her husband and tutted. Greg wet his index finger and raised the digit in the air. Doreen looked quizzical.

"I'm just seeing which way the wind's blowing".

"Don't be so disgusting", replied the Outings Secretary.

"Okay, let's get on", requested Robin. "Any other business?"

No-one had any other points to raise.

"Right, meeting closed at 10.42 p.m. May I have my pens back, please", asked Colin as the sound of scraping chairs echoed around the hall.

*   *   *   *   *

The first Wednesday in June witnessed a downpour that caught many suburban communities on the hop. Early morning sunshine gave way with undue haste, severe cloudbursts covered an area from Bromley in the east to Isleworth in the west, and from Chelsea in the north to Stoke D'Abernon in the south, with surprisingly little falling on nearby Cobham.

By the time Albert had tested the barrels and unlocked the Club doors the fickle English weather pattern had once again been turned on its head. The clouds had cried themselves dry and the evening sunshine highlighted the glinting, oily colours in the rain water, as it flowed along the guttering and into the drains.

As time passed various group members discussed their recent modelling feats or their latest purchases. Others sought new ideas for building even larger, but ever lighter, layouts. The check-jacket brigade were overheard by Robin debating the advantages and disadvantages of Brunel's broad gauge system.

Meanwhile, close to the doors, Doreen and Derek had set up a table with two chairs, hoping to attract a sizeable reserve list for their forthcoming excursions.

Sitting on a bar stool Mick slowly turned his head towards the Outings Secretary and her assistant. "You'd think they would be happy with one full coach, wouldn't you?"

Greg, standing beside him, nodded agreement.

134

Mick tutted. "Christ, she'll never be off that tannoy. Every time the second coach is out of sight Big Tits'll be telling the driver to slow down, so that Derek's lot can catch up".

"I never thought you went on any of the Club's trips?"

"There was one, my one and only. The Durdles organised a jaunt to the Severn Valley Railway, two-coach job". Mick turned his body towards Greg as he continued. "Talk about Red Victor One to Red Victor Two, she kept yapping to the driver of the second coach. In the end he got so fed up he told her he couldn't reply because the equipment had developed a fault. It was obvious to everyone else that he'd turned it off - though that possibility had never occurred to Doreen!" Greg smiled. "Anyway, it was a family day out, Derek hired the videos for both coaches. He took the 'Long Good Friday' and 'Mad Max'. One poor tot, aged five, was so upset at seeing Mel Gibson's wife run over that she promptly spewed up all over her mother's dress! Her mother, needless to say, was not best pleased. Meanwhile, on the other coach, some nasty little sod shouted out 'boo' at the wrong moment and a ten year old girl shot out of her seat, hit her head on the luggage rack and had to be taken to the casualty department of a hospital in Warwick suffering from a six inch gash and concussion. She and her parents stayed there all day, while the coach continued to Kidderminster. Not unnaturally we were so late in arriving that we missed our train and had to take the next, which was full to the gunwhales with a group of geriatrics from Eccles. It would have given Saga Holidays a bad name - the day was not a success!"

"Why on earth did Derek pick two films like that?"

"Because someone told him they were good on-board family entertainment".

"Who would say that?"

Mick's eyes twinkled. "Could have been me, well, don't have any kids, do I!"

The doors burst open. Pete walked in with Rita by his side. He donned a charcoal pin-striped suit, set off with a multi-coloured fish tie, whilst Rita wore a mid-green towelling track suit, which enhanced her figure admirably.

"Your vanity knows no bounds", commented Greg, looking at Pete's hair which had obviously been the subject of a recent perm.

"Like my cars, sunshine, like my cars", Pete quipped in response. Rita raised her eyebrows as Pete placed an arm over her left shoulder.

"Right, chaps and chapesses, what we having?" Pete rubbed his hands together; Albert stood ready. "Usual for Reet, Mick and Greg'll have the same again, and make mine a pint of hand pull - what's on, anyway?"

"Young's Special", replied Albert with affection. "Nice pint, that".

Colin bounced towards the bar, seemingly engrossed in conversation with Robin.

" ..... I feel that the various merits you describe have yet to be accepted by the public at large", Colin was heard to say.

Robin placed one hand on the bar top and wearily wiped his face with the other.

"You look harassed", said Greg.

"So would you, talking to him for, what, thirty-eight seconds at the most".

"It sounded like an in-depth subject, what on earth were you talking about?"

"You could certainly be forgiven for assuming it was in-depth. I just happened to mention that I thought it was a good idea moving the hand dryer in the Gents toilet to the opposite wall - Colin just took off!"

Both men laughed. Pete shouted across to them. "So, my little Clipboard, what would you like? Robin, you having one?"

"Thanks, Pete, I'll have a Scotch", replied the Chairman.

Albert finished pouring the drinks that had been ordered, then waited, one hand resting on the cider dispenser. Colin stood, pointing a finger at the various pumps. Standing on tiptoe he surveyed the bottles whilst mumbling an elongated "Mmmmmm".

"Shall I?" said Albert, looking at the assembled members. There was a unanimous nodding of heads and the barman pulled through half a pint. As he placed the tankard in front of Colin, the Clubroom Manager and Secretary raised a finger and announced, "I'll have a half of, oh, you've guessed".

"Didn't take much guessing", said Albert sardonically.

"Aaah, well, one day I'll surprise you".

"What, by joining another club?" suggested Mick eagerly.

"Take one for yourself", offered Pete, as he handed over a twenty pound note.

Albert acknowledged Pete's generosity by holding up a half pint of Young's Special. Pete Balfour turned towards Colin, grinned inanely and for the benefit of all at the bar announced, "Someone we know's been out with that Tanya, and that someone refused to accept her hospitality". Pete emphasised the last word.

Colin reddened, turning away slightly. "Mmmmm".

Pete nudged Colin's arm. "Come on, then, tell all. Uncle Peter wants to know all the details!"

"Leave him alone", scolded Rita, before adding, "I'm just going to pop to the loo". Colin looked in her direction, as if seeking further words of support.

"'E's all right, come on, Colin, cat's out the bag".

Mick slowly stepped down from his stool and walked to the other side of Colin, who felt intimidated by his two fellow members. He looked to one and then the other. Mick held his pint glass around the rim, from his left hand a cigarette slowly burned. The Club Treasurer smiled, in a way befitting a predator when cornering an injured animal. All eyes focused on Colin.

Pete Balfour persisted. "Baz 'as given me a brief outline but I'm a bit sort of, hazy, about, you know". He rolled his hands in mid air, encouraging Colin to expand on information received.

Colin was extremely agitated. "We just went to the cinema and then I was invited back for a cup of coffee. That's all". He stared straight ahead towards the optics.

Pete shook his head dolefully. "That's funny, because I was led to believe that you were offered more than just coffee!"

Jeers went up from those around.

"You turned down this 'ere blonde bombshell, did you?" asked Mick, who tutted mockingly.

Robin felt uneasy about the mickey-taking. "Come on, chaps, I think you've gone far enough".

"Certainly gone further than Colin did", shouted Pete, slapping his victim hard on the back.

Colin angrily shrugged off Pete's physical attentions and without uttering a word burst from between Mick and Pete, his head bowed. Colin quickly made his way towards the rooms at the far end of the building. Mick dragged on his cigarette, his eyes squinting momentarily. "You'd have thought he'd have had a better sense of humour than that, wouldn't you?"

"Don't understand him", queried Pete. "Can you honestly see anyone in their right mind turning down the chance to go to bed with a slapper like Tanya?"

"Beats me", replied Mick, as he continued to look towards the far end.

"I have to say it's difficult to imagine Colin being comfortable in the company of any female", observed Greg.

"You're still here, then?" asked Mick, as he turned towards his fellow member. "Knowing how pedantic he is, she probably hadn't filled in all the necessary forms in triplicate".

Pete wagged his finger knowingly, seeking the attention of all. "I think he balked at the prospect of 'aving to go through with something that might end up being messy!" Shrieks of laughter could be heard coming from the direction of the bar. Rita, taking her usual short steps, walked back towards the men, their faces still displaying the broadest of childish grins.

"What have you been saying to Colin?" Rita was clearly annoyed.

Pete downed the rest of his pint. "'E should learn to take life a bit more lightly, 'e's too bloody serious".

"Well, that's him, isn't it? Pity you can't take it a bit more seriously, Pete Balfour".

Pete dismissed his wife's retort. "P'raps it was because 'is other half was a girl! Maybe Colin prefers chaps!"

Robin considered that the conversation had gone far enough. "When you lot have finished with your character assassination, I suggest one of you finds Colin and apologises. For one thing, he was clearly embarrassed and, for another, it was bugger all to do with any of us". He glanced swiftly at Rita. "I'm sorry for swearing".

Rita half smiled. "That's all right, Robin, I've heard worse when Pete's sleeping". Robin seemed reassured.

"Well, go on then, someone apologise. Mick? Pete?"

Pete held up both hands and turned. Poking his head around the library door he enquired as to Colin's whereabouts.

"Just passed him in't bog", responded Lankie.

Pete stood at the next urinal to the one Colin was using. "Pointing Percy at the porcelain, are we?" He was devoid of a more imaginative comment.

Colin took a while to answer. "Yes, why, will Baz need to be told?"

"I asked for that. Look, I'm sorry, Clipboard, didn't mean any harm. Didn't expect you to get funny about it, it's only a bit of a laugh after all".

"Yes, and at someone else's expense, as usual". Colin bent slightly forward as he fastened his zip. Pete was unhappy that his apology had not been unquestioningly accepted. Colin walked towards the sink and commenced washing his hands.

Pete shuffled his shoes. "It does seem a bit strange, though, that a bloke gets it 'anded on a plate and then throws the plate away, when it's still stacked with boiling 'ot goodies". He looked in the mirror in an effort to gauge Colin's reaction. "I mean, anyone might think you were, well, a bit of a Bertie woofter".

At that moment Mick appeared in the doorway. He was about to crack a joke but seeing their faces, thought better of it. Colin appeared flustered but continued rubbing his hands under the newly positioned dryer, before walking in a more decisive fashion than was usual. Standing on tip-toe he was face to face with Pete Balfour. "That's about as far as you can see, isn't it? If you're not rutting like a rabbit, then you're obviously a homosexual. Does it ever occur to you that someone might, just might, not possess the same degree of frenzied, lustful, primeval yearnings that seem to be so important to you - a position I find sadly at odds with your marital status!"

With that he rushed past Pete, ignored Mick and hurried out of the toilets. "Game, set and match to Colin", quipped the Club Treasurer.

"Well, he's nowhere to be found", sighed Robin, as Pete appeared in the doorway.

"His car's gone", added Greg.

"Hardly surprising, is it?" remarked the Chairman. "Right, Mick, Greg, I'd be obliged if you could organise the raffle".

"I think I'm going to have one of my heads", said Mick, holding his left hand against his forehead.

"You'll get one of my boots if you don't help", replied Greg.

Mick turned sharply. "Funny, it's gone".

With the winning tickets redeemed, third prize, as usual, inclusive of Harold's ten-penny contribution, the Treasurer and the Archivist stood looking at the "O" gauge layout, operated by those Mick termed "clinically dead".

"You were quiet", said Mick.

"When?"

"When Pete was attempting to unravel the mystery of Tanya's failed attempt to seduce Colin".

"Oh, it didn't need any contribution from me. You two were doing well enough on your own".

"No, that's not it". Mick turned towards his friend. "There's more to

139

it than that". Both men continued to watch as a mixed goods train was being assembled in the sidings at Chipping Waltham. A Dean Goods ambled around, coupling and uncoupling an assortment of box vans and open wagons, one containing coal and two carrying agricultural equipment.

"That's a nice touch", remarked Greg, pointing to a chocolate and cream six-wheeled coach that was being marshalled at the head of the train. The Treasurer was only half listening.

"I've got it, you wanted to impress Rita".

"Rubbish!"

Mick chuckled. "True rubbish, though. Consciously or subconsciously you wanted to be on the same side. I was bloody right all along - you do fancy her, don't you?" His pleasure at finding an Achilles heel was obvious. Before Greg could think of anything that might improve his defence, Mick had sauntered towards the bar. Greg knew he wouldn't say anything directly to Rita. Not that there was anything substantial to say, but he was right, although it had been subconscious. "Clever Clogs", he thought.

"That lot drink like fish", said Albert, as he downed yet another half of Special. He nodded in the direction of a small group who were obviously enjoying themselves.

"Who are they?" enquired Mick.

Doreen overheard the conversation and almost skipped towards the bar, leaving Cedric, who had just offered to pay one adult fare for the mystery tour. "That's Dave", she announced. Mick's face remained vacant. "Dave Warburton, the new member. He's brought along five of his little friends". Mick glanced at the group once more. "I wouldn't call them little".

"Oh, just my term of endearment". Doreen grinned, Mick smirked.

"Don't tell me, they're interested in going on a Club trip".

"Several, actually. How did you know?"

"Just call it male intuition".

Doreen returned to the desk where Cedric waited patiently. "Now, dear, where were we before I was interrupted?"

"Before you poked your nose in", thought Mick.

Greg came up behind Mick and in a low voice asked, "What do you call an aversion to railway enthusiasts?"

"I don't know, what **do** you call an aversion to railway enthusiasts?"

"Anoraknaphobia!" Mick groaned.

"I know, I know, but you'll still be telling someone in the office tomorrow, won't you?" Mick nodded in agreement, discreetly pointing to the newcomers.

"And there they are, the latter-day spotter personified. The guy on the right, with three inches of skin showing through that hedge, is the new member David - or Dave, according to Doreen".

"Oh, right, the chap who's interested in diesels?"

Mick eagerly pointed a finger at Greg. His eyes grew wide. "Dave Diesel", he announced.

"Well, they're certainly wearing regimental uniform. Jeans, gaudy coloured anoraks, three are sporting beards and judging from the number who wear glasses, I reckon they're a fairly academic lot".

"And drinkers, according to Albert".

"So they can't be all bad, then".

Mick continued studying the group. "Computers and education, that's the area that lot work in".

It was shortly after 10 p.m. that Mick and Greg introduced themselves. Three were indeed in computers, one was a teacher, another worked for Customs and Excise, whilst Dave Warburton managed a paint ball adventure centre.

Greg offered to help with the evening's takings. He and Mick cashed up as Albert closed down the bar.

"He's looking better, isn't he", observed Greg, as he completed building a second ten pound pile of one-pound coins.

Albert had just walked past the office, his hands clutching spent glasses. Mick chewed the end of a pen for several seconds and then in a quiet voice proceeded to tell Greg about Vi's condition. He wasn't so much seeking reassurance of his decision to take Albert with Vi on her next appointment, an arrangement already known to Mrs. Buchanan and the hospital consultant, but more an unburdening of his own situation.

"Let's get this right, you're going to ring Graham and tell him about his own mother's illness?" Mick nodded. "But shouldn't that come from Albert? After all, he is Graham's father".

Mick placed both arms on the desk, as if to stress his proposed course of action. "I've spoken with Vi, so has Kate. Albert and Graham are hardly on speaking terms, let alone good friends".

Greg pursed his lips. "I just think you could be accused of, well, interfering. Don't you think it's a bit risky? I mean, I'd hate to see it spoil a good relationship. You obviously mean a lot to them. I could tell that by what Vi said when Albert was in hospital".

Mick was deep in thought. "And them me", he murmured.

"Pardon?"

"Sorry, I mean, they mean a lot to me as well".

Greg pushed the door shut in case Albert should pass by again. "Mick, I can understand why Vi wants Albert to be given all the facts directly by the consultant, I can understand her wanting you to be with them, but ringing Graham is personal. I think you're taking a bit of a gamble".

"Greg, what concerns me is that Albert can't talk to Graham. Christ, Graham hasn't exactly shown much thought for either of them. D'you know how many times he's rung over the last few weeks?"

Greg shrugged his shoulders.

"Once". Mick raised a finger as if to substantiate the figure.

Sitting back, legs crossed, Greg commented, "With all due respect, Mick, you don't exactly have a track record for giving a toss about other people's problems, so why d'you feel so strongly about the Buchanans?"

Mick pondered for several seconds and then stood up. He adjusted his trousers. "Let's just say they're a bit special". He smiled weakly, ushering Greg out of the office.

Seeking Albert's attention Mick shouted, "Come on you old bastard, it's going home time".

Albert acknowledge Mick's request and slipped on his jacket. Lights out and alarm on, the barman settled into the front passenger seat of Mick's car as Greg lowered the driver's window of his Ford Mondeo.

"Just checking, Mick, the pouch is dropped at the High Street Branch, not Cavendish Road?"

Mick nodded.

"I wonder if we'll see Colin next Wednesday", added Greg.

"You never know, he might have his hands full again - although thinking about it, he never quite got round to having them filled the first time, did he!"

*   *   *   *   *

142

CHAPTER FIVE

The Durdles hurried about ushering fellow travellers towards their allocated seats. Those who made up the "live steam crew", sat together as usual, on one side of the coach, towards the rear. Opposite them were the dozen or so members of the public, who had either replied to one of Doreen's ad's in the local paper, or who were, by now, "seasoned friends of the SRC" - another term used by the Outings Secretary. The gang of four who operated "Pennytown" sat in front of them. Reg and Gwladys were placed opposite. Reg always found their ramblings and coarse jokes amusing, although it caused Mrs. Bowen more than a little irritation and discomfort, which suited Doreen! Mrs. M. and Colin had been put together, the Outings Secretary working on the assumption that as they were by themselves, it was only right and proper to pair them. She felt the arrangement to be particularly appropriate as Mrs. M. was approximately the same age as Colin's mother. Cedric found himself next to Harold and promptly set up a discussion on the merits, or otherwise, of afforestation in the Scottish Highlands.

In pole position on the seats closest to the driver a printed card stating, "Outings Secretary & Assistant", sat in all its fluorescent Day-glo glory, as if awaiting royalty. Doreen strutted towards the front of the coach, having made much of checking the stock of refreshments. She stopped in her tracks and sniffed. Backing up she lowered her head and sniffed again. Between her feet lay a brownish mark.

"Can we all check our shoes, please. Someone's trodden in something rather nasty". Mumbles and sniggers could be heard as first one shoe, and then the other, were checked by the travellers.

"Own up, who's responsible", Doreen barked, whilst tapping a finger on Cedric's head rest.

A hand rose slowly. Colin was apologetic. "Sorry". He hobbled on one leg down the aisle towards the steps.

"Well, do something quickly", reproached Doreen. "We haven't got all day - honestly, men". She raised her eyebrows.

The co-driver emerged with a mop and proceeded to clean the affected area. Colin could be seen wiping his footwear at arm's length with tissue paper. He used almost a packet.

"That's right, Colin", shouted Doreen from just inside the coach. "Get it all off, we don't want you smelling all day!"

With that Doreen faced down the coach and clapped her hands. Derek stood behind her grinning. "Right, everybody", she began, "I know that most of you have travelled with John before - John, show your face". John turned and waved with confidence.

"And this is our co-driver, Dave. Go on, stand up, let the dog see the rabbit". Doreen gesticulated, urging him out of his seat. She laughed, Dave blinked and smiled nervously.

Colin tried to appear as inconspicuous as possible whilst he made his way back to his seat. "Sorry", he said softly. Doreen nodded.

"All right, Colin, but look where you tread in future. It's not very nice for other people".

"It wasn't very nice for me", Colin mumbled as he took to his seat once more.

Doreen continued. "I won't introduce everybody by name, but welcome anyway". She put her hands together. "If it's all right with you, John, we'll be away - don't want to keep our destinations waiting!" She chortled loudly, eyeing those around her for a response. Several grinned, others had already tuned in to their personal stereos. Doreen gave two blasts on her guard's whistle. John accepted the signal. The coach pulled away.

"Great, super, terrific", said Derek, as he gave the thumbs-up sign. He sat, but Doreen remained standing, almost rigid. She looked along the aisle so as to check that no-one was walking about. It was not a habit she approved off unless the traveller was visiting the toilet, and then only if the journey was well into its second hour and the perpetrator was known to have a dicky bladder.

The 7 o'clock start brought about only light conversation, many preferring to sleep, as far as is possible in a coach. Colin had not mentioned the incident with Pete and Mick that had taken place some three weeks previous. He appeared to be his usual self, talking to the pair as if nothing had happened. Here on the coach journey he engaged himself in a limited amount of small talk with Mrs. M. She felt elevated to a position of high office, being allotted a seat beside the Clubroom Manager **and** Secretary.

"Fancy sitting next to you", she said, "and getting the window seat". Colin smiled politely.

With little early morning traffic to hinder their progress, coffee and Gwladys's Welsh cakes were served almost immediately. Doreen handed out serviettes to all, explaining that although it was generous of Gwladys to provide light refreshments, being home made they were very prone to crumbling, and the last thing John and Dave wanted was more clearing up.

Kingston, Hampton Court and Sunbury had been speedily negotiated. Traffic on the M3 was light and having taken the A303 just west of Basingstoke, a stop was made for breakfast.

Heading westwards once more, Doreen exchanged words with the driver. She then took hold of the microphone and stood at the end of the aisle. She tapped its head then blew into it. "I've just been having a few words with John and I'm glad to announce that we're on schedule". She held out her free hand, as if to rebuff the advances of an amorous admirer. "No, I'm still not saying where our destinations are, but I can tell you that we're only a short distance from the first - of three!"

She paused, and was duly rewarded. Mumblings rose above the drone of the engine. Ooohs and aaahs abounded. Husbands and wives nodded, acknowledging Doreen's announcement with surprised satisfaction.

"I suppose we'll need our coats", enquired Gwladys.

"No", replied Doreen curtly. "If you had needed them, I would have told you, wouldn't I?" Her smile was less than sincere.

A shrill, high pitched whistle temporarily deafened her, and those close by. Hands jumped to cover ears. "John, John", Doreen shouted, as she flapped one hand at the driver, whilst holding the microphone as far away as possible. John fiddled with a dial and then gave the thumbs-up sign. Doreen continued. "As I was saying, we will be arriving at mystery destination number one in about fifteen minutes and staying for about an hour - thank you".

Mick sank into his seat and closed his eyes. Kate nudged him in the ribs. "Stay awake", she whispered.

John, the driver, indicated, decelerated and turned left off the main road and down a slip lane. Picking up the microphone once more Doreen announced, "Consider this to be the aperitif". She smiled knowingly.

145

"Can't do without it", said Mick. Kate shook her head.

Indicating once more the coach pulled into a car park. There were a smallish number of cars present. A conglomeration of ancient buildings surrounded the main two-storey structure. A river ran alongside. The uneven surface brought to life those who had slept for the best part of the journey, including Harold, who had remained asleep throughout the breakfast stop.

Jock nudged Yorkie, who rubbed his eyes and stretched.

"Where the bloody 'ell are we?" he enquired.

"Errr, I dinnae ken, but we're way past Andover". Yorkie appeared none the wiser.

Derek grinned inanely as Doreen declared, "It's a silk farm".

As they alighted from the coach, some took off with the enthusiasm of intrepid explorers, others stretched their legs, while a few members remained on board, deeming a site visit unworthy of their attention, due to the lack of steam power available.

At 10.55 a.m. Doreen stood by the entrance to the coach and blew her whistle. Bodies scurried from the car park towards her.

"Fun, wasn't it?" she said as fellow travellers returned to their seats. Most smiled courteously. Jock was not so impressed.

"Och, all those wee things moving aboot the racks reminded me of the maggot box I keep beneath the sink". Doreen winced.

"That's nice for you", she said dismissively.

Derek stood at the front of the aisle checking for empty seats. "Only one unaccounted for", he said, "not bad for a first blow of the whistle - great!"

"Who's missing", enquired Doreen, looking at her watch.

"Colin", replied her husband.

In unison and without prompting many Club members raised an index finger into the air and exclaimed, "Aaaah". Robin leant forward. "Mick, leave it at that, you know how sensitive he is". Mick held up his hand in acknowledgement. "Just enjoying myself", he replied, grinning.

"Sorry, John, I'll have to go and look for him", said Doreen. As she approached the Reception doors Colin appeared. "Didn't you hear my whistle?"

"No".

"Well, everybody else did!" Doreen's reply was haughty. Colin fingered his chin.

"Ah, I think the sound of the toilet flushing may have deadened your audible signal". Doreen tutted and changed the subject.

Cheers went up as Colin appeared in the doorway.

"Wrong coach for the second eleven", exclaimed Pete. Greg smirked and took a second look at the Clubroom Manager **and** Secretary. Colin was dressed in a white shirt and immaculately creased cream slacks, set off with white socks and tan sandals. His jacket, neatly laid out along the rack above his head, was also cream. It sported the SRC blazer badge, which Mrs. Mabey had sewn onto the pocket two summers previously, plus lapel badges representing the Ffestiniog and Talyllyn Railways.

Doreen was thankful that everyone had been found and seated by 11 a.m., her planned departure time which had to be adhered to.

As they continued along the A303 Kate browsed through the brochure she had bought at the farm shop.

"It appears that the Chinese started making silk in about 2640 BC, Mick". She received no reply. "Mick", she said more forcefully, nudging him once more.

"What!" His tone was irascible.

"It says here that the Chinese Empress Si Ling Chi dropped a silkworm's cocoon into hot tea and discovered that the liquid loosened the filaments enough to be unwound". Mick gestured with his hands.

"You mean she just happened to be playing with a cocoon, drops it into a cup of PG Tips and exclaims, 'I think I'll wear that next time we have a girls' night out!"

Kate ignored her husband as he closed his eyes once more.

"The Saracens brought silk production to North Africa, Spain and Italy ....."

She read to herself for several seconds, then continued aloud. "It seems that the silkworm spins the cocoon about itself in a continuous series of figure eight's".

"Fascinating", replied Mick. "I think the only smart silkworms are the semi-cultivated chaps who bugger off before the drowning process begins". His eyes remained closed.

Vi leaned forward towards Mick and Kate. "I've seen Torvill and Dean do that!"

"What, drown?" asked Mick.

"No, do those figure eight's".

The coach driver turned right onto the A36, passing through Warminster and Frome before turning left along a B road just south of Radstock. Only a few minutes elapsed before their vehicle entered a large parking area. Several coaches and a good number of cars were already present. Doreen stood once more, holding onto the upright railing as John reversed.

"If the silk farm whetted your appetite, then this will tantalise the taste buds even further before we visit the piece de resistance". She turned smugly to the driver. "I got that off 'Masterchef'. Now here, you **will** need your warmer clothing". Doreen clasped her hands together. "Derek and I have arranged for a complete tour of this working mine museum. We'll be split into two groups, I'll be taking seats 1 to 26 as the first party - excluding seat number 2, which is Derek's of course! Derek will look after all of you in seats 27 to 52. At the end of the official guided tour our itinerary allows us to meander about and explore at leisure. I will just add one thing here - for those of you worried about your stomachs - food has been arranged at our next stop - our main course, so to speak! So, without further ado, numbers 1 to 26 come along with me. John, that includes you. Dave, you go with Derek".

Mick looked at his wife and raised his eyebrows. Kate started laughing. "Is she always like this?"

"About 24 hours a day, I would imagine". They joined the snake headed by Doreen and the driver.

On arrival at the reception area the two parties under the auspices of the Durdles were once again halved. The guide explained that fifteen persons was the limit for each journey down the mineshaft. Doreen asked Robin to take responsibility for group 1A, as she referred to them, whilst Lanky was to oversee group 2A.

Ex-miners kitted out the visitors with helmets, complete with lights, plus waste bands containing breathing apparatus, should the unexpected occur. Doreen said that it wasn't likely to, but that it added to the atmosphere anyway.

They descended some eight hundred feet before stepping into a cold cavern that had three tunnels leading from it. The jovial guide, Ted, offered a mixture of history and anecdotes as the first party listened intently. Electric lights were positioned along the walls, fire doors were opened and closed as they made their way ever deeper into the confines of another era. Water dripped continuously and ran along gulleys beside the now rusting tramway tracks.

The guide stopped periodically, taking time to describe the workings of the surviving pumping equipment. Wooden wagons were still to be seen, some filled with coal extracted during the last week's workings several years ago. Stools, where pit ponies stood when off duty, lay empty, save for the straw and name tags still tacked to wooden cross members. "Pixie, Queenie and Violet", stated Ted. The visitors sighed. "They all feel more sorry for the ponies than they do the men", he continued. "We get more questions about them than anything. Still, time to move on". They walked into a conspicuously narrower tunnel. In slightly officious tones Ted requested, "The electric light finishes here, so turn on your lights, please". Some few hundred yards on he stopped and asked everyone to switch them off and stand still. "There", he said softly, "this was the ponies' view". All agreed that the lack of light, coupled with the constant trickle of water, brought about an extremely eerie scenario. The whole place felt damp, everyone felt lonelier. Suddenly a voice shrieked, followed almost immediately by a thud. The guide appeared distraught.

"What was that, everyone okay?"

Lights were turned back on, many flashing directly into the eyes of fellow visitors. Gradually their beams followed the same path, forming a great pool of light. Lying half on the floor and half in a gulley a lightish coloured mass moved slowly. It muttered. It was Colin. Ted hastened through the enquiring bodies. "You all right, sir?" he asked with genuine concern. Pairs of hands leant forward, lifting him up. Kate put a hand to her mouth. Mick whispered, "Well, Doreen's not going to be pleased, she won't let him back on Johnny-Baby's coach looking like that".

Colin's jacket hung limply, the left sleeve and back of the garment were marked with coal dust, his trousers stained and dirty.

"What happened?" asked the guide.

"Ah, well, I dropped my packet of Extra Strong Mints, you know the ones with the four x's on them. I just bent down, suddenly ....." He motioned with his arm, making a scooping movement.

"Don't fuss", said Greg, "he's not dead".

"More's the pity", exclaimed Pete, "wouldn't have to take him back with us". The mineshaft echoed to the mirth. Colin grinned half-heartedly.

"Didn't he have a heavier coat or anorak?" asked Vi.

"Apparently he forgot it", answered Mrs. M.

A further few minutes' walk brought them to the cage from where the group ascended. Once on the surface they spread out into small groups and couples, with the exception of Colin who headed for the toilets.

"I haven't done anything this strenuous in years", said Albert, as he sat back in the eating room that basked in the appropriate, if unimaginative, title of the "Pit Head Cafe".

"Doreen suggested we only have a cup of tea", commented Vi, who had taken the Outings Secretary at her word.

Kate acknowledged Vi and then said, "That silk wasn't cheap, was it?"

"I remember silk stockings in the war, buying them off American GI's at the camp". Vi's eyes were slightly glazed as if rediscovering a lost age.

"It was all right for them", sighed Albert. "What was it? Oh, yes - overfed, oversexed and over 'ere!"

Mick slouched, a cigarette hanging from his left hand.

"You're only jealous, Albert Buchanan", said his wife in a mocking way.

"Yeah, but just the oversexed bit!" He grinned youthfully. His whole face lit up, and momentarily and ex-sergeant looked many years younger. "Bin a good day, so far". He looked at Kate. "I know you're not, well, coachy people, but we're both glad you came along with us. Made all the difference, it has". He placed his bony hands on Kate's and smiled.

"Actually, it's been quite entertaining so far", offered Mick.
"Doreen's an entertainment in herself, like being on another planet", commented Kate.

"If only she was", thought Mick, "if only she was".

Pete and Greg examined the various outbuildings, reading the potted histories as they drifted around the site. For Greg, his day was without any interruption of thought. His father-in-law was spending two weeks with Sally's sister. Although they did not have the room to look after him on a permanent basis, it had been agreed from the outset that their house in Barton-on-Sea, Hampshire, would be second home to him. It allowed Sally some relief, if not freedom, from the continual worry regarding her father's possible whereabouts. Alan Hargreaves was becoming more forgetful and the situation would only deteriorate. Today, however, while Greg was away playing trains, as Sally put it, if for no other reason than to tease, she, the children and dog were driving to Richmond Park for a picnic.

At "Ballocks" there had been a disconcerting calm. Rita had not mentioned the fact that she knew Pete had lied to her about being with his father on that Sunday. It had been over four weeks since Bert Balfour had phoned his son at the office, yet when Pete had arrived home with a thousand and one excuses going round in his head, outstretched arms and a loving kiss had welcomed him, instead of the expected tirade of abuse. Pete remembered thinking that this was Rita being devious, a trait which he felt, upon reflection, was not in keeping with her true character. He had walked slowly behind her into the dining room, expecting the worst, but the smell of steaks cooking and the ambience created left him feeling vexed as to which way she was jumping.

Over the last few weeks Pete had noticed small, subtle changes. Rita would phone him at the showroom to see when he expected to be home. She emphasised that she wasn't checking up, but wanted the meal to be on time. When Pete had arrived, he had been waited on hand and foot, a drink prepared, the bath already running. The odd motoring magazine had been purchased. Rita had even swatted up on the forthcoming season's Grand Prix, her interest progressing to the point where she could match racing team with driver.

But what, he thought, did it all mean? For the first few days he had expected one almighty row, but the possibility had diminished with each new dawn and yet, he still felt unsure of their real relationship. Had she blanked it out? Had she decided to put more effort into their marriage - as it appeared she might have done - or was this the lull before the proverbial storm? He would phone her, he thought. Reet would like that. After all, she wasn't going anywhere.

Pete Balfour's mobile phone was a problem. Owned for over two and a half years he had never told his wife of its existence. The last thing Pete wanted was a phone call during an "awkward" moment. Whilst it went everywhere with him, it was never to be seen when Rita was around. Switched off and hidden away in the car boot, it remained out of sight. On the rare occasions he did use it to phone her, Pete would say, "I'm with so-and-so, and I've just borrowed their dog and bone, so I'd better be quick ....."

"Did you see a phone in Reception?" asked Pete, as he and Greg walked between two rows of coal wagons, now condemned to static display as a tourist attraction.

"God, you haven't got a bit on the side round here, have you?" enquired Greg.

"No, I'm just going to ring Reet, see how she is, like".

151

"Funny, the words 'Pete Balfour' and 'caring' don't spring readily to mind as being entirely conducive".

Pete smiled amiably and headed for the main entrance. Greg stood surveying the site, now considerably reduced in size since its heyday, when it was both employer and centre of local life.

Doreen once again blew for time, and from outbuildings, the shop, the Pit Head Cafe, and crevices deemed worthy of exploration, bodies presented themselves in double quick time. Others simply strode across as if purposely bucking the system. Mrs. M. considered it her duty to look after Colin. She had waited patiently outside the gents' toilet, while the Clubroom Manager **and** Secretary endeavoured to make good, as far as was possible, the damage done some hundreds of feet underground. Further examination of Colin's jacket revealed a rip just below the elbow and the separation of the left sleeve from the shoulder. When worn, the jacket gave Colin an unbalanced appearance. The neat crease in his slacks had disappeared in part, due to the washing and rubbing which in the event, had had the effect of transferring the stains and marks over an even greater area of his clothing.

John, the driver, had laid a rug across the seat and back; Mrs. M. tucked it in.

"There you are", said Doreen to Colin, as he sat down. "Mrs. M. has made it nice and cosy for you - just like home". She patted the rug.

"I don't sit on a rug at home", Colin replied irritably.

"No, well, you probably don't dress like that at home either". Doreen smiled in a superior fashion.

Pete caught up with Greg who was taking one last glimpse at the wagons.

"Got through, 'elped 'er make it through the day". Pete beamed.

"You don't half fancy yourself".

"True, but I'm one amongst thousands, sunbeam. One amongst thousands!"

They ambled towards the coach. "You've taken your time". Doreen looked at her watch. "I thought you were strays".

Having been counted on board Pete stopped on the first step, turned suddenly and looked intently at the Outings Secretary, his silver shell suit catching the sun as he did so. In a low, husky voice he said slowly, "Not so much of a stray, more of a tom". He emphasised the last word, narrowed his eyes, not looking away from Doreen. Motioning both hands as paws, he roared loudly. Doreen giggled girlishly. Both men returned to their seats.

"You could score there", said Greg mockingly.

"You **could**", reflected Pete. "The point is, would you want to - would anyone want to?"

"Derek did!" Both men looked quizzical.

"All present and correct", yelled Derek, giving a salute to his wife before adding, "Great, smashing, super".

"Well, then, John, anchors away - or should I say brakes off". Doreen laughed at her analogy. The doors hissed closed as the driver manoeuvred the coach out of the car park. Many of the travellers had guessed the third and last destination, but none dared mention their prediction within earshot of the Outings Secretary. As they travelled on the final leg of the outward journey, Doreen collected the microphone. They had just turned left onto the road leading to Shepton Mallet.

"On the right was Downside Abbey. You've just missed it. Also, on your right is the village of Gurney Slade. Many of you not in your first flush of youth will remember the name from the Anthony Newley TV series shown in the 1960's. Out of interest Max Harris's orchestra played the title theme, which was in the Hit Parade - as they called it then - not that I remember, of course". She laughed loudly and attempted to sing the tune. Heads shook, some from a complete lack of musical memory and others from a complete lack of appreciation with regard to Doreen's vocal abilities, likened by Jock to the sound emitted by a Scottish wildcat during an operation to remove its testicles. Lanky asked if he had ever witnessed such surgery. Jock said that he had not, but if it did take place, that was surely the sound it would emit. Lanky tensed his groin and shivered.

Doreen continued. "We will shortly be passing the village of Oakhill, which once housed a famous brewery. Thanks are due to Albert for that piece of information ....."

Shepton Mallet was admired and discarded. Once on the A361 an ebullient Doreen stood once again. "This, ladies and gentleman, is our main course".

A little further on a plume of smoke could be seen. There was a sense of anticipation within the confines of the coach. Even before the doors were open the gangway was blocked by eager beavers desperate to soak up the atmosphere and fill their stomachs.

"Many of you will know", said Doreen, blocking the aisle so as to make escape impossible, "that we have arrived at Cranmore, home of the East Somerset Railway, founded by that well-known conversationist and artist, David Shepherd".

"Conservationist", corrected Jock.

"Whatever", said Doreen, now perched on the step nearest the door and unseen by most of those travelling. There was a lot of jabbering as news of the railway spread towards the toilet end of the coach.

"Oooooh", mouthed a couple of women. "Fancy, David Shepherd", said another. One male member of the public asked, "Isn't he a cricketing vicar during the week?" An elderly couple shook their heads dolefully, indicating a complete lack of recognition at the mention of his name. Doreen's head could be seen bobbing as the air operated doors hissed open once more. She held aloft a neatly constructed sign, hitherto unseen by the day trippers, being some fourteen inches long by three inches high, it bore the stencilled legend, "Surbiton to Cranmore - And Back".

"Would you all stand by the coach until I have a word with David". She seemed flustered.

A young man in overalls locked his Ford Cortina and walked across the car park towards the station entrance.

"Excuse me, cooee", Doreen waved. The young man walked over.

"Can I help you?"

"We're from Surbiton", said Doreen with pride.

"That's nice". The young man scratched his head, appearing to be none the wiser.

"We're from the Surbiton Railway Club". She gestured to those behind her. "David, your boss, is expecting us. I'm Doreen Durdle, Outings Secretary, and you are?"

"Ralph".

"Well, Ralph, I'd be obliged if you could take us to your leader". She laughed, nudging his arm.

"Oh, God", exclaimed Mick to those around him. "She'll really be in her element this time. David this, David that, bet she asks him to autograph her ticket".

Colin was looking and feeling particularly downhearted. Greg commented that their fellow Committee member was making an excellent attempt at impersonating the ugly duckling. Pete had been quick to announce that he, of course, looked every part the swan!

As Ralph was about to continue towards the station with Doreen literally treading on his heels, such was her zeal, David Shepherd appeared at the end of the path leading to the platform. Striding across, his hand was held out in anticipation.

"Mrs. Durdle", he called out.

"Doreen, please".

"Doreen it is, then". She blushed.

"Young Ralph here was about to bring us over. This is my husband, Derek, who assists me with our little sorties, and this is Robin, our Club Chairman". Hands were shaken, pleasantries exchanged.

"I must apologise for not being here to greet you personally but one of our visitors was purchasing a print and wished for it to be signed".

"Oh, that's okay, I think we can safely say you'll be required to sign a few more before the day's out". So saying Doreen gestured to her shoulder bag. The artist smiled with the merest show of embarrassment. Derek was grinning like the legendary Cheshire cat. "Great, no problems, smashing".

"Well", said the Railway's founder", if everybody would like to follow me ....." As he turned he caught sight of a dishevelled character loitering to one side of the visitors.

"Excuse me, but this is a private party, I ....."

Doreen looked around. "Oh, it's all right David". She caught hold of his arm. "That over there is our Clubroom Manager and Secretary".

David Shepherd seemed startled. "Oh". Colin waved tentatively.

"Is he all right?" enquired Ralph.

"Oh, yes", said Doreen, "he just slipped down a mineshaft".

"Shouldn't he be dead, or at least badly injured?" David Shepherd fingered his chin.

"No", said Doreen, laughing. "I mean he **slipped** down a mineshaft, not slipped **down** a mineshaft". She then explained the story. David Shepherd's response was encouraging. He placed an arm around Colin's shoulders. "Come on, Colin, let's find you some clothes while you're here. We must be able to fit you up with something".

"Ah, thank you", said Colin, as he bounced alongside, a smile now developing.

Having discussed the afternoon's timetable with Robin and Doreen the visitors were led to the recently constructed restaurant. Noisily, everyone took up places at the prepared tables.

Some three quarters of an hour had elapsed when Albert exclaimed, "I really needed that". He sighed and wiped a serviette around his mouth.

"Doesn't eat like this at home". Vi pointed to her husband's empty plate.

"Must be the air", observed Kate.

Robin stood up and cleared his throat. "Hmm, hmm. In the temporary absence of our Outings Secretary I would just like to remind you that our train will depart in 15 minutes and we'll all be travelling in the rear coach marked 'Reserved for SRC'".

Mick leant towards his wife. "She's probably telling our host how much she admires his surrealist touches, his pre or post modernist perceptions".

"Sounds more like Salvador Dali".

"You know that and I know that, but I doubt if Doreen knows the difference!"

The visitors assembled on the platform. Doreen strutted back across the railway line and waved to David Shepherd as he re-entered the signal box which had been turned into an art gallery and museum.

"Ah, you're back. Great, super, smashing", said Derek rubbing his hands.

Doors opened, passengers boarded the coaches and those with cameras and camcorders took final shots before claiming their seats. The engine whistle blew, doors slammed closed and the guard waved his flag. Once in motion, fingers pressed against the windows pointing out landmarks and artefacts. Heading westwards the train passed the old stone siding, all admired the engine shed, soaking up the atmosphere and smell. Windows were slid open or lowered, enabling the train's occupants to capture as much sulphuric steam as they could manage. For some it was a first time journey behind a steam engine, for others, it was a nostalgic return to a form of transport last encountered over thirty years ago. One or two of the older men relaxed in a way their wives had forgotten, basking in the sound made by the coach wheels as they bridged the rail joins, dee- dum, dee- dum - dee- dum, dee- dum.

More than once a father leaned towards his children and said, "This is the very same engine I used to travel behind when I went on holiday to Wales". The only difference in the story being the destination. Cornwall, Skegness, Blackpool, Mallaig. It never was the same engine, but more often than not, they believed it to be.

With the gradient steepening, open fields allowed splendid views of Somerset's undulating countryside. Past Merryfield Lane Halt and through Doulting Cutting, the train ran downhill among wooded areas which opened up as the train approached the terminus at Mendip Vale.

The sun was still shining brightly, with only the softest of breezes in the air, as virtually all the train's passengers alighted at Cranmore West during the return journey. This was the station one required if a tour of the maintenance centre was to be partaken.

Having stepped off the engine's footplate, David Shepherd escorted the SRC party on a work's tour. He was particularly pleased to point out the brick-built two road engine shed.

"'Ow long's this been here?" asked one of the party.

"We built it in 1973", replied the line's founder with due pride.

"It's not very old then, is it? I thought it was, well, old. You've not kept up with the times, have you?"

Placing his hand against the brickwork David Shepherd emphasised the thinking behind their decision to build the engine shed in that style. "The shed's been built to a traditional design, dating back over one hundred years. It's in keeping with the character and atmosphere we're trying to create", he enthused.

Heads nodded and murmurs of accord could be heard. The original enquirer, however, was not convinced. "Oh, I understand that, it's just that I thought you'd have used a bit more imagination. For a start, concrete blocks - after all, they're much cheaper". His eyes lit up. "And you can always paint your engines on the outside wall, show people what's inside". The man snapped his fingers and added excitedly, "Or you could paint one of your elephant scenes - I mean, you're used to that!" The man seemed pleased with his suggestion, but added with resignation, "Still, you've built in now".

"Quite", remarked David Shepherd.

Doreen sidled up. "It's all right, David, he's not a member of our Club, he just replied to our ad in the local paper". She made much of emphasising that he was not a genuine enthusiast but merely a daytripper with limited understanding. Doreen then swung around and glared at the traveller concerned.

Most of the fifty two members of the party, plus John and Dave, the drivers, followed limpet-like as they explored the various sheds, huts and outbuildings. Colin, however, was not of like mind. He ventured off, poking around in corners, opening doors marked "Private" and entering into conversation with volunteer workers. One such young man was painting a coach in British Railways Southern Region green. Having made his way back towards the main party Colin bounced through to those at the front. "Mr. Shepherd, Mr. Shepherd", he called, his index finger remained raised even when the founder's attention had been received.

"Yes, Colin, d'you know, you look just like one of our chap's in that boiler suit. Still, it's more used to getting covered in dirt than your flannels". He smiled.

"Ah, yes, well, I was wondering if I might, well, if I could purchase a small amount of your SR green paint. I'm currently restoring a Southern name board at home and I'm not in possession of the correct shade - not that I'm fully convinced your chap has matched it accurately, but then, the memory does play tricks and you never can tell until the finished article is subjected to daylight. That, as they say, is the acid test".

"Quite", came the reply once more. "Anyway, tell the chap you saw that it's quite okay for you to have some".

"Oh, right, thank you", said a beaming Colin, as he bounced more forcefully back towards the painter.

With the tour completed, the train whistle sounded once more and the excursionists boarded for their return to Cranmore. With time in hand to explore before the coach departed, small groups made their way in turn to browse around the signal box's upper floor containing the art gallery.

"Did he say earlier that he went to Africa to paint those elephants?" asked Vi, pointing to one of the many wildlife prints on display.

"Yes", replied Albert.

"Seems a waste of time going out there, doesn't it? Mind you, p'rhaps he didn't know they'd got some in London Zoo. I mean, they probably don't have posters about it down here".

Kate, who was standing alongside, smiled. Mick shook his head.

Albert looked at the date on one of the animal paintings. "D'you know, he painted this one over twenty years ago, gal".

"Fancy. He probably doesn't paint them now 'cos there's none left - d'you reckon I ought to tell 'im about those ones in the zoo ....."

Colin had taken the container of paint with him on his wanderings, despite suggestions that he should leave it somewhere safe and retrieve it prior to departure. This idea had not been well received by Colin, who worried that it might be forgotten or lost. He walked up the steps to the signal box clutching the container, the top of which was covered by a circular layer of polythene secured by means of an elastic band.

His intention was to show David Shepherd the amount of paint he had obtained so that a monetary value could be placed upon it. The reply he received was that a donation would be sufficient. Colin was advised to be careful whilst walking around the station site with the container. He was, however, politely asked to take the paint out of the gallery as there were a lot of people milling around, the point being made that "accidents do happen".

"Aah, right", was all Colin replied before bouncing his way down the stairs.

Those who heard the conversation held their breath. A sense of relief was visible on the artist's face as he signed yet another print.

As the late afternoon heat began to subside, Doreen, still grasping her sign that had been affixed to the inside of the coach window for the duration of their journey, started fidgeting around the lower steps of the signal box. She ushered out those remaining in the gallery and informed everyone, loudly, that they were to remain on the platform as there was to be a surprise event taking place.

"Is this where she gets tied to the rails?" asked Greg.

"Robin, Robin", Doreen shouted across the track. "Could you make yourself available, please. Thank you".

David Shepherd walked slowly down the steps, having closed the gallery door behind him. In one hand he held a box, long, yet shallow. Walking alongside Doreen they made their way over to the platform. Robin was standing a pace forward from the rest of the party. Doreen asked for complete silence and attention. She coughed, adjusted the top button of her low cut blouse and clasped both hands in front of her.

"While you were finishing off your dinners - which I know you all enjoyed - I was having a little chat with David". She looked up at him admiringly. "I expect you were all wondering why Robin gave you details of our itinerary instead of me?"

"No", called out Mick. Doreen blinked her eyes disdainfully and continued.

"Well, unbeknown to anyone at the Club, other than the Chairman ....."

"Not even Derek?" enquired Pete.

"Our Chairman **and** Derek, I asked David if he would be prepared to donate a print for auction on one of our running nights, so that the money raised could be presented to our charity". She paused, looking over the heads of those she knew well. "For the benefit of new members and those of you who are friends of the SRC I would like to briefly explain that we support our local hospital with small donations that help towards the purchase of equipment. I might add here that I myself ....."

"Briefly", interjected Mick, "you did say briefly". Kate nudged her husband.

"Well, anyway, Mr. Shepherd - David - has been more than generous. He offered to paint an original and asked me to choose an appropriate subject, and you won't see a print of this one over there". She pointed to the gallery. "So, without further ado, Robin, will you step this way, please", she ordered, moving him bodily to the artist's left side.

Cameras were extracted from cases, camcorders were held shoulder high.

"It gives me great pleasure to present you with this painting of your - Clubrooms". David Shepherd hesitated before sliding the frame out of its box. He shook hands with the Club Chairman, who then led the applause as the artist held his painting against his chest for all to see.

"I sent several photographs", said Doreen, "from lots of different positions so that David got the complete picture". She almost laughed out the words.

"Who's the fat tart standing outside the door?" asked one of the party, as he attempted to get a closer view of the said painting.

"That's me", replied Doreen haughtily. She turned quickly towards the artist. "I'm not saying it's not a good likeness, David, it's probably difficult for him to see, in this light - the sun, it plays tricks ....."

"It's a very generous donation", commented Robin. "I'm sure the eventual owner will be delighted to sit at home and view the fine building that constitutes our Clubrooms. You've captured it very well ....." He highlighted some of the features with his right hand before finally picking out the smiling female figure. "..... not least of all, our Outings Secretary, Doreen, seen here standing proudly by the Club entrance. I would now like to thank ....." Robin was stopped in his tracks. In an attempt to obtain a better view Colin had stumbled forward. Pete and Greg were pushed aside as Colin fell. The container flew out of his hands, the elastic band snapped and the polythene cover disappeared over the platform edge. Green paint shot forward, gasps of surprise and astonishment could be heard from all assembled.

Colin lay spreadeagled. He raised his head slowly. Doreen's hands covered her mouth. Robin was stroking his forehead in amazement at the incredulity of it all.

David Shepherd stood frozen to the spot, his donated painting still held at chest height. Green paint ran down his forehead and dripped off the tip of his nose. He opened his eyes and blinked, then blinked again. His shirt sleeves were splattered, as were his trousers. Further investigations were to reveal that his shoes had not escaped attention either. The painting, however, had borne the brunt of the onslaught. By coincidence, although considered later by Mick to be more than a slight case of irony, the Club's entrance and Doreen's likeness had escaped the unwanted coating.

Colin offered to give the railway owned boiler suit back to David Shepherd, suggesting that he might require a change of clothing, but having stood upright once more and realising the difference in height was several inches, Colin's offer drifted into a mumble.

"Not been your day, has it, my little Clipboard", quipped Pete.

Colin did not reply. Doreen ran about like a headless chicken, following her guru as far as she could, before he disappeared into private quarters in an attempt to clean himself up. If only there was something she could do. There was - strangle Colin! Hurriedly making her way to where the Clubroom Manager and Secretary was changing, she burst in to find him standing in only his vest, pants, socks and sandals. The boiler suit fell from his hands as he endeavoured to cover himself up. He was startled by the overbearing figure blocking out the sunlight, the extent of which would have been almost the same had the door been shut. "Colin", she screamed, "how could you do such a thing? Have you seen his face? He's green, and not with envy. Well, what have you got to say for yourself?"

Colin shuffled his left foot sideways across the floor. "Mmmmm, yes, sorry, but it was an accident".

"So, and I've no doubt your mother will confirm, were you!" Hands on hips and finger pointing admonishingly, Doreen continued to chide her fellow Committee member. "You were **told** to leave that pot of paint until we departed, but oh no, you had to go and take it around with you like a prize toy. What were you going to do when you got home? Take it to bed with you instead of your favourite teddy. Honestly, Colin, I just despair!"

Colin looked down and aimlessly picked up his flannels which hung over the back of a chair. He proceeded to dress. All previous concern about his lack of attire now seemed unimportant. Doreen stood there; she could see how hurt he was. Wringing her hands together she said,

"I'm sorry, Colin, it's just that I had so much planned for the day, it wasn't easy finding a time when Mr. Shepherd - David - would be here. I wanted the handing-over ceremony to be - well - right". Colin looked up at her in the manner of a scolded dog.

"Sorry".

Her cold face weakened. She regretted her wounding comments. That measure of invective was generally reserved for Gwladys who, it had to be said, had behaved without fault throughout the day. Reg had taken it in good part when asked not to go running about on the engine shed roof.

"I'll leave you to it, then. See you on the coach", Doreen said softly, as she backed out of the room. Colin nodded. She shut the door gently, paused, checked her watch and reopened the door forcefully. "Colin, four minutes, don't be late!"

In a strange way Colin felt reassured by her familiar sharp tone. Derek was waiting for her nearby. "Oh, there you are. Been a great day, hasn't it? Smashing".

"Oh, Derek, it's been a disaster".

"No it hasn't". Doreen looked up at her husband.

"But what's David going to think of us?"

"He's going to think that we've got an accident-prone member who really is a pretty decent chap". He tightened his grip on her shoulder as they walked towards the coach which fellow travellers were now boarding. As they stood, taking one last look at the train, in particular the carriage in which they had ridden, Derek added, "Decent, but bloody irritating!"

Subconsciously shaking herself back into life Doreen shouted, "Derek, can we have a head count, please". Derek obliged.

"Fifty one", he called, "only Colin to come. A mock cheer went up.

"'Ere comes Clipboard", shouted Pete, as he espied the missing member walking alongside David Shepherd.

Once aboard the coach Colin returned to his rug-covered seat. Doreen, Derek and Robin stood just inside the doorway talking to the railway's founder. "I am so sorry about what's happened", offered Robin, "and I also have to apologise to you for the ignorance you had to put up with outside the engine shed. Still, I did notice the man hand you something - I assume it was a donation".

"Not exactly", replied David Shepherd, "it was his business card - wholesale breeze and concrete blocks!" Both men chuckled.

Robin then beckoned the artist forward to address his fellow pilgrims. "Well, thank you all for coming, it's been a pleasurable and a somewhat different day". He smiled. "You'll be delighted to know that the painting is not terminally damaged and I'll undertake to send it to you in due course". He self-mockingly touched his forehead and lightly tapped his nose. "And I'm not as green as I was previously, either", he added, looking around. Spontaneous applause broke out.

Colin suddenly jumped out from his seat, hitting his head on the luggage rack. "One thing I think you should know, Mr. Shepherd, having seen the green paint in the light, so to speak. I feel fairly certain that you are, in fact, a shade out, but ..... on reflection ..... I don't suppose ..... "

Robin had been about to rescue the situation when Doreen cut in, now restored to her former, indefatigable self, "Thank you, David, once again for your magnanimous gesture - now, you have my address so you can send the picture, haven't you?"

He gestured in the affirmative, waved goodbye and stepped off the coach. The waving was reciprocated as Dave, the co-driver, pulled the coach cautiously out of the car park.

Out of the corner of her eye Doreen could see young Ralph walking back towards his Ford Cortina. "This is where we came in", she said to herself as she sank back into her seat. Doreen glanced downwards, resting on her knees and clasped tightly between her hands lay the signed print she had purchased in the gallery. She laughed inwardly. Doreen had often told friends that her life had started A.D. - After Derek, how she wished it had stopped B.C. - Before Colin.

There was much chatting and laughter as the troops made their way back to Surrey. Doreen's stencilled sign was temporarily attached to the nearside portion of the front window. One or two of the younger passengers were fast asleep before the A303 had been reached. John, the driver, now relieved of duty, nattered tirelessly to the Durdles. Yorkie read pages from the latest "Thomas the Tank Engine" saga. Less than one hour had elapsed before Dave signalled left and pulled into the grounds of a large public house, whose signboard proclaimed that coaches were welcomed. Most alighted.

Pete and Greg considered enquiring if the landlord would jokingly ask Colin to leave as he was not suitably attired, but they thought better of it. Mick, Kate, the Buchanans and Mrs. M. sat at the same table. Colin felt less conspicuous sitting in the corner, sharing the break with Reg,

Gwladys, Harold and Cedric.

Albert lowered his glass and licked his lips. "Nice drop of bitter, this Eldridge Pope". His satisfaction was obvious. "What else they got on, Mick?"

The Treasurer looked above the ex-sergeant's shoulders towards the bar. "Palmers, Marstons and Gales".

"Coo, that's good. Three more halves and no two the same!"

"We're off in half an hour, not half a week", said Vi. "Anyway, you'll only keep going to the loo if you have two pints and you know Doreen doesn't like people roaming about".

"Oh, don't take any notice of her", advised Mick, "you roam where you like, providing it's on the coach, of course!"

Albert smiled, finished his half and having taken orders, went to the bar for refills.

Kate, Vi and Mrs. M. became engrossed in conversation as Albert waited to be served. Mick glanced casually at the three women. A thought struck him as he sat there, divorced from their female discussion. No-one sitting watching could possibly tell that one of these women was going to die before too long. There was no difference in their enthusiasm or their laughter, only their age, and that counted for little. Cancer showed scant regard for youth. He lit up another cigarette and stretched out in the chair, his feet reaching the far side of the table. He remained in that position. Albert was right, he thought, they weren't coachy people but when asked if he and Kate would go with them for the ride, he'd readily agreed.

Mick was so immersed in his ponderings that he became oblivious to all sounds emanating from the saloon. Subconsciously turning a beer mat end on end, he reflected on his life as a child growing up in South West London. He'd teamed up with Graham as they seemed to share the same interests, but as with many youngsters those interests turned into passing phases. Graham never retained the fascination of any hobby for more than a few weeks, whilst Mick found himself developing an attachment to railways, in particular, trainspotting. It was something he could do on his own. With the aid of an Ian Allan ABC, notebook and pen, he would cycle to Surbiton Station and stay for hours. Sometimes he would meet up with like-minded children. Sandwiches and drinks would be shared and a common bonding develop. It was only when cycling home that the elation would cease. There was no-one to talk to, no-one to share the joy at "copping" all fifteen Lord Nelsons or all thirty

Merchant Navies. That, Mick contemplated, was the only real aspect of their respective lives that he and Graham shared. Neither had brothers nor sisters.

Back in his well-appointed, detached house, with detached parents, he spent many hours alone making his own amusement. Neither Mick's mother nor his father showed any interest in his schooling or his hobbies. They always turned up for parents' evening but it was more out of duty than concern. "Well done", his father would say when told of his son's achievements. It was, however, said without any feeling or expression. It had never occurred to him that his parents only stayed together for his sake, which, on reflection, had only served to increase the tension between the adults and to contribute towards Mick's continuing isolation.

No wonder he sought solace in the terraced house in which the Buchanans lived during Mick's younger days. Regardless of the weather Mick always felt warmer in their two-up, two-down. Whereas he revelled in the friendliness of an open fire, Graham would complain that his parents were "not with it". Nothing they had, nor bought, was ever good enough for Graham, who made a point of remarking that the rank of sergeant wasn't exactly a success story. "Leopards don't change", thought Mick, "just look at the bitch Graham married. A clone, if ever I saw one".

He had been present at their wedding, officially invited by Graham and Camilla. He had, in reality, attended at the request of Albert and Vi. Camilla's family had all but ignored the Buchanans and their relatives. The incivility was never mentioned but the hurt on their faces said it all. It was the hands on the shoulders or the embracing arm which Mick remembered. There were always words of encouragement, the Buchanans would never let an unfinished story lapse; they were always eager to hear the next instalment.

Mick enjoyed football and it was the Buchanans who came to see "young Clayton" play for the school team in his one and only appearance, and that was as a substitute, but from the cheering and calling the pair of them made you could be mistaken for assuming that they were his parents. And where were his parents? They were so wrapped up in their own misery, they never noticed their son.

Mick recalled the day of his 18th birthday. He had returned home from work at the local engineering company where he was serving his apprenticeship, to find his parents standing almost to attention in the lounge. "Got something to tell you, Michael", his father announced coldly. "We're getting divorced. Arrangements have been made for you to stay with your mother, when she moves". He spoke as if she wasn't there. "Not far away, Michael, won't affect your work". That was all he said before turning and walking over to the armchair, where he picked up the Evening News and commenced reading, whilst puffing away at his pipe. His mother outlined their plans, which clearly did not include Mick other than in the short term. He now realised more than ever that his presence was nothing other than an unfortunate irritation. It was, Mick reminded himself, the only time he could remember crying, apart from when a so-called friend, Roger Walker, smacked him full in the face for kissing his kid sister. Talk about kiss-and-tell. Mick smiled. Never before had he felt so alone, so dejected. Indelibly inscribed was the memory of running up to his room where he vented years of frustration and anger. Neither parent appeared in the doorway. Vividly he recalled the slow walk back downstairs. The house was silent. He opened the lounge door to find his father still sitting in the same spot. His mother was rearranging flowers on the window sill. It all seemed to unreal. His father looked up at him. "Good boy, got it all out of your system, then. All for the best you know, Michael". No-one had even considered asking him if he thought it to be for the best, or for that matter, what he wanted from life.

Mick's eighteenth had metaphorically unlocked the shackles of pretence. They could now disregard any feelings of guilt, such as they were. Both parents had been involved in affairs for years. Not for Mick a surprise party or a night out, only a surprise. They had bought him a watch and with it a card. The picture on the front cover was of an MG sports car, with a young man and, Mick assumed, his girlfriend, both smiling in carefree fashion. Had his parents ever been like this? On opening the card and reading the printed inscription Mick read with disbelief that of his mother's handwriting, "All our love, Mum and Dad". What a joke! Mum? Dad? Love? They wouldn't recognise hypocrisy if it hit them in the face, he thought.

Mick took to lodging with a work mate. Within months he had rented his own flatlet. Evening classes and further education, paid for by his employers, led to qualifications, higher wages and a reasonably pleasant bachelor flat. He became popular amongst his peers, never being one to hold back a view or make his point known. Mick worked hard to attain his present status, that of junior partner in a small, structural engineering company. And who had been there to follow his rise up the ladder? The Buchanans. They were never impressed by other people's material wealth, merely by the person concerned. And what of his parents now? Mick subconsciously shrugged his shoulders. The divorce had been quick and amiable, with both parties moving almost immediately. He received letters, but never reciprocated. He did hear that his mother had moved to Amberley in Sussex during the early seventies, while his father had apparently taken up residence with the last of a long list of short affairs somewhere in Norfolk. Not a word had been spoken to either parent in over twenty years. "Twenty years". The figure came as a shock to Mick, his cigarette still burning away in his hand. For all he knew both couples were still together. Had either remarried?

Mick often wondered if his childhood insecurity was responsible for his lack of trust in others. He'd had several relationships spread over a good number of years. Some had lived with him, but he always shied away from talk of commitment.

For many years he had moved around the country living where the contract took him. All the really exotic places, thought Mick. Preston, Scarborough, Fraserburgh, Goole. Now that had been fun, Goole. That was where he had met Kate. Mick had found that being laid back and seemingly disinterested attracted females who liked a challenge. Kate, however, was different. She gave nothing away. It was stalemate. He discovered for the first time that it was he who was doing the running. It took two years for either to discover their true feelings. They had now been married for ten years. Kate's parents were homely people who had taken Mick to their hearts. Southerners, they'd moved up to Yorkshire when Kate was sixteen. Independent by nature she shared a flat with three other girls. Starting as a trainee at the local bank she had "clawed her way" as she put it, through the male dominated ranks to reach the status of branch manager at her employer's office in Kingston upon Thames. Mick hoped they would still be together when he was Albert's age. How unfair it was that the Buchanans should be the recipients of such cruel fate. Their devotion and happiness had never been called into question. So how could Vi's number be called out of the hat in such a way? "Vi Buchanan - cancer!" said the ticket held aloft by a higher being during the "great death draw" as Mick saw it. Where was her God, Mick said to himself, pursing his lips unknowingly.

The three women were still chattering as Mick recalled that Sunday night after the Buchanans had returned home. Mick called Graham who seemed furtive and distant. No change there, he'd thought. He did sense, however, that something was wrong. Mick had been his usual direct self. He had told Graham that he would not have considered phoning had it not been important to his parents. But what response had he received? "You always were their favourite, in the frame for a hand-out, are we?" It had been at this stage that Mick started to tell a few home truths. He had pointed out that it wasn't unreasonable for Graham's parents to expect a conversation with their only grandson now and again, or to receive a photograph taken less than six months previously. Had not the thought of his mother dying broken any ice with him. Graham had remained silent for a moment but that was the extent to which any feeling had been shown.

Mick had asked about Camilla but was told to mind his own business. Mick's signing off message still rang in his ears. "I always used to think of you as an ungrateful bastard, and you've made a vocation out of it, but just for once in your miserable life think of someone else for a change. Think about your mum and dad - and Jamie. He'll probably never forgive you when he grows up, and I tell you what, you'll never get another chance".

With that he had slammed down the receiver, exclaimed "bastard" with venom and then sat for some time reflecting on the situation. That call had taken place the night before Albert was due to visit the specialist with Vi. As promised he had gone with them, hoping to be able to tell them that their son and grandson were coming over, if for no other reason than to take the sting out of the consultant's unchanged diagnosis. In the event, he hadn't mentioned the phone call. Albert had just sat there motionless when told of Vi's true condition. The consultant had been as open as possible. He had pulled no punches, been sympathetic and in a peculiarly honest way, reassuring. Vi had sat throughout, eyes cast down upon her handbag which lay flat across her lap. Mick had told Kate later that day that he had felt like a spare part. No-one had said anything for what seemed like ages, although in reality it was merely seconds. The journey home had not been pleasant. Every red light seemed like an eternity. The traffic appeared heavier than on previous journeys. Every time Mick thought about starting a conversation the words seemed so inconsequential, so unnecessary, so trite.

Just prior to arriving back at the Buchanans's bungalow Albert spoke for the first time. "Did you know?" he asked. Mick glanced into his rear view mirror. Vi looked at him, encouraging a positive response. Mick nodded. "Ah", was all Albert said.

Normally he would have been offered tea. It was almost a standing order but this time he helped Vi out of the rear passenger door and returned to the driver's side, mumbled "cheerio" and drove home. It had been some two hours later that the phone had rung. Mick knew instinctively that it would be Albert. He enquired as to whether Mick and Kate could pop round later for a "chat". Mick could not remember seeing Kate cry but tears welled up in her eyes the moment he told her they'd been invited that evening. "What do I say, Mick?"

"I think we listen". He tried to reassure her.

Mick's thoughts then drifted to that evening.

"I suppose deep down I knew something more serious was wrong with Vi", Albert had said, taking hold of his wife's hand, "But you try, well, to hide it away, don't you? Vi never said anything. It was just that ......" He paused and blinked. "..... Just that, after forty odd years of marriage you get an inkling when ....."

Albert swallowed heavily and gripped his wife's hand more tightly. He never got to finish the sentence. The visit had not been pleasant and it didn't get any better despite things now being out in the open. Vi tried to contain her feelings but burst out crying in the kitchen when making ham sandwiches for everyone, not that anyone was hungry. It just seemed the proper thing to do. Kate had held Vi close and comforted her. There were no great revelations, even fewer decisions, but the Buchanans needed to talk and sort out things in their mind. On the way home Kate remained very quiet. As they pulled into their drive Kate spoke at last. "They really do love you, Mick". He uttered something unintelligible, mainly through a sense of embarrassment then, clearing his throat, he looked directly at his wife and spoke more audibly. "And what did Vi say? You're the daughter they never had". Nothing else was said.

Since that date there had been precious little change in Vi. Certainly today she seemed full of life - if that was the right phrase. "Full of life", Mick repeated quietly.

"What was that, Mick?" asked Albert, placing the tray on the table with gusto. Mick looked up.

"Oh, nothing - miles away". He smiled jovially.

Within a very short while Doreen's whistle blew, conversations

169

ceased immediately. The landlord looked up, as did most of the local patronage.

"Just calling time on our lot", explained the Outings Secretary, "but in our case I'm calling time to get back to Surbiton, and then home!" She looked round at her fellow travellers, "And then we can all go up the stairs to Bedfordshire and count engines!"
Chairs scraped across the floor allowing the occupants to make for the coach.

"Harold Fidler, where do you think you're going, then?" asked Doreen loudly. Heads turned in Harold's direction.

"To the loo".

"Well, make sure you're not in there all night. Some of us have been up a long time". Vi and Mrs. M. laughed at Doreen's comment. The Outings Secretary stood looking at her watch as last gulps were taken and emptied. Harold emerged in double quick time.

A regular customer stood by the bar somewhat bemused by the proceedings. Doreen looked at him and said "What's the betting he'll still need to go before we get home!"

"I'd enjoy telling Doreen where to take her overdraft", said Kate with a wicked grin.

"In her case, I think it's an underdraught", added Mick, as the Outings Secretary adjusted her cleavage once more.

"Does she have a problem?" enquired Kate.

"Only if there's a captive male audience", observed Mick as they made their way outside.

Coffee was served and the last of Gwladys's Welsh cakes were devoured by those who were hungry, and it appeared that many were. Derek carried a black plastic bin liner and collected all the discarded cups and other items of rubbish. Doreen noticed one fellow traveller attempting to throw away a leaflet which had been picked up at the silk farm, but the Outings Secretary made her take it home, saying the least she could do was to leave it in her doctor's surgery, as other people would be interested, even if she wasn't.

John then stood in the aisle and conducted the sing-song, an integral feature of any tour, according to Doreen.

"Thank you, thank you for travelling with SRC tours", said the Outings Secretary to all as they alighted and made their way along the car park to their respective vehicles.

As the last doors closed and the occupants drove slowly out of the

Club grounds, Doreen waved for the final time. In her left hand she held the drivers' collection bowl, which she had handed along the coach just east of the Fleet services. She gave the contents to John. "There you are, boys, you can share that between you. I've had a little look through, though, you've got about eighteen pounds - okay?"

So saying, Derek brought forward his car, lowered the window and shouted, "Great, smashing, cracking day". He gave the thumbs up sign and waited patiently as his wife kissed both drivers goodnight. She then skipped across to the passenger door, making much of waving, as Dave pulled away down the lane. Having sat down and connected her seat belt she placed her stencilled sign on the dashboard, facing out. "Well, we're not home yet", she sighed, in answer to Derek's quizzical look.

"Great", replied Derek, enthusiastically.

"It had not been an unsuccessful day", she thought, despite all attempts to the contrary. "Yes, all in all, she'd pulled it off again".

*   *   *   *   *

CHAPTER SIX

The last Monday in June was Committee night. Colin dutifully crossed off the names of those present. There were no apologies for absence. The biggest smile was worn by Doreen who, having blotted out the previous day's disaster, namely Colin, could hardly contain herself as she awaited the moment when Robin would offer his thanks and appreciation. This would lead to the applause which she felt sure would follow spontaneously.

Drinks and crisps were dispensed around the table. The meeting started at 8.03 p.m. Colin read out the minutes. Mick's statement concerning the Club's finances were concise, as usual, there being little change from his previous month's address.

Greg assured the Committee that Southworth was now in excellent running order and had attained the standard required, enabling the layout to represent the SRC on its trip northwards.

"Got its BS 5750, has it?" enquired Mick. "So who's going with you?"

"Colin, Derek, Pete and Harold".

"I'm driving the hired van", said Derek. "Colin and Harold are coming up with me, Pete and Greg are going up in one of Pete's cars. Great, huh?"

Mick smiled before throwing a glance at Greg. "Don't tell me, he's got something to look at up there. Wouldn't be female by any chance, would it?"

"Don't think so, but we couldn't get five in a van and anyway, Pete said his petrol was tax deductible!".

There were no new applications for membership but Colin, acting in his capacity of Clubroom Manager did express his desire to increase the price of soft drinks and crisps by six pence and two pence respectively.

"That's one and tuppence on drinks and five pence on crisps", bemoaned Reg.

"Well, 24p a packet, certainly", acknowledged Colin.

"Four and nine in real money ....." Reg tailed off, shaking his head in resignation.

"We can't keep looking back", commented the Chairman.

"I thought that's why we were here", Mick suggested.

"I think Robin meant ....." Colin raised his finger in an effort to add weight to his remark, but Robin cut in.

"Mick was just being his usual facetious self".

"Aaah".

Mick looked towards Colin who had fallen silent. "Cut short prior to completion again. Story of your life, isn't it".

Greg and Derek laughed out loud, Doreen tutted. Reg chortled like a small boy listening to his first "rude" joke. Robin and Colin remained straight-faced as Mick lit up his third cigarette of the evening.

The Maintenance Report took up some little time as Reg was keen to inform the Committee of his progress during the intervening period. Robin offered his thanks, making special mention of the diligence with which the newly appointed Maintenance Officer was tackling the myriad of unfinished tasks. Doreen was not to be disappointed. Robin laid on the superlatives lavishly. Even Mick deigned to add that she had done a good job, but spoiled the praise, in Doreen's eyes, by suggesting that a special thanks be given to Colin for turning out to be the cabaret's star.

Any Other Business brought the longest discussion of the evening. Robin had received two letters; the contents of the first related to membership.

"Dave Warburton", the Chairman stated, "has written indicating his friends' desire to join the Club, but they are 'undecided' due to the Club's apparent disregard for diesel traction'. Mr. Warburton goes on to mention that various other chaps in his circle would also be interested in joining if a diesel group could be formed within our ranks, with a view to arranging tours and possibly in the longer term, building a modern image layout". He looked around for comment.

"I told you he was strange", said Colin.

"You don't contribute much, do you?" remarked Greg, "and when you do, it's not really worth it".

Robin banged the table calming the jollity. "Can we get on now, please", he implored.

173

"Even four new members would bring in another hundred quid", said Mick. "Not a figure to be sneezed at". He turned towards Greg. "A bit like Rita's, in fact". Greg smiled smarmily.

"But the point is", said the Chairman, in slightly louder tone than usual, that we **do** need fresh blood and we must keep up with events".

"Who's going to organise these trips to diesel engine sheds?" enquired Doreen.

Robin noted her concern. "I'm sure Mr. Warburton and his friends would be only too pleased to acquire some of the tricks of the trade you've picked up over the last few years as Outings Secretary".

Doreen smoothed her hands across her bust. Robin continued. "I just feel that some expansion of our sights would be no bad thing". Doreen seemed placated.

"Traction depots", offered Reg.

"What?"

"They're called traction depots, not engine sheds. They were called engine sheds in the days of Ian Allan's ABC's - two and six pence each and worth every penny. Two and six!"

"Yes, yes", pleaded Robin, "can we get on".

"Tell him 'yes'", said Mick as he slumped in his chair. "If he wants to form a group within the Club that specialises in all things non-steam, then let him do it".

Robin smiled. "Do I take it that we are all in agreement in adopting a broad church approach?"

"You've been listening to too many party political broadcasts, coming out with phrases like that - or have you been taking lessons from Cedric?"

Robin was eager to continue. "I'll take it as a yes. Letter number two comes from another recently joined member".

"Where - at the hips?" quipped Mick.

"Is he on something?" asked Colin.

"..... one, Jeremy LeGrand". Robin spoke loudly, emphasising the French accent. "He writes to say that he is concerned about the Club's long term aspirations and that he would like to meet members of the Committee to discuss the opportunities his experience in advertising and PR might bring, etcetera, etcetera". Robin looked up at those around him. "Basically, he's got a few ideas about raising funds more readily and would like to have a chat outside of our usual running night. I suggest that Mick, as Treasurer, Colin and myself have a word with Mr.

LeGrand and see what he has to say for himself". The nodding of heads confirmed Robin's proposal and a tentative date was discussed.

"I can't place him", pondered Derek, as he finished off his second packet of plain crisps.

"You'd know him if you saw him, only been down a few times. He's the one who keeps practising his golf swing when he talks to you", Greg informed his fellow members.

Derek snapped his fingers. "Oh, I know the one, flashy looking type - executive suits. He's only here a short while before he disappears again. Obviously got a lot on. Great, yeah, got him!"

"Smug bastard, I think you mean, "added Mick, as he rocked back on his chair. "Still, I suppose he might have something to offer - other than golf lessons, that is".

The meeting was called to order and Colin registered its termination at 10.22 p.m.

Wednesday evening passed without even the most fleeting appearance of Jeremy LeGrand. On Thursday morning Robin rang his office. A very efficient but distant receptionist told the Club Chairman to hold for a minute. It turned out to be several; the duration of the wait being made less bearable by the synthetic jingling of "Greensleeves". Just prior to the completion of yet another rendition, the tune was suddenly cut.

"LeGrand", announced the PR consultant smoothly, his voice rich and clear.

"Morning, it's Robin here ....."

"Robin? Sorry? Robin who?"

Robin took the receiver away from his ear and looked at it. "I was about to tell you", he thought, but continued. "Robin Harmsworth from the Surbiton Railway Club".

"Oh, **that** Robin. My, the world's just full of them today!"

"I'm just ringing regarding the letter you sent me. I wonder if we could arrange a meeting for some time next week?"

"Sure thing, Oscar, just check my windows". Robin listened as electronic bleeps of differing tone appeared to take on a life of their own.

"Is Thursday week okay, say, 8 p.m.?" enquired Robin.

"Thursday week, let's see. Uhm, twenty hundred hours? Yes O.K."

"Fine".

"Where?"

What about the Goat's Head", suggested Robin.

"Sounds cool, Oscar, just programming it in. See you at GH - got to dash - bye-ee!"

"Bye", replied Robin, who was not convinced that his parting word had been heard before Jeremy's receiver had been replaced.

He then rang Mick who confirmed that he would be available. Robin was not so lucky when trying to contact Colin.

"His desk's opposite mine", informed a colleague cheerfully, "but I've no idea where he is. Gone walk about, I expect". Robin smiled to himself.

"Does he do that often?"

"Well, I'd say there's more chance of his desk being Colin-free than Colin-lumbered". The Club Chairman was intrigued.

"What does Colin do?"

"**That**", replied Colin's fellow worker, "is a question we've all been asking for a number of years".

"Are you never subjected to time and motion studies?" Robin asked jokingly.

"Yes, we are, and that's the amazing part. He appears to have fooled them as well". Both men laughed.

Colin returned Robin's call later that afternoon. The Club Chairman probed as to where Colin had been earlier in the day, but completed the conversation none the wiser. It wasn't that the Clubroom Manager and Secretary had been furtive or evasive, it was just that Robin came off the phone still unsure of what Colin actually did. Confirmation was given, however, of his ability to attend the forthcoming meeting.

*   *   *   *   *

During the week Greg's father-in-law returned from the Hampshire coast. Sally felt that two positive aspects had come from his fortnight's holiday. One, it had given her, and to a lesser extent, Greg, a break they didn't realise would be so apparent and two, her sister was now more mindful of the problems Sally was encountering, day in, day out.

Harold waited patiently for Baz to visit him, his clutch being in such worn condition that a hill start was now almost an impossibility. The "Southworth" stalwart had mentioned the mechanic's non-appearance to Pete Balfour on two consecutive running nights and during the mystery trip. Promises that, "he'll be over tomorrow, trust me", had failed to produce even an apologetic phone call.

*   *   *   *   *

The following Tuesday morning, as Albert and Vi were settling down for a cup of tea, the doorbell rang twice. Albert looked at his watch. "You expecting anyone, gal?"

Vi shook her head. The Club barman raised himself from his chair and walked over to his front window where he drew back the corner of the curtain. Standing on the front step were the two policemen he'd met previously. On opening the door, they'd smiled, asking if he could spare a few minutes of his time. Vi stood with her left hand pulling limply at her bottom lip, the other played with her apron. Albert re-introduced the detective sergeant and his assistant. Vi curtsied slightly. They sat together on the settee, as the D.C. explained from the armchair opposite that two men had been arrested in connection with another assault on an elderly lady. Despite taking place over a mile away the circumstances were similar. It transpired that this particular victim had attended a bingo session the previous evening. She had bid goodnight to her friends and commenced walking through what she had always considered to be a safe short-cut. Two men had appeared just inside the opening, blocking her path. She had tried to walk on, but had frozen with fear. Her handbag had been snatched but pride had got the better of reason and she had kept hold with terrier-like tenacity. Jerking the handbag away the woman had fallen, only to be dragged along until her strength had been sapped. Suffering from shock, cuts and bruises, she had, however, managed to give a good description.

"But how were they arrested?" enquired Vi.

"It appears that they attempted the same type of theft less than half an hour later, but were spotted by a motorist. They scarpered but he had the good sense to ring on his car phone, whilst driving round the local streets. Our boys picked up the pair of them in under ten minutes".

"So, what happens now?" asked Albert, as he held out his hand, which Vi instinctively met and squeezed tightly.

"Well, sir, we'd like you to come down to the station with us and see if you can identify either of them".

Albert looked worried, Vi even more so.

"It shouldn't be too distressing, sir", offered the constable, sensing the old couple's concern.

177

"No", replied Albert, it's not that, "I just don't want to let anyone down by not picking the right ones - or not picking anyone at all".

The detective sergeant gestured with both hands. "All you've got to do, sir, is to take your time and see if any features strike the memory. It does happen". He smiled reassuringly.

Albert fetched his jacket. "Won't be long", he said, as he squeezed his wife's arm. Vi smiled weakly.

It had been an upsetting start to the week. On Monday, Vi had made the journey to see the consultant once more. Mick had been unable to take them but Nobby stood in gamely. There was no real change in her condition, other than a tendency to feel slightly more tired. Albert did notice that his wife's appetite had to be nursed along. She often failed to finish a meal, but Albert would encourage her. "You've got to eat", he'd say. Vi would smile warmly and take another couple of mouthfuls. Despite their original objections to outsiders being involved a Health Visitor had been appointed to "pop in and see how things were progressing", as the hospital administrator had put it. Albert found it an odd phrase to use in the circumstances. As far as he could see, the only thing that was progressing was his wife's cancer.

Mrs. Buchanan had been asked to spend a few days in hospital to undergo some tests, but had declined, saying that she had come to terms with her future, or the lack of it and if it was God's will that she went that way, so be it.

Although it was but a short period of time, to Vi her husband's visit to the police station seemed like an eternity. She looked careworn as Albert unlocked the varnished door and called out her name.

"Well?" she asked quietly. "How did you get on?"

"They were very nice, the police ....."

"I expect they were", Vi interrupted impatiently, "but what happened?"

Albert sat down and sighed heavily. "There was something about one of them, but I couldn't be sure. Still, Mrs. Hallett, the lady who was attacked, recognised them, so did the other one who was about to be robbed. You know, the one the man saw from the car".

"Well, that's something - what happens next?"

"They go before the beak tomorrow. Dependent on what he says, they'll either get bail or custody. I know what I'd like to give 'em!" Both hands formed themselves into fists.

"Don't upset yourself, Alb, it's not worth it - they're not worth it".

Albert ran his fingers lightly through his grey hair, then leaned forward. "The second lady, Mrs. Carlisle, asked if I was going to court tomorrow. I said I wouldn't be, so she's took our number and she's going to ring us, let us know what's happened to the little bastards".

"Albert", Vi scolded, "there's no need for that".

Albert tutted and thumbed through the magazine rack. He ignored the Woman's Own and the Woman's Realm, his fingers coming to rest on a gardening part-work issue he had decided to collect. Tucked inside the cover was the copy of Beekeeping Weekly he had been given some time before. "I must ask Nobby about that", said Albert to himself as he consigned the magazine to the rack once more.

*   *   *   *   *

Wednesday evening's gathering was swollen by the arrival of yet more diesel enthusiasts. There were mumblings amongst the check-jacketed brigade. It happened to be the "O" gauge group's running night and Chipping Waltham was sporting a brand new goods shed. It was the work of one of the group's members and had taken several months to build, paint and weather, proceeded by an equal length of time researching the prototype; the resultant model being worthy of the layout and well received by all.

This particular group, more than any other within the club, felt threatened by the intrusion of what one of their number described as "New Wave Enthusiasts". He pointed out that he had seen pictures, not only of Stonehenge at summer solstice but also of the legendary Woodstock rock festival and he knew what sort of people those with beards were like. In defence of these guests the opposite view was offered, stating that the only similarity between New Age Travellers - scrounging bastards, as Mick suggested - and the potential new members were the beards and hair sported somewhat longer than expected by those feeling aggrieved. The fact that all were employed, the majority in academic posts, cut no ice whatsoever. Stickers were affixed to Chipping Waltham's front boards declaring the layout to be a "diesel-free zone". This format lasted only briefly before Tippex was applied and the word "zone" replaced with "area", considered to be infinitely less offensive and more in keeping with the Cotswolds.

"For someone who considers that anybody with an interest in diesels is odd, Colin's certainly making a fortune out of the raffle with that lot", observed Greg to the Treasurer.

One pound coins poured into the beer mug as Colin bounded around the Club rooms. Having financially exhausted the gathering he approached the Treasurer and Archivist, who had recently been joined at the bar by Pete Balfour.

"Excellent response", said Colin, jangling the mug. He raised the index finger of his free hand. "Greg, I've just had a request from that Dave chappie. He'd like to order some books from us". After searching through trouser and jacket pockets Colin produced a list for Greg to peruse. "A few bob's worth here, sort of a bulk order, I'd say".

Colin peered over Greg's shoulder whilst bouncing vigorously on the soles of his feet. Pete studied Colin's movements, then turned to Mick. "Has he got something stuck up his backside?"

"Are his brains big enough to get wedged?" offered the treasurer.

Colin ignored his fellow members. "Anyway, I think the raffle money must be around the £38 mark. Not bad, is it?"

"Little things", said Mick as he wandered back towards the office.

Greg walked over to Dave Warburton with the intention of thanking him for the book order. Colin stood in at Chairman's Announcement Time due to Robin being away on business. New and prospective members were, as usual, welcomed to the Club. The generosity shown by Dave and his friends towards the raffle had mellowed Colin's suspicion of their interests to the point where he mentioned the possibility, not only of a potential diesel-only layout, but also the arranging of tours to traction depots in the not too distant future. He then proceeded to read out a letter received from a regional railway organisation to which the Club was affiliated. They were inviting entries for an annual poetry competition.

"They should be of no more than four verses and relevant to railways in general", Colin disclosed.

"The broad church approach, I believe", whispered Greg to Mick, who pursed his lips and lit up another cigarette.

"Final day for entry is 30th August, so we've got just under eight weeks to put on our thinking caps". Colin looked around. "I'm prepared to act as a clearing house in this matter, so if you can all let me have your scribings in plenty of time, I'll send them off en masse".

"You could send them altogether, as well", shouted someone at the back of the hall, much to the amusement of those gathered within. There was, however, a distinct lack of enthusiasm to Colin's rallying call, so he promptly proclaimed the amount collected for the raffle. "Forty two pounds and sixty pence", he shouted, eagerly awaiting the mock oooohs and aaaaahs that traditionally accompanied the announcement of the total raised.

"Where's the dreadful duo tonight?" enquired Mick.

"Derek's in bed with flu, apparently", replied Greg.

"Could be worse, could be in bed with Doreen!" considered Mick.

Once again, two of "Pennytown's" custodians claimed gold and bronze, whilst a check-jacketed member won silver. He promptly asked Greg to order a book known to have been out of print since 1975. He looked disappointed on being given the news but the Archivist did point out that it was the fourth time in as many months that he had requested the title and the corresponding number of times that he had been given the same answer.

"Unreal", said Greg to himself as the check-jacket returned to his place among those whom Mick described as clinically dead.

The fourth share of the spoils went to one of Dave Warburton's guests, the redemption value being £6.60. Greg engaged himself in conversation with the last prizewinner in an effort to explain the raffle system, but could be seen backing off during his discussions.

"Christ", he said to Mick a little later, "don't go too close, his breath is decidedly 'iffy'."

"Halitosis, is it?" Mick scowled.

Greg looked back at the unfortunate fellow. "In his case it's more like halibutosis".

"Oh, so **he's** the one lumbered with the last of our out-of-date scampi crisps!"

Harold once again tackled Pete Balfour regarding Baz's recurring non-appearance, and once again the car salesman promised "on 'is mother's life" that the mechanic would sort out the problem tomorrow "without fail". Harold seemed satisfied. The fact that Pete's mother had died two years previously was not something Harold had readily taken into consideration.

Dave Warburton walked over to the bar and ordered another six pints of Gales H.S.B. and one orange juice.

"D'you lot drive home afterwards?" asked Greg, sitting on a bar stool devouring his second packet of Worcester sauce flavoured crisps.

Dave turned and smiled through his forest of beard. "No, we've got a twelve seater outside and we all take it in turn to play the part of the poor sod who can't drink".

Greg was impressed with the self-discipline. "Oh, I see". He pointed to the counter. "Hence the orange juice".

Dave nodded. "I hear I've been Christened 'Dave Diesel' by your Clubroom Manager and Secretary.

"Oh, he's cottoned on, has he. Actually, it was our Treasurer, Mick, who first uttered the immortal phrase. I suspect Colin was eavesdropping. You can't keep secrets here, can you", said Greg humorously. "And he's made sure you know his full title, as well!"

"Yes, actually he's quite enthusiastic about a couple of ideas I've mentioned to him".

"What were they?"

"Well, I thought we might organise - with Doreen's blessing, of course ....."

"Of course", interrupted Greg.

"..... a trip under the tunnel on the new Eurostar, and a weekend to one of the diesel gala do's that the preserved railways organise".

"Sounds good. You should get a lot of support, well, from some sections of the membership anyway". Greg smiled.

"Oh, I know it's not everyone's cup of tea, but we expect a lot of our friends to be interested", said Dave seemingly encouraged.

"Well, good luck", offered Greg as a parting comment.

Once served Dave Diesel returned to where his friends were standing, heads bowed. They were surveying a map of track alterations in the Watford area.

"Nice pint, that", commented Albert, his eyes having followed the tray's progress across the hall. Greg turned towards the Club barman.

"So, Mick tells me they've caught the little toe rags".

"That's right", replied Albert, as he wiped the inside of a pint mug. "During the identity parade there was something about one of them. I told the police but I couldn't be definite". Albert threw the towel over his left shoulder and leant forward. "I tell you what, though - it did make me laugh. The sergeant told me they once had to find a line up at 10 a.m. for a one-legged suspect. As 'e said, there aren't too many people like that walking - or hobbling - passed the station at that time of day".

"Or any other!", joked Greg.

The rest of the evening passed without incident or revelation, although Pete Balfour did manage to sell a B-plated Fiat Panda in black to one of the Club's members, as a first car for his daughter. Pete had pointed out that **normally** a car of that age, with an extremely low mileage, and in black, which was always regarded as a premium colour, would fetch around £500. However, this was a "friend", a description he used whilst placing an arm around the potential customer's shoulder. The car was offered for sale, as seen, no guarantee implied, given, indicated or stated for £400 - cash, of course! Pete liked to add a rider to the "cash, of course" phrase, emphasising that it was easier due to the paperwork it **didn't** create.

Mick drove Albert home after closing time. Both men noticed Vi standing beside the bay window curtain, which she had pulled a discreet distance to the side. By the time Albert had alighted the front door had been opened. Vi stood silhouetted by the hall light. "You all right, gal?"

Mick looked across the passenger seat towards them. Vi beckoned the Club Treasurer. Subconsciously pressing the remote locking pad attached to the car key, Mick walked quickly, hands in pockets, to where the Buchanans stood. "Have you got a minute?" Vi asked gravely.

"Sure". Both men followed.

Albert looked at Mick and shrugged his shoulders. As soon as they were seated Vi informed them that Mrs. Carlisle had rung as promised. Vi was very precise. "She said she was sorry she didn't ring earlier but her son and daughter-in-law took her back to their home. She's a widow and she completely forgot to ring".

"So?" asked Albert, "is there a point to this story?"

"So", replied Vi, "they got bail". Albert's face was one of disbelief.

"Now there's a surprise", said Mick.

Vi pointed her finger. "No, that's not the surprise". She paused. "The surprise is knowing who the little blighters are".

Albert and Mick sat bolt upright. Vi took a slip of notepaper from the mantelpiece. Albert furrowed his eyebrows. "Wayne and Stephen Maynard, 48 Ormskirk Close". Albert looked at his wife, then quickly glanced at Mick.

"Mrs. M.'s two lads?" he said disbelievingly. Vi nodded. No-one said a word. Mick lit up a cigarette.

"It might not have been them who did me", suggested Albert.

"Oh, but it was, Alb. That Mrs. Carlisle said they'd admitted two other attacks. Yours and another old boy in Worcester Park".

"I'm bloody dumbfounded". Albert shook his head.

Mick walked over and collected an ash tray from the table. "I wonder what our cleaner's thinking now", he said, as he noted the inscription on the circular tin receptacle. "A Present from Grange-over-Sands" it read, alongside a coat of arms and a line drawing of the locality.

*   *   *   *   *

"Strange what some people collect", said Colin, noticing Mick's gaze around the walls of the Goats Head Public House. It was bedecked with frames, some contained luncheon vouchers, others, telephone cards. Mick stretched out, raised his arms above his head and yawned. "But some people are strange", he considered, motioning towards the door. "Only here an hour, he's taken three phone calls and made two himself - dear me, what a busy little executive he is!"

"Come on", said the Chairman, "what do you honestly make of Jeremy LeGrand?"

Colin looked towards Mick, took a sip of cider and enthused, "Well, I was jolly impressed, quite a go-getter".

"That is the same as prat, isn't it?" asked the Treasurer.

"What I mean is that he certainly has got some interesting ideas". Colin perused his notes. "Jeremy said that by signing up with this brewery we would be able to revamp our bar area, totally at their expense. They would also be able to supply a new cold tray - which we desperately need - and improve the interior, signage, etc."

"But at what cost, Colin?"

"Well", Colin replied, fingering through his notes once more. "We would lose the freedom to buy our beers from small independents, but Jeremy did say that Greater London Breweries will soon be producing real ale again, so we won't be losing out".

"Colin's right", agreed Robin looking serious. I'm not sure we can afford to turn down a chance like this". The discussion continued for some time.

"At the end of the day", said Mick, "there's no such thing as a free lunch and there's one minor point you've both overlooked in what appears to be a burning desire to throw away control of our Club".

Colin looked puzzled.

"Go on", said Robin.

"Jeremy's company wants somewhere to entertain guests and like all go-getters" - Mick looked at Colin, who smiled - "no, Colin, that wasn't a compliment, like all go-getters, he'll want it on the cheap. After all, put against hotels, we are cheap. I can see that most evenings the hall will be hired out and who's going to do the bar duties? You can't expect Albert to cover all events. We all know he's willing, but even so".

"Surely if we're hiring out the hall, paid staff could be found?" suggested Colin.

"Well, you're the Clubroom Manager, so you'll have to organise it".

Colin finished his half pint of Stowford Press, sat back and crossed his arms. "I perceive it as being an extremely exciting project". His backside was visibly moving off the chair, such was his level of excitement.

Mick shrugged his shoulders. "I don't like it. Don't tell me you've failed to notice just how plastic he is. Oscar this, Oscar that - he even beats Pete for the home perm look! And to be fair to Pete, he doesn't have his tinted as well. To sum him up, he's the sort whose family motto would read, 'All or everything'".

Robin smirked. "All the same, Mick, I think we ought to call an Extraordinary Committee Meeting to discuss it further."

Mick stood, legs astride, hands in pockets. "Well, just remember, I'll go along with the majority view, but don't ever say I didn't tell you, it'll end in tears". He emphasised the last four words.

Colin recoiled slightly. "Aaah", he murmured.

As Robin returned the three spent glasses to an appreciative barmaid Colin looked at his watch.

"You're not going to turn into a pumpkin, are you?" enquired Mick.

"No, I was just wondering whether it was too late to pop into Pete's, as I have a coach of his which has been subject to a re-spray".

"Not Southern Railway green is it, by any chance?" enquired Robin wryly, as the three men walked into the car park.

"Aaah", replied Colin, "it's blood and custard, actually".

"Oh, 'cos if you're ever short of green paint, I know a place in Somerset where they stock the right colour - although it might be just a shade out!" joked Mick.

Colin chuckled. "Mmmmm, I assume you're referring to a certain incident I'd rather forget! I wonder if Mr. Shepherd's managed to clean up that painting yet".

"He's probably been more concerned with cleaning himself up".

Colin found this comment particularly amusing, his shoulders falling and rising noticeably. Having recovered from what Mick described as 'full moon syndrome', Colin raised his index finger. "Out of interest, perhaps one of you might know, why is Pete Balfour's house called 'Ballocks'. It sounds a bit, well, you know ...."

"Ah", responded Mick, mimicking Colin's stance, "as it happens, I can answer that one. The 'Bal' is from 'Balfour' and the 'locks' is from Rita's maiden name, 'Lock'".

"Could have called it 'Lockball', I suppose", added Robin, fingering his chin.

"Or 'ReetenPeet'. No, I think I prefer 'Ballocks', at least it doesn't pretend to be anything other than a pathetic attempt at a play on words. Oh, Colin, just a pointer, don't forget to stand to attention when you ring the doorbell - it plays 'Rule Britannia'". Mick unlocked his car.

"Does it really?" asked Robin, somewhat incredulously.

"'Fraid so. Apparently, every time it's played he's reminded of that patron saint of entrepreneurs, Margaret Thatcher".

"Not another bit on the side", suggested Robin, laughing.

Colin removed the Krooklok, setting off some five minutes after the departure of his fellow Club members. He'd sat pondering on the evening's developments, feeling elated at the praise bestowed on him by Jeremy LeGrand. Colin searched for music to match his mood. He chose the "Trish Trash Polka". As the car headed towards "Ballocks", Colin thought to himself. "How perceptive of Jeremy to notice my forward vision". He adjusted the rear view mirror to such an angle as to permit only his grinning face within the confines of the rectangular tinted glass reflector. "Tonight, I'm a happy Colin", he said aloud.

*   *   *   *   *

Having left his Volvo in a parking bay that Robin felt offered a modicum of security, he walked along Ormskirk Close towards the Maynards' house. He noted a well-kept garden. It appeared as an oasis of civilised life amongst a desert of what he considered self-inflicted deprivation. The houses were basically sound but the effects of mis-use and abuse were constantly witnessed. Abandoned and defective cars and vans occupied land formerly given over to flower beds and lawns. The once green verges had not escaped as tyre marks dug deeply into the now well-formed grassless ruts, broken saplings stood testament to the council's failed attempt to rejuvenate and brighten up the estate.

An Alsatian snapped and snarled within the confines of it's owner's domain. Tethered by chain and ropes some twenty feet away from its makeshift kennel, it howled pitifully as Robin quickened his pace. He approached an opening between a privet hedge which had been allowed to expand in all directions. Two rotting posts marked the entrance. There was no gate. Robin advanced with trepidation. Ringing the bell, but receiving no response, he resorted to knocking loudly. Glancing towards the door frame he noticed the remains of a hand-written message, advising visitors that the bell was temporarily out of order. Robin turned, facing the sunlight. Of the eight houses he could see from the Maynards' slab concrete porch, six sported satellite dishes which clung uncomfortably to the textured magnolia-painted walls, all facing their power source, like spring flowers towards the sun.

Mrs. M. appeared at the side gate, beckoning the Club Chairman through to the kitchen. "Sorry about the tradesman's entrance but we're redecorating the hall". Robin had been told to expect that as an opening line. He'd also learned that it had been subject to redecoration for the past five years at least. Mrs. M. seemed nervous.

"Would you like to come through to the lounge?"

"Thank you", responded Robin, smiling in a way calculated to relieve tension and embarrassment.

They entered a plain room which featured a commendably neat mahogany coffee table, with smoked glass inlay. Also present was a patterned three-piece suite and a wide-screen television, which stood conspicuously in the corner of the room close to the Crittall windows. The Club's cleaning lady made the point of walking over to the gas fire, which although not conveying heat, was still switched on so as to show off the realistic log fire effect.

"Nice, very nice", commended Robin, as the cleaner patted its polished top. Her smile was stilted. Robin could see she felt awkward and seized the initiative.

"Mrs. Maynard, look, I don't want you to feel that any of this unfortunate incident reflects on you at all. I rang and asked to come round because I knew it would be difficult".

Mrs. Maynard sighed. "You can say that again".

"Mr. and Mrs. Buchanan don't blame you".

"Don't they?" She looked the Chairman straight in the eyes. "I would if I were them, I'm their mother. They've never been what you'd call easy. Right from day one they've been an 'andful, but I never, ever, thought they'd go and do anything like this - I'm so sorry, would you like to sit down?"

187

Robin acknowledged her request and took to one of the armchairs. She fidgeted. "I expect everyone at the Club knows?"

"Actually, no", said Robin with conviction. "The Buchanans were informed of the identities of Albert's attackers by one of the ladies who recognised them at the I.D. parade". The cleaner stared blankly as she picked her left thumb nail.

"We left it late, you see. Brian, my husband, never was that interested. I was thirty-six before Stephen came along, and once we had 'im I always felt he should have a mate to grow up with. Even Brian seemed pleased, but the novelty soon wore off. He never liked being woken from his sleep. D'you know, 'e never changed a nappy, never played with them, left it all to me. Once he was able to sign on the social because of 'is bad back, that was it. How was I supposed to stop two strapping lads like that from going out whenever they wanted to? They haven't taken any notice of me in years. Mind you, Brian's never noticed them in all their lives."

There was an uneasy silence before Robin continued. "I was going to add that Vi and Albert have only told Mick who, as you may or may not know, is a close family friend. I happened to be with Mick last night when he told me of the Buchanans' concern for you. I stress it is only Mick and I who know, although you don't need reminding that the local paper will name them when the next issue comes out". He gestured emptily with his hands.

"Today", said Mrs. M., "it comes out today. It'll be all round the estate by now. I'll be getting all the looks, the stares, the name calling. It's happened before", she said wearily, "so we won't be any different, will we?" She looked up. "D'you know where they are now, Stephen and Wayne?" Robin shook his head. "They're out breaking up cars for spares down the scrap yard, they couldn't give a cuss, and where's their father? Placing a bet at the bookies. Mind, they'll all expect their teas on the table as if nothing's happened". She paused, and then asked softly, "Do I still have a job - or what?"

"As far as I'm concerned you do, and that goes for the rest of the Committee. **You're** not on trial".

"Honestly, Mr. Harmsworth, as soon as I found out they were responsible I wanted to ring Albert and Vi and say sorry. No, that's not quite true, not if I'm honest with myself. I know it's an awful thing to say, but I never wanted to see either of them again - you know, face them. Funny, isn't it, I'd never really known Albert, 'cos our paths didn't

188

cross that often, but since his accident I've got to know them quite well. You know, going round for a chat with Vi". Mrs. Maynard sat upright, took a deep breath and placed her outstretched palms on her knees. "Friends, I actually thought I'd made friends ....."

Robin listened until he felt she'd got some, if not all of it out of her system. "If I were you, I'd ring them - and don't worry about your job. Anyway, I'd better be going".

Mrs. Maynard blew her nose, nodded and showed Robin out through the side gate. Several times Mrs. M. dialled the Buchanan household, several times she replaced the handset. Her sense of guilt finally overcame embarrassment and she listened intently as the dialling tone gave way to the clicking sound, which in turn changed to the all too familiar ring-ring. Her hands were sweating, she felt sick.

"Hello", said a male voice, "Hello".

"Albert?"

"Who's that?" he said, neither confirming nor denying identity.

"It's Joyce Maynard". There was a brief pause.

"Oh, hello", Albert said slowly, appearing suspicious, although not intentionally so.

"Look, I feel awful about - you know. I had no idea - sorry, I'm not very good at ....." She broke down.

Albert heard her sobbing. He placed his free hand over the mouthpiece and spoke to Vi, who was sitting nearby. "It's Joyce Maynard". Vi instinctively put her hand to her mouth.

Mrs. Maynard continued, having composed herself. "Look, I'd like to come round and see you both, I'd like to talk. Frankly, I feel so bloody ashamed".

"There's no need, we don't hold you responsible, Joyce".

"Maybe, but they're my children, or were. I bore them, I ....."

She did not, could not continue. The receiver was replaced and although Albert was given no indication of an arrival time, he knew it would be later that day. Within an hour Mrs. Maynard knocked on the door. She'd walked the fifteen minute journey from her estate. All three made small talk, somewhat stilted, before Albert took a deep breath, expanded his chest and grasped the nettle.

"This isn't getting us anywhere. It happened, I'm alive and I've got a lot to live for". Vi looked down. She knew he was saying it for her. "You're the same Joyce Maynard regardless, it doesn't change nothing, you're not to blame". Vi nodded agreement but remained silent.

"What about my job?"

"What about it?"

"Do I still have it or are you going to get Mr. Harmsworth to ask me to leave? - I'd understand".

"What good would that do? How many times do I have to say it, Joyce, what's done's done. We none of us can turn the clock back. What I think of that pair is unprintable". Albert hesitated, changed position slightly, then continued. "But they are your sons. We have a son of our own, so I know what the word 'disappointment' means, but flesh and blood is, well ....." He smiled faintly, Vi wrung her hands together, her eyes still cast down.

Mrs. Maynard looked at the slightly hunched female figure and then at Albert. After a brief lull in the conversation she began to speak concisely and without falter. "I told Mr. Harmsworth that for once in my life I'd found some really nice people to be friends with". She looked directly at Albert. "We knew each other, didn't we, but only when we happened to be down at the Club at the same time. Been like that for years".

Albert nodded. "But ....."

Mrs. M. continued. "Whatever you say now, however much you say it's not my fault, I still feel that you'll always look on me as their mother. I don't blame you, I'd feel the same". With that, Mrs. Maynard stood up, straightened her jacket. "Thanks for seeing me, I'll probably see you at work, Albert. I'm sorry I ....." Her strength was sapping. She looked around the room, as if literally searching for words.

Albert's tone was comforting. "I know, love". He led the way towards the front door.

"Goodbye", called out Vi, but the cleaner had already gone.

*　*　*　*　*

An extraordinary Committee meeting was called for the following week. All attended and listened intently to the various proposals announced by the Chairman. Each recommendation was unerringly supported by Colin. Robin expressed his concern regarding the Club's long-term future and that in his opinion, they should proceed with the project which, according to Mr. LeGrand, would have to be implemented whilst the brewery were "hot", as he put it. Mick stayed silent throughout Robin's overtures, remaining slumped in his usual position, ash falling

190

onto the floor tiles.

There then followed a lengthy debate, during which Mick pulled himself close to the table and laid out his reservations. One by one other members gave their views. Reg was of the opinion that his maintenance programme could receive a substantial financial boost if the profits from the regular meetings that Jeremy almost guaranteed were channelled into the upkeep of the Club, as indicated. Therefore, Reg was in favour.

Doreen was as impressed with the sharp suits and smooth talk as Colin and had readily been won over. In her case, the fact that Jeremy had mentioned to Doreen "in confidence" that he felt her managerial skills were wasted on trips, her self-esteem had been boosted to even greater heights. Derek, true to form, adopted Doreen's view. "Great, good idea, super" was the extent of his comment, combined naturally with a vigorous rubbing of hands as if to emphasise his commitment.

Greg considered that whilst he found the financial offer and the redecorating package attractive, he certainly had doubts about the long term implications. A vote was taken, the result being 5-2 in favour of the proposals.

"So", Mick said, as he lit up another cigarette, "Greedy brewery bastards won, proper people lost".

"Good that", Derek remarked, grinning broadly, "I thought Mick was going to say 1-nil. Of course, you never know how somebody's spelling 'one' or 'won' when it's being said to you ....."

His conversation tailed off but he continued to shake his head in acknowledgement of the Treasurer's turn of phrase.

"What happens now? asked Colin. The Chairman was thoughtful.

"Well, I suggest that you, Colin, type up the notes outlining the proposals and give them to all members attending Wednesday evening. Those members who aren't here can have them posted. Oh, and don't forget country members, past presidents, etc. We then meet Jeremy next Monday, when he's bringing along the brewery's architect chappie to explain the detailed plans. If everybody ....." Mick looked up and frowned. "..... if the majority of members are in favour when these plans are unveiled, we'll go ahead". Robin sat back satisfied that the course he was steering was the correct one. Colin raised an index finger.

"Aaah, so those not present on Wednesday will then have a chance to pop along for the vote the following week. I see, good, uhm".

Mick shook his head from side to side. "So what we're actually saying is that those who spend bugger-all time here, and even less money, will be invited to have just as big a say as those who come week-in, week-out. Well, that could swing the decision in favour of LeGrand's grand slam".

"Good one, that", Derek said, giving the thumbs up. "Mick's got a point".

Robin looked concerned. "Mick, it could easily go the other way". The Treasurer was not impressed.

Come Wednesday, Colin, Derek and Doreen combined forces to ensure that all members received a copy of the proposal on arrival. It was very much the centre of conversation, being enthusiastically supported by certain sections of those present. Robin, however, gauged the reaction to be closer than he'd anticipated, or hoped. The live steam crew, "Pennytown" and the check-jacket brigade formed a previously unthinkable alliance, supporting Mick's suspicions. They, like the Treasurer, failed to see the long-term advantages of what seemed to be change for change's sake and a loss of control, not to mention the refurbishment of a hall that had only recently been redecorated.

Colin was as surprised as the Chairman and echoed Robin's comments that those against showed a lack of foresight.

The following Monday was not a pleasant day, as far as Mick was concerned. He, Colin and Robin, had made themselves available, for the official detailed presentation. They were all waiting at the Club when Jeremy LeGrand appeared, as agreed, dead on 9.30 a.m.

"Hi", said the executive, with a fixed grin. "Let me introduce Roy, Greater London Brewery's chief architect, and Nigel, administrative co-ordinating executive - designate. Isn't that right, Oscar?" Jeremy laughed. Nigel flexed his facial muscles, the end result could never be described as a smile.

Two heavy ash trays held down the architect's drawings. He pointed eagerly to the various proposed alterations. They were fairly drastic. Out would go the traditional oak bar top with carved front panelling and brass foot rail. In its place would be an easy-to-clean, hygienic-to-use work top, capable of accepting boiling pans without cracking or burning - a fact that fell on deaf ears as far as the Treasurer was concerned. Concealed lighting with dimmers, plus replacement disco spotlights, with associated strobe lighting, were an integral feature of the bar surround, as Roy termed it.

All the way through the examination of the plans Jeremy stood practising his golf swing. Colin noticed his mentor looking at the wall only some four feet away, standing as if he had just followed through. Colin sensed that Jeremy's view was different from his own. "Can you see the ball?" he asked.

"Sure". Jeremy held his position. "It's just to the right of that copse, and still flying".

Colin was impressed. "Do you ever get a hole in one?" He craned his neck in an effort to see the picture as painted.

"Every time, Oscar", came the smooth and measured reply. "Every time".

The spell was broken. Mick demanded loudly, "What's this?"

"Oh, that, that's the name of the bar - the Railway Inn".

"Not exactly original, is it? Tacky, yes, but ...... and what about this?" Mick poked his finger impatiently at yet another feature.

"That's the Greater London Brewery logo".

"But it's bloody everywhere". Mick pointed to even more sections of the drawing. "You never said anything about logos, it'll probably only be fashionable for the next six months and then either Jeremy or one of his cohorts will suggest a change of image, just like a premier league football strip. Am I wrong?"

"But yes", came the reply. Roy was taken aback. "Mr. Clayton, we've only just adopted the softer image, you know, family values, etc. That's why we're keen to support an organisation such as yours".

Still swinging his imaginary golf club Jeremy added, "Exactly, Oscar".

"Anyway", said Robin, in an effort to defuse the situation, "it's a small price to pay. We've discussed it over and over again. What with all these new EC health and safety regulations we're going to have to make changes, and fast".

"Health and safety rip-offs", Mick replied tersely.

Roy looked around before focusing his attention on Mick, who now stood apart from his colleagues. "D'you not like the clean lines, the sophisticated design embracing all that's new in the world of modern thinking? Are you not excited by the ambience we're creating?" The architect gestured theatrically with his hands. "In a word, we're offering you pizzazz".

"That's eight, if you split we're into we are", replied Mick sneeringly.

"I think Roy meant 'pizzazz' as the one word", Colin offered tentatively.

"Shut up, Colin". Mick was clearly irritated. He turned, visibly snubbing the architect and the brewery's Administrative Co-ordinating Executive - Designate, and faced Robin. "You got us into this with his help". He pointed dismissively at Colin. "I sincerely hope I'm wrong and that this is what the membership want, but just remember, we fought hard to get that bar top out of St. Pancras Station buffet in the sixties, we struggled to get the bloody thing back and now you, who is supposed to be upholding **real** traditional values, are prepared to see it go. I just hope you and your plastic facade will both be very happy together. As far as I'm concerned, and if it's all right with Jeremy Oscar and Roy Oscar, should the vote go against us, I'll remove the bar and fittings and make sure it's given a good home elsewhere". Mick's tone had become more brusque with every sentence. Having given vent he stormed out of the building without another word. The hall was momentarily silent. Colin looked up at Jeremy.

"So, how often do you play?"

*   *   *   *   *

"Can you call Kate", Mick's secretary asked, on his arrival back at the office. Mick listened as his wife informed him that Vi had been taken to hospital at 8 a.m. that morning. It transpired that she had felt unwell during Sunday but had said nothing. Albert became concerned with the pain she was obviously experiencing and called the doctor. After some questions and the obligatory prodding and poking, an ambulance was summoned.

Mick arrived at the hospital with Kate and Albert some time after 7 p.m. Vi seemed more relaxed, according to her husband, than she had appeared earlier in the day. She was, however, still in considerable pain. A consultant, whom Albert and Mick had seen previously, offered little comfort. Other factors were to be taken into consideration regarding Vi's health; her life could not be prolonged; other organs were now beginning to fail. The consultant pointed out that there would be days when she would feel better than others, but the general trend would be one of not so gradual decline.

"D'you think that's it, Mick?" Albert asked as they drove back to the Buchanans' home.

Mick stole a glance towards his wife in the rear view mirror as he replied. "What do you mean?"

"Well, d'you reckon she'll come out again?"

"Look, I'm sure Vi's getting the best care and attention she could get anywhere".

"Mick, you're not answering me question".

"I wouldn't insult you by lying, Albert, we've both heard the consultant's opinion. We know what's going to happen, we ......"
Mick hesitated. " .....Albert, this isn't easy ....."

Mick indicated, turning into the Buchanan's side road. He involuntarily shrugged his shoulders. "If - if anything happens, she's got round the clock care and they can cope a lot better and a lot easier with her there under observation. I know it's asking a lot, you've just got to try not to worry". He half smiled as the car pulled into the kerb.

Kate leaned forward from the rear seat and placed her hands on Albert's shoulders. "She's not in any immediate danger, so don't feel guilty about coming home for a few hours".

Albert mumbled something but neither of the Claytons heard. It didn't seem appropriate to ask him to repeat it. They all sat in silence for a few seconds before the barman was seen back into his house.

*   *   *   *   *

195

CHAPTER SEVEN

Early on Wednesday evening Colin posted the architect's proposed plans on the notice board. This particular Club night would prove to be the litmus test. There had to be a unanimous decision in favour of the proposals. To Mick, the for's and against's seemed biased in favour of the brewery's scheme. There was too much emphasis on health and safety and the fear of Brussels.

Robin and Colin spent some two hours explaining, expanding upon and generally enthusing about the proposed alterations, which could all be installed and made ready during August, which was the Club's quietest month. No Committee meetings took place and traditionally the Wednesday evening attendance was at its lightest. Mick and Greg talked to as many members as possible, voicing their reasons for not supporting the brewery scheme, and also their suspicions of those concerned.

"Have you noticed how many new faces there are here tonight, Greg? Faces that are unseen month after month. They're only here because of the proposals, creaming themselves because their opinion's been sought. The only thing I'd ask them to do is leave". Greg concurred with Mick's observations.

When all the arguments had been exhausted and the summing up completed, voting slips were handed out by Colin and Doreen. Albert was behind the bar at this time. It was a particularly busy evening for him. Derek had offered to help 'person' the bar, as he put it. Although a non-voter, Albert expressed his concern and made known his views to all those he served. Some twenty five minutes had elapsed before Robin stood up. A pin could be heard dropping. He cleared his throat and looked around the hall.

"The vote for the proposed sponsorship and associated developments in conjunction with Greater London Breweries plc is as follows: those in favour - 48, those against - 42. There was one spoiled paper". There was more a sense of loss from the traditionalists than there was elation from those victorious.

"Even my comment about Jeremy the Saviour not being here didn't swing it", said Mick dejectedly. Pete and Greg said nothing. "I can't believe so many people fell for it". Mick looked around. "There's at least fifteen so-called members here tonight who you don't see from one year to the next, but they have the same rights as you and me - bastards!"

Mick left early that night. Besides arranging a time when work would commence on the new bar so that the oak example could be extracted without damage, little was seen of the Club's Treasurer over the next few weeks. He and Kate were more than a little tied up with the Buchanans. Vi was by now continually in discomfort, unable to sleep properly and requiring constant attention. Albert could no longer provide the care she needed and having been discharged and subsequently readmitted, it was agreed that she should spend some time in the local hospice.

Albert made little of his non-appearances on Club nights to the majority of members, most of whom were aware that Mrs. Buchanan was 'unwell', but that was the extent of it. Albert had also asked for temporary leave from the Hippodrome, where a reluctant manager agreed to find impermanent cover.

In contrast, Robin and Colin spent a considerable amount of time being 'involved' in the improvements, as both men perceived the alterations to be. Jeremy LeGrand tended to make appointments to see Colin on a more regular basis, continually praising his dedication and attention to detail. The clerical assistant felt his status increased almost as much as his confidence. He no longer felt the need to discuss detailed decisions, as he saw them, with Robin. After all, he was the Clubroom Manager **and** Secretary. His accumulated flexi-time was rapidly consumed within the month of August, towards the end of which the new bar and cold shelf were in position and functioning. Concealed lighting had been installed, as had the replacement disco spotlights and other specialised electrical gadgetry. The main hall walls were repainted in the brewery house colours, with logos replacing the vintage carriage mirrors and maps. These were consigned to the storeroom.

Patio furniture with umbrellas - also sporting the GLB logo - graced the tiled floor, which although not replaced, had been subjected to the attentions of an industrial cleaner and coated with an easy-to-clean wax finish. However, it tended to take on the appearance of a stained ice-rink.

197

Curtains, once again in house colours with logo, completed the internal renovations, save for the bar sign shaped like a curved Great Western Railway nameplate, which spanned the centre of the flush finished canopy.

On the penultimate Wednesday before the York weekend there appeared to be a marked contrast in the reaction of the two sides. There were several members genuinely pleased with the outcome, more however were dismayed by the cold and clinical result that had replaced the former, friendly railway orientated surroundings.

The "Pennytown" group, whose turn it was that week, arrived on the previous Sunday in an attempt to erect their layout as usual, only to be told by persons unknown that the hall had been hired for a conference that day. Members were made to feel distinctly unwelcome. The following evening was also booked, resulting in the proprietary layout only having two evenings on which to operate their locomotives and rolling stock.

Complaints were made to Robin, who in turn directed them to Colin who, as Clubroom Manager, entered all bookings into sheets, copies of which were pinned upon the notice board. Sadly, all of August's and September's were missing - as was Colin. A number of people, Robin included, remembered seeing him around opening time but by 8 p.m. at the latest, all sightings had ceased.

Mick made much of the fact that with the exception of one lone soul, all those distant, or inactive members who attended and voted for the alterations, were now conspicuous by their absence. Derek and Doreen took advantage of the new style patio furniture, ousting Cedric and Harold from where they were discussing the various theories surrounding the "Immaculate Conception", the Outings Secretary and her assistant commandeered their now vacant table and chairs. Installed by the hall doors they wrapped a banner around the umbrella's fringe. It read, "SRC Tours, in association with GLB PLC", their respective logos placed either side of the wording, in the manner of bookends.

Last minute instructions were given to those present who would be travelling to York a week Saturday.

"Is this it?" Mick asked of Robin, on looking around the hall. "Have we finished converting the SRC into the Los Crapos night spot?"

"Colin did mention the odd plant would be appearing, to complement the surroundings ....."

Mick butted in. "Christ, you're at it now! Complement the

surroundings?" He tutted.

Robin continued, ignoring the interruptions. "And a sign, I believe, is being fixed over the doorway". Mick tutted again. Robin shrugged his shoulders and walked away.

The weekly raffle was of modest proportions, befitting the low turnout. One or two members voiced their opinions about the alterations at Chairman's Announcement Time, but Robin explained, and not to everyone's satisfaction, that there would always be the familiarity factor with every new look. The greatest rumblings came from the recently appointed relief barman who, having just become accustomed to the old bar, found himself having to adjust to a whole new way of life. The most complex item appeared to be the vandal-proof, burglar-proof computerised till, which required at least a degree (with honours) to understand the instructions, let alone its operation.

Each round took twice as long to serve. Robin once again played down the situation, stating that all new systems had their teething troubles. Most felt that the Chairman's back was against the wall on this issue as well.

Mick left the Club before 9.30 p.m., calling in on Albert. Vi's condition was relatively unchanged, due mainly to the hospice staff administering greater doses of pain relieving drugs. On his return home Mick rang Graham. The only reply came from an answerphone, which invited the caller to leave a message. Mick did not. He had only just replaced the receiver when it rang. Turning quickly on his heels, Mick answered sharply. "Yes".

"That was quick, you sitting on it?"

Mick recognised Greg's voice. "No, walking away from it, but don't bother yourself".

"You left early, I was just wondering if everything was all right?"

Greg was aware of Mick sighing.

"Nothing that a pole up a backside wouldn't cure. Seriously, I've got to get up early - Bromsgrove by 10 o'clock, and anyway, I wasn't so taken by the surroundings - sorry, ambience - that I felt like staying to the bitter end. Talking of bitter, what is that liquid we're dispensing now? The proverbial gnat's piss would be preferable!"

Greg laughed. "Colin said last week that GLB were providing us with real ale, but that's all we've got so far".

"Bastards"

"Anyway, the other reason I called was to find out whether you'd be there next Wednesday".

"No, I'm away in Dorset from Tuesday to Thursday, I'll be back in the office Friday for an hour or so, before Kate and I leave for Goole".

"That's nice".

"You don't mean that, do you?"

"No - you coming to the exhibition while you're up there?"

"Yeah, be over some time on Saturday morning. My drive into York was going to be an enjoyable one, dreaming of steam, but now Kate and her mum are coming as well, so I'll be dropping them off in town and making my way over".

"Bringing Kate's dad?"

"No, he wouldn't leave his beloved garden for the real thing, let alone a toy, as he sees it!"

Greg laughed. "Right, well we're all set, we're loading the van on Thursday".

"I can see it's going to be a riveting journey. Imagine being subjected to Derek, Colin and Harold prattling on for hours. It's the van I feel sorry for! Bet you're pleased you're going up with Pete?"

"Absolutely, providing he doesn't carry on giving me details of his latest conquests, or even worse, how he managed to sell a Mercedes to someone who came in looking for a Metro". Both men laughed and signed off.

*   *   *   *   *

Considerably weakened, Vi Buchanan remained aware of her surroundings and those around her. Nobby continued to help out running the Club's barman to the hospice during the day. Once there Albert would stay with his wife, even while she slept, going home during the evening with Mick or Robin.

The ward no longer held any surprises for Albert. The mere fact that his wife was entering a hospice initially filled him with foreboding and a deep sense of guilt. The soft pastel colours, the fresh flowers, the dependable smile and the care had all but eliminated those fears. It comforted him to realise that not every patient was waiting for God.

On the last Saturday in August Vi lay in bed, Albert held her hands, stroking them gently as he talked about their garden, South London as it used to be, friends they knew from way back. Neither mentioned that most of them were no longer alive. Vi smiled, seemingly content to discuss things that shouldn't have seemed important. Mick and Kate sat on the opposite side of the bed facing Albert. Listening to their conversation Mick thought that perhaps these were the important things. After all, the Buchanans whole life embraced the ordinary.

Vi looked across at Kate, grimaced slightly as she adjusted her position and in a low voice said, "If you can, make sure that husband of mine doesn't go buying butter, does 'im no good at all. Make sure 'e buys that poly-whatsit stuff - Flora, or one like it".

Doors opened, footsteps were heard. Vi, answering a question put to her by Kate, suddenly cut off. Her jaw dropped. The startled look on Vi's face encouraged the others to turn their heads. Standing at the foot of the bed were Graham and Jamie. Mick glanced the slightest of smiles towards Kate. Vi slowly raised her arms, her nightdress sleeves falling back towards her elbows, revealing painfully thin arms. She beamed broadly. Albert stood, looking somewhat stunned. Their son seemed shy about venturing any closer; his right hand rested on Jamie's shoulder.

"Hello, son", said Albert, extending his hand.

Graham hesitated momentarily. "Mum, Dad", he said quietly. Pulling Jamie closer to him he shook his father's hand. Then, as if on the command of an unseen signal, both men took one step forward and held each other. Albert's bony hands almost dug into his son's back. Releasing his grip slowly Albert moved back beckoning Graham, who mumbled something incoherently before sitting beside his mother. Her arms, which had remained outstretched in anticipation, trembled visibly as she wrapped them around him.

Albert, seated once more, held his grandson's hand as Jamie unfolded a story concerning an injured koala bear. Mick smiled at the innocence of it all. Jamie's eyes grew larger and his voice louder before he completed his tale. Coaxed from his grandfather's side he edged close to his 'nan', as he referred to her when living in England. Vi was mesmerised. She kept blinking, looking at son and grandson in turn, as if to check that it wasn't a dream. The weak smile on her face held constant, her eyes never fully dry.

Kate nudged Mick who stood, checked his watch and said, "Time we were going". Graham broke off from his conversation. "Sorry, I haven't said hello properly". Mick nodded. Hands were shaken across the bed. Kate could tell Vi was pleased with the last gesture - it was more than symbolic. Vi winked, clutching Kate's hand before Kate kissed her lightly on the cheek.

It was shortly after 7 p.m. that Graham phoned Mick to ask if they could meet for a quick drink later that evening - just the two of them.

Shortly after 9 p.m. Mick strode across the bar holding two pints of Bass. They sat at a table away from the general throng. "Jamie's helping dad in the kitchen", Graham said during the small talk that followed his initial greeting. The stilted conversation appeared to be leading nowhere until Graham said, "Look, Mick, I know we were never the greatest of friends, and I'm not unaware that it was mainly my fault, all my fault probably, but I've always appreciated what you've done for mum and dad. Selfish, of course, as it meant I could get on with doing my own thing - you know, cosseting Camilla". He laughed nervously. "..... without having to worry about them".

Mick started to reply but was stopped at Graham's insistence. "Sorry, Mick, but I must finish. May not get the chance again". There was an embarrassing, albeit brief, silence. "Camilla and I have split up".

"Oh, is that why ....."

"I couldn't say anything over the phone, either to you or mum and dad. I've lost nearly everything. It's been pretty nasty and unpleasant, really. All those years, all those bloody wasted years".

Mick sensed Graham becoming slightly emotional. "You've got Jamie". There was another silence, somewhat longer.

"Ah, yes, Jamie. I could have lost him too, you know, Mick. I could tell from the eyes, poor kid. He never knew how I was going to be - what mood I'd be in, but I've come through it".

Mick pursed his lips before responding. "So where does all this leave Jamie - between you and Camilla?"

"One of the easier passages, that. There was no custody struggle. Jamie was always an inconvenience to her so it was by mutual agreement, much to the chagrin of the lawyers who thought they were going to make a packet out of our parting, but still ....."

Graham sipped from his glass, the liquid went down slowly. Mick's eyes never left his companion's. Graham continued. "Still, all water under the bridge, eh".

"Leaves you both free to get on with your lives".

"We both were before the divorce proceedings. Camilla is now living with your all-Australian macho-man, Neville - or Nev, as he prefers to be called - and I'm ....." his voice became shaky, "There's something else you should know - someone else you should know. Her name's Corinne. She was waiting in the reception area when I brought Jamie into the ward".

Mick looked surprised. "Do mum and dad know?"

"Yes, I introduced her shortly after you left. To be honest, I didn't know what kind of reception I'd get, so I thought it best to take Jamie in with me". He smiled. "Coward, aren't I? However, I think they both like her". He pointed to Mick's empty glass.

"Half, I'm driving".

Graham asserted himself and walked to the bar, taking the empty glasses with him. Mick spread himself and lit up another cigarette. For all the tension, he thought, in a strangely ironic way, Graham seemed more relaxed than for many years. He'd filled out in the face, his features were no longer so sharp. Young Jamie had shot up. That mop of blonde hair would hopefully be the only feature inherited from his mother. Mick smiled openly at his deliberation.

"I'll have to get used to warm beer again", said Graham, as he placed the glasses on the table.

"Thought you'd be a confirmed amber nectar man by now".

Graham looked serious once more. "Not going back, actually. Well, only to clear things up".

As they sipped their beers Graham expanded on his plans. A contact here in England had offered him a job at their head office in London and Corinne, a nurse, had applied to a teaching hospital. They would, in due course, be looking for a house 'somewhere in the area'.

"Mum and dad'll be pleased, no doubt".

"Yes, yes, they are. Mick, the other thing I have to say is that I didn't mean it on the phone when I said you were only helping out for the inheritance". Graham looked down at the table and fiddled with his glass, before looking back at Mick. "Jealousy is a dreadful thing. All my life I've felt as though I've been in your shadow". Mick was genuinely taken aback.

"Me, I never had parents who cared at all. You know that, not one bloody iota. That's the strange part of this, isn't it. I was always jealous of you".

"I can see that". Graham seemed sidetracked by his own thoughts. "I can see that", he repeated for no reason, his eyes staring blankly.

"Well, are we going to meet Corinne?"

"Of course, would you and Kate come over for an evening - say one day next week?"

"We'd love to. Where? Your parents?"

"Yes, I'll ring you with a date and time. Okay?"

"Fine, look forward to it - out of interest, where are you staying? At the bungalow?"

"No, didn't think that was prudent, Corinne and I sharing the same bed".

"See what you mean, they might not have taken to that". Quickly Mick added, "that's a change for you".

"What is?"

"Thinking of others, I'm warming to this Corinne already".

Graham grinned and explained that the three of them were staying less than a mile away in a small guest house, a hire car having been provided by his future employers. Shaking hands they parted on terms Mick could never have foreseen only weeks previously.

*   *   *   *   *

Pete and Greg strolled across the car park. The sun was still warm, birds were chattering, busying themselves in the bushes that surrounded sections of the fencing. The unexpectedly loud revving of a car engine caused Pete to walk smartly into the Club rooms. Harold's Austin Princess entered the car park in a frenzy of noise, followed by a cloud of polluted air, which hung lazily above the ground for several minutes. Pete Balfour faffed around in the library but was captured by Harold some time after 8 p.m. "I'll ring him now" said Pete as he walked outside with Harold in hot pursuit. "The reception's better out here". Dialling Baz's number and making a point of uttering every digit, he turned slightly away from Harold, then indicating connection, commenced a diatribe of abuse, designed to make even the thickest of skins wilt. After completing the one-sided conversation, Pete palmed down the aerial with gusto. "That's told him, he'll be over Saturday morning while we're playing trains in York".

Harold was concerned. "I didn't want him getting into any trouble".

"'E needed telling". Pete pointed menacingly. "The one thing I can't stand is people being let down".

He slapped Harold on the back and walked into the hall. Harold seemed impressed with Pete's handling of the situation and promptly bought him a drink. Pete's general air of bon-homie lasted only a short time. There was, as yet, no draught bitter available.

"The keg's very good - apparently", offered Colin apologetically. He was asked various questions relating to running times for the Club's layout. His replies were evasive, to say the least. Colin defended his corner by stating that pressure of work had caused him to be behind with the following month's hiring schedule, but that all would be in place by the time the York weekend was over.

Resigned rumblings echoed around the patio furniture. Doreen took to drinking variously coloured concoctions out of wide-brimmed Babycham style glasses, complete with fruits, olives and the mandatory parasol.

At Chairman's Announcement Time Doreen dutifully held aloft the now restored painting. Reg immediately found a suitable space where it could remain on display until such time as it was auctioned. The suggested spot was curiously considered unsuitable by the Clubroom Manager and Secretary. In fact, every alternative that Reg offered was found to be inadvisable, undesirable or inappropriate and all for no sound reason.

It became clear to many that Colin would rather have not been at the Club at all. There was a brief glimpse of his old self when he rang the bar bell and called 'Order' so that any last minute poems could be entered for the regional competition.

"The thirtieth's gone", shouted someone close by.

"I know", replied Colin, "but due to the lack of entries being submitted on time, I managed to secure a stay of execution for another seven days". He looked around hoping for a positive response from somewhere in the hall. There was none. "Oh, well, right, in that case we'll be sending off a single entry on behalf of the SRC".

"Still going t'send it en masse?" shouted Lanky, emphasising the 'en'. Colin shuffled uncomfortably from sole to sole.

"Well, the main thing is that we're represented".

"By who?" enquired Reg.

"Me, actually".

"Come on, my little Clipboard, let's hear it", said Pete coarsely.

"Mmmm, I don't think that will be very necessary or required". He squirmed visibly.

Chants of "We all want to hear it" gathered momentum around the hall. Colin's hands went up. The raucous outcry subsided. "If you really insist", said Colin suddenly and markedly more poised, "it's only a little thing ......"

"We know that, but what about the poem", shouted Pete, who nearly fell over laughing at his own joke.

"It's just a token, it won't win", said Colin, extracting a folded sheet from the file he carried under his right arm. He loosened his tie, coughed anxiously and commenced:

"How many times I've ridden through
that ageing edifice
that once was live to the smell of steam.
Power, toil and grace.

With Paddington now left behind
Slough and Reading passed
The countryside would soon stretch out,
with fields of corn at last.

Pangbourne, Goring and Streatley too,
standing proudly on the Thames.
They think they are the gateway,
but they only can pretend.

For the rails that take us to the west
must pass a station first,
that ageing edifice so dear
- our very own Tilehurst."

"Boom, boom", shouted a large group in unison, who then commenced a round of nudging and pushing, whilst laughing boisterously. The group included all of "Pennytown"'s members. As Colin headed towards the bar Greg caught up with him. "You're right, it won't win. In fact, you've brought a whole new meaning to the word 'crap', haven't you?"

"Ah", mumbled Colin as he looked at his watch. The poem was neatly refolded and placed in the file. "Got to dash - an appointment, you see".

Greg didn't get a chance to respond. Colin had scurried out of the door and into the car park, starting his car in what for him was double-quick time. Head close to the steering wheel he drove with pace out into the lane, not indicating as he turned, a sure sign that all was not well.

*   *   *   *   *

Mick arrived back from his sojourn to Dorset at 7.30 p.m. to discover that Vi Buchanan had passed away some four hours previous. She went to sleep with her family by her side. She never awoke. The Claytons were invited round that evening, Graham insisting that they came, despite Kate's reservations about "disturbing" them. Mick momentarily thought twice about their going to Goole the following day, but realised that not only would it have been unfair on Kate and her parents, but that now, Albert **did** have his family around him.

It wasn't a pleasant journey but one Mick knew he would have to make sooner rather than later. Albert was taking it well. Kate knew that Graham's homecoming had softened the blow beyond all expectations. Corinne appeared to be a very caring person and it was obvious during their brief visit that Jamie enjoyed her company. Nobby dropped in to pay his respects; he stayed only briefly. On seeing him to the door Albert asked of his neighbour, "Nobby, I've been meaning to ask you, why did you think I'd want to read a magazine on bee keeping?" Nobby looked vacant. Albert walked over to the magazine rack and extracted the said periodical. "There, that's what you bought me when I was laid up". Nobby looked at the title, then at the cover. Slowly his eyes refocused on the title. "I remember now, I found it in the optician's waiting room, when I went to get my eyes tested". He chuckled. "Thought it said 'Beer Keeping Weekly'. Sorry!"

Little was said on the way home, but as Mick pulled on the handbrake and turned off the ignition, he faced Kate. "Well, everyone got their wish. It's just that for Vi, it was her last".

*   *   *   *   *

It was a bright, sunny morning. Pete Balfour shut the boot of his car and swaggered back into the airy confines of "Ballocks". Rita was fussing around, making sure her husband had everything packed for the trip to York. Whistling tunelessly Pete scanned the loft for any remaining stock he considered worthy of public viewing. He occasionally sold models that had either been built because of the challenge the kit or design afforded, or because the locomotive had been superseded by a more

207

detailed example. This weekend was no exception. Downstairs once more he carried his suitcase out to the car. Rita watched him from the doorway. Dressed in a maroon tracksuit and gold high-heeled shoes her hair had been tied back, the crimped tresses seemingly breaking free from the constraining band that secured them, allowing it to cascade like a frozen waterfall.

"Have a nice time, love", she said, as Pete sorted out boxes on the rear seat. "Hope you sell them all".

"Probably make more out of this lot than selling a decent motor".

"Decent? When was that?"

"Cheeky cow", replied Pete, before winking in her direction.

The phone rang. Rita ran back into the kitchen. Pete waited momentarily to see if it was for him. "Keys", he thought, "where are the keys?"

Turning quickly he strode into the hall to find them sitting on the stand just inside the doorway. It was obvious the call was not for him. "Is he? Oh, oh, oh I know. Really?" was all he could hear. Rita was engrossed in her conversation. He waved just as she exclaimed loudly, "Christ Almighty, he didn't, did he?" Here, he thought, were the sounds of a woman wallowing in gossip.

"I'm going", Pete shouted, before blowing her a kiss.

Rita waved good-bye as Pete launched himself out of the front door. By the time she'd surfaced her husband was well on his way to Greg's house.

"So, how are you?" Sally asked on Pete's arrival, noted by the twin horn on his BMW.

"All the better for seeing you, darlin'", replied the car salesman in his usual disarming way.

"Flattery will get you everywhere", quipped Sally, who instantaneously snapped her fingers mockingly, before adding, "Sorry, I meant it will get you a cup of tea and a biscuit!"

"I'll settle for that, then". Pete rubbed his hands together and bellowed a laugh.

Greg appeared. Close by the door were several boxes of stock, together with an overnight bag.

"Shouldn't be without a bit of variety", commented Pete, as he filled the remaining areas of the back seat and boot. Greg looked around to make sure Sally wasn't in ear shot. "Your case is large enough for two, we're not picking up anyone on the way, are we?"

Pete grinned. "No, the way Reet's been the last couple of months, well, she's really done me proud - drink ready when I gets 'ome, steak done as I like it - d'you know, she 'ad me feeling quite guilty at times, so guilty in fact that I've been leaving the slapper early!"

Shutting the boot once more he turned to Greg. "Anyway, it does them good to be left wanting more".

Greg shook his head. "To quote Mick - 'bastard'".

Pete smiled. "Well, I can't give up a way of life overnight, can I? It takes willpower. But I'm cutting down!"

"On what?"

Pete was thoughtful as they walked back into the house. "Well, I've given up the sheep!"

Greg raised his eyebrows. Pete nudged him in the ribs. He laughed bawdily. As they sat drinking the tea which Sally had brewed upon Pete's arrival, her attention was drawn to the dining room where, on the table, lay a number of boxes all of the same length. "Are they to go, as well?"

Greg moved slightly to gain a better view. "Bloody hell, yes, they've got to be packed. They're all for sale".

"You selling them?"

"Well, now we've settled on a particular period and location on which to base our layout these locos can't run on it".

"Why, are they a different size?"

"No, it's just that ..... Oh, it doesn't matter. Drink up".

Packed and ready they departed once Sally had kissed her husband goodbye. "Don't I get one?" asked Pete, looking doleful. Sally tutted. "You never know what I'll catch!" Pete feigned hurt.

"Oh, for God's sake, go away and play with your trains but don't honk that horn again - dad's still asleep". Sally waved until they were out of sight.

They stopped at a service station for brunch some time after 11.30 a.m. "I assume they got away all right this morning", mused Greg.

"Yeah, course. Mind, stacking the layout into the van last night helped". Greg acknowledged Pete's reply, as he added sugar to his tea. Stirring gently he said, "I'm surprised Harold's missus lets him out for a whole weekend, but then again, I did hear that she's told him to drink half a pint of milk before touching anything alcoholic. Apparently he doesn't drink much at home".

"Or at the Club. Tight git! Christ, how the other 'arf live, I .....

209

Bloody hell! I should have told Baz to go round to Harold's tomorrow morning. I promised faithfully".

"What, as faithfully as you promised Rita?"

"Cruel, ever so cruel - yes", Pete replied, mimicking Frankie Howard's delivery of a line.

As Greg cut the fat off a slice of extremely streaky bacon, Pete extracted his mobile phone from a waist pouch, and dialled. Greg dipped his head in embarrassment, as the whole restaurant was treated to one side of a conversation in which Pete became embroiled in other issues, namely a customer's allegation that the invoice price was two hundred pounds in excess of the original marked-up figure. He also had to calm down a dissatisfied punter, as Pete referred to him, who had returned for the third time, only to find the car lot's owner unavailable once more.

"Is Baz in charge while your away?"

"Yeah, 'e sort of takes care of things. 'Ang about, I only forgot to mention 'Arold's car again. Oh well, 'e can't be in two places at once, can 'e? I'll tell Harold that Baz went over but there was no reply. Get 'im round next week now".

"Harold's supposed to believe that, is he?" asked Greg doubtfully.

"'E 'as so far". Greg tutted and smiled, then grimaced as he witnessed Pete scoop up the juices on his plate with a piece of bread roll. "Waste not, want not", said Pete on seeing Greg's stare.

They arrived in York around 2 p.m. Having checked in at their hotel, chosen specifically for its close proximity to the exhibition halls, they met up with the other three just over an hour later.

"What's the hotel like?" asked Derek, full of his usual zeal.

"Not bad, not bad at all", Greg replied. "Surprisingly, they managed to find two singles for Pete and I".

Harold asked, "What, single beds?"

"No, single rooms. You and Colin are sharing and Derek will have a double room to himself as Doreen will be joining him tomorrow".

"We have got single beds, though, haven't we?" Colin was anxious, although he did not wish to induce Pete into another round of sexual innuendo.

"You'll have to check for yourself, Colin, but I'd imagine so".

Colin wasn't happy. "So, how did you two get separate rooms. The organisers pointed out that accommodation would be based on two sharing".

"I smiled sweetly", said Pete, who subconsciously pulled in his stomach and expanded his chest.

Greg joked. "He smiled smarmily, actually".

"Funny, though", added Pete, "for some reason I've only got this room for tonight, then they're moving me along the corridor where I've got meself a double - room 44. I reckon the receptionist must fancy me!" He became louder. "That's what's going to 'appen. She's going to pop in during the night. Who's a lucky boy, then?"

"Dream on", said Greg.

"Come on, chaps", said Colin, "let's get this layout out and up".

"Great, terrific", concluded Derek.

Stewards directed them to their marked out position. Nods and acknowledgments were meted out as they, along with other exhibiting groups, trundled backwards and forwards with sections of what looked like over-sized jigsaw pieces. Little by little the pattern took shape. Layouts came to life as final touches were applied. Trade stands were set up in preparation for the following two days' business.

"They seem a very friendly bunch", stated Harold, as he received the meal and coffee vouchers allocated to the five members.

Stock was brought in from the van and Pete's BMW. All the group worked quietly. There was little time for conversation. By 6 o'clock the layout's trackwork and pointwork had been checked to everyone's satisfaction. After a heady bout of locomotive testing, rakes of coaches and wagons were assembled in sets to await their turn on the running lines.

The van was parked up for the weekend, all five members travelling around in Pete's BMW.

"You look happier", commented Greg, on meeting Colin in the bar. Colin responded in a low voice.

"We **do** have separate beds".

Greg's reply was in measured, scholarly tone. "That was worrying you, wasn't it?"

"Well, you know". Colin looked up at Greg. "Two men of differing ages ....."

Greg changed the subject. "So, what are you having?"

Colin went through his usual ritual of surveying the entire liquid contents of the bar and exclaimed loudly when he chanced upon a northern brew unheard of down south.

"So", asked Greg, after what seemed a lifetime, but was, in fact, just under two minutes, "once again, what are you having?"

"Oh, I think I'll just have a half of cider".

They were joined by the other three. "It was never really in doubt". Greg sighed as he concluded giving his order to the barman, who had pointed out, quite politely, albeit forcibly, that there were other customers waiting.

As they walked to the table Pete had selected, Colin said, "I'll put his attitude down to his being a gruff Yorkshireman. They do have a reputation, you know".

"So do you", thought Greg, "so do you".

Pre-prandial drinks completed, Harold, Derek and Colin enjoyed the set meal as per the financial restraint imposed upon them by their hosts, Greg and Pete preferring to pay the difference and eat a la carte.

After dinner all five sat in the hotel's tastefully decorated mock Edwardian bar. Colin was the first to expire. He started to yawn and stretch at about 9.30 p.m. Looking at his watch, he announced, "Well, I'm off - early start. Lots to remember, you know. Route plans, schedules, etc." He raised an index finger as he stood. "Still got to sort out a way of marshalling those cattle wagons".

"Not forgetting the mineral train", added Greg mockingly.

"No, I won't forget the mineral wagons. Must make sure they're in correct order".

Colin's reply was very serious. He bid everyone goodnight, adjusted his tie and the sleeves of his blazer, then bounced across the deep piled burgundy carpet towards the lift.

At a nearby table two women, who had taken temporary residence some time earlier, were joined by a third. Pete noted Greg becoming distracted.

"You thinking of using your pass-out to good effect?"

"Not me, it's you I'm thinking about!"

"Why?"

Greg leaned forward. Harold and Derek followed suit. "That woman who's just sat down over there with the other two". Greg nodded in her direction. "She keeps looking at you".

Pete moved around the table and sat on the chair earlier vacated by Colin. He fidgeted several times in order to get a better view, but the woman's face continued to elude him. Just as he was about to rejoin the conversation she suddenly looked round. Pete jumped up. "Margie", he shouted. "Gordon Bennett, gal. What you doing 'ere?"

"It is you, Pete Balfour?" A broad smile developed on her face.

Greg watched as the woman made her excuses and left her friends. She stood about five foot five, with a good figure, attractive face and bleached, blonde hair. Greg increased her age from thirty something to forty something as she neared. Pete kissed her on the cheek, introducing her to his friends.

"This is Margie".

"Gathered that", pronounced Harold.

"We go back, well, years". They both laughed.

Having exchanged pleasantries the car salesman encouraged Margie towards the open floor several feet away from their respective friends. Greg observed the situation with interest. Within ten minutes she had walked back to her table, finished her drink and collected her handbag. She said something to the other two women, waved and slowly chassised across to where Pete stood. She glanced a smile at Greg before Pete put his arm around her waist and glided her across the floor, following the route Colin had taken to the lift lobby. As the woman turned out of sight, Pete looked around, clenched his fist and gestured to the three men.

"Nice meeting an old friend, isn't it?" said Harold.

Derek bubbled. "Yeah, great, super, ace".

Greg sat looking at the pair of them. "Why couldn't I have chosen another hobby?" he thought.

*　　*　　*　　*　　*

Colin arrived at the exhibition halls early on Saturday morning so as to prepare the cattle train, though he found it difficult to improve upon Greg's arrangement of the mineral wagons. By 9.30 a.m. "Southworth" was ready to meet its public. Four of its five operators were ready to meet their public. Pete Balfour was conspicuous by his absence.

At 9.50 a bell sounded, indicating that only ten minutes remained before the expected deluge of paying visitors was to commence. The organisers were not to be disappointed. For some it was like the winter sales, swooping on stands in anticipation of a bargain before swiftly moving onto the next, until the halls had been exhausted, only to follow the same pattern all over again, but in a more genteel fashion.

Certain layouts would be dismissed with derision, whilst others would be observed for long periods in utter reverence, such are the diverse interests of the railway enthusiast.

213

Greg and Derek worked the up and down main lines. Harold operated the branch line and Colin acted as points man on the fiddle sidings, making sure that the stock was changed regularly so as to retain the audience's attention. A large screen divided the front viewing area from the rear half of the layout, blocking the public's view of the fiddle yard, cutting off direct vision between the operators and the points man. Colin enjoyed this task as he controlled which trains ventured out onto the running lines, and when.

Contact was maintained by a series of bell codes. Although unseen, Colin's presence was always known to the public, due to his continuous unmelodic rendering of the Coronation Scot and the theme tune from the "Railway Children"!

Harold ceased working the branch line some time around 11 a.m. and slowly eased himself under the railway boards in order to obtain four coffees. Pete was still nowhere to be seen.

Doreen had managed to obtain the services of John and Dave for the trip north. Stopping outside the hotel she stood by the coach steps and handed out leaflets to all, concerning the proposed pre-Christmas shopping trip to France - by ferry.

"Something for you to read with your aperitif, or whatever".

Having checked in, the travellers made their way to the outside world, following Doreen's various suggestions. For many, the exhibition was the prime reason for their visit to the county town. Included in their number was Rita Balfour. Six weeks previously she had had a discreet word with Doreen as to whether there would be a spare seat available. Despite a reserve list of would-be travellers, Doreen was not one to forget favours. She remembered how helpful and supportive Rita had been on that working Sunday in May when Reg had fallen through the Club house roof. There was only one cancelled seat. It was duly made available to Rita.

The car salesman's wife had decided to take a more active interest in all her husband's hobbies, but other than accompanying him to the Club occasionally she never felt she contributed to his love of railways at all. This time she was to surprise him. Buying a programme Rita eagerly sought out "Southworth"'s location. "Lower Hall, Stand B3", she read to herself. Clip-clopping down the stairs in her bright green shoes, several heads were to turn in an effort to gain a further view of her well-formed stocking-free legs. Rita wore a bright green flared skirt with cream blouse. She had spent Friday afternoon at the hairdresser's, the result of which had changed her facial shape considerably. Gone were the crimped mouse-with-highlights colour of recent months. Gone too was most of her hair. Now cut short and dyed with a red tint, it was brushed forward from the crown and layered, giving her an impish look. Doreen had commented that the new style Rita paraded reminded her of Sarah, in "Emmerdale". Rita liked being compared to a soap-star, even if it was by Doreen.

By the time she reached Stand B3 there was a sizeable crowd surrounding the layout. Making her way to the side she finally made contact with Colin. "Where's Pete?"

Colin looked, then looked again. "Ah, oh, it's you. Didn't recognise you under that, uhm, wig - sorry, hairstyle". He chuckled. "Well, he's not here yet, probably imbibed a little too heavily". Colin then fingered his chin.

"You all right, Colin?"

"Yes, sorry, it's just that I've got a slight hitch with cattle wagon number 21".

Rita looked puzzled and shrugged her shoulders. She tried to have a word with Greg but there were too many spectators holding camcorders and cameras, thwarting her attempts to attract Greg's attention, whilst Derek was discussing the layout with visitors eager to improve their various modelling techniques and skills.

Obtaining a pass-out from the front door steward, Rita walked briskly back to the hotel. "Mrs. Balfour, Room 44. Can you tell me which room my husband was booked into last night, please".

"Oh, yes", replied the effeminate male receptionist, whose eyes widened and contracted with every word uttered. "Mr. Balfour was in Room 52. Same floor, just along the corridor". He pointed in the direction, his arm hanging limply.

Rita turned towards the lift as the uniformed employee continued. "I'm sorry we couldn't give your husband the room you asked for upon his arrival, but all the doubles were pre-booked last night".

"That's all right, thank you", replied Rita, her eyes warm and friendly. "My husband's slept in so I'm just going to surprise him".

Passing the room where she had deposited her case some fifty minutes earlier, Rita stood outside Room 52 like a delinquent child waiting to be called in by the headmaster. She took a deep breath. She felt a tingling inside. A "Do Not Disturb" sign hung from the doorknob. Not for a long time had she felt like this.

215

Rita re-appraised the situation. It was really as if an elicit affair was about to be encountered. She undid the second button of her blouse and instinctively smoothed some imaginary stray hair back from her forehead before knocking. Giving the slightest of coughs she announced in a tone that was formal, "Special delivery for Mr. Balfour".

The door opened, Pete stood naked, except for a black leather G-string. Rita stared at the figure before her. She blinked, her surprise matched only by that of her husband, whose stomach automatically pulled itself in. Something across the room drew her attention. In the mirror opposite the door she glimpsed a female head disappearing below the bedclothes. Pete said nothing. Her eyes stared disbelievingly; her mouth remained open. Rita pushed the door back and demanded, "What the bloody hell's going on?"

A lump lay concealed beneath the covers. Rita stood hands firmly planted against her hips. Pete turned and put his hand to his forehead. Rita ordered, "Get up, you bitch!" Pete winced. There was no response.

"Get up, you **deaf** bitch". Rita's voice was faltering. She turned to her husband. "Who, or what, is in there, Pete?" He gestured ineffectively.

Rita prodded the prone figure, who squealed, jerking slightly. Pete Balfour paced the room. "Don't make a scene, Reet".

"Don't make a scene", Rita shouted, pulling a pillow from the bed. "Don't make a bloody scene! I'll give you, don't make a scene". She was vaguely aware of a female voice moaning, "Oh no, oh no", as Rita began to pound her husband. Pete tried to hide his face and called on his wife to desist. She did not. Instead, she injected more venom into the crescendo of abuse she poured on him. For a split second Rita noticed Pete looking towards the door through the hands which covered his face. She turned quickly and espied the female trying vainly to creep into the bathroom. Clad only in pants and bra she held a dress close to her visibly shaking body.

"It moves, then!"

"Reet, listen, it was a mistake, an unfortunate coincidence. Marge, tell 'er". Pete was standing with his lower back pushed into the edge of a chest of drawers.

"Marge, is it, mistake, is it?" Rita's eyes were fiery, her cheeks flushed. Margie stood silent, locked against the bathroom wall.

"So, slag, where did you pick him up from? I assume he was drunk". Rita looked her up and down in a belittling manner. "Christ, he'd have to be, to go to bed with you!"

Pete thought it best to stay where he was and say nothing. Rita bent the lower half of her body towards the immobile figure, her arms closed in by her sides, exuding greater strength of stature. Margie looked in Pete's direction. "You're not going to let her talk to me like this, are you?"

Pete raised his hands slightly and grinned apologetically. Sensing that she was going to receive little or no help from her previous night's lover, Margie turned once more towards Rita.

Rita demanded. "How much?"

"What?"

"How bloody much did he pay you? Was it by the hour, or did he want you for the all-night session so you could go through your full list of services". Rita looked on her like dirt.

"How dare you, I ....."

"It must have been by the hour, 'cos he's never managed to stay interested any longer than that".

"Well, that's your fault", blurted Margie.

"You what!" screamed Rita, as she lunged forward. Her right hand swung from behind her back with great force, landing palm flat across Margie's left cheek. Margie cried out, stunned and bewildered by the onslaught.

Pete stood as if his feet were set in concrete. "Reet", he called weakly. In a manner which suggested his wife had just noticed him she turned slowly, as Margie held her left hand to her face. "You bastard", Rita screeched, as a porter appeared in the doorway.

"I'm sorry, but there's been a complaint".

"Yes, it's over there". Rita scowled and pointed vigorously towards her husband. "He's the complaint. Over-active glands!"

Pete Balfour slowly rose from the cowering position he had unaccountably found himself to be in. Realising the attention being given to his near nakedness by the porter he once again pulled in his stomach and drew back his shoulders. "There's been a little misunderstanding", he said in a low voice.

Sensing more security now that the hotel employee had arrived, he moved cautiously towards the door. The porter's head kept moving from Pete to Rita, and back. He said nothing, but continued to frown. Suddenly, as he was about to go, he caught sight of the other female still standing against the wall, dress in right hand, her left nursing a throbbing cheek.

"Have you been holding an orgy, sir?"

Rita shrieked. "Do I look dressed for an orgy, you prat".

"Well, no, madam, but ....."

"I've dressed in Southern Region colours for him". Rita looked directly into her husband's eyes. He sensed a mixture of anger and disappointment and turned away with embarrassment. Glaring at Margie Rita flounced out of the door, brushing past the porter. The sound of the quickening footsteps faded. Pete walked over to his lover, but she pushed him away.

"What have I done?" he asked.

The porter stood by the door and coughed discreetly. Pete backed up. "'Ang on, Marge, the man needs, well, recompense for his troubles".

She looked on incredulously as Pete delved into his suit trouser pockets and unravelled a roll of notes. His stomach fell forward, giving the unsuspecting eye no clue as to the whereabouts of his only garment of clothing. Extracting a note of ten pound denomination, he calmly placed it into the porter's open palm and winked. The employee touched his cap. "If you're sure everything's all right now, sir", he said, in a tone more in keeping with hope than expectation.

Having gently closed the door and walked away, his shoulders automatically hunched as he heard a smacking noise, followed by a number of thuds before all went quiet. Standing still once more the porter's ears picked up a low moaning noise. "That's definitely the sound of a tom in pain", he thought, smiling to himself. As he returned to the reception area the previously partly-dressed female ran out of the foyer, tears streaming down her face. Heads turned. Only the porter knew the story.

Harold returned with the coffees. "Sorry I've been so long, there was a queue, and they'd run out of change, which didn't help those in front. Typical, isn't it, mid-morning and no change".

Greg accepted the tray offered to him across the boards before Harold made his way back underneath.

"Colin", Greg shouted. "Coffee up".

"Ah, thanks", replied the points man, still engrossed in the complexities of his re-arranged parcels train. "Saw Rita earlier".

"Where?" exclaimed Greg, popping his head around the partition.

"Oh, she called in to see Pete. A surprise, I gather".

"It'll be a surprise all right. What did you tell her?"

"Well, I said Pete was probably having a lie in? Why?"

Greg scratched the back of his head with his left hand, his mind struggling to come to terms with the marital explosion he visualised taking place, unless someone did something quickly.

"Oh, Christ", he exclaimed.

Colin looked aghast. "We do have a viewing public to consider", he whispered. "I've no doubt some will be church-goers".

"They could be joined by a new member if I don't get to Pete first".

"Sorry?" said Colin, unaware of the situation. "Why would Pete want to go to church?"

"To pray for his life - that's if he's still got one. Look, if you see Pete, keep him here. Tell him Rita's turned up, and make sure you tell Derek and Harold. They'll understand - hopefully".

"But ....."

Greg scrambled under the boards. "Caught short, Greg?" enquired Derek on seeing his fellow operator merge into the crowd. "Do one for me while your there. Great, super".

As Greg made his way between the slow moving hordes towards the staircase Rita strode across in the opposite direction towards "Southworth". He missed her by a couple of feet, but he wasn't looking for a red-headed, close-cropped female.

There were slightly less visitors in the immediate vicinity of "Southworth". Rita noticed Harold, who was concentrating on running his trains. Derek was talking across the boards with Mick, who had just arrived. Rita's attention was drawn to a table positioned next to the Club layout. There, displayed on sections of rail, stood over twenty locomotives, all priced on fluorescent yellow card in Pete Balfour's inimitable style. Rita's eyes flashed from model to model, from card to card.

"GWR 47XX, real pearler of a loco - £250", "BR Britannia, genuine beauty, under priced at £495", "SR West Country, showstopper, this is the bizzo, £525". Derek looked in Rita's direction. Mick followed his gaze.

"Ah, hello", said Derek, sensing something was awry, but not being able to fully put his finger on it. "Shouldn't you ....., aren't you ...... isn't ...... like your hair. Great, super!"

Rita hadn't heard a word. Her muscles became tense, her back straightened. Years of pent-up anger which had bottled up inside now reached bursting point. "You bastard", she shouted.

Mick, like a lot of people within earshot, seemed taken aback. "I thought I had the patent on that one", he whispered to Derek, who was still controlling the outer track, Harold having taken over from Greg on the inner.

"Bastard", she repeated. People started to look round. Some stopped and stared, others scurried away, not wishing to be involved. Rita took one final step towards the table and tossed the large "For Sale" sign in the air. Derek followed its progress, allowing his train to overrun the station platform. This action incurred Colin's wrath as he'd overshot the starter signal, causing havoc to Colin's schedule.

"Look what you've done", bellowed Colin. "You've fouled the points. The up express will be late now!"

Grabbing hold of the first locomotive she raised it from the table, turned and coolly opened her hand, allowing the engine to crash onto the floor. The twisted, broken model was swiftly followed by a second, then a third. Derek looked horrified. Harold tapped his chin. Colin was still trying to complete his rake of parcel vans. Trains came to a halt on all the surrounding layouts. Traders stopped trading as customers diverted their attention towards Rita who, by now, was exclaiming "bastard" to the sound of each locomotive splattering upon the parquet flooring. Wheels, motors, cabs, boilers, mangled tenders and indefinable metal pieces lay scattered. Such was Rita's anger that no-one moved close enough to stop her, although Harold asked Mick if he thought it was due to what he termed, "woman's problems".

All Derek could do was to point in her direction and utter a very feeble "But".

Mick stood throughout legs astride, hands in pockets, adding up the cost of the models from the now redundant price tags. "£250, £425, £730, what was that, another £250 - £980".

As Rita ceremoniously, and with feeling, hurled the final model down onto the floor, the car salesman's wife spat out the same expletive for the final time. She seemed drained of energy, her shoulders hunched. She bent forward, head bowed. Mick picked up the remaining card and read out aloud. "Oh, £275, I'd have thought Pete could have got three and a half for that. Still it's all academic now".

People mumbled, shrugged shoulders and went about their business as two security officers with peaked caps and epaulettes on their jackets hurried through the crowd. They enquired as to what had happened. "An internal matter, I'd say", offered Mick.

Rita surveyed the remains that covered the area surrounding the now empty table, empty save for a few lengths of rail. "What have I done?" she gasped in horror. Her face one of total disbelief, she bit her bottom lip. "What have I done?" she repeated more softly, almost unknowing.

"About six and a half thousand quid's worth, according to these price tags. Mind you, given Pete's mark up I'd say that Glass's Guide would price them at about two grand trade!"

Rita wasn't listening. She stood transfixed. Derek was still pointing. "But ....."

"But what, Derek?" asked Mick, somewhat irritated.

Derek blinked. "But they're not all Pete's".

Rita gasped. "What?" She stepped back, as if to disassociate herself from her actions.

"Half of those models belonged to Greg. Pete just marked them up for him. He said he knew how much they would make. He ....."

Mick almost collapsed laughing. Doreen came into view. She hurried across to where a very broken Rita stood and cradled her in her arms. She then escorted Rita to the ladies' cloakroom.

Shortly afterwards Greg appeared with Pete, who sported a black eye. He also walked very slowly, appearing to be in some discomfort. His hands were clasped in front of his groin, as if to form a shield. Colin's head appeared around the partition. "Nearly forgot, Greg gave me a message earlier ....."

He surveyed the scene, looked at each in turn, mumbled, "Aaah", and retired once more behind the screen from where he recommenced whistling the "Coronation Scot". Pete looked at Mick, who still had difficulty containing his mirth, then to Greg, who was clearly furious. Pete's gaze finally rested on Harold, who enquired quietly, "I know what I meant to ask you, do you reckon Baz would have managed to fix my car this morning?"

Having checked out of the hotel Rita caught the London-bound train. Once back home she collected as many clothes and items of sentimental value that her car could hold and drove to Marcia's. This was a journey not without incident, as the accelerator jammed just east of Forest Hill. The end result of this mechanical problem meant that by the time she reached Homerton, the engine was knocking continuously.

The "Balfour" incident, as Colin referred to it, had done the rounds by meal time. Naturally, the story had been exaggerated and embellished along the way, so that nearly everybody had a different tale to tell. For

Doreen, the rest of the weekend went without further misadventure.

"Southworth" had proved to be a very popular layout with the crowds, being fully staffed from just after Saturday lunch time, Pete Balfour having taken over from Colin behind the screen.

At 3.50 p.m. on Sunday afternoon the bell rang, advising the public that only ten minutes remained to view their favourite layout or haggle with a trader over that coveted second-hand item.

By 5 p.m. the layout had been disassembled and stacked into the van, Pete and Greg returning in the BMW.

Dave, the relief driver, was given the all clear whistle by Doreen at around the same time, giving him his cue to commence the journey south. Mick and Kate left Goole shortly after lunch, deciding to tour across the Isle of Axholme and on through Gainsborough before picking up the A1 east of Newark.

"So why have we got to call in at the Club?" asked Kate, as they turned off the road leading to Guildford.

"Robin assumed, quite reasonably, that we'd get home before the coach or van, in which case I could give the spare keys to the relief barman. Apparently, there's a function of some kind on tonight at the Los Crapos Night Spot".

"Still not happy about the renovations", Kate joked.

Mick mumbled "bastards" under his breath as he pulled into the lane leading to the Club house.

"That's new", murmured Kate, leaning out of the window.

"What the ....." Mick's eyes darted between the lane ahead and the previously unsullied Club room roof. As he unlocked the gates Kate drew Mick's attention to a newly erected sign.

"Didn't you used to have a board which said 'Surbiton Railway Club' along with the times of opening?"

Mick walked towards where his wife was standing. His head moved from side to side in disbelief as he read the inscription:

**Greater London Breweries PLC Social Centre
The Railway Inn
Available for hire - 7 days a week
Clubroom Administrator - Mr. J. LeGrand
Clubroom Manager - Mr. C. Mabey**

Mick turned to Kate. "What **are** they playing at? No-one gave them permission to do that. Not even Robin's that foolish". He looked up at the Club roof. "But I know a man who is!"

Walking slowly around the buildings, with Kate two paces behind, Mick continued to take in the full extent to which GLB plc had exerted its power and influence. Facia boards, some four feet high, now ran the entire length of the Club room. In large letters they read, "The Railway Inn". The wording was surrounded by the GLB logo, the brewery's full name appearing at either end of the facia. Mick raised his hands in disgust. "Where does it mention **our** Club?" he asked aloud.

On entering the building they walked into the hall where Kate looked around her. "What was it, Los Crapos?" She sniggered. Mick nodded, but said nothing.

"You weren't wrong. Mind, some of these plants are nice. Trouble is, they've gone overboard. There's more here than in Kew Gardens".

Mick scowled. "They're bloody everywhere, standing to attention by the wall, hanging from the ceiling, it's like an evergreen Wookey Hole".

The relief barman appeared, said "Hello" and set about arranging the tables in preparation for the evening function. Leaving Kate to gawp, Mick continued through to the office, where he sought out the file marked "SRC/GLB PLC". He spent some forty minutes sifting through documents, solicitors' letters, related legal papers, most of which he'd never previously seen. So engrossed was the Club Treasurer that he failed to respond to Kate's verbal observation that the coach had returned. Many of the travellers went straight to their cars, all trying to exit at the same time, the result being an entanglement comparable to Piccadilly Circus during the rush hour.

"How tropical", commented Greg sarcastically as he entered the office, pointing to yet another six foot specimen of the broad leafed variety, standing sentinel against the gents' toilet.

"You're back, then?"

"Got here two minutes after the coach. The others are just finishing unloading. Derek's going to be parking the van up overnight".

Outside in the car park Derek walked over and joined his wife as she stood on tiptoe waving to John and Dave as their coach made its way slowly down the lane.

""Don't forget", shouted Doreen, "it's viva la France next time!"
A hand waved out of the driver's window.

The last of the travellers had now dispersed. Harold waited for the Durdles as they were giving him a lift home. Colin was behind the bar talking to the barman about GLB plc's failure to produce the promised draught beer and cider.

Robin approached Mick and Greg as they continued to study the files. The Club Chairman was clearly bewildered by what he had seen.

"Something like, 'I told you so' springs to mind". There wasn't the slightest hint of humour in Mick's tone.

"I never agreed to this", defended Robin. "I've never seen half of this paperwork. The only signature we keep coming across is Colin's. It's just ....."

He drew his hand across his forehead.

"Oh, we know that much", sympathised Greg, "and I bet you don't know about the running nights either". He handed over the Club's diary. Robin looked bewildered as he scanned page after page.

"Well, there aren't any", he said at length. "They're all taken up with lectures, conferences, dis ....."

Mick interjected. "That's right, which means we can't play trains any more, we can't talk trains any more, we can't do anything down our Club any more - and we all know why?" Robin stared ahead blankly, deciding not to interrupt. Mick's voice became louder. "That bloody Colin's gone and signed our Club over to that smarmy example of Thatcherism. No wonder he was cagey about publishing the diary as usual. Where is the sloth-some little creature?"

"Steady on", said Robin. "In a way he's been the victim of manipulation".

"Victim of his own failure, you mean".

"Stowford Press is a particularly fine example of the cider maker's art", said Colin to the barman who feigned interest. Mick and Robin stormed out of the office, along the corridor and into the hall, followed quickly by Greg. "Where's Colin?" exclaimed Mick to his wife, who sat reading a paperback on one of the patio chairs. Kate pointed nonchalantly to the bar area. "The butler did it", Mick spluttered, as he pushed between the white plastic furniture.

"Oh, that'll save me a few pages!"

Pushing the bar door open Mick was confronted by the relief barman. "Where's that little arsehole you were talking to?"

"I don't know". The casual employee appeared bemused. "One second he was here, wittering on about cider, the next - well, he heard you shouting and disappeared out of the back door".

Robin and Greg made for the main entrance. Mick caught up with them as the doors were flung open.

"Colin, Colin, C- o- l- i- n!!" shouted Mick, but to no avail.

The three Committee members witnessed a fleeting glimpse of him as he raced out of the car park and down the lane in his Metro Vanden Plas. Harold sat on the wall, watching the farcical actions of all concerned. Talking to no-one in particular, he muttered, "I expect his mother called to say tea was ready".

"Nice one that, great, super", remarked Derek, grinning broadly as Pete Balfour eased himself slowly into the driver's seat of his BMW. His expression demonstrated clearly the discomfort caused when sitting in a confined space with legs pressed together. His face cracked mildly as he passed slowly by but no-one was sure whether the contortion was through humour or pain.

"Nice to go home to a car that's got a new clutch". Harold was genuine in the belief that his beloved Austin Princess would now be so fitted.

Mick, Robin and Greg continued to view the outside of their Club rooms in stunned silence as Doreen caught hold of her husband's arm. Derek, who was blissfully unaware of his colleagues' displeasure, looked at his wife, pulled her close, then followed her stare across a row of elms. A slight breeze played with the hem of Doreen's skirt as she reflected aloud. "We've had some good tours so far and there's still the Christmas trip to France to look forward to. Yes, all in all, it's been a very successful year".

The response was predictable. "Great, super, terrific". Doreen squeezed her husband's hand. There was a momentary silence as they continued to gaze contentedly into the sunset. Derek then announced softly, "All's well with the world".

Doreen rested her head against Derek's arm and declared "As long as all's well in Surbiton, that's what really matters!"

THE END

You might like to read the reviews and comments regarding other books and CDs published by Trouser Press.

All books are available direct from Trouser Press, PO Box 139, Aldershot, Hants, GU12 5XR, P & P £2.25 per book, £1.50 per talking book (CD)

FROM WHERE I SIT
by Anthony Mann
ISBN: 978-0-9516501-0-3
Price: £6.99 (second re-print)

What the critics say:
"Set to become a humour classic..... the find of the year" - *WH Smith's Bookcase Magazine*

"Liberals with a heart condition beware" - *Croydon Advertiser*

"An amusing collection of personal experiences, anecdotes and memories" - *Surrey Mirror*

"The book earns the author full marks for humour, determination and street-wise common sense" - *Aldershot News & Mail*

AS I WAS SAYING
by Anthony Mann
ISBN: 978-0-9516501-1-0
Price: £5.50

"Courageous enough to write what most of us think....." - *Surrey Advertiser*

"A humorous look at life as it really is" - *Croydon Advertiser*

"Rude, insensitive, arrogant, self-opinionated, sexist – he is also very, very funny" - *Wandsworth Borough News* (author's note: I particularly warmed to that review!)

THE FURTHER THOUGHTS
OF CHAIR MANN
by Anthony Mann
ISBN: 978-0-9516501-7-2
Price: £5.99

"The book for all Millenniums, not just this one" - *Author*

"Lively reading for your holiday? Commuter train? Outside toilet? – this is the book for you!" - *Author again*

"I don't know why he doesn't get a proper job!" - *Author's mother*

LAST MANN STANDING
by Anthony Mann
ISBN: 97809516501-6-5
Price: £6.99

"...I have just completed reading your latest work 'Last Mann Standing' - a gift from my cousin who bought a copy following your recent address to their U3A. Suffice to say, I am still aching with laughter..."

"...Just to let you know that I am more than half way through 'Last Mann Standing'. It's a laugh a minute. I very much admire your perceptive view on the modern world, which in short is a bloody awful mess!..."

"...I always know when my husband has been reading one of your books, as he stumbles around the house for the next year sounding like 'Victor Meldrew". Best wishes from Basingstoke, yes I know, but someone has to live here!..."

The following are talking books, each lasting 2 ½ hours
(two discs per CD)

A MANN AT LAST
by Anthony Mann
ISBN: 978-0-9516501-4-1
Price: £11.99

Equality! Political correctness! Tolerance – you'll find none
of it here. News, views and comments on life's little problems
– like life itself.

From the over-stated, to the under-staffed, the over-blown, to
the under-estimated – all human life is here. Compensation,
asylum, minority rights, fox-hunting, no turn is left unstoned.

"Thought provoking", "Wonderfully entertaining"
"Hilarious", "Like a breath of fresh air"
(These comments were uttered by friends of the author, or those
accustomed to taking backhanders.)

A MANN FOR ALL REASONS
by Anthony Mann
ISBN: 978-0-9516501-5-8
Price: £11.99

Enjoy listening as the CD unfolds and all human frailties
are exposed.   From the under-stated to the over-staffed, the
under-blown to the over-estimated – all human life is dissected
and reassembled.

"Refreshingly thought-provoking", "A cynical view of the
Septic Isles"
(These comments were uttered by the same friends who listened
to above CD. Trainspotters don't have many friends.....)